SLEEPWALK AND OTHER STORIES

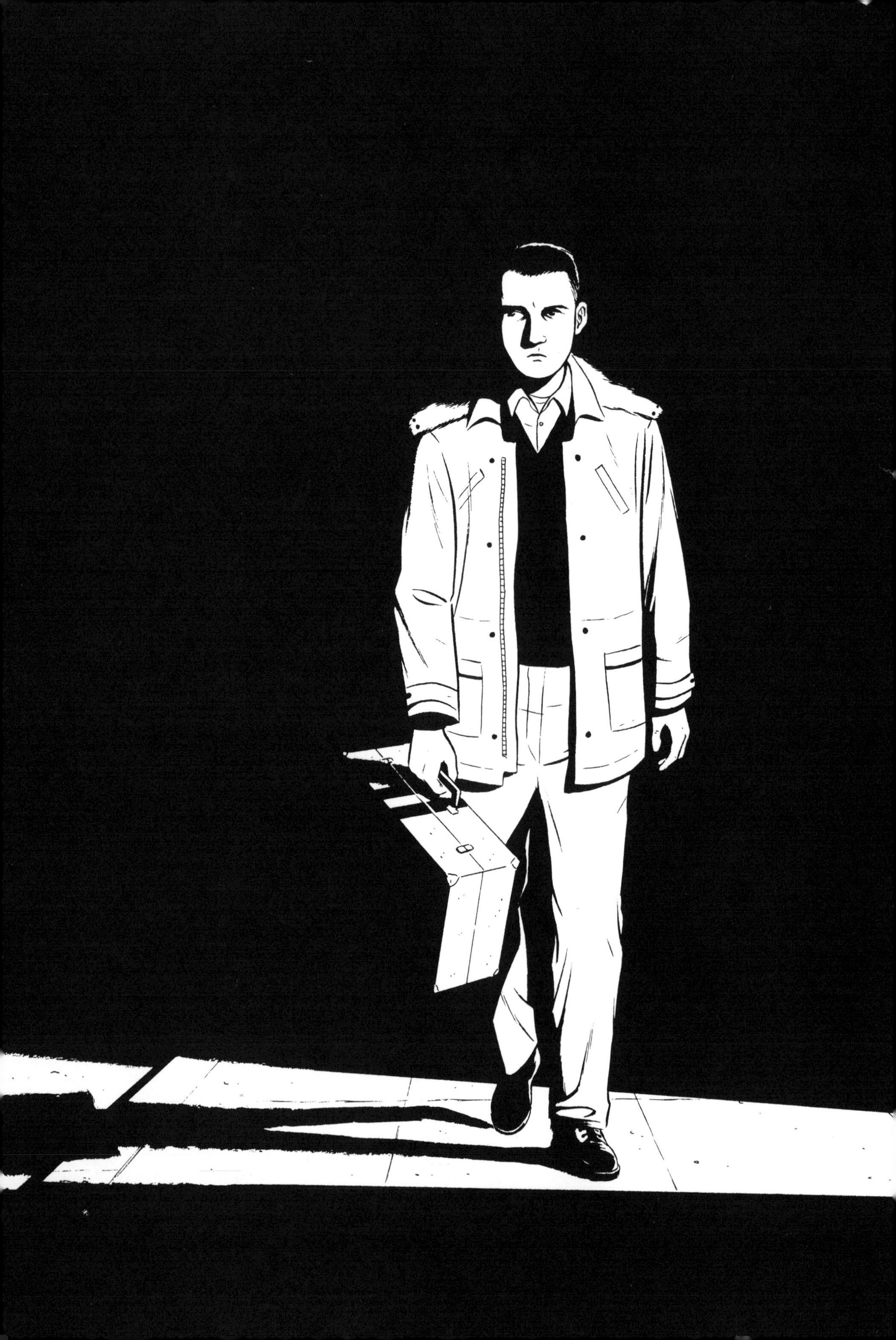

SLEEPWALK AND OTHER STORIES

ADRIAN TOMINE

DRAWN AND QUARTERLY

MONTREAL

ALSO BY ADRIAN TOMINE

32 Stories

Summer Blonde

Scrapbook (Uncollected Work: 1990–2004)

Shortcomings

Scenes from an Impending Marriage

New York Drawings

New York Postcards

Killing and Dying

The stories presented here were originally published in issues one through four of Adrian Tomine's comic book series *Optic Nerve*.

Color separations / computer expertise: John Kuramoto

First hardcover edition: 1997
First softcover edition: 1998
Second softcover printing: 2002
Third softcover printing: 2004
Fourth softcover printing: 2007
Fifth softcover printing: 2011
Sixth softcover printing: 2015

Printed in Malaysia
10 9 8 7 6

Library and Archives Canada Cataloguing in Publication
Tomine, Adrian, 1974–
     Sleepwalk and other stories / Adrian Tomine.
ISBN 978-1-896597-12-6
     I. Title.
NC1429.T66S43 1998   741.5   C99-019535-X

Published in the USA by Drawn & Quarterly, a client publisher of:
Farrar, Straus and Giroux
Orders: (888) 330–8477

Published in Canada by Drawn & Quarterly, a client publisher of:
Raincoast Books
Orders: (800) 663–5714

www.drawnandquarterly.com
www.adrian-tomine.com

CONTENTS

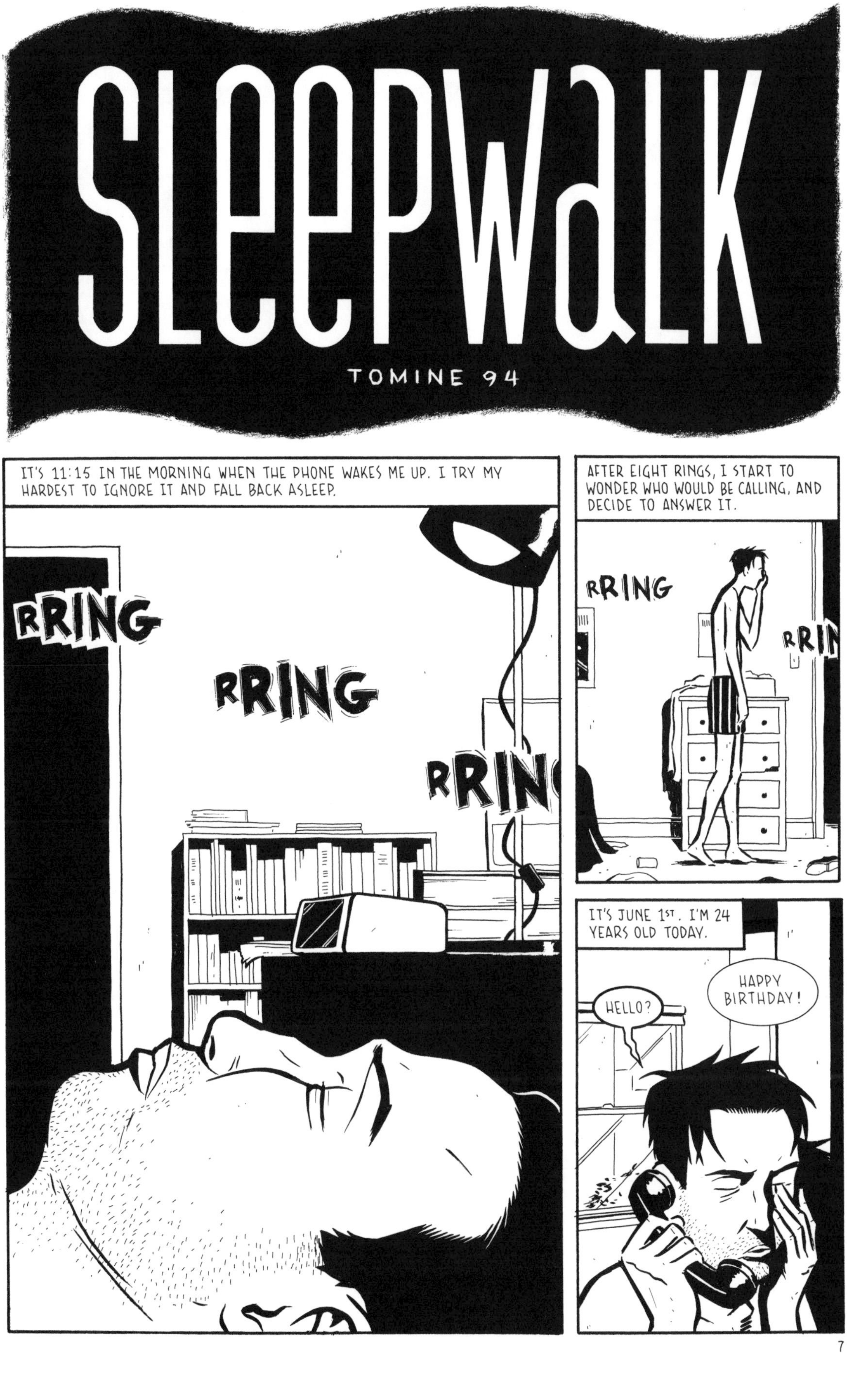
SLEEPWALK
TOMINE 94
IT'S 11:15 IN THE MORNING WHEN THE PHONE WAKES ME UP. I TRY MY HARDEST TO IGNORE IT AND FALL BACK ASLEEP.
RRING
RRING
RRIN
AFTER EIGHT RINGS, I START TO WONDER WHO WOULD BE CALLING, AND DECIDE TO ANSWER IT.
RRING
RRIN
IT'S JUNE 1ST. I'M 24 YEARS OLD TODAY.
HELLO?
HAPPY BIRTHDAY!

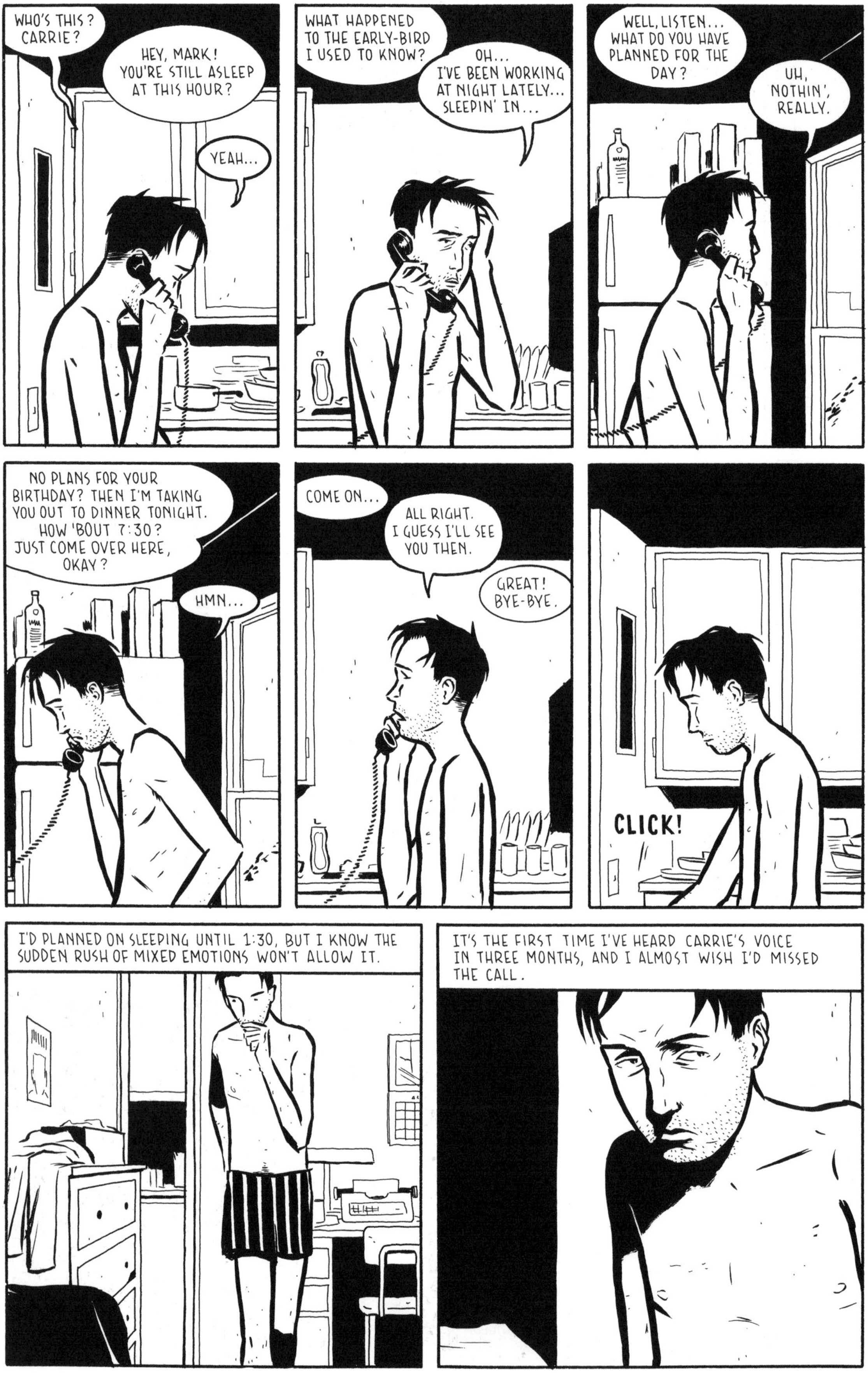
WHO'S THIS? CARRIE?
HEY, MARK! YOU'RE STILL ASLEEP AT THIS HOUR?
YEAH...
WHAT HAPPENED TO THE EARLY-BIRD I USED TO KNOW?
OH... I'VE BEEN WORKING AT NIGHT LATELY... SLEEPIN' IN...
WELL, LISTEN... WHAT DO YOU HAVE PLANNED FOR THE DAY?
UH, NOTHIN', REALLY.
NO PLANS FOR YOUR BIRTHDAY? THEN I'M TAKING YOU OUT TO DINNER TONIGHT. HOW 'BOUT 7:30? JUST COME OVER HERE, OKAY?
HMN...
COME ON...
ALL RIGHT. I GUESS I'LL SEE YOU THEN.
GREAT! BYE-BYE.
CLICK!
I'D PLANNED ON SLEEPING UNTIL 1:30, BUT I KNOW THE SUDDEN RUSH OF MIXED EMOTIONS WON'T ALLOW IT.
IT'S THE FIRST TIME I'VE HEARD CARRIE'S VOICE IN THREE MONTHS, AND I ALMOST WISH I'D MISSED THE CALL.

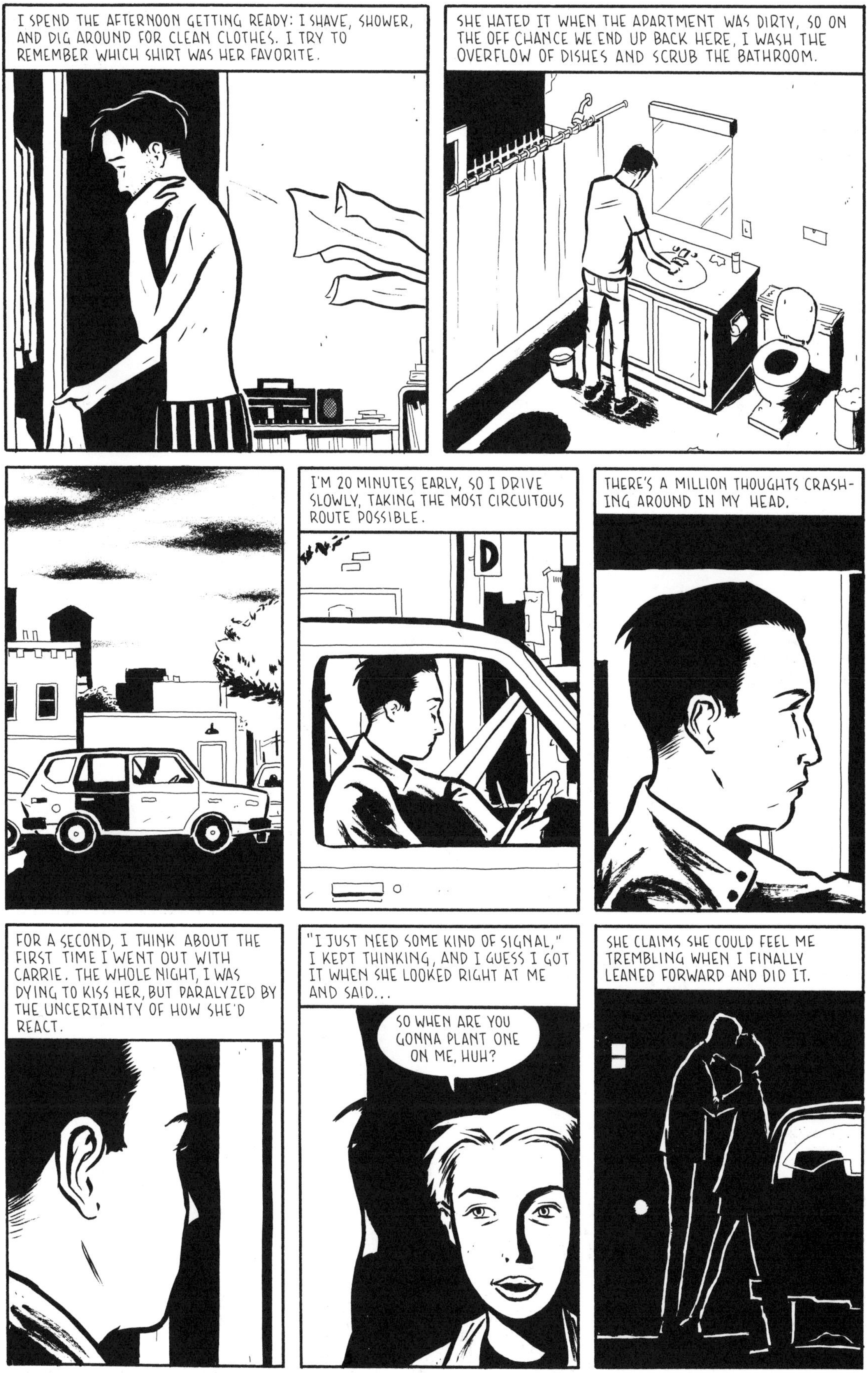
I SPEND THE AFTERNOON GETTING READY: I SHAVE, SHOWER, AND DIG AROUND FOR CLEAN CLOTHES. I TRY TO REMEMBER WHICH SHIRT WAS HER FAVORITE.
SHE HATED IT WHEN THE APARTMENT WAS DIRTY, SO ON THE OFF CHANCE WE END UP BACK HERE, I WASH THE OVERFLOW OF DISHES AND SCRUB THE BATHROOM.
I'M 20 MINUTES EARLY, SO I DRIVE SLOWLY, TAKING THE MOST CIRCUITOUS ROUTE POSSIBLE.
THERE'S A MILLION THOUGHTS CRASHING AROUND IN MY HEAD.
FOR A SECOND, I THINK ABOUT THE FIRST TIME I WENT OUT WITH CARRIE. THE WHOLE NIGHT, I WAS DYING TO KISS HER, BUT PARALYZED BY THE UNCERTAINTY OF HOW SHE'D REACT.
"I JUST NEED SOME KIND OF SIGNAL," I KEPT THINKING, AND I GUESS I GOT IT WHEN SHE LOOKED RIGHT AT ME AND SAID...
SO WHEN ARE YOU GONNA PLANT ONE ON ME, HUH?
SHE CLAIMS SHE COULD FEEL ME TREMBLING WHEN I FINALLY LEANED FORWARD AND DID IT.

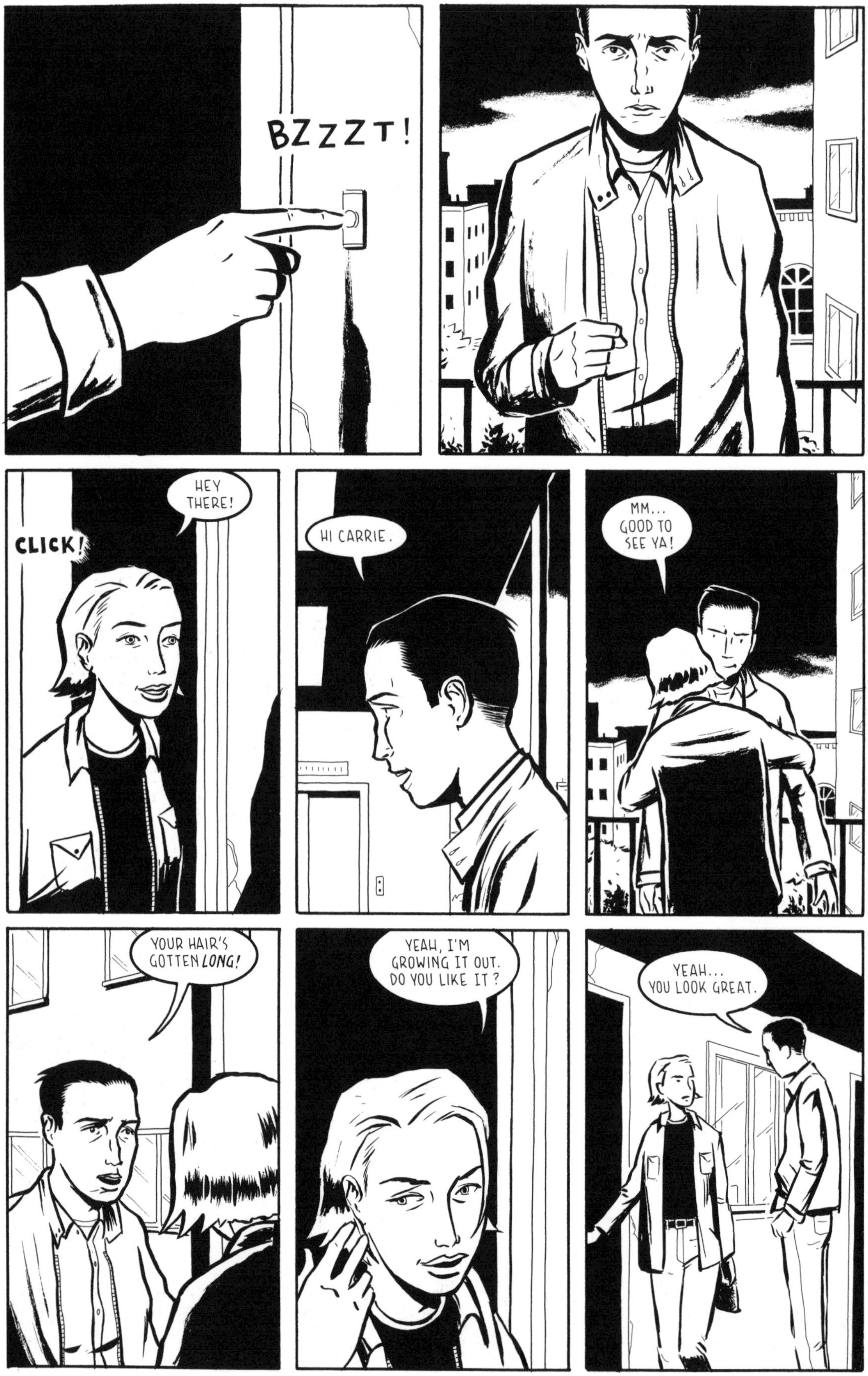
BZZZT!
HEY THERE!
CLICK!
HI CARRIE.
MM... GOOD TO SEE YA!
YOUR HAIR'S GOTTEN LONG!
YEAH, I'M GROWING IT OUT. DO YOU LIKE IT?
YEAH... YOU LOOK GREAT.

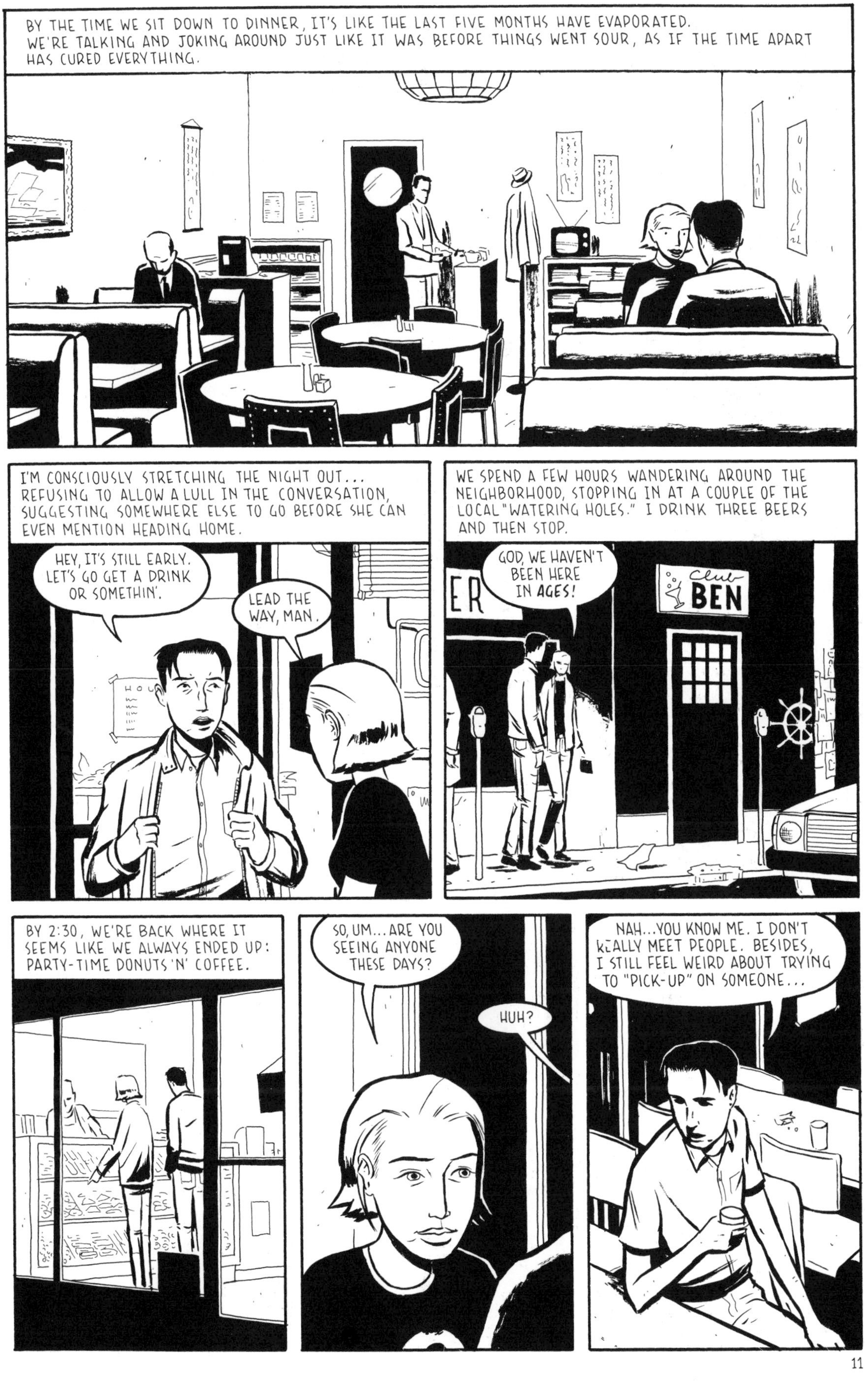
BY THE TIME WE SIT DOWN TO DINNER, IT'S LIKE THE LAST FIVE MONTHS HAVE EVAPORATED. WE'RE TALKING AND JOKING AROUND JUST LIKE IT WAS BEFORE THINGS WENT SOUR, AS IF THE TIME APART HAS CURED EVERYTHING.
I'M CONSCIOUSLY STRETCHING THE NIGHT OUT... REFUSING TO ALLOW A LULL IN THE CONVERSATION, SUGGESTING SOMEWHERE ELSE TO GO BEFORE SHE CAN EVEN MENTION HEADING HOME.
HEY, IT'S STILL EARLY. LET'S GO GET A DRINK OR SOMETHIN'.
LEAD THE WAY, MAN.
WE SPEND A FEW HOURS WANDERING AROUND THE NEIGHBORHOOD, STOPPING IN AT A COUPLE OF THE LOCAL "WATERING HOLES." I DRINK THREE BEERS AND THEN STOP.
GOD, WE HAVEN'T BEEN HERE IN AGES!
ER
Club BEN
BY 2:30, WE'RE BACK WHERE IT SEEMS LIKE WE ALWAYS ENDED UP: PARTY-TIME DONUTS 'N' COFFEE.
SO, UM... ARE YOU SEEING ANYONE THESE DAYS?
HUH?
NAH... YOU KNOW ME. I DON'T REALLY MEET PEOPLE. BESIDES, I STILL FEEL WEIRD ABOUT TRYING TO "PICK-UP" ON SOMEONE...

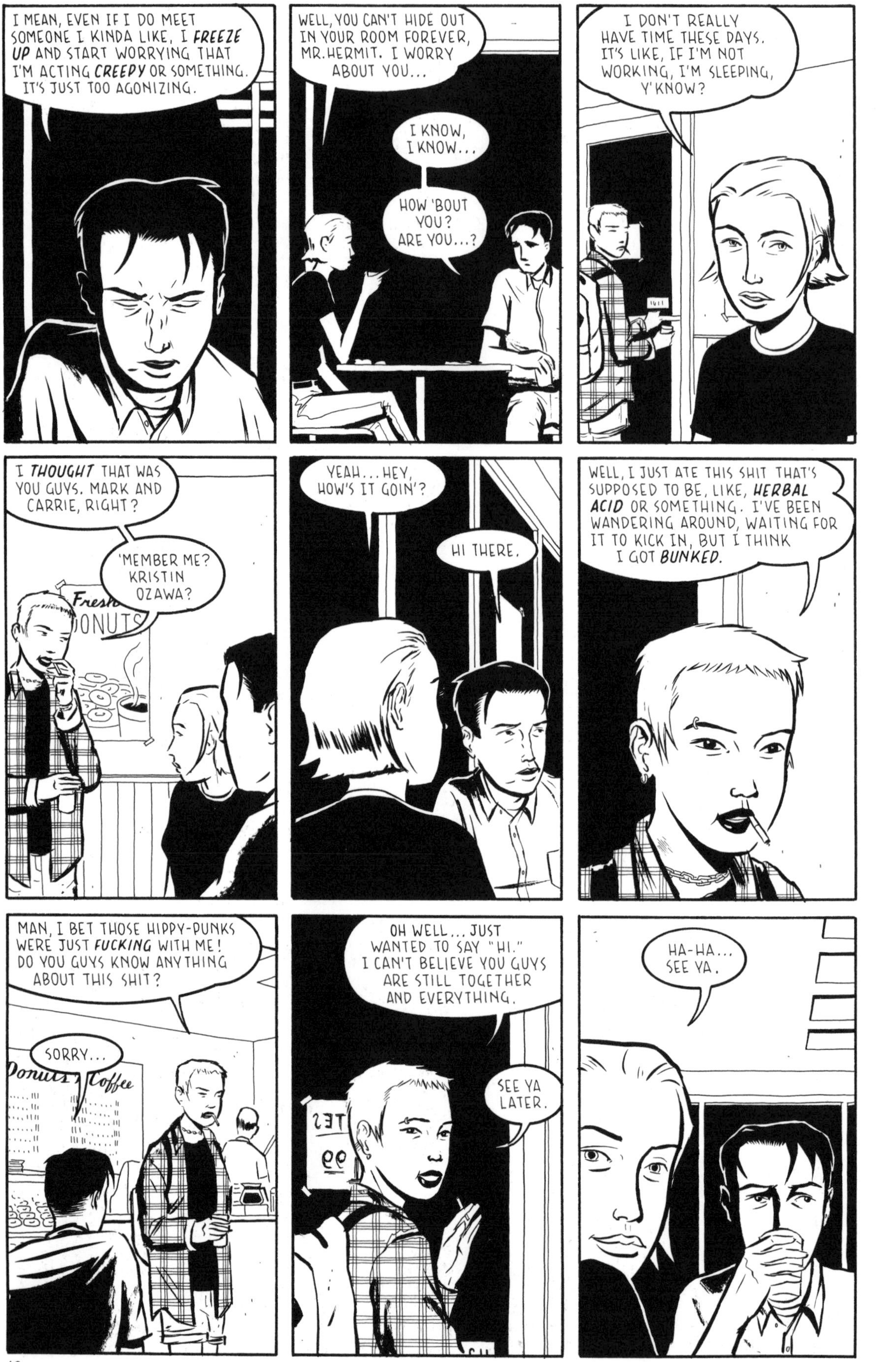
I MEAN, EVEN IF I DO MEET SOMEONE I KINDA LIKE, I FREEZE UP AND START WORRYING THAT I'M ACTING CREEPY OR SOMETHING. IT'S JUST TOO AGONIZING.
WELL, YOU CAN'T HIDE OUT IN YOUR ROOM FOREVER, MR. HERMIT. I WORRY ABOUT YOU...
I KNOW, I KNOW...
HOW 'BOUT YOU? ARE YOU...?
I DON'T REALLY HAVE TIME THESE DAYS. IT'S LIKE, IF I'M NOT WORKING, I'M SLEEPING, Y'KNOW?
I THOUGHT THAT WAS YOU GUYS. MARK AND CARRIE, RIGHT?
'MEMBER ME? KRISTIN OZAWA?
YEAH... HEY, HOW'S IT GOIN'?
HI THERE.
WELL, I JUST ATE THIS SHIT THAT'S SUPPOSED TO BE, LIKE, HERBAL ACID OR SOMETHING. I'VE BEEN WANDERING AROUND, WAITING FOR IT TO KICK IN, BUT I THINK I GOT BUNKED.
MAN, I BET THOSE HIPPY-PUNKS WERE JUST FUCKING WITH ME! DO YOU GUYS KNOW ANYTHING ABOUT THIS SHIT?
SORRY...
OH WELL... JUST WANTED TO SAY "HI." I CAN'T BELIEVE YOU GUYS ARE STILL TOGETHER AND EVERYTHING.
SEE YA LATER.
HA-HA... SEE YA.

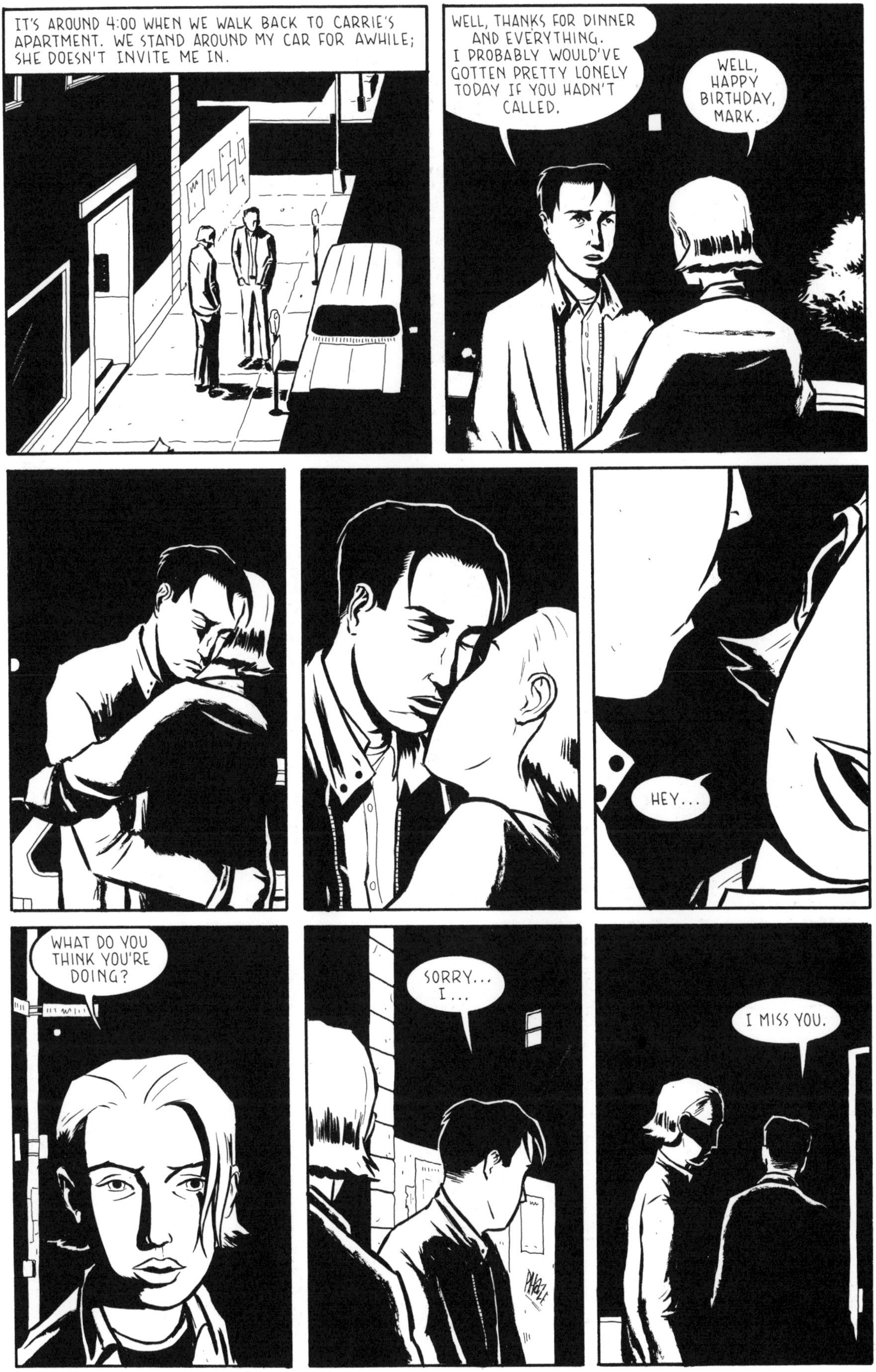
IT'S AROUND 4:00 WHEN WE WALK BACK TO CARRIE'S APARTMENT. WE STAND AROUND MY CAR FOR AWHILE; SHE DOESN'T INVITE ME IN.
WELL, THANKS FOR DINNER AND EVERYTHING. I PROBABLY WOULD'VE GOTTEN PRETTY LONELY TODAY IF YOU HADN'T CALLED.
WELL, HAPPY BIRTHDAY, MARK.
HEY...
WHAT DO YOU THINK YOU'RE DOING?
SORRY... I...
I MISS YOU.

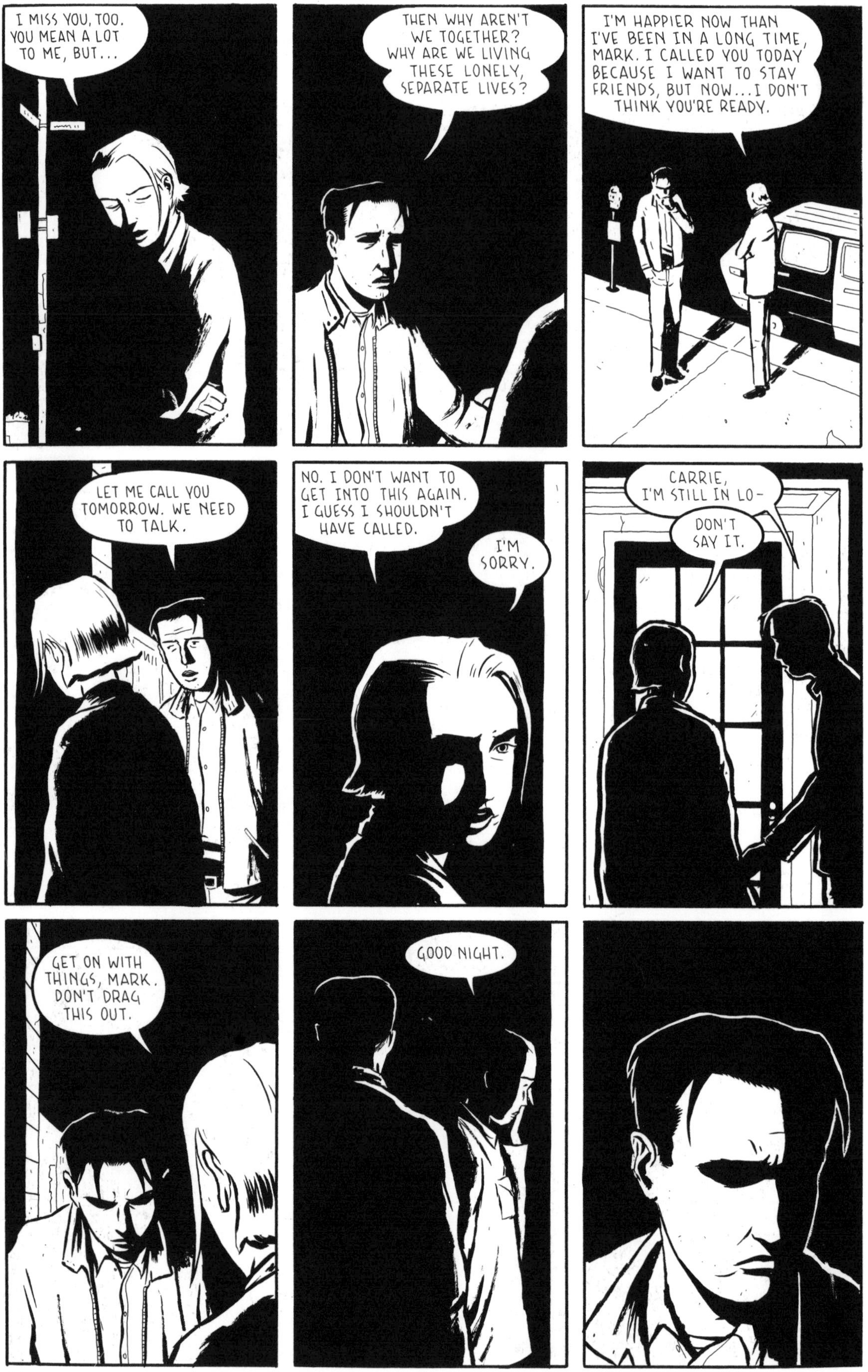
I MISS YOU, TOO. YOU MEAN A LOT TO ME, BUT...
THEN WHY AREN'T WE TOGETHER? WHY ARE WE LIVING THESE LONELY, SEPARATE LIVES?
I'M HAPPIER NOW THAN I'VE BEEN IN A LONG TIME, MARK. I CALLED YOU TODAY BECAUSE I WANT TO STAY FRIENDS, BUT NOW...I DON'T THINK YOU'RE READY.
LET ME CALL YOU TOMORROW. WE NEED TO TALK.
NO. I DON'T WANT TO GET INTO THIS AGAIN. I GUESS I SHOULDN'T HAVE CALLED.
I'M SORRY.
CARRIE, I'M STILL IN LO–
DON'T SAY IT.
GET ON WITH THINGS, MARK. DON'T DRAG THIS OUT.
GOOD NIGHT.

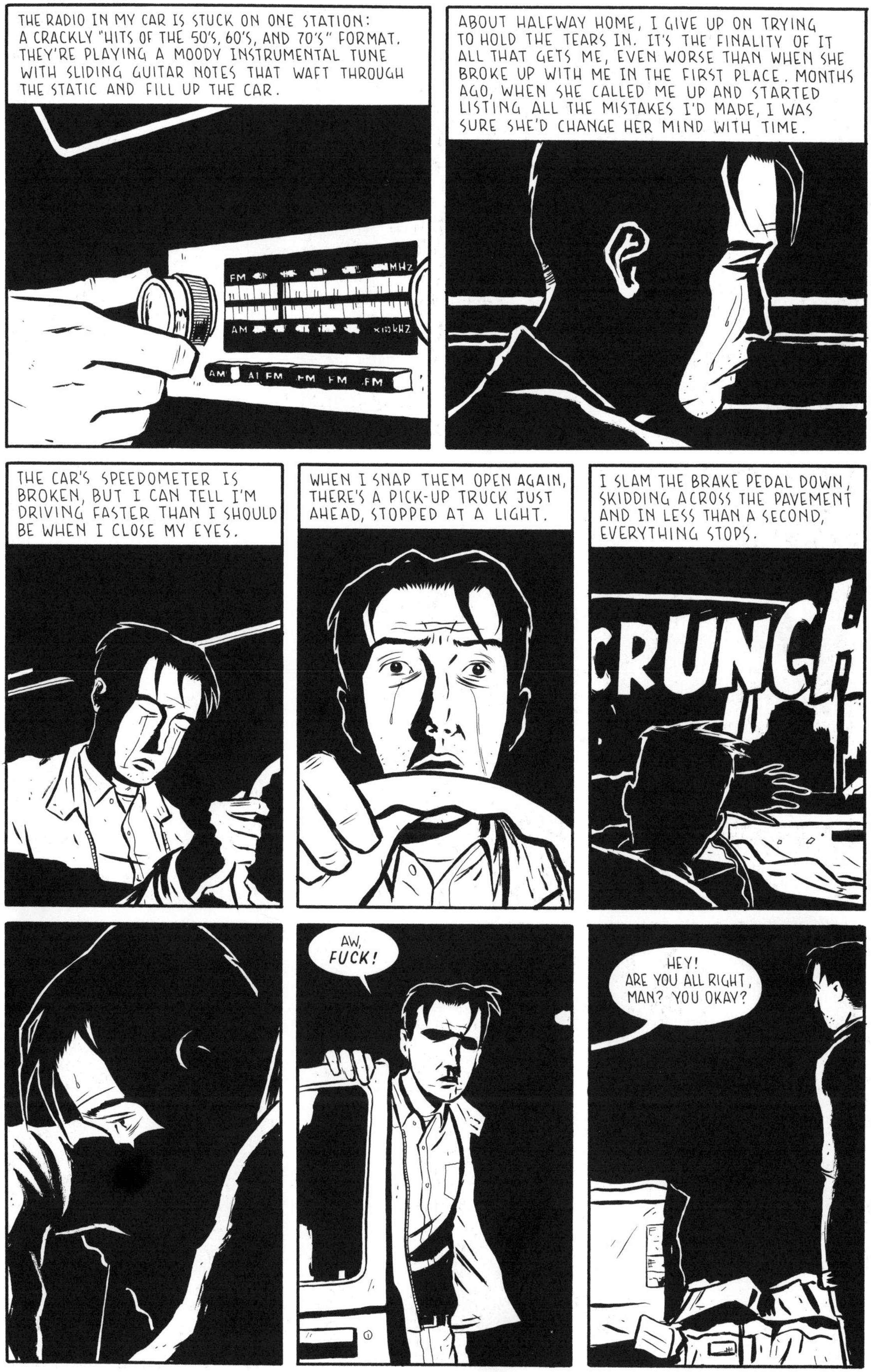
THE RADIO IN MY CAR IS STUCK ON ONE STATION: A CRACKLY "HITS OF THE 50'S, 60'S, AND 70'S" FORMAT. THEY'RE PLAYING A MOODY INSTRUMENTAL TUNE WITH SLIDING GUITAR NOTES THAT WAFT THROUGH THE STATIC AND FILL UP THE CAR.
ABOUT HALFWAY HOME, I GIVE UP ON TRYING TO HOLD THE TEARS IN. IT'S THE FINALITY OF IT ALL THAT GETS ME, EVEN WORSE THAN WHEN SHE BROKE UP WITH ME IN THE FIRST PLACE. MONTHS AGO, WHEN SHE CALLED ME UP AND STARTED LISTING ALL THE MISTAKES I'D MADE, I WAS SURE SHE'D CHANGE HER MIND WITH TIME.
THE CAR'S SPEEDOMETER IS BROKEN, BUT I CAN TELL I'M DRIVING FASTER THAN I SHOULD BE WHEN I CLOSE MY EYES.
WHEN I SNAP THEM OPEN AGAIN, THERE'S A PICK-UP TRUCK JUST AHEAD, STOPPED AT A LIGHT.
I SLAM THE BRAKE PEDAL DOWN, SKIDDING ACROSS THE PAVEMENT AND IN LESS THAN A SECOND, EVERYTHING STOPS.
CRUNCH
AW, FUCK!
HEY! ARE YOU ALL RIGHT, MAN? YOU OKAY?

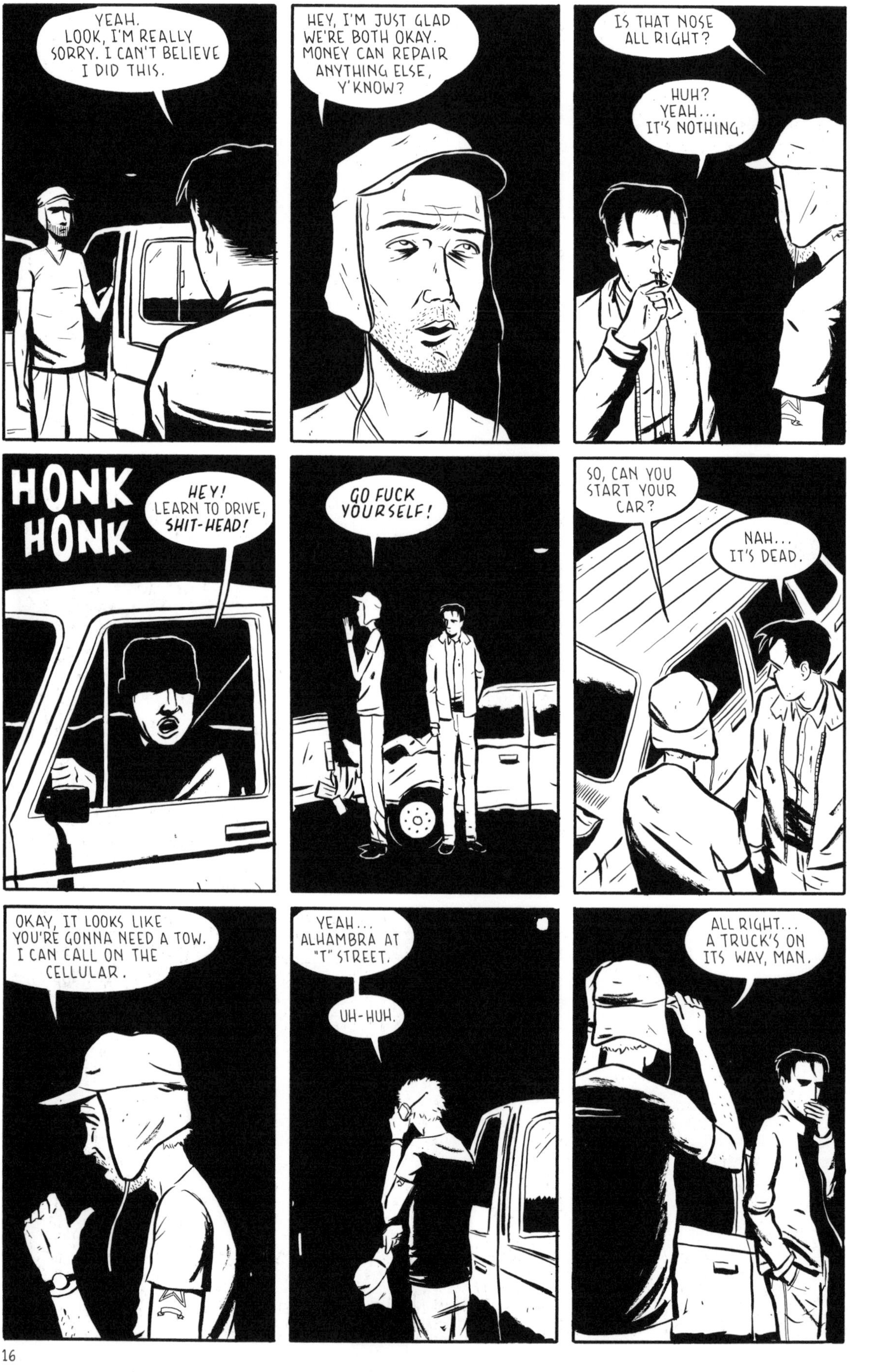
YEAH. LOOK, I'M REALLY SORRY. I CAN'T BELIEVE I DID THIS.
HEY, I'M JUST GLAD WE'RE BOTH OKAY. MONEY CAN REPAIR ANYTHING ELSE, Y'KNOW?
IS THAT NOSE ALL RIGHT?
HUH? YEAH... IT'S NOTHING.
HONK HONK
HEY! LEARN TO DRIVE, SHIT-HEAD!
GO FUCK YOURSELF!
SO, CAN YOU START YOUR CAR?
NAH... IT'S DEAD.
OKAY, IT LOOKS LIKE YOU'RE GONNA NEED A TOW. I CAN CALL ON THE CELLULAR.
YEAH... ALHAMBRA AT "T" STREET.
UH-HUH.
ALL RIGHT... A TRUCK'S ON ITS WAY, MAN.

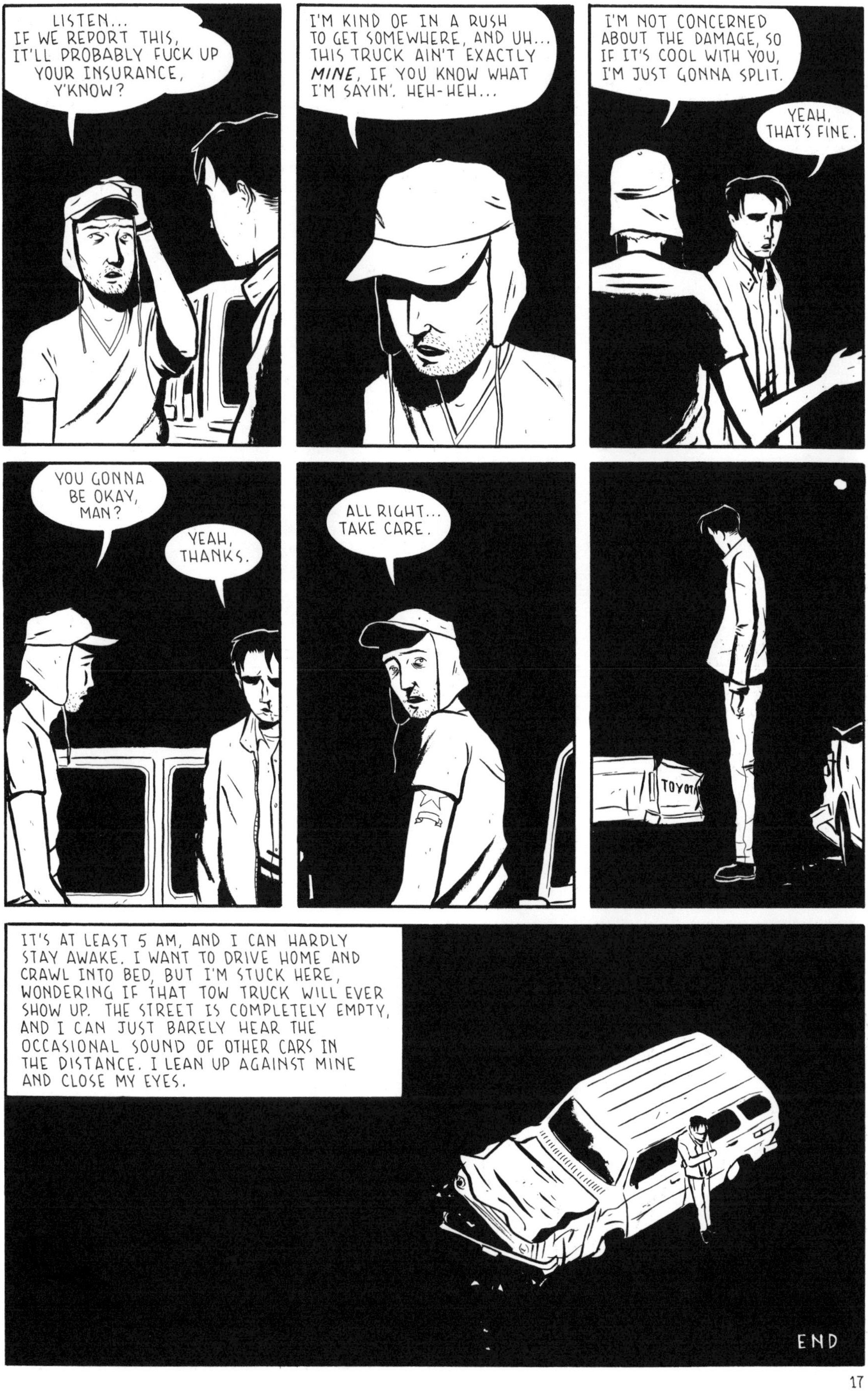
LISTEN... IF WE REPORT THIS, IT'LL PROBABLY FUCK UP YOUR INSURANCE, Y'KNOW?
I'M KIND OF IN A RUSH TO GET SOMEWHERE, AND UH... THIS TRUCK AIN'T EXACTLY *MINE*, IF YOU KNOW WHAT I'M SAYIN'. HEH-HEH...
I'M NOT CONCERNED ABOUT THE DAMAGE, SO IF IT'S COOL WITH YOU, I'M JUST GONNA SPLIT.
YEAH, THAT'S FINE.
YOU GONNA BE OKAY, MAN?
YEAH, THANKS.
ALL RIGHT... TAKE CARE.
TOYOTA
IT'S AT LEAST 5 AM, AND I CAN HARDLY STAY AWAKE. I WANT TO DRIVE HOME AND CRAWL INTO BED, BUT I'M STUCK HERE, WONDERING IF THAT TOW TRUCK WILL EVER SHOW UP. THE STREET IS COMPLETELY EMPTY, AND I CAN JUST BARELY HEAR THE OCCASIONAL SOUND OF OTHER CARS IN THE DISTANCE. I LEAN UP AGAINST MINE AND CLOSE MY EYES.
END

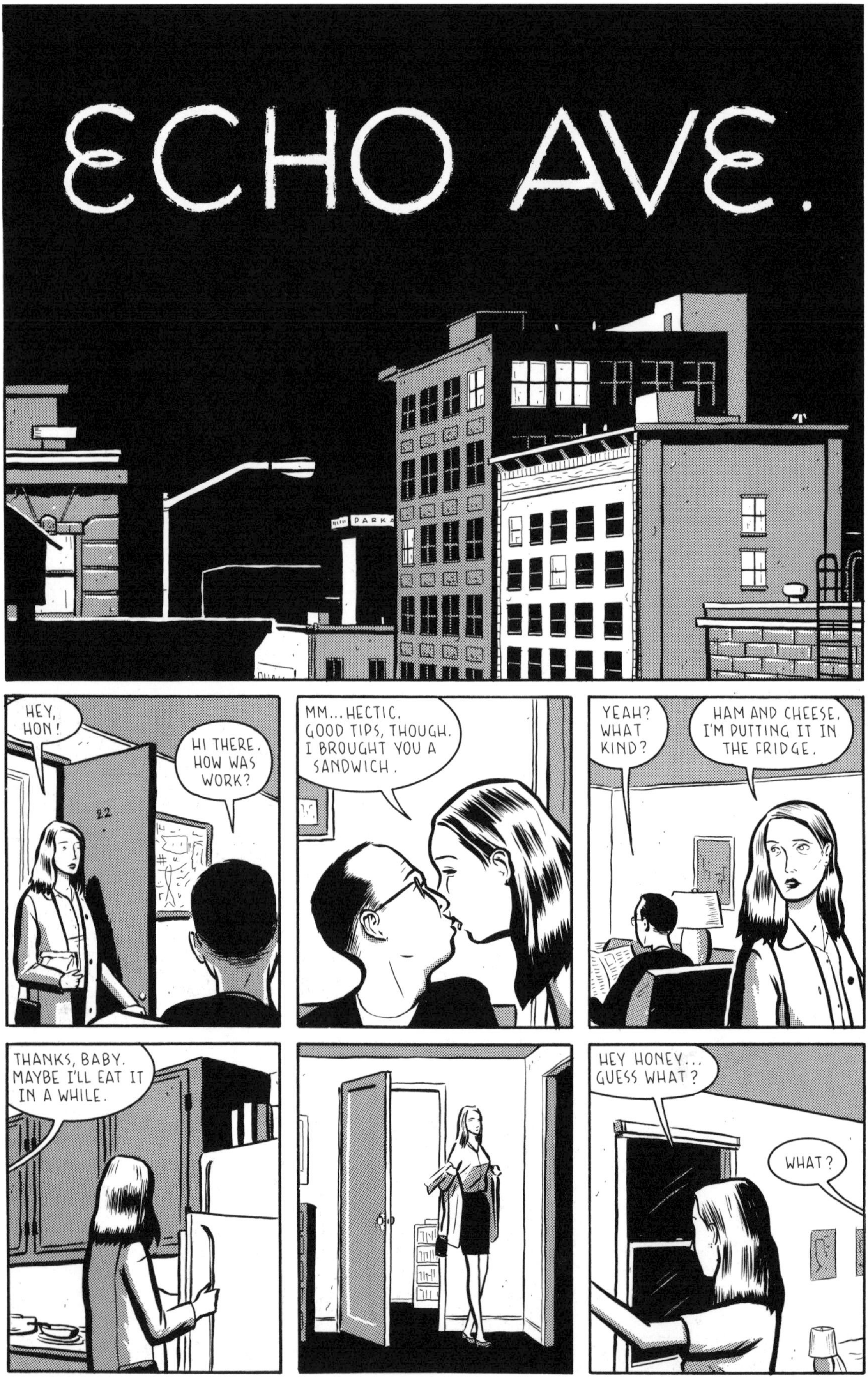
ECHO AVE.
PARKA
22
HEY, HON!
HI THERE. HOW WAS WORK?
MM... HECTIC. GOOD TIPS, THOUGH. I BROUGHT YOU A SANDWICH.
YEAH? WHAT KIND?
HAM AND CHEESE. I'M PUTTING IT IN THE FRIDGE.
THANKS, BABY. MAYBE I'LL EAT IT IN A WHILE.
HEY HONEY... GUESS WHAT?
WHAT?

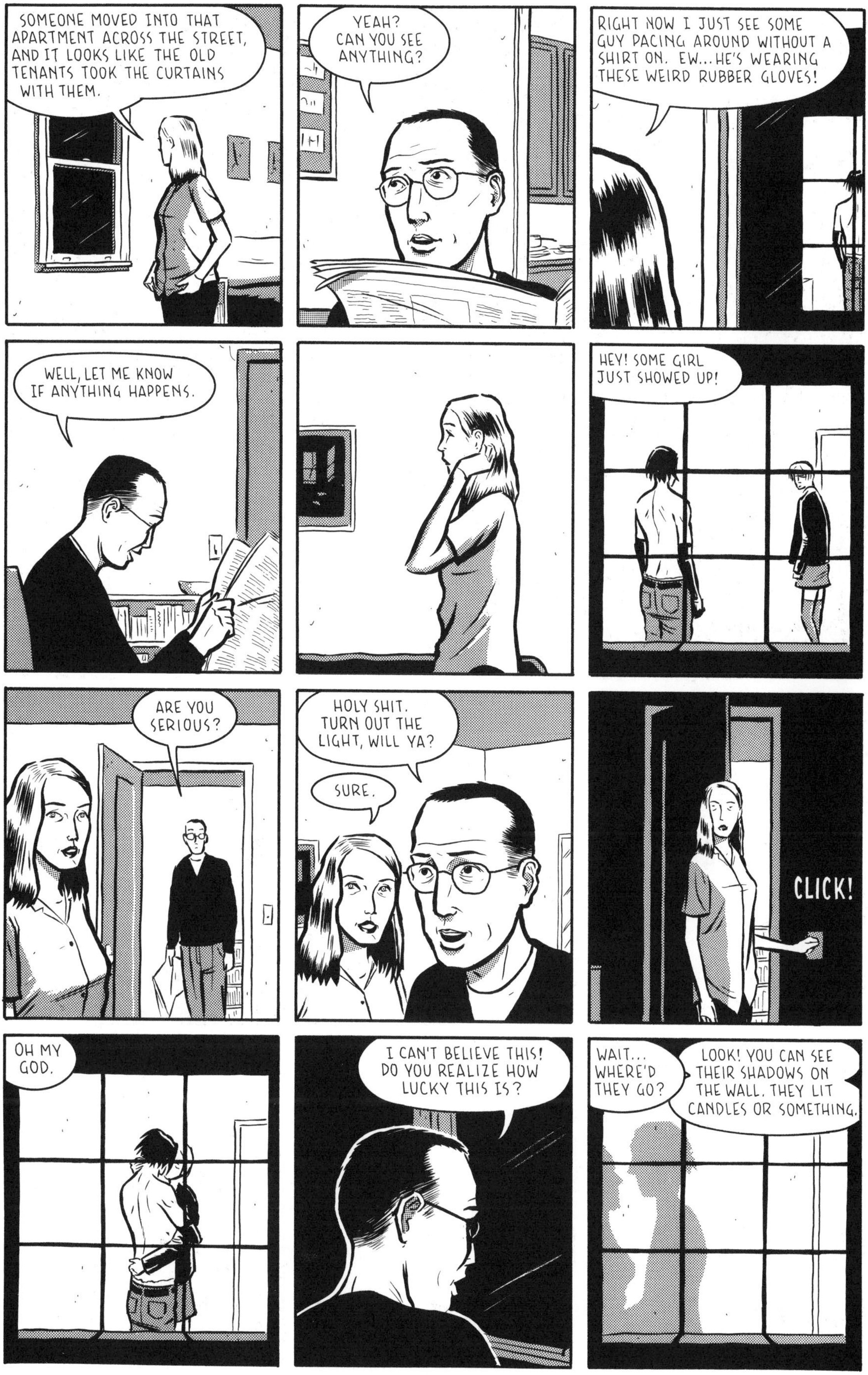
SOMEONE MOVED INTO THAT APARTMENT ACROSS THE STREET, AND IT LOOKS LIKE THE OLD TENANTS TOOK THE CURTAINS WITH THEM.
YEAH? CAN YOU SEE ANYTHING?
RIGHT NOW I JUST SEE SOME GUY PACING AROUND WITHOUT A SHIRT ON. EW...HE'S WEARING THESE WEIRD RUBBER GLOVES!
WELL, LET ME KNOW IF ANYTHING HAPPENS.
HEY! SOME GIRL JUST SHOWED UP!
ARE YOU SERIOUS?
HOLY SHIT. TURN OUT THE LIGHT, WILL YA?
SURE.
CLICK!
OH MY GOD.
I CAN'T BELIEVE THIS! DO YOU REALIZE HOW LUCKY THIS IS?
WAIT... WHERE'D THEY GO?
LOOK! YOU CAN SEE THEIR SHADOWS ON THE WALL. THEY LIT CANDLES OR SOMETHING.

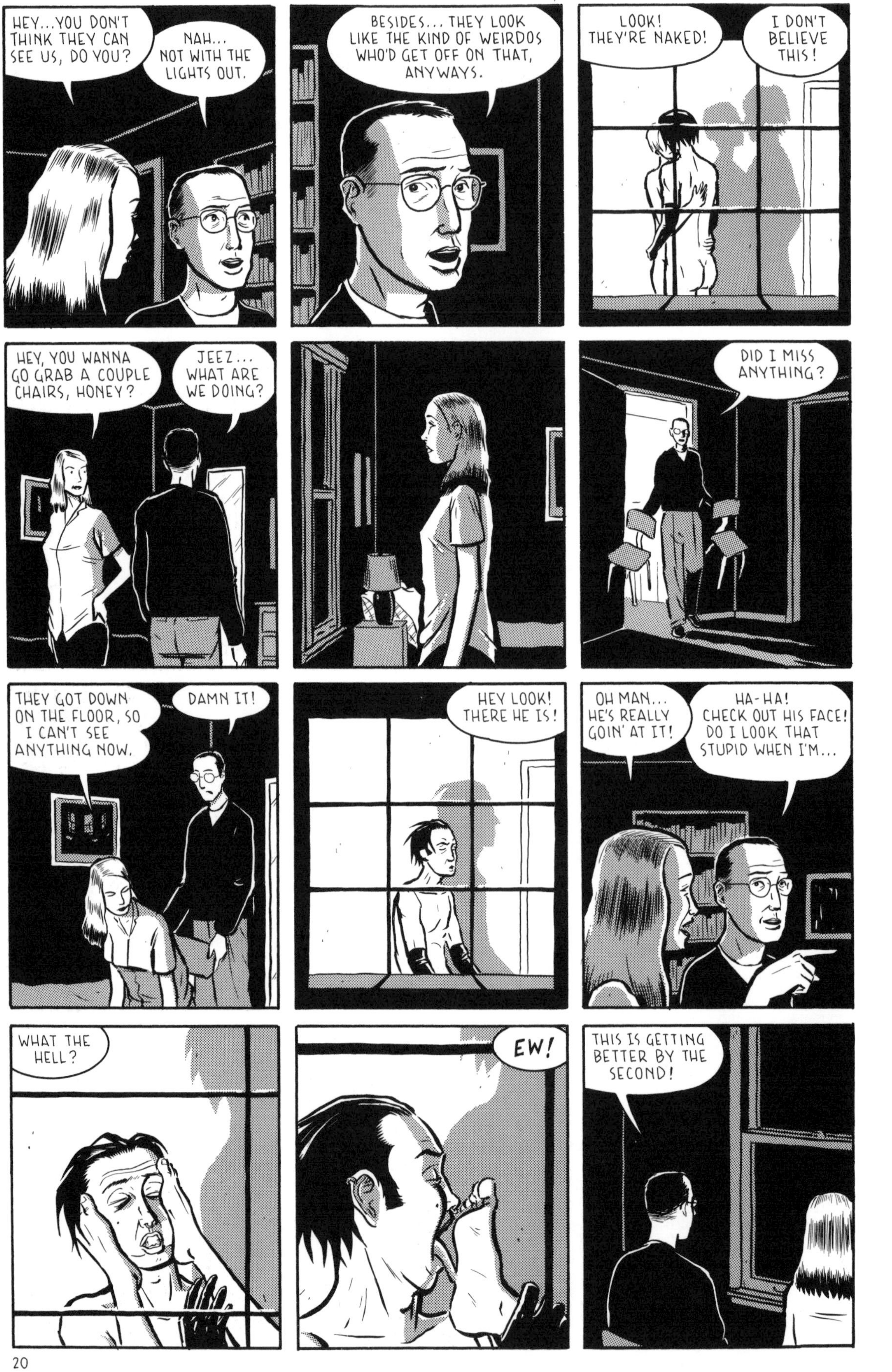
HEY...YOU DON'T THINK THEY CAN SEE US, DO YOU?
NAH... NOT WITH THE LIGHTS OUT.
BESIDES... THEY LOOK LIKE THE KIND OF WEIRDOS WHO'D GET OFF ON THAT, ANYWAYS.
LOOK! THEY'RE NAKED!
I DON'T BELIEVE THIS!
HEY, YOU WANNA GO GRAB A COUPLE CHAIRS, HONEY?
JEEZ... WHAT ARE WE DOING?
DID I MISS ANYTHING?
THEY GOT DOWN ON THE FLOOR, SO I CAN'T SEE ANYTHING NOW.
DAMN IT!
HEY LOOK! THERE HE IS!
OH MAN... HE'S REALLY GOIN' AT IT!
HA-HA! CHECK OUT HIS FACE! DO I LOOK THAT STUPID WHEN I'M...
WHAT THE HELL?
EW!
THIS IS GETTING BETTER BY THE SECOND!

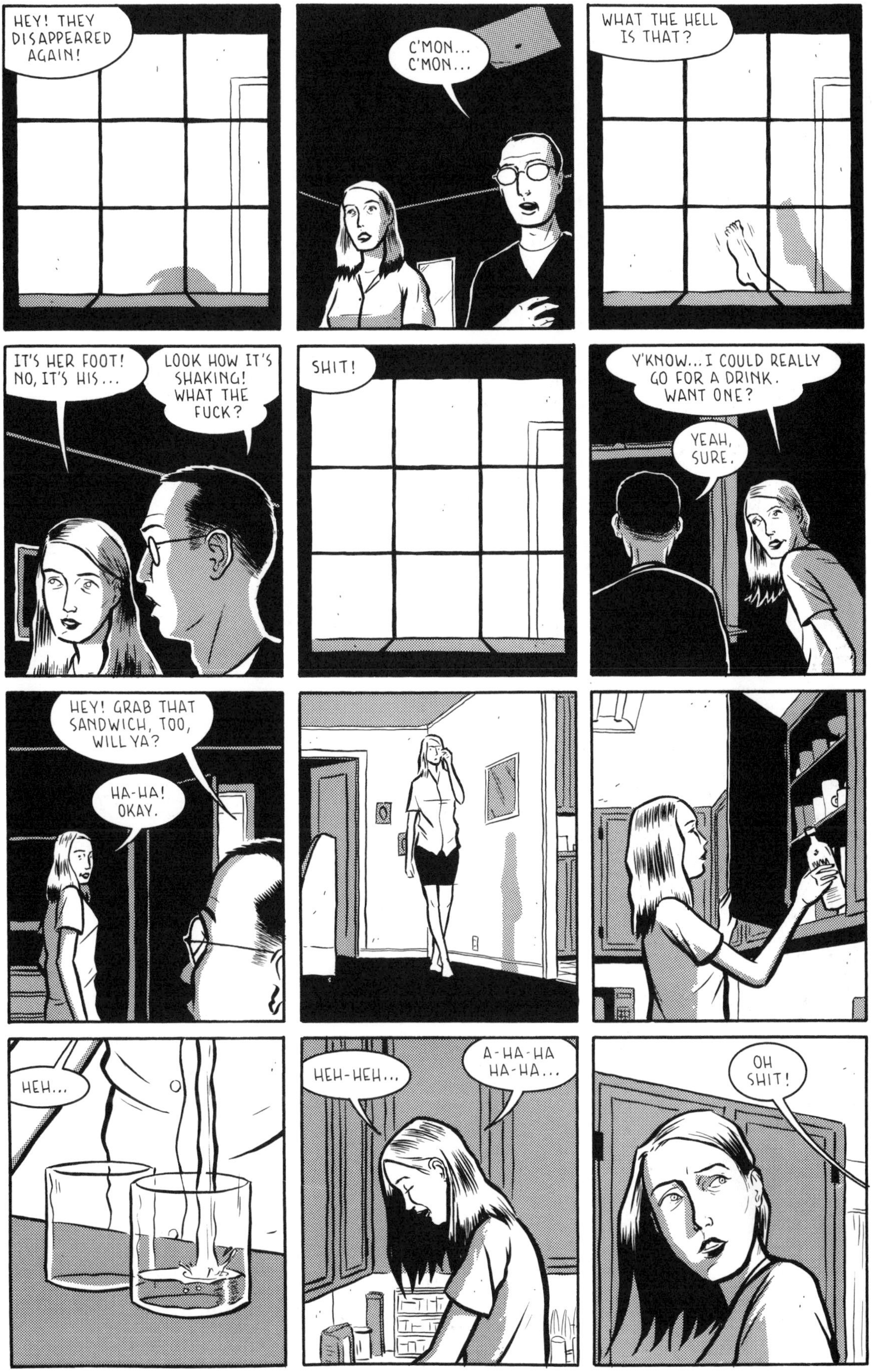
HEY! THEY DISAPPEARED AGAIN!
C'MON... C'MON...
WHAT THE HELL IS THAT?
IT'S HER FOOT! NO, IT'S HIS...
LOOK HOW IT'S SHAKING! WHAT THE FUCK?
SHIT!
Y'KNOW... I COULD REALLY GO FOR A DRINK. WANT ONE?
YEAH, SURE.
HEY! GRAB THAT SANDWICH, TOO, WILL YA?
HA-HA! OKAY.
HEH...
HEH-HEH...
A-HA-HA HA-HA...
OH SHIT!

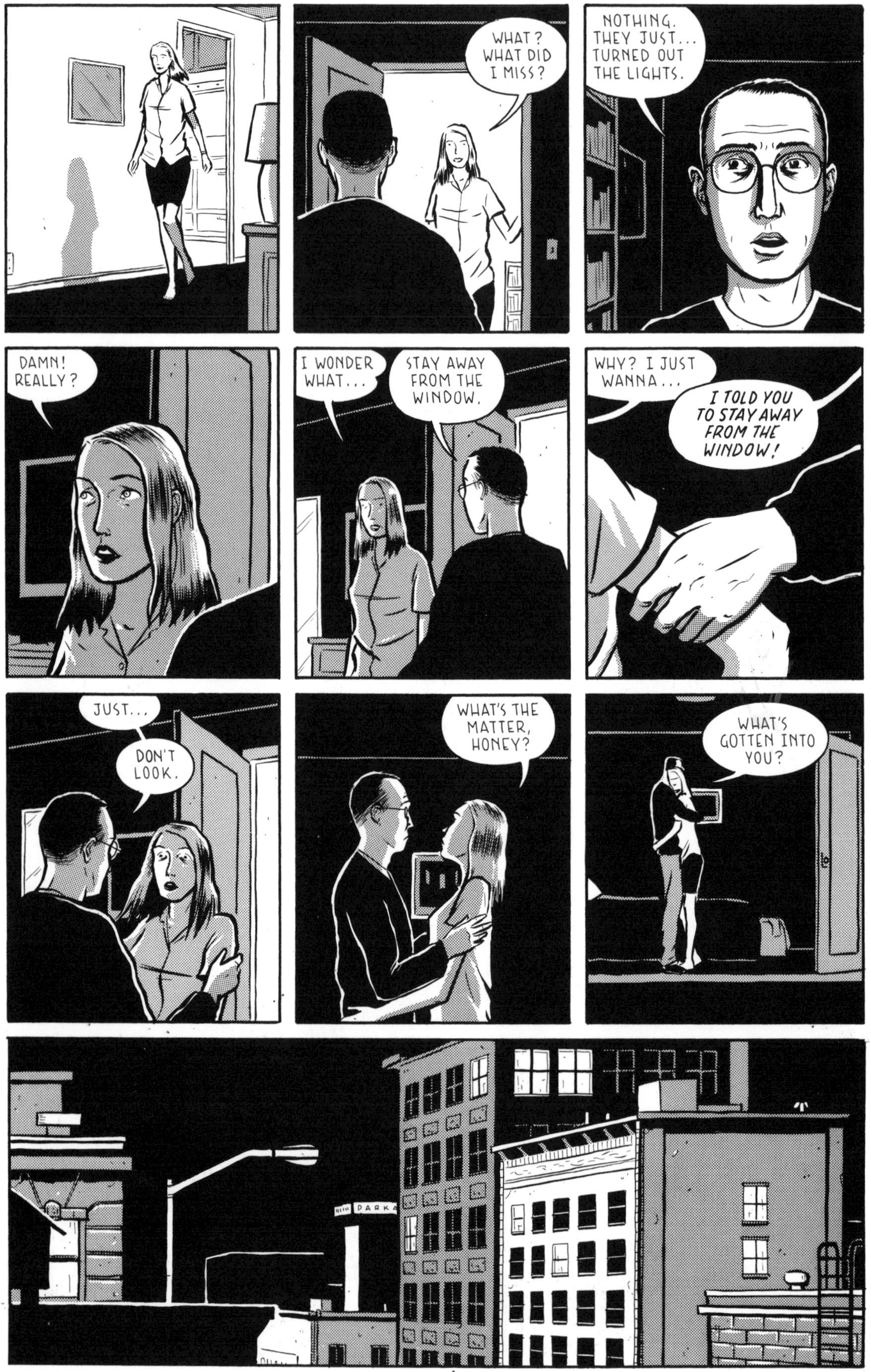
WHAT? WHAT DID I MISS?
NOTHING. THEY JUST... TURNED OUT THE LIGHTS.
DAMN! REALLY?
I WONDER WHAT...
STAY AWAY FROM THE WINDOW.
WHY? I JUST WANNA...
I TOLD YOU TO STAY AWAY FROM THE WINDOW!
JUST...
DON'T LOOK.
WHAT'S THE MATTER, HONEY?
WHAT'S GOTTEN INTO YOU?

TOMINE 94

LONG DISTANCE

TOMINE 1994

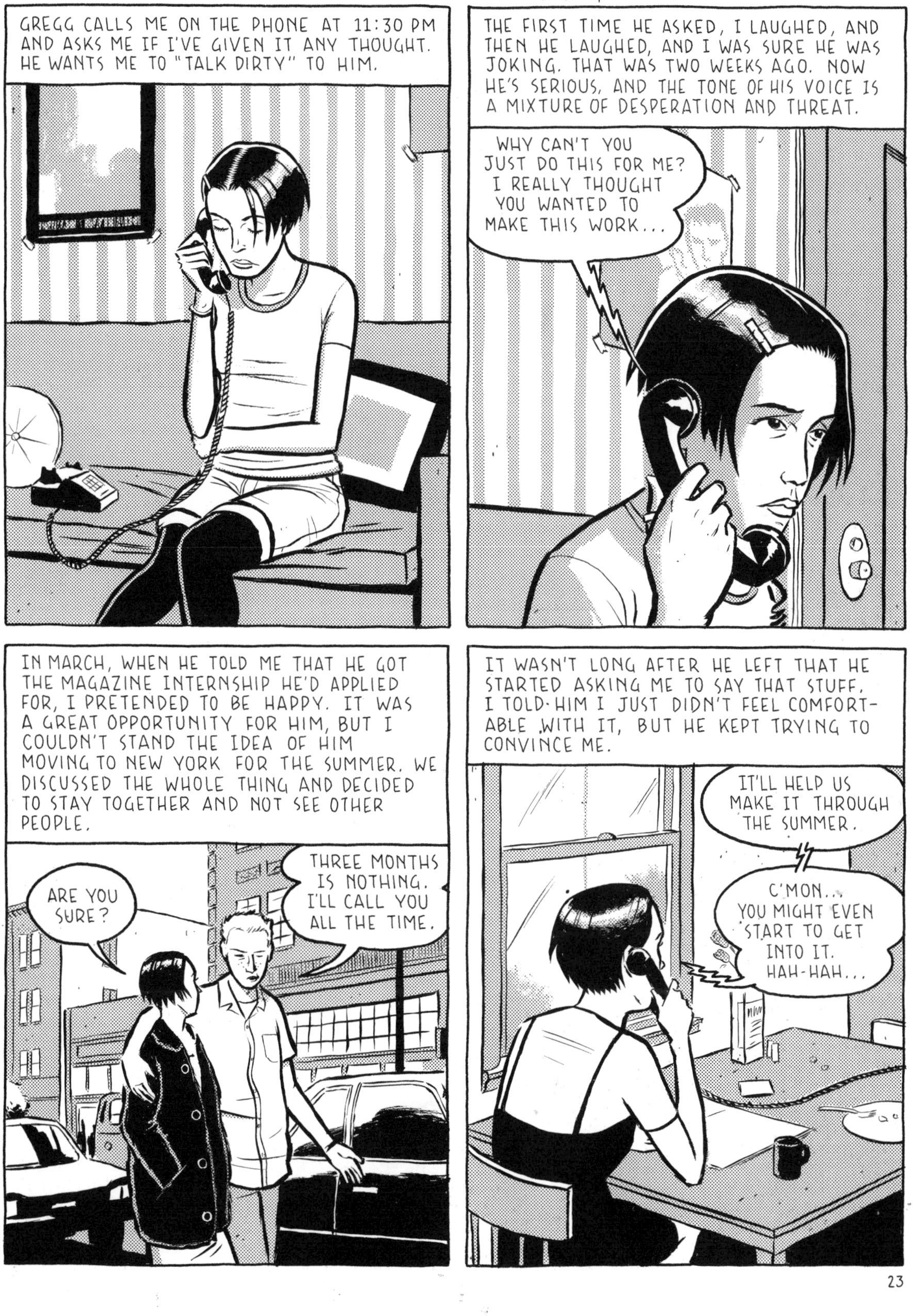
GREGG CALLS ME ON THE PHONE AT 11:30 PM AND ASKS ME IF I'VE GIVEN IT ANY THOUGHT. HE WANTS ME TO "TALK DIRTY" TO HIM.
THE FIRST TIME HE ASKED, I LAUGHED, AND THEN HE LAUGHED, AND I WAS SURE HE WAS JOKING. THAT WAS TWO WEEKS AGO. NOW HE'S SERIOUS, AND THE TONE OF HIS VOICE IS A MIXTURE OF DESPERATION AND THREAT.
WHY CAN'T YOU JUST DO THIS FOR ME? I REALLY THOUGHT YOU WANTED TO MAKE THIS WORK...
IN MARCH, WHEN HE TOLD ME THAT HE GOT THE MAGAZINE INTERNSHIP HE'D APPLIED FOR, I PRETENDED TO BE HAPPY. IT WAS A GREAT OPPORTUNITY FOR HIM, BUT I COULDN'T STAND THE IDEA OF HIM MOVING TO NEW YORK FOR THE SUMMER. WE DISCUSSED THE WHOLE THING AND DECIDED TO STAY TOGETHER AND NOT SEE OTHER PEOPLE.
ARE YOU SURE?
THREE MONTHS IS NOTHING. I'LL CALL YOU ALL THE TIME.
IT WASN'T LONG AFTER HE LEFT THAT HE STARTED ASKING ME TO SAY THAT STUFF. I TOLD HIM I JUST DIDN'T FEEL COMFORTABLE WITH IT, BUT HE KEPT TRYING TO CONVINCE ME.
IT'LL HELP US MAKE IT THROUGH THE SUMMER.
C'MON... YOU MIGHT EVEN START TO GET INTO IT. HAH-HAH...

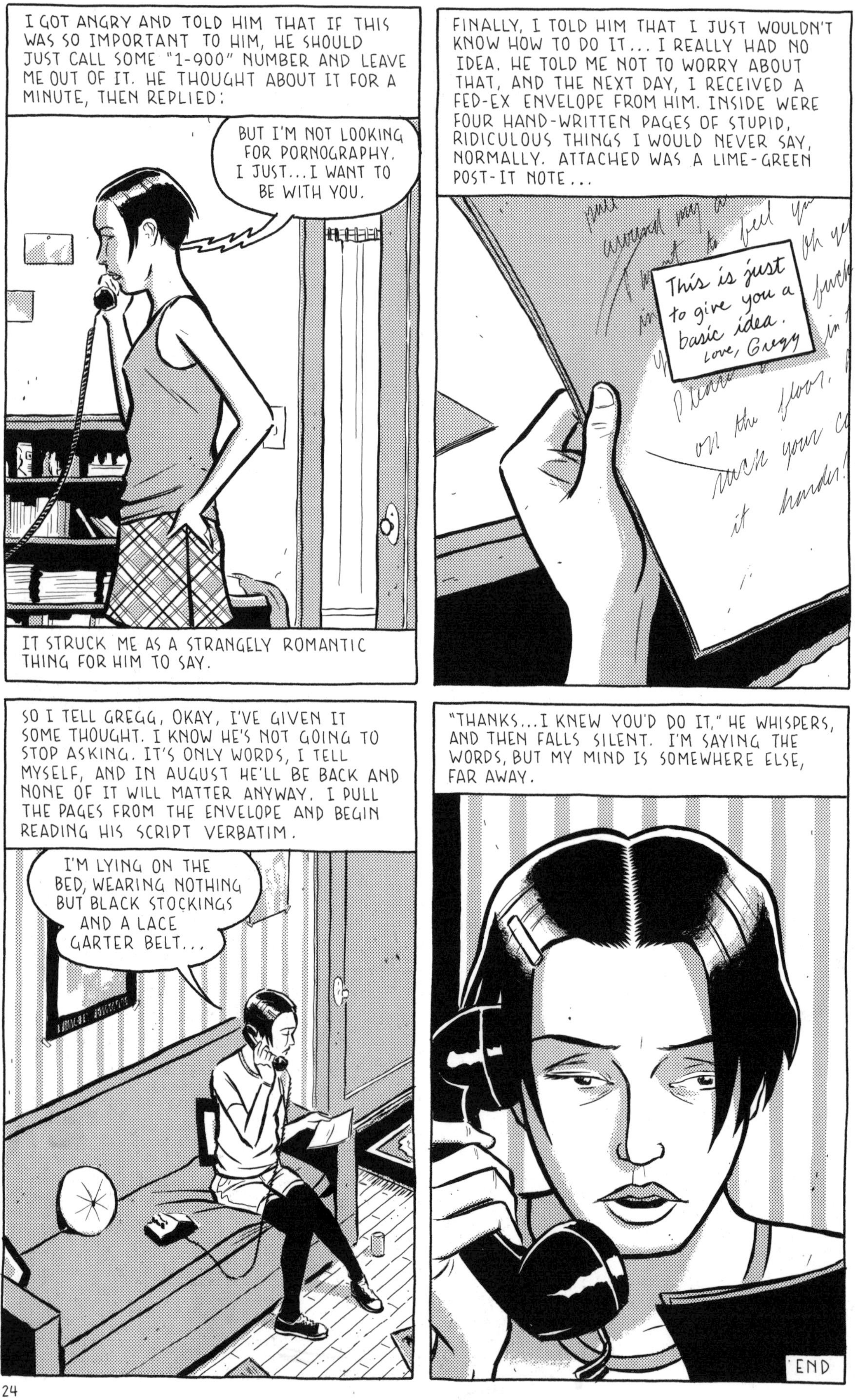
I GOT ANGRY AND TOLD HIM THAT IF THIS WAS SO IMPORTANT TO HIM, HE SHOULD JUST CALL SOME "1-900" NUMBER AND LEAVE ME OUT OF IT. HE THOUGHT ABOUT IT FOR A MINUTE, THEN REPLIED:
BUT I'M NOT LOOKING FOR PORNOGRAPHY. I JUST... I WANT TO BE WITH YOU.
IT STRUCK ME AS A STRANGELY ROMANTIC THING FOR HIM TO SAY.
FINALLY, I TOLD HIM THAT I JUST WOULDN'T KNOW HOW TO DO IT... I REALLY HAD NO IDEA. HE TOLD ME NOT TO WORRY ABOUT THAT, AND THE NEXT DAY, I RECEIVED A FED-EX ENVELOPE FROM HIM. INSIDE WERE FOUR HAND-WRITTEN PAGES OF STUPID, RIDICULOUS THINGS I WOULD NEVER SAY, NORMALLY. ATTACHED WAS A LIME-GREEN POST-IT NOTE...
This is just to give you a basic idea. Love, Gregg
SO I TELL GREGG, OKAY, I'VE GIVEN IT SOME THOUGHT. I KNOW HE'S NOT GOING TO STOP ASKING. IT'S ONLY WORDS, I TELL MYSELF, AND IN AUGUST HE'LL BE BACK AND NONE OF IT WILL MATTER ANYWAY. I PULL THE PAGES FROM THE ENVELOPE AND BEGIN READING HIS SCRIPT VERBATIM.
I'M LYING ON THE BED, WEARING NOTHING BUT BLACK STOCKINGS AND A LACE GARTER BELT...
"THANKS... I KNEW YOU'D DO IT," HE WHISPERS, AND THEN FALLS SILENT. I'M SAYING THE WORDS, BUT MY MIND IS SOMEWHERE ELSE, FAR AWAY.
END

Drop

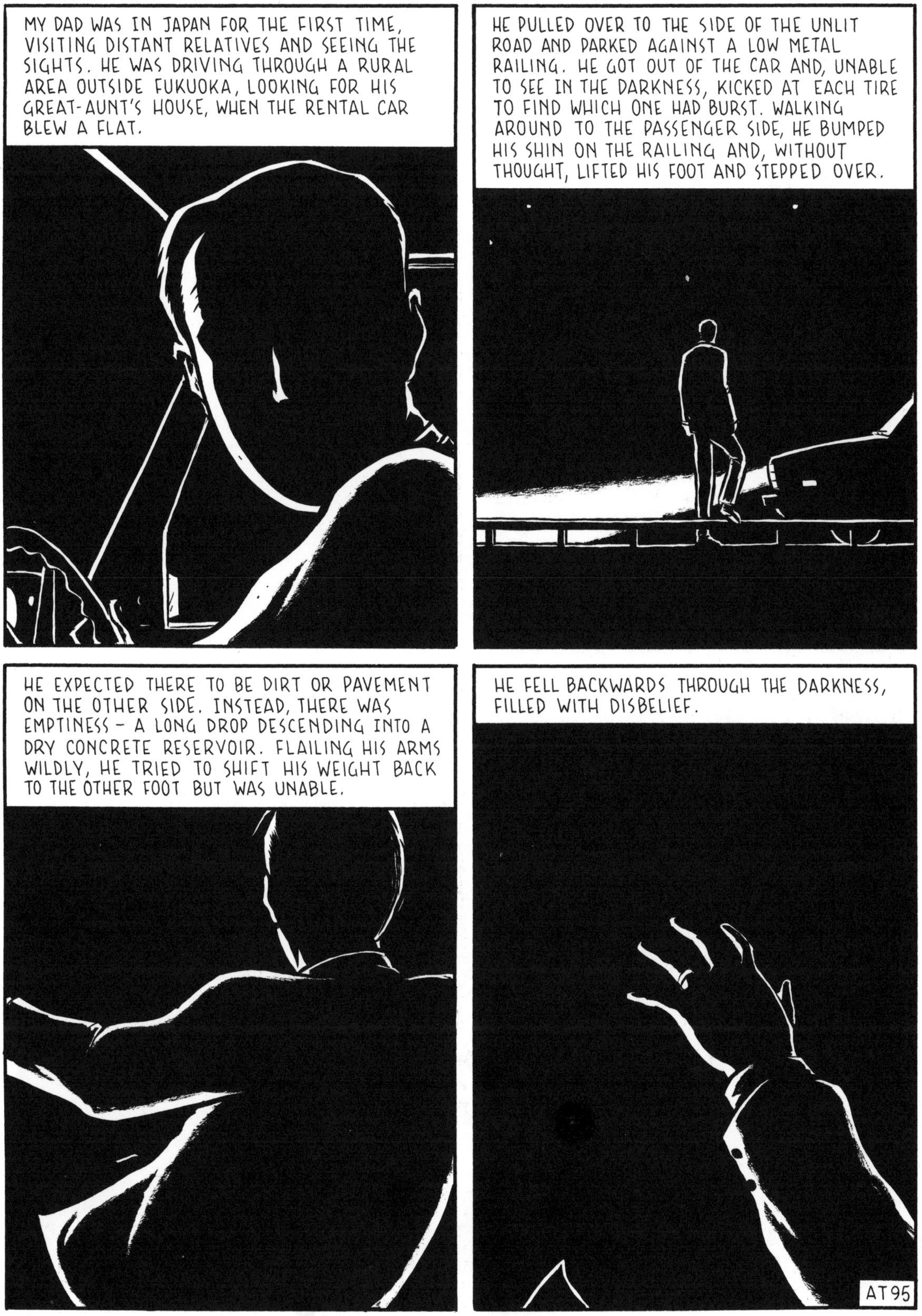
MY DAD WAS IN JAPAN FOR THE FIRST TIME, VISITING DISTANT RELATIVES AND SEEING THE SIGHTS. HE WAS DRIVING THROUGH A RURAL AREA OUTSIDE FUKUOKA, LOOKING FOR HIS GREAT-AUNT'S HOUSE, WHEN THE RENTAL CAR BLEW A FLAT.
HE PULLED OVER TO THE SIDE OF THE UNLIT ROAD AND PARKED AGAINST A LOW METAL RAILING. HE GOT OUT OF THE CAR AND, UNABLE TO SEE IN THE DARKNESS, KICKED AT EACH TIRE TO FIND WHICH ONE HAD BURST. WALKING AROUND TO THE PASSENGER SIDE, HE BUMPED HIS SHIN ON THE RAILING AND, WITHOUT THOUGHT, LIFTED HIS FOOT AND STEPPED OVER.
HE EXPECTED THERE TO BE DIRT OR PAVEMENT ON THE OTHER SIDE. INSTEAD, THERE WAS EMPTINESS – A LONG DROP DESCENDING INTO A DRY CONCRETE RESERVOIR. FLAILING HIS ARMS WILDLY, HE TRIED TO SHIFT HIS WEIGHT BACK TO THE OTHER FOOT BUT WAS UNABLE.
HE FELL BACKWARDS THROUGH THE DARKNESS, FILLED WITH DISBELIEF.
AT95

Lunch Break

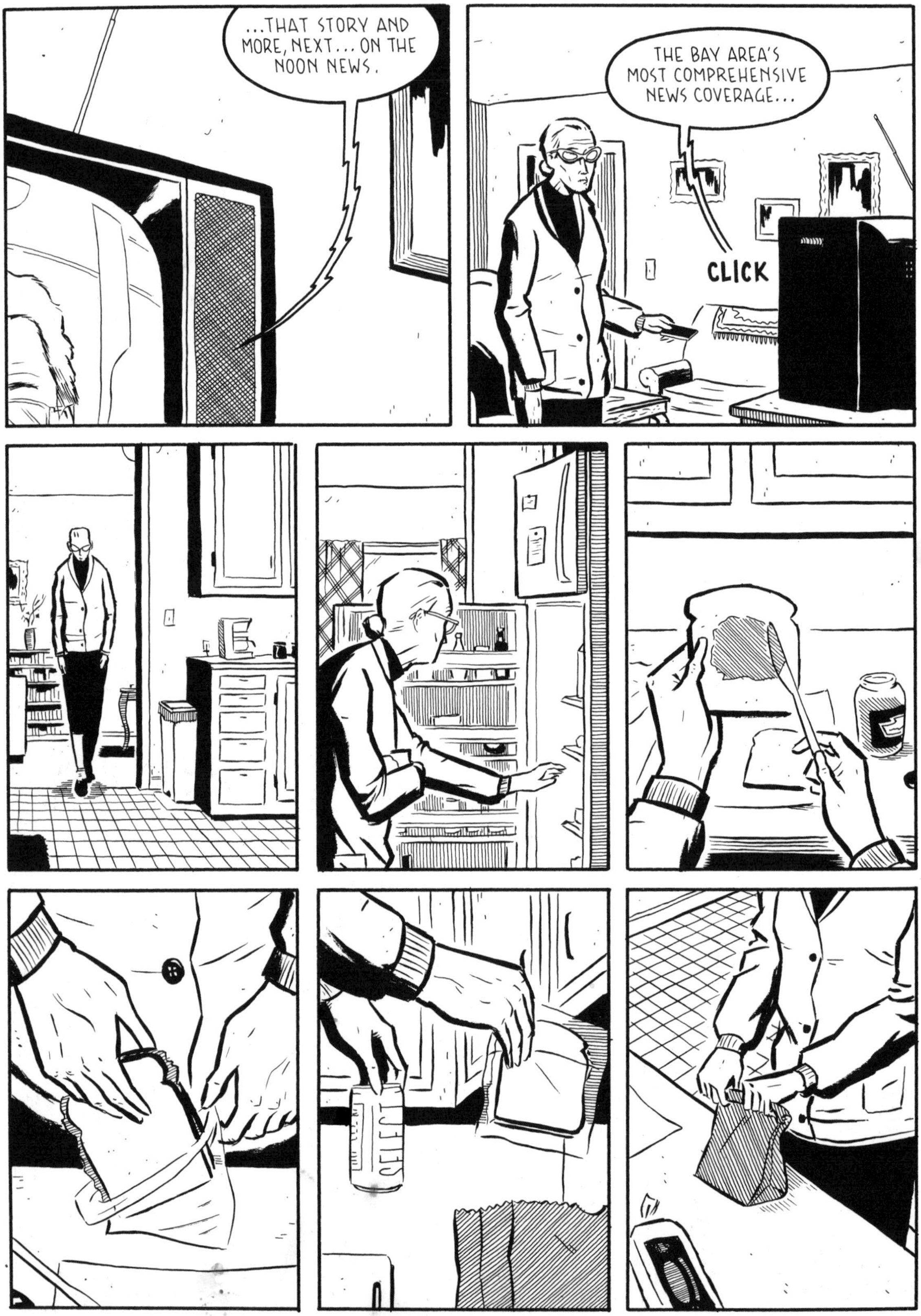
...THAT STORY AND MORE, NEXT... ON THE NOON NEWS.
THE BAY AREA'S MOST COMPREHENSIVE NEWS COVERAGE...
CLICK

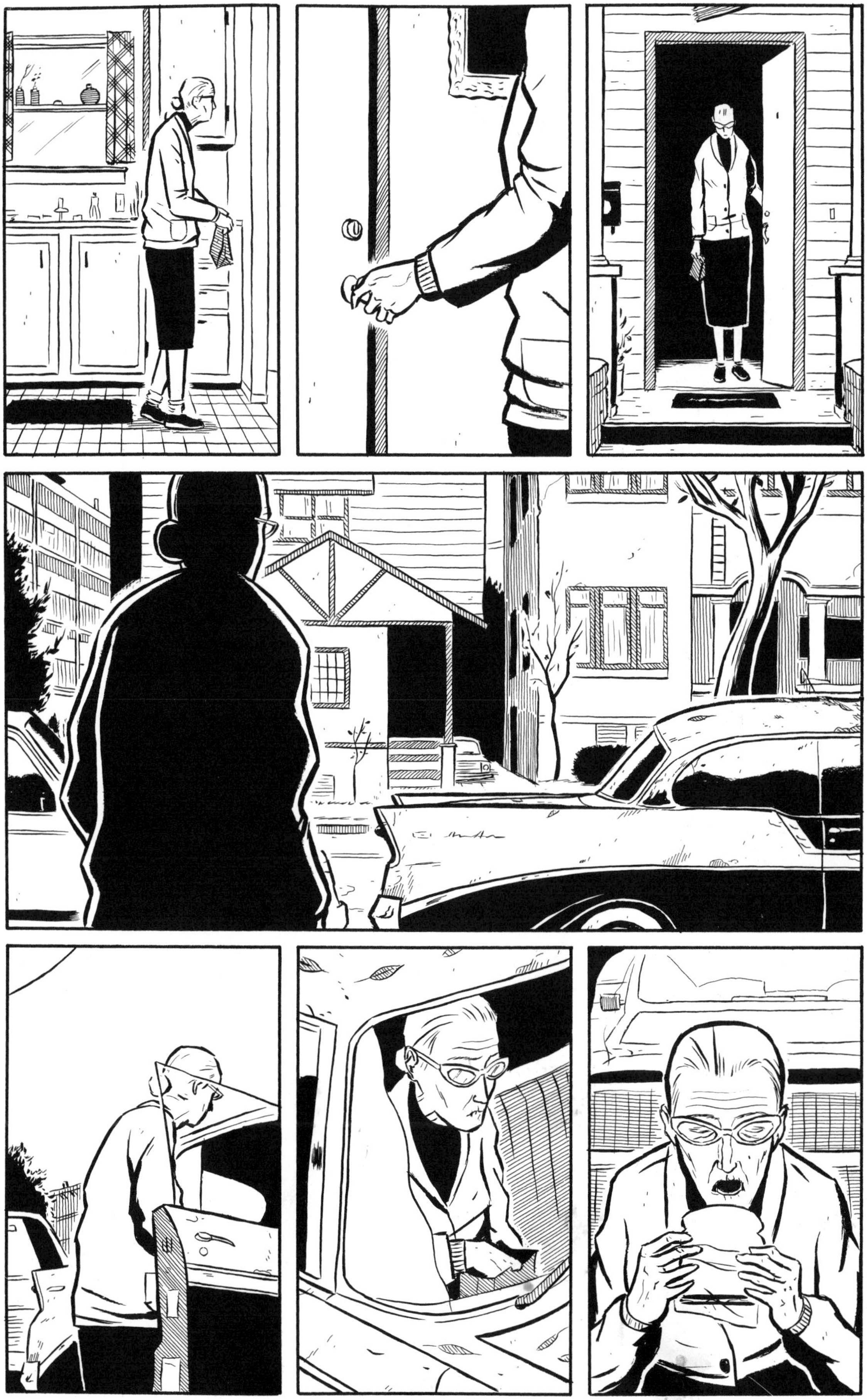

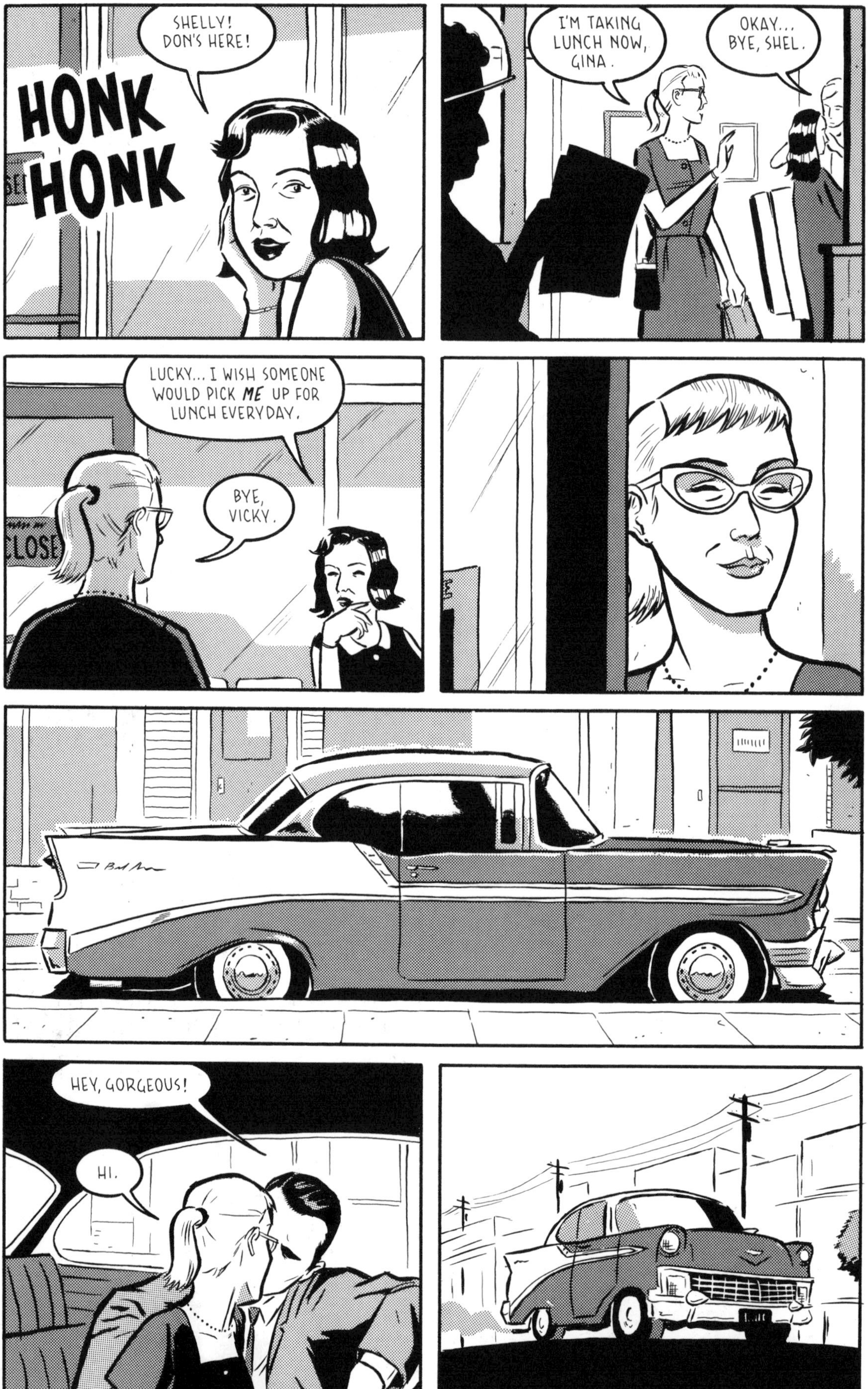
SHELLY! DON'S HERE!
HONK HONK
I'M TAKING LUNCH NOW, GINA.
OKAY... BYE, SHEL.
LUCKY... I WISH SOMEONE WOULD PICK *ME* UP FOR LUNCH EVERYDAY.
BYE, VICKY.
HEY, GORGEOUS!
HI.

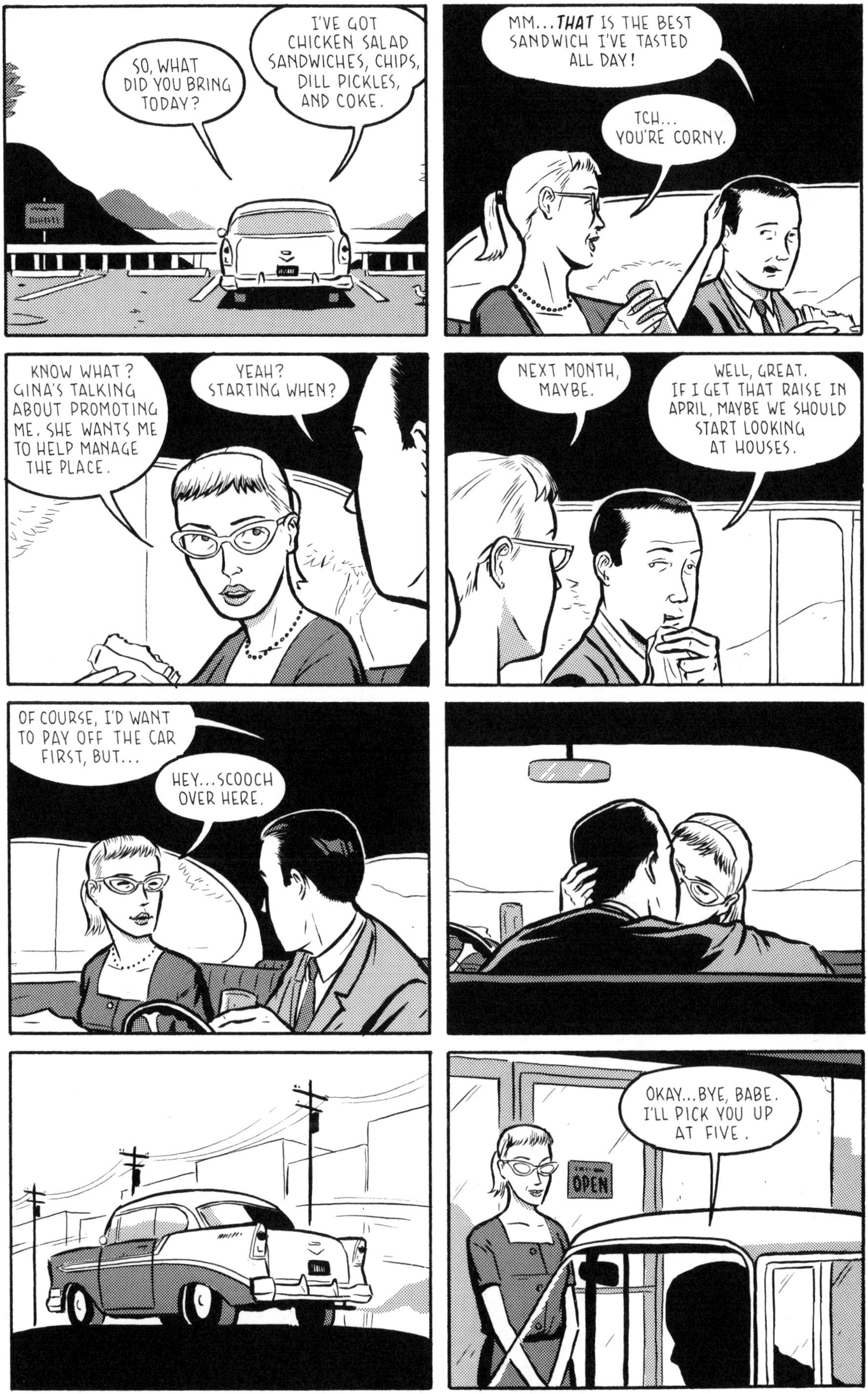
SO, WHAT DID YOU BRING TODAY?
I'VE GOT CHICKEN SALAD SANDWICHES, CHIPS, DILL PICKLES, AND COKE.
MM...**THAT** IS THE BEST SANDWICH I'VE TASTED ALL DAY!
TCH... YOU'RE CORNY.
KNOW WHAT? GINA'S TALKING ABOUT PROMOTING ME. SHE WANTS ME TO HELP MANAGE THE PLACE.
YEAH? STARTING WHEN?
NEXT MONTH, MAYBE.
WELL, GREAT. IF I GET THAT RAISE IN APRIL, MAYBE WE SHOULD START LOOKING AT HOUSES.
OF COURSE, I'D WANT TO PAY OFF THE CAR FIRST, BUT...
HEY...SCOOCH OVER HERE.
OPEN
OKAY...BYE, BABE. I'LL PICK YOU UP AT FIVE.

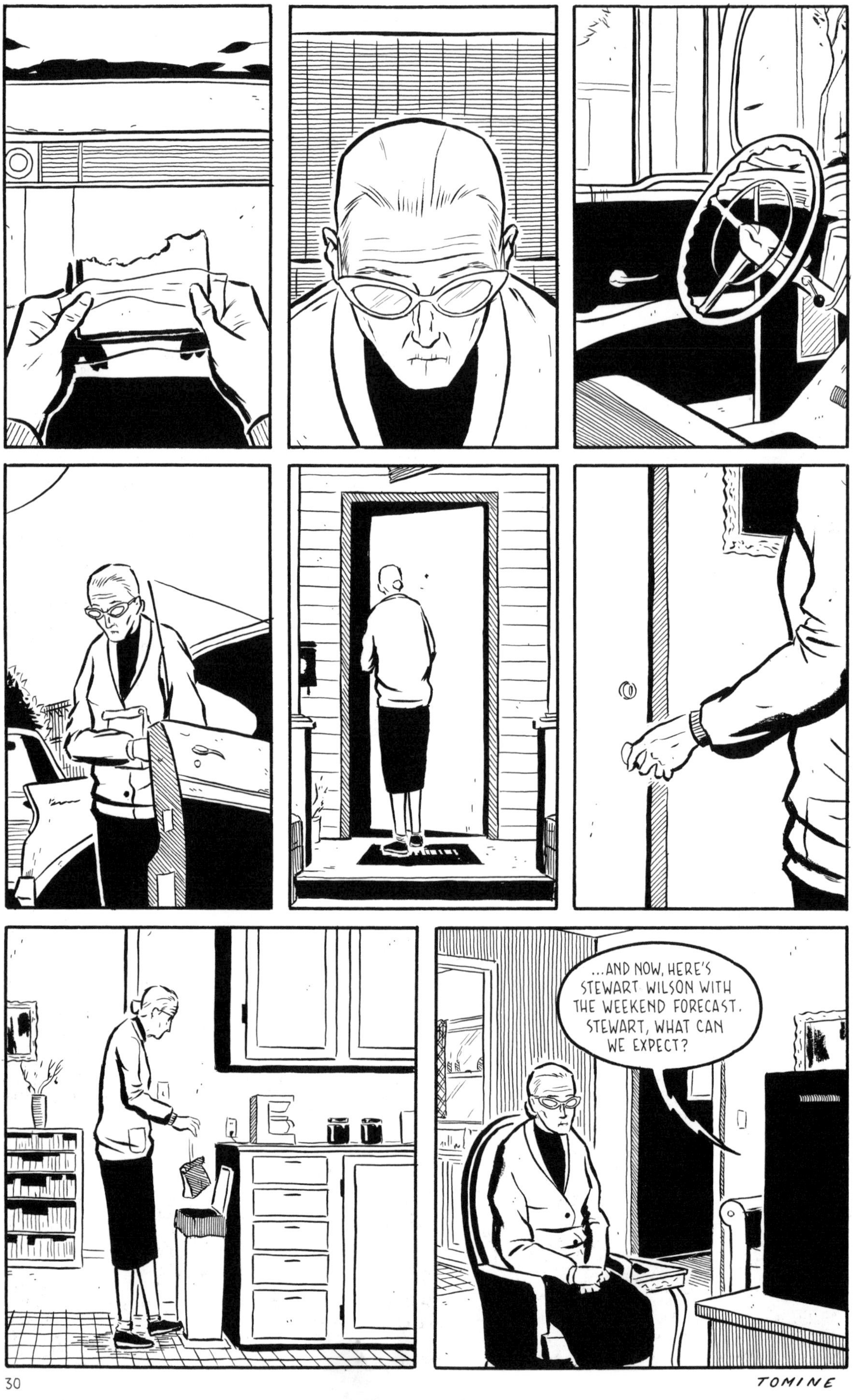
...AND NOW, HERE'S STEWART WILSON WITH THE WEEKEND FORECAST. STEWART, WHAT CAN WE EXPECT?

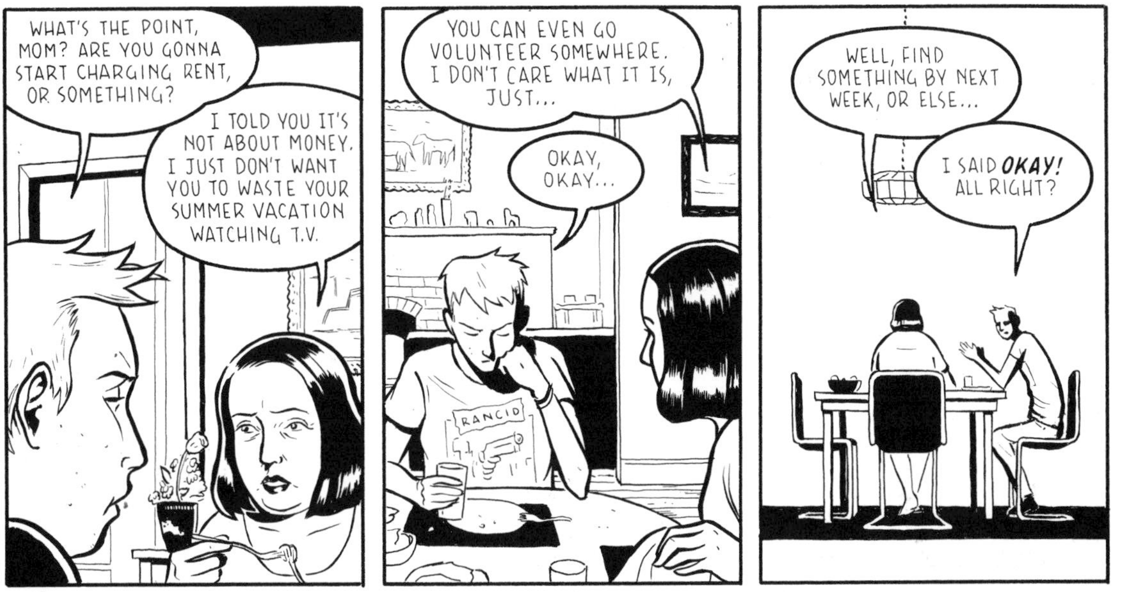
WHAT'S THE POINT, MOM? ARE YOU GONNA START CHARGING RENT, OR SOMETHING?
I TOLD YOU IT'S NOT ABOUT MONEY. I JUST DON'T WANT YOU TO WASTE YOUR SUMMER VACATION WATCHING T.V.
YOU CAN EVEN GO VOLUNTEER SOMEWHERE. I DON'T CARE WHAT IT IS, JUST...
OKAY, OKAY...
RANCID
WELL, FIND SOMETHING BY NEXT WEEK, OR ELSE...
I SAID **OKAY!** ALL RIGHT?

SUMMER JOB

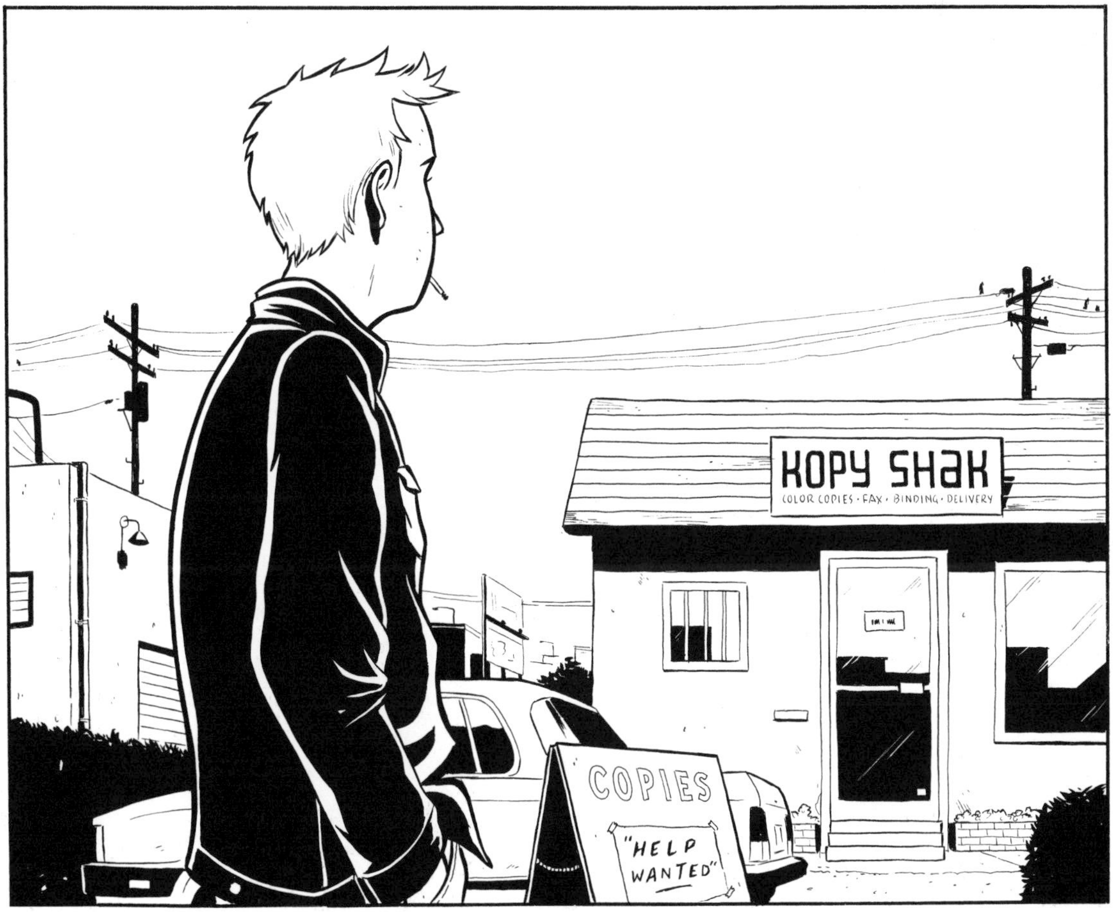
KOPY SHAK
COLOR COPIES · FAX · BINDING · DELIVERY
COPIES
"HELP WANTED"

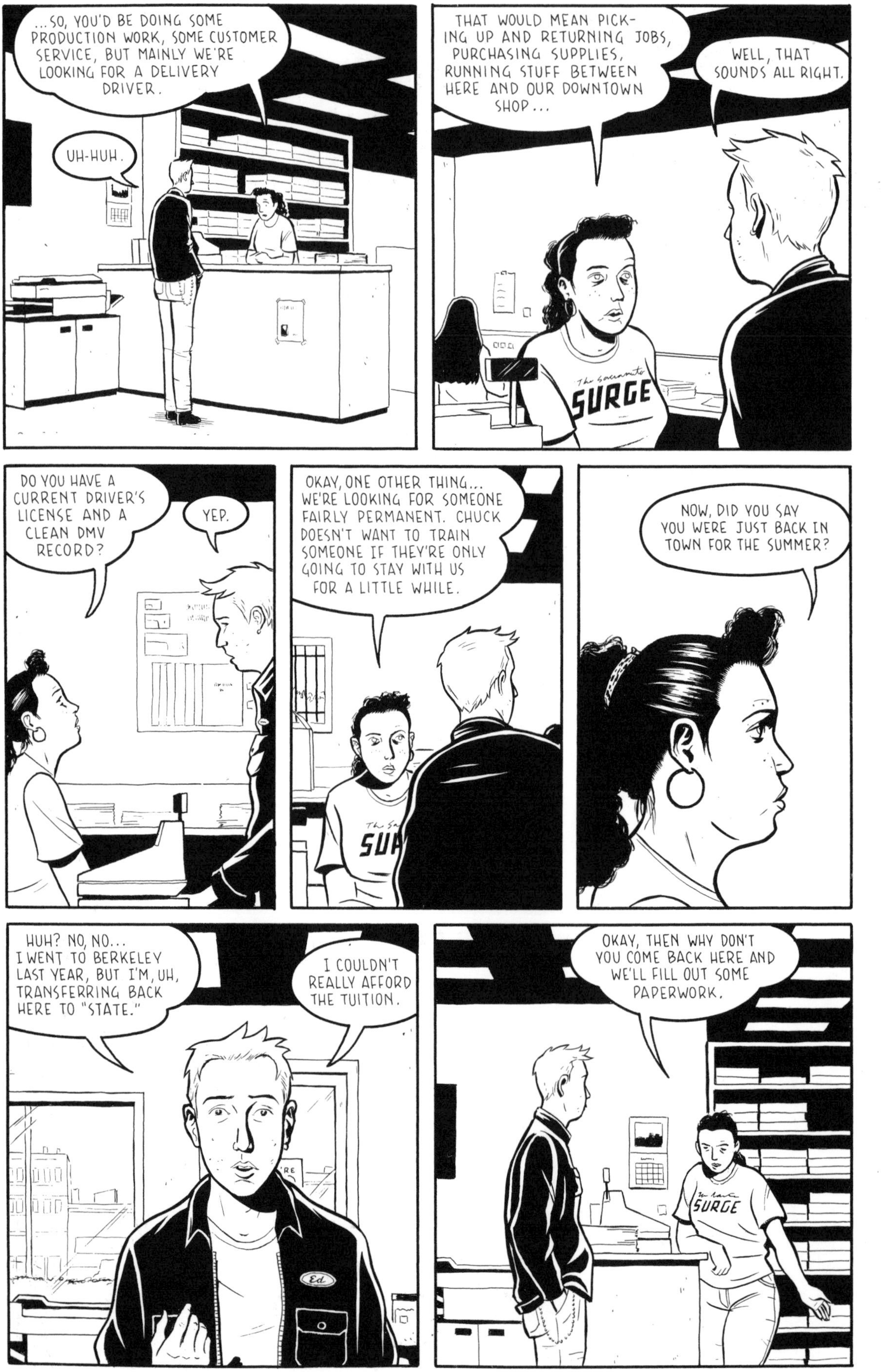
...SO, YOU'D BE DOING SOME PRODUCTION WORK, SOME CUSTOMER SERVICE, BUT MAINLY WE'RE LOOKING FOR A DELIVERY DRIVER.
UH-HUH.
THAT WOULD MEAN PICKING UP AND RETURNING JOBS, PURCHASING SUPPLIES, RUNNING STUFF BETWEEN HERE AND OUR DOWNTOWN SHOP...
WELL, THAT SOUNDS ALL RIGHT.
SURGE
DO YOU HAVE A CURRENT DRIVER'S LICENSE AND A CLEAN DMV RECORD?
YEP.
OKAY, ONE OTHER THING... WE'RE LOOKING FOR SOMEONE FAIRLY PERMANENT. CHUCK DOESN'T WANT TO TRAIN SOMEONE IF THEY'RE ONLY GOING TO STAY WITH US FOR A LITTLE WHILE.
NOW, DID YOU SAY YOU WERE JUST BACK IN TOWN FOR THE SUMMER?
HUH? NO, NO... I WENT TO BERKELEY LAST YEAR, BUT I'M, UH, TRANSFERRING BACK HERE TO "STATE."
I COULDN'T REALLY AFFORD THE TUITION.
Ed
OKAY, THEN WHY DON'T YOU COME BACK HERE AND WE'LL FILL OUT SOME PAPERWORK.
SURGE

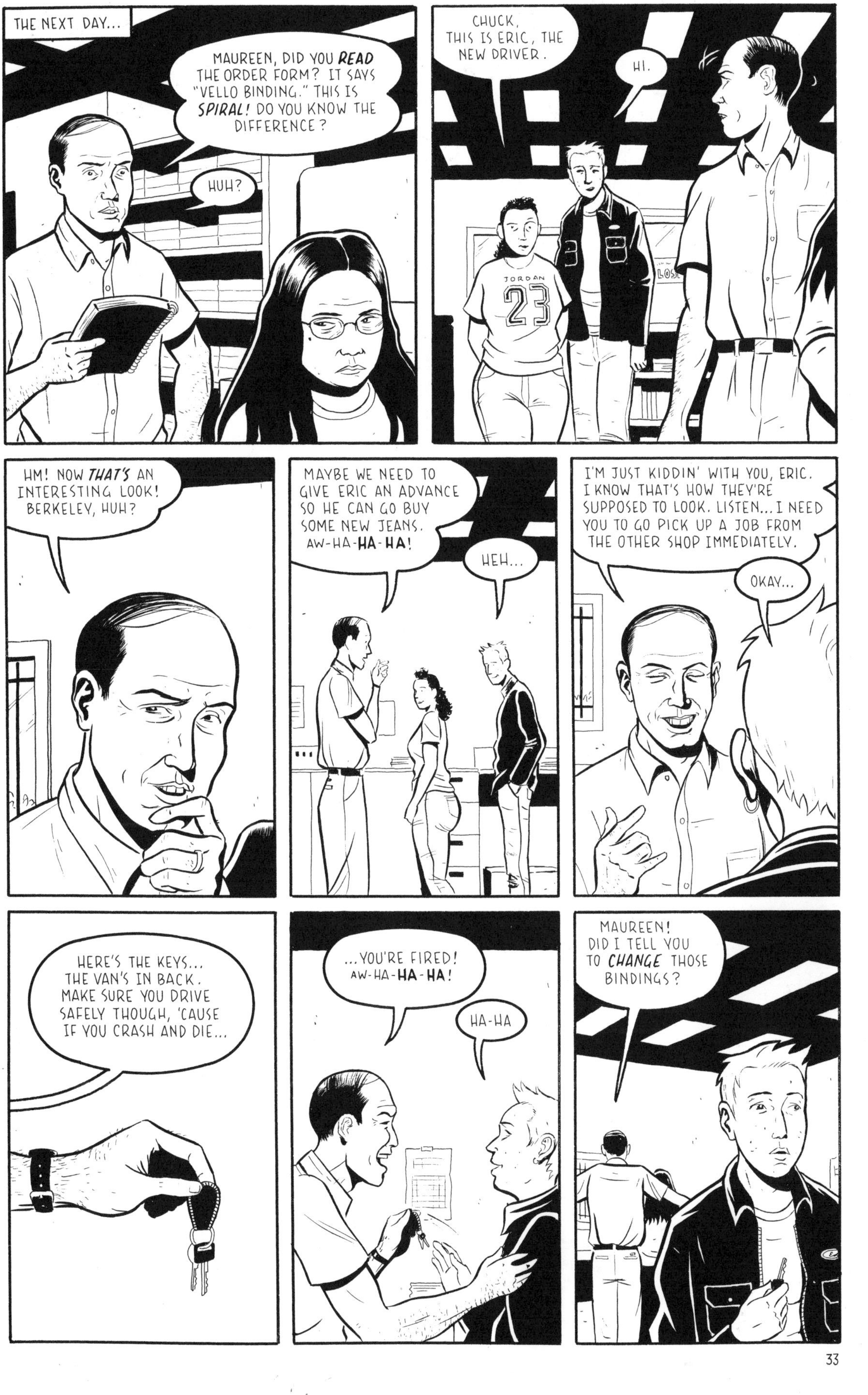
THE NEXT DAY...
MAUREEN, DID YOU READ THE ORDER FORM? IT SAYS "VELLO BINDING." THIS IS SPIRAL! DO YOU KNOW THE DIFFERENCE?
HUH?
CHUCK, THIS IS ERIC, THE NEW DRIVER.
HI.
JORDAN 23
HM! NOW THAT'S AN INTERESTING LOOK! BERKELEY, HUH?
MAYBE WE NEED TO GIVE ERIC AN ADVANCE SO HE CAN GO BUY SOME NEW JEANS. AW-HA-HA-HA!
HEH...
I'M JUST KIDDIN' WITH YOU, ERIC. I KNOW THAT'S HOW THEY'RE SUPPOSED TO LOOK. LISTEN... I NEED YOU TO GO PICK UP A JOB FROM THE OTHER SHOP IMMEDIATELY.
OKAY...
HERE'S THE KEYS... THE VAN'S IN BACK. MAKE SURE YOU DRIVE SAFELY THOUGH, 'CAUSE IF YOU CRASH AND DIE...
...YOU'RE FIRED! AW-HA-HA-HA!
HA-HA
MAUREEN! DID I TELL YOU TO CHANGE THOSE BINDINGS?

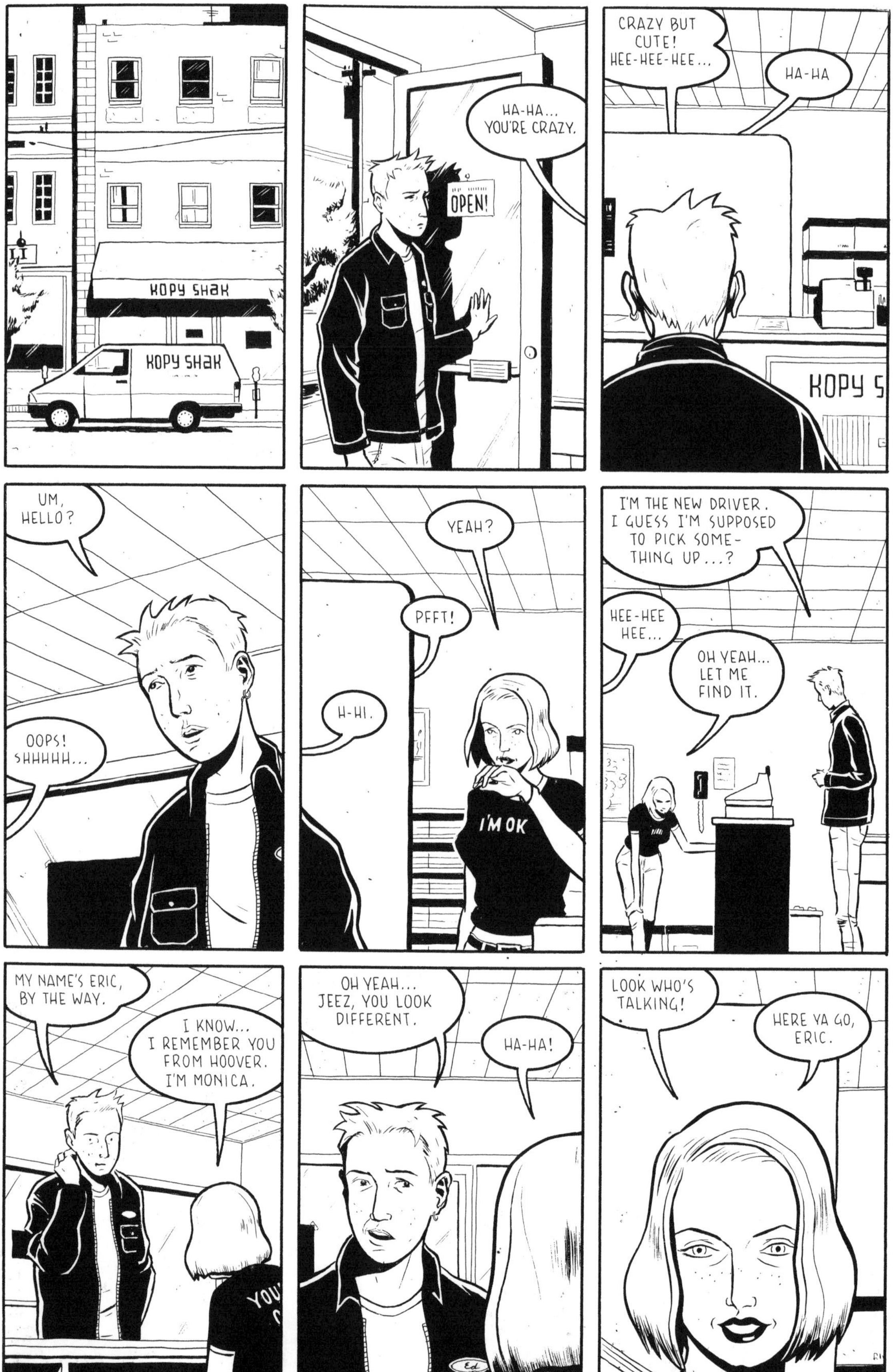
KOPY SHAK
KOPY SHAK
OPEN!
HA-HA... YOU'RE CRAZY.
CRAZY BUT CUTE! HEE-HEE-HEE...
HA-HA
KOPY S
UM, HELLO?
OOPS! SHHHHH...
YEAH?
PFFT!
H-HI.
I'M OK
I'M THE NEW DRIVER. I GUESS I'M SUPPOSED TO PICK SOME-THING UP...?
HEE-HEE HEE...
OH YEAH... LET ME FIND IT.
MY NAME'S ERIC, BY THE WAY.
I KNOW... I REMEMBER YOU FROM HOOVER. I'M MONICA.
OH YEAH... JEEZ, YOU LOOK DIFFERENT.
HA-HA!
LOOK WHO'S TALKING!
HERE YA GO, ERIC.

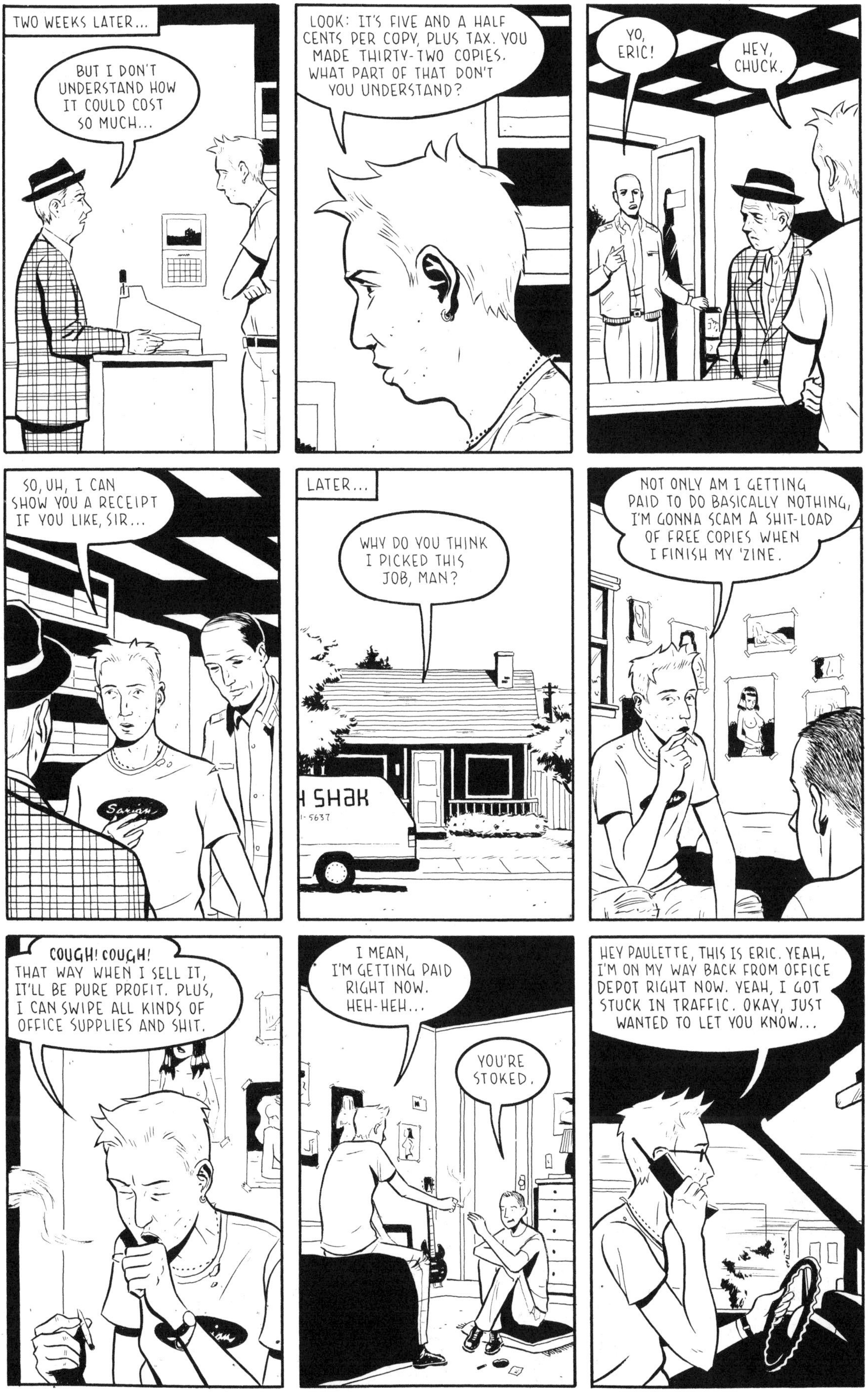
TWO WEEKS LATER...
BUT I DON'T UNDERSTAND HOW IT COULD COST SO MUCH...
LOOK: IT'S FIVE AND A HALF CENTS PER COPY, PLUS TAX. YOU MADE THIRTY-TWO COPIES. WHAT PART OF THAT DON'T YOU UNDERSTAND?
YO, ERIC!
HEY, CHUCK.
SO, UH, I CAN SHOW YOU A RECEIPT IF YOU LIKE, SIR...
LATER...
WHY DO YOU THINK I PICKED THIS JOB, MAN?
H SHAK
NOT ONLY AM I GETTING PAID TO DO BASICALLY NOTHING, I'M GONNA SCAM A SHIT-LOAD OF FREE COPIES WHEN I FINISH MY 'ZINE.
COUGH! COUGH!
THAT WAY WHEN I SELL IT, IT'LL BE PURE PROFIT. PLUS, I CAN SWIPE ALL KINDS OF OFFICE SUPPLIES AND SHIT.
I MEAN, I'M GETTING PAID RIGHT NOW. HEH-HEH...
YOU'RE STOKED.
HEY PAULETTE, THIS IS ERIC. YEAH, I'M ON MY WAY BACK FROM OFFICE DEPOT RIGHT NOW. YEAH, I GOT STUCK IN TRAFFIC. OKAY, JUST WANTED TO LET YOU KNOW...

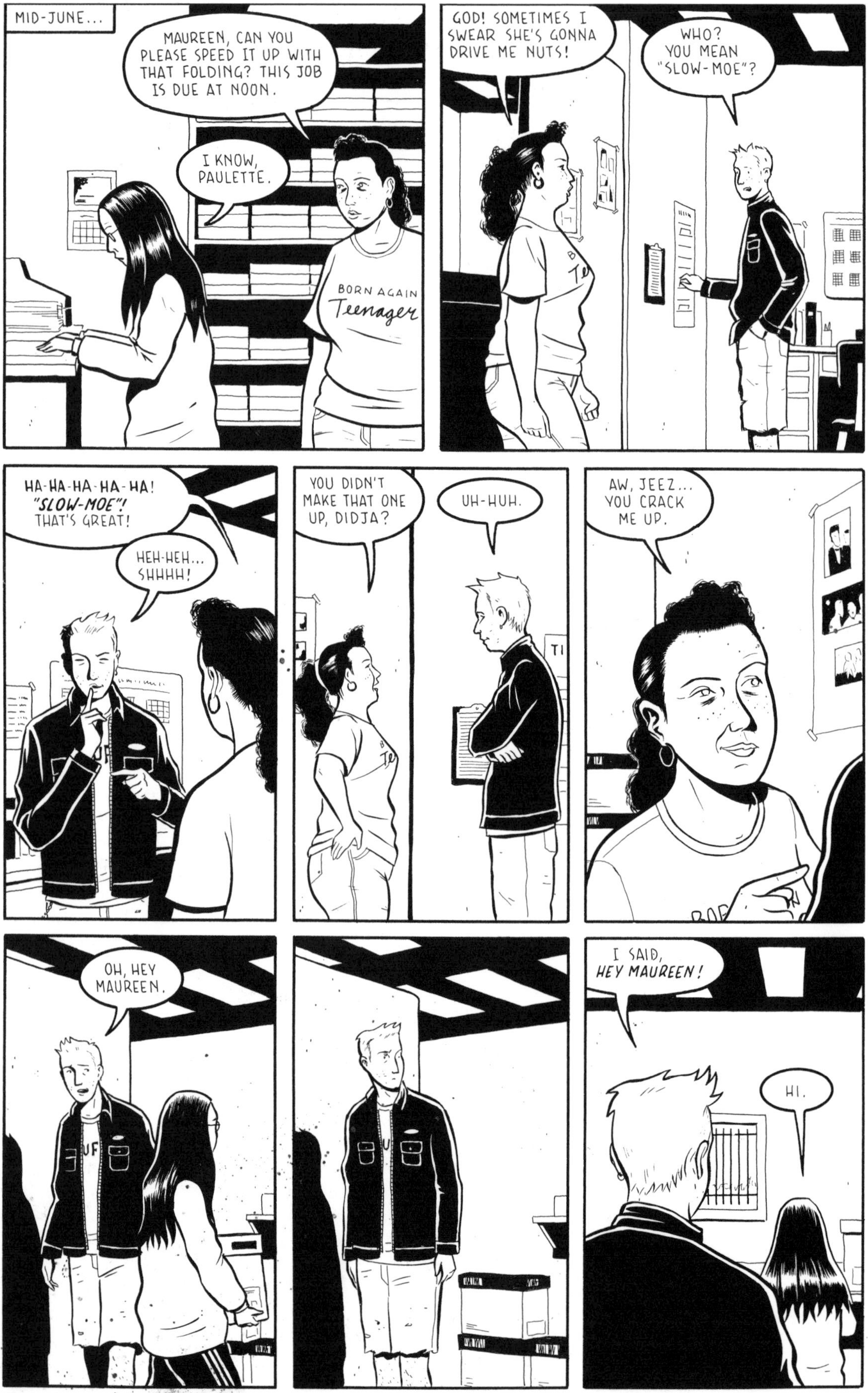
MID-JUNE...
MAUREEN, CAN YOU PLEASE SPEED IT UP WITH THAT FOLDING? THIS JOB IS DUE AT NOON.
I KNOW, PAULETTE.
BORN AGAIN Teenager
GOD! SOMETIMES I SWEAR SHE'S GONNA DRIVE ME NUTS!
WHO? YOU MEAN "SLOW-MOE"?
HA-HA-HA-HA-HA! "SLOW-MOE"! THAT'S GREAT!
HEH-HEH... SHHHH!
YOU DIDN'T MAKE THAT ONE UP, DIDJA?
UH-HUH.
AW, JEEZ... YOU CRACK ME UP.
OH, HEY MAUREEN.
I SAID, HEY MAUREEN!
HI.

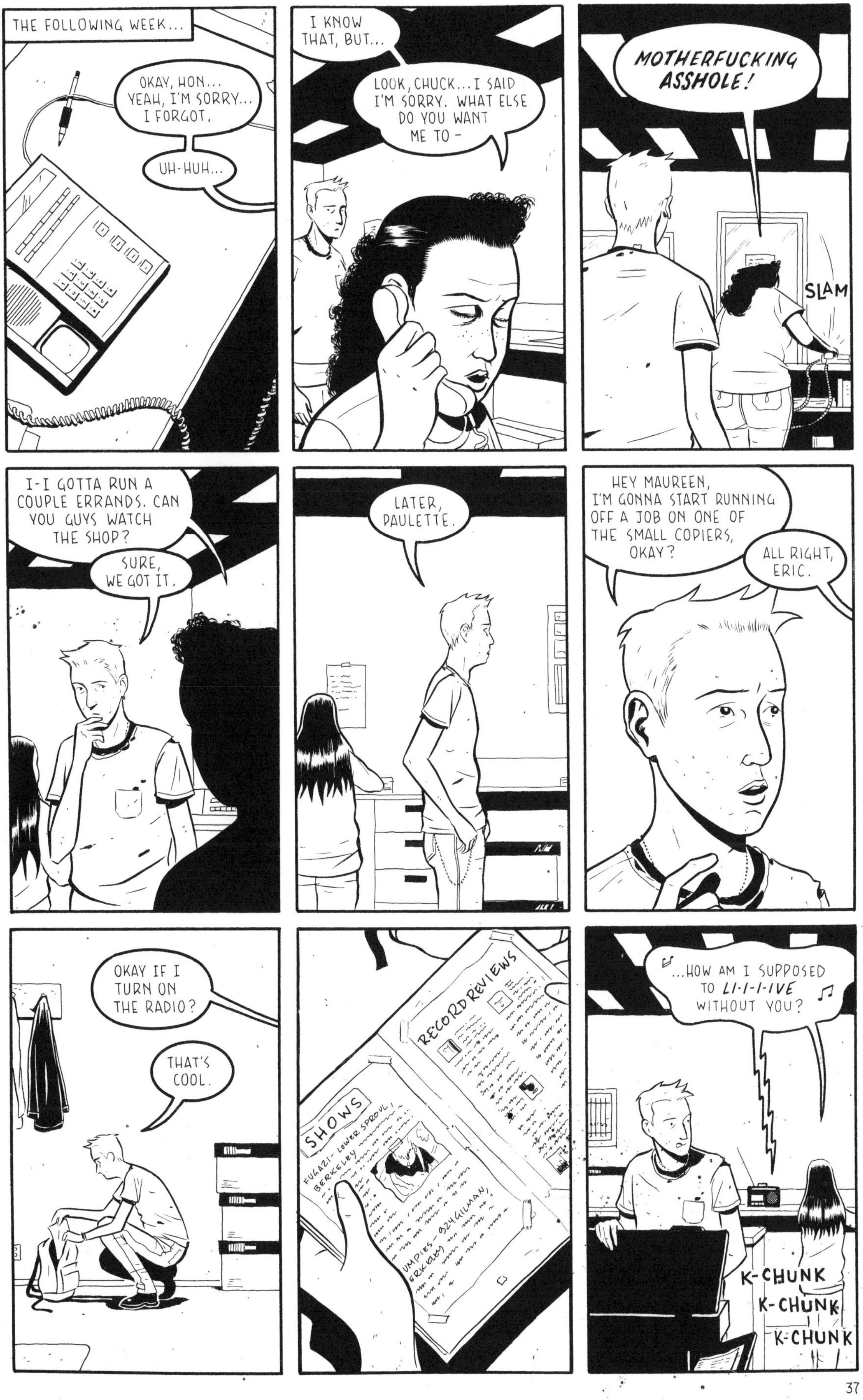
THE FOLLOWING WEEK...
OKAY, HON... YEAH, I'M SORRY... I FORGOT.
UH-HUH...
I KNOW THAT, BUT...
LOOK, CHUCK... I SAID I'M SORRY. WHAT ELSE DO YOU WANT ME TO -
MOTHERFUCKING ASSHOLE!
SLAM
I-I GOTTA RUN A COUPLE ERRANDS. CAN YOU GUYS WATCH THE SHOP?
SURE, WE GOT IT.
LATER, PAULETTE.
HEY MAUREEN, I'M GONNA START RUNNING OFF A JOB ON ONE OF THE SMALL COPIERS, OKAY?
ALL RIGHT, ERIC.
OKAY IF I TURN ON THE RADIO?
THAT'S COOL.
RECORD REVIEWS
SHOWS
FUGAZI - LOWER SPROUL, BERKELEY
UMPIES - 924 GILMAN, BERKELEY
...HOW AM I SUPPOSED TO LI-I-I-IVE WITHOUT YOU?
K-CHUNK
K-CHUNK
K-CHUNK

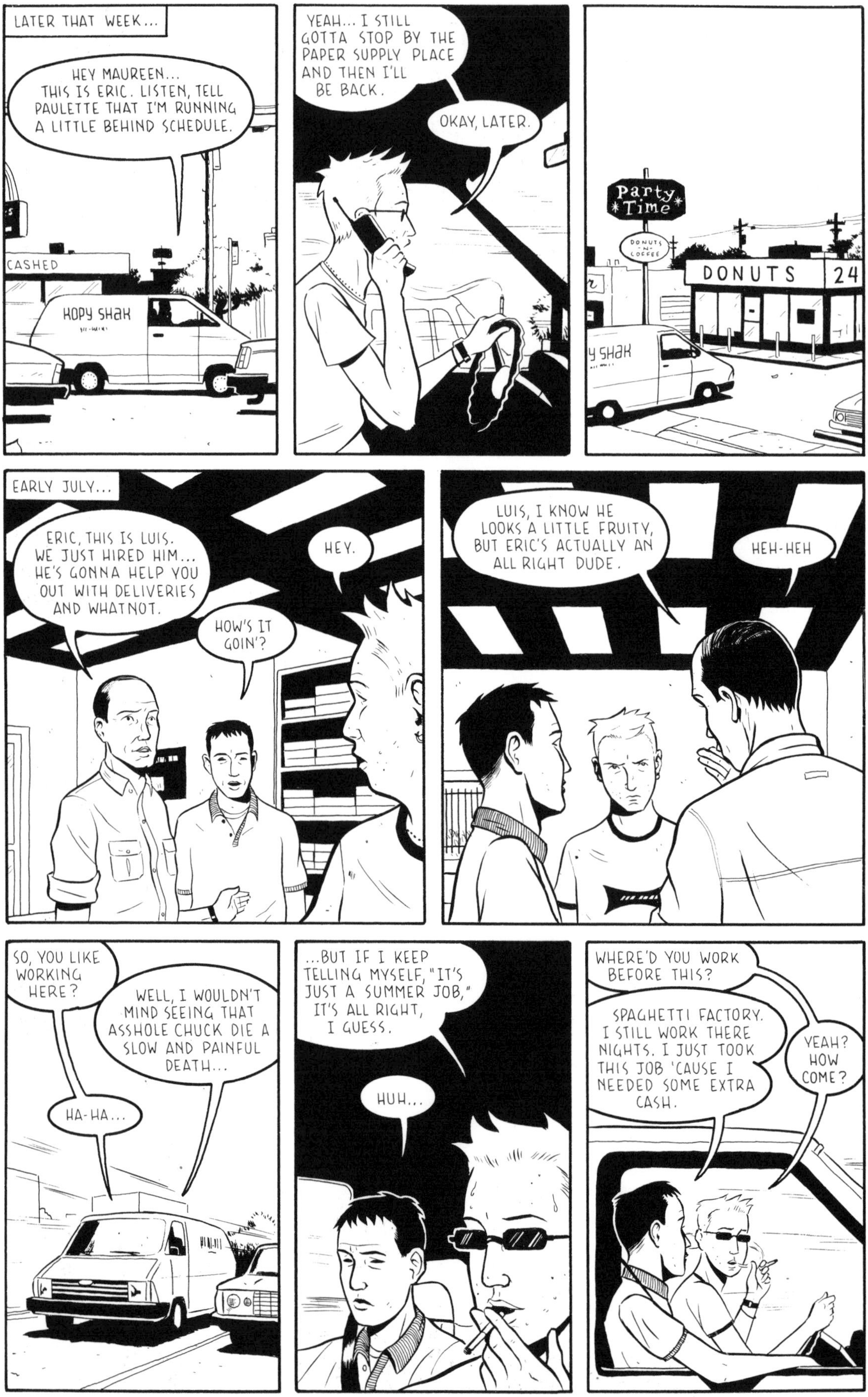
LATER THAT WEEK...
HEY MAUREEN... THIS IS ERIC. LISTEN, TELL PAULETTE THAT I'M RUNNING A LITTLE BEHIND SCHEDULE.
CASHED
KOPY SHAK
YEAH... I STILL GOTTA STOP BY THE PAPER SUPPLY PLACE AND THEN I'LL BE BACK.
OKAY, LATER.
Party Time
DONUTS -N- COFFEE
DONUTS
24
EARLY JULY...
ERIC, THIS IS LUIS. WE JUST HIRED HIM... HE'S GONNA HELP YOU OUT WITH DELIVERIES AND WHATNOT.
HEY.
HOW'S IT GOIN'?
LUIS, I KNOW HE LOOKS A LITTLE FRUITY, BUT ERIC'S ACTUALLY AN ALL RIGHT DUDE.
HEH-HEH
SO, YOU LIKE WORKING HERE?
WELL, I WOULDN'T MIND SEEING THAT ASSHOLE CHUCK DIE A SLOW AND PAINFUL DEATH...
HA-HA...
...BUT IF I KEEP TELLING MYSELF, "IT'S JUST A SUMMER JOB," IT'S ALL RIGHT, I GUESS.
HUH...
WHERE'D YOU WORK BEFORE THIS?
SPAGHETTI FACTORY. I STILL WORK THERE NIGHTS. I JUST TOOK THIS JOB 'CAUSE I NEEDED SOME EXTRA CASH.
YEAH? HOW COME?

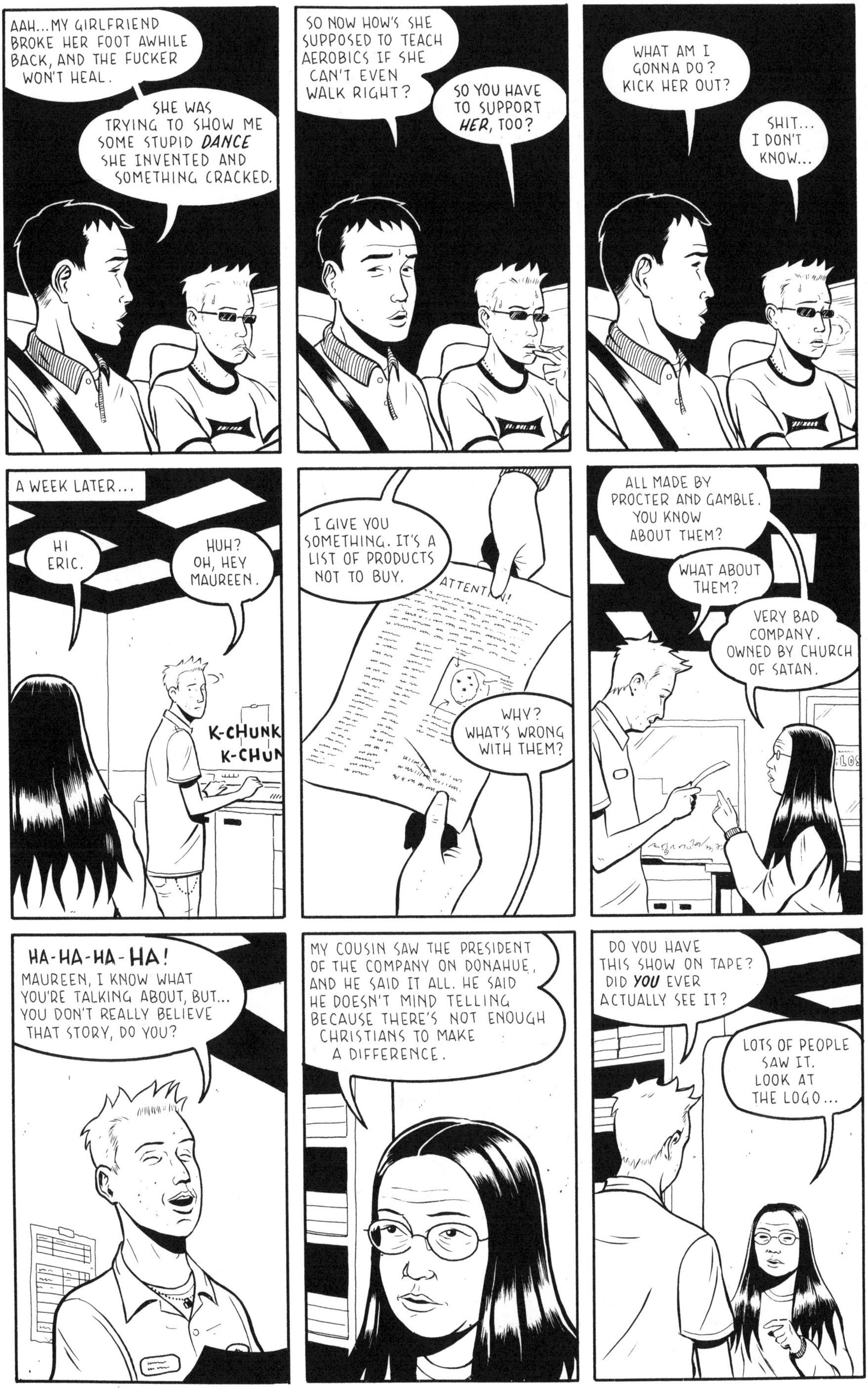
AAH...MY GIRLFRIEND BROKE HER FOOT AWHILE BACK, AND THE FUCKER WON'T HEAL.
SHE WAS TRYING TO SHOW ME SOME STUPID DANCE SHE INVENTED AND SOMETHING CRACKED.
SO NOW HOW'S SHE SUPPOSED TO TEACH AEROBICS IF SHE CAN'T EVEN WALK RIGHT?
SO YOU HAVE TO SUPPORT HER, TOO?
WHAT AM I GONNA DO? KICK HER OUT?
SHIT... I DON'T KNOW...
A WEEK LATER...
HI ERIC.
HUH? OH, HEY MAUREEN.
K-CHUNK
K-CHUN
I GIVE YOU SOMETHING. IT'S A LIST OF PRODUCTS NOT TO BUY.
WHY? WHAT'S WRONG WITH THEM?
ALL MADE BY PROCTER AND GAMBLE. YOU KNOW ABOUT THEM?
WHAT ABOUT THEM?
VERY BAD COMPANY. OWNED BY CHURCH OF SATAN.
HA-HA-HA-HA! MAUREEN, I KNOW WHAT YOU'RE TALKING ABOUT, BUT... YOU DON'T REALLY BELIEVE THAT STORY, DO YOU?
MY COUSIN SAW THE PRESIDENT OF THE COMPANY ON DONAHUE, AND HE SAID IT ALL. HE SAID HE DOESN'T MIND TELLING BECAUSE THERE'S NOT ENOUGH CHRISTIANS TO MAKE A DIFFERENCE.
DO YOU HAVE THIS SHOW ON TAPE? DID YOU EVER ACTUALLY SEE IT?
LOTS OF PEOPLE SAW IT. LOOK AT THE LOGO...

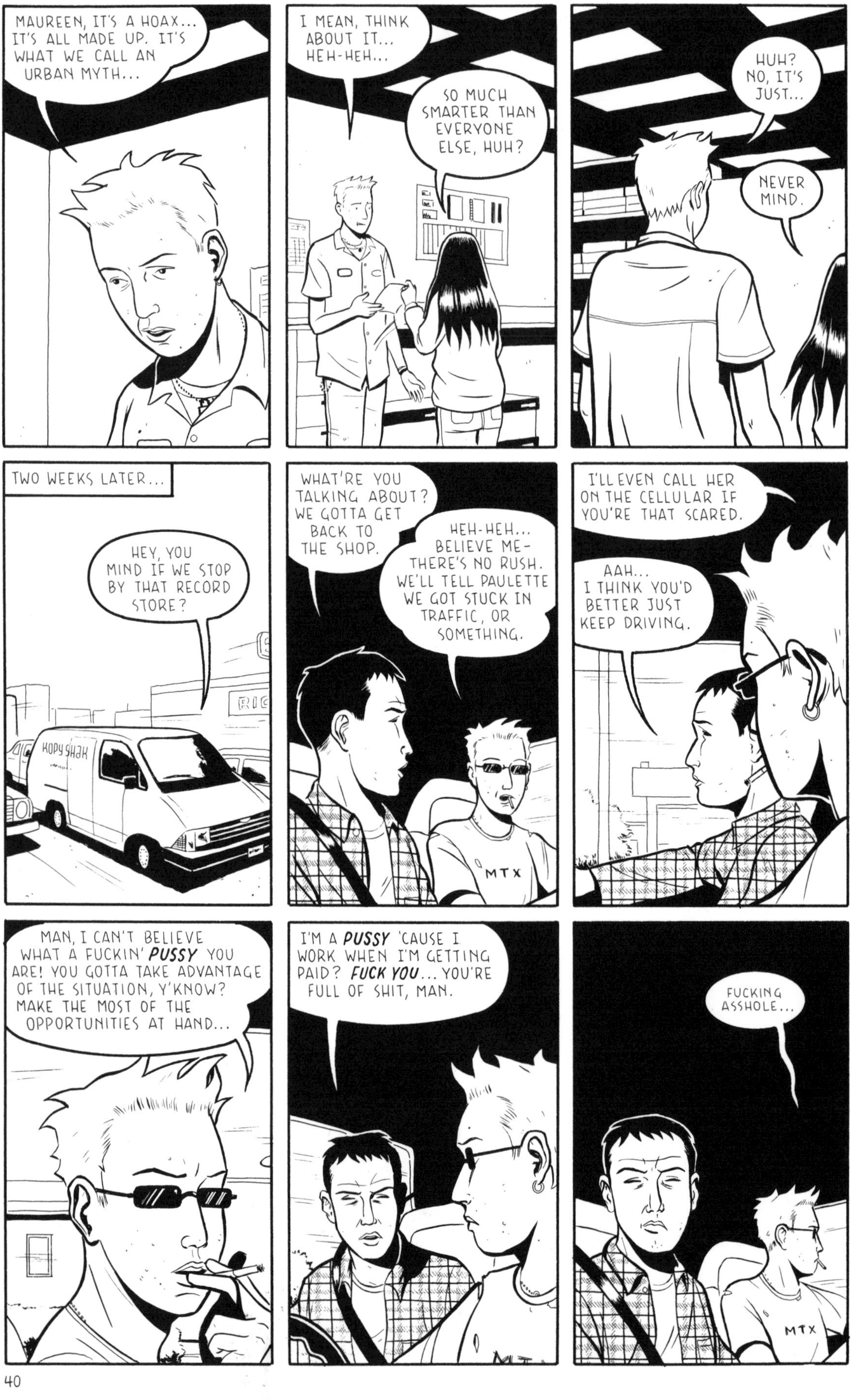
MAUREEN, IT'S A HOAX... IT'S ALL MADE UP. IT'S WHAT WE CALL AN URBAN MYTH...
I MEAN, THINK ABOUT IT... HEH-HEH...
SO MUCH SMARTER THAN EVERYONE ELSE, HUH?
HUH? NO, IT'S JUST...
NEVER MIND.
TWO WEEKS LATER...
HEY, YOU MIND IF WE STOP BY THAT RECORD STORE?
KOPY SHAK
WHAT'RE YOU TALKING ABOUT? WE GOTTA GET BACK TO THE SHOP.
HEH-HEH... BELIEVE ME– THERE'S NO RUSH. WE'LL TELL PAULETTE WE GOT STUCK IN TRAFFIC, OR SOMETHING.
MTX
I'LL EVEN CALL HER ON THE CELLULAR IF YOU'RE THAT SCARED.
AAH... I THINK YOU'D BETTER JUST KEEP DRIVING.
MAN, I CAN'T BELIEVE WHAT A FUCKIN' **PUSSY** YOU ARE! YOU GOTTA TAKE ADVANTAGE OF THE SITUATION, Y'KNOW? MAKE THE MOST OF THE OPPORTUNITIES AT HAND...
I'M A **PUSSY** 'CAUSE I WORK WHEN I'M GETTING PAID? **FUCK YOU**... YOU'RE FULL OF SHIT, MAN.
FUCKING ASSHOLE...
MTX

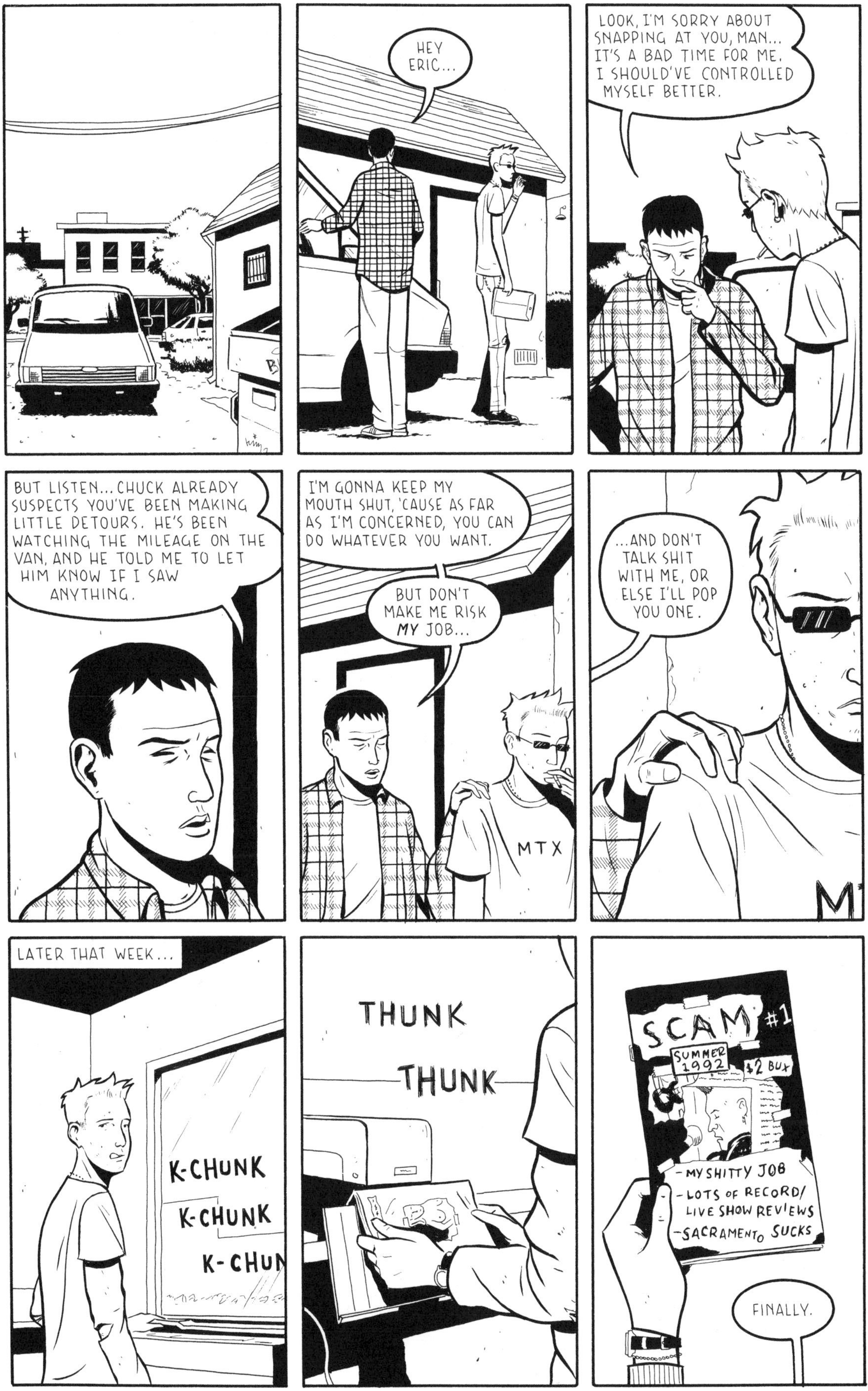
HEY ERIC...
LOOK, I'M SORRY ABOUT SNAPPING AT YOU, MAN... IT'S A BAD TIME FOR ME. I SHOULD'VE CONTROLLED MYSELF BETTER.
BUT LISTEN... CHUCK ALREADY SUSPECTS YOU'VE BEEN MAKING LITTLE DETOURS. HE'S BEEN WATCHING THE MILEAGE ON THE VAN, AND HE TOLD ME TO LET HIM KNOW IF I SAW ANYTHING.
I'M GONNA KEEP MY MOUTH SHUT, 'CAUSE AS FAR AS I'M CONCERNED, YOU CAN DO WHATEVER YOU WANT.
BUT DON'T MAKE ME RISK MY JOB...
MTX
...AND DON'T TALK SHIT WITH ME, OR ELSE I'LL POP YOU ONE.
LATER THAT WEEK...
K-CHUNK
K-CHUNK
K-CHUN
THUNK
THUNK
SCAM #1
SUMMER 1992
$2 BUX
-MY SHITTY JOB
-LOTS OF RECORD/ LIVE SHOW REVIEWS
-SACRAMENTO SUCKS
FINALLY.

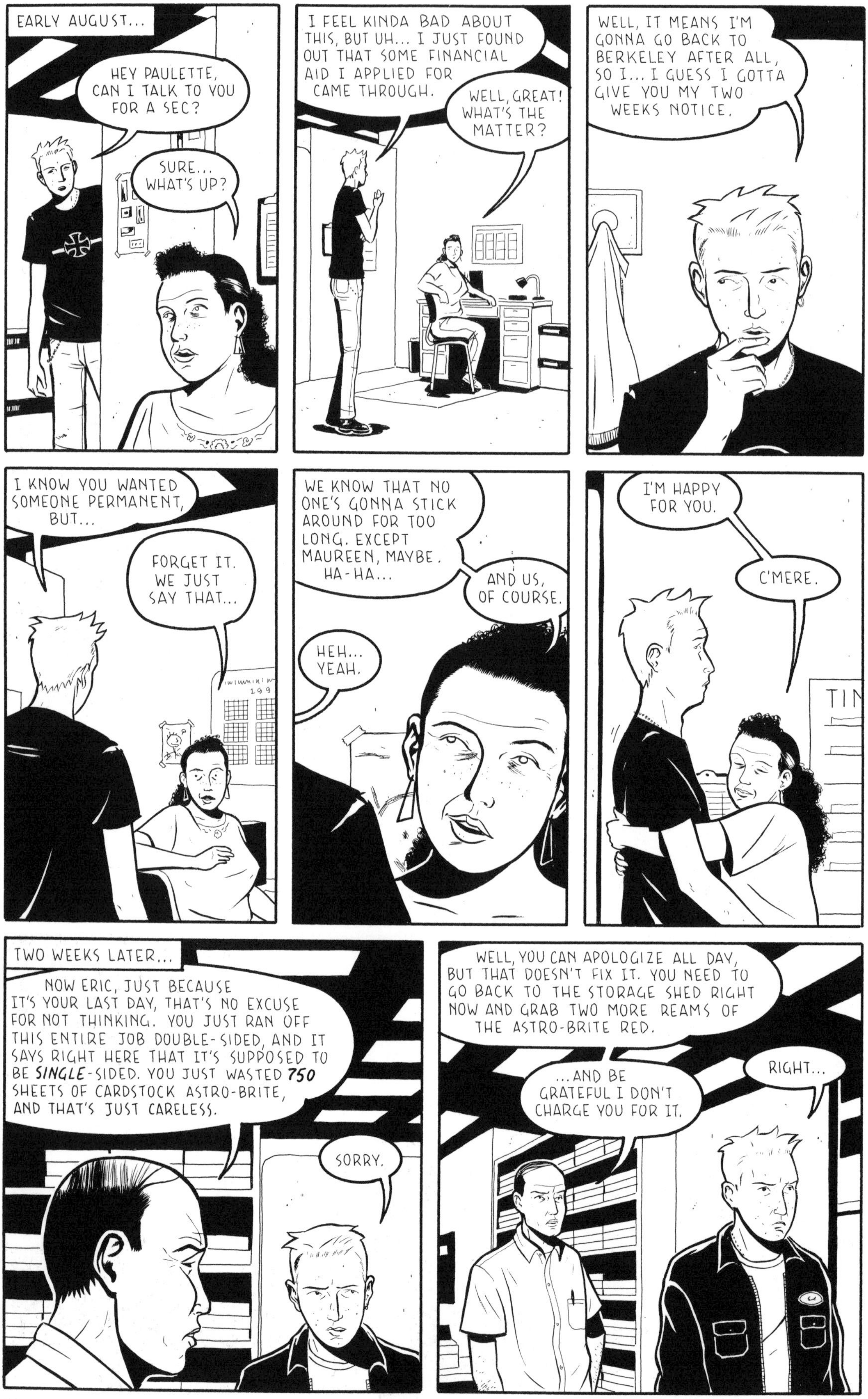
EARLY AUGUST...
HEY PAULETTE, CAN I TALK TO YOU FOR A SEC?
SURE... WHAT'S UP?
I FEEL KINDA BAD ABOUT THIS, BUT UH... I JUST FOUND OUT THAT SOME FINANCIAL AID I APPLIED FOR CAME THROUGH.
WELL, GREAT! WHAT'S THE MATTER?
WELL, IT MEANS I'M GONNA GO BACK TO BERKELEY AFTER ALL, SO I... I GUESS I GOTTA GIVE YOU MY TWO WEEKS NOTICE.
I KNOW YOU WANTED SOMEONE PERMANENT, BUT...
FORGET IT. WE JUST SAY THAT...
WE KNOW THAT NO ONE'S GONNA STICK AROUND FOR TOO LONG. EXCEPT MAUREEN, MAYBE. HA-HA...
AND US, OF COURSE.
HEH... YEAH.
I'M HAPPY FOR YOU.
C'MERE.
TWO WEEKS LATER...
NOW ERIC, JUST BECAUSE IT'S YOUR LAST DAY, THAT'S NO EXCUSE FOR NOT THINKING. YOU JUST RAN OFF THIS ENTIRE JOB DOUBLE-SIDED, AND IT SAYS RIGHT HERE THAT IT'S SUPPOSED TO BE SINGLE-SIDED. YOU JUST WASTED 750 SHEETS OF CARDSTOCK ASTRO-BRITE, AND THAT'S JUST CARELESS.
SORRY.
WELL, YOU CAN APOLOGIZE ALL DAY, BUT THAT DOESN'T FIX IT. YOU NEED TO GO BACK TO THE STORAGE SHED RIGHT NOW AND GRAB TWO MORE REAMS OF THE ASTRO-BRITE RED.
...AND BE GRATEFUL I DON'T CHARGE YOU FOR IT.
RIGHT...

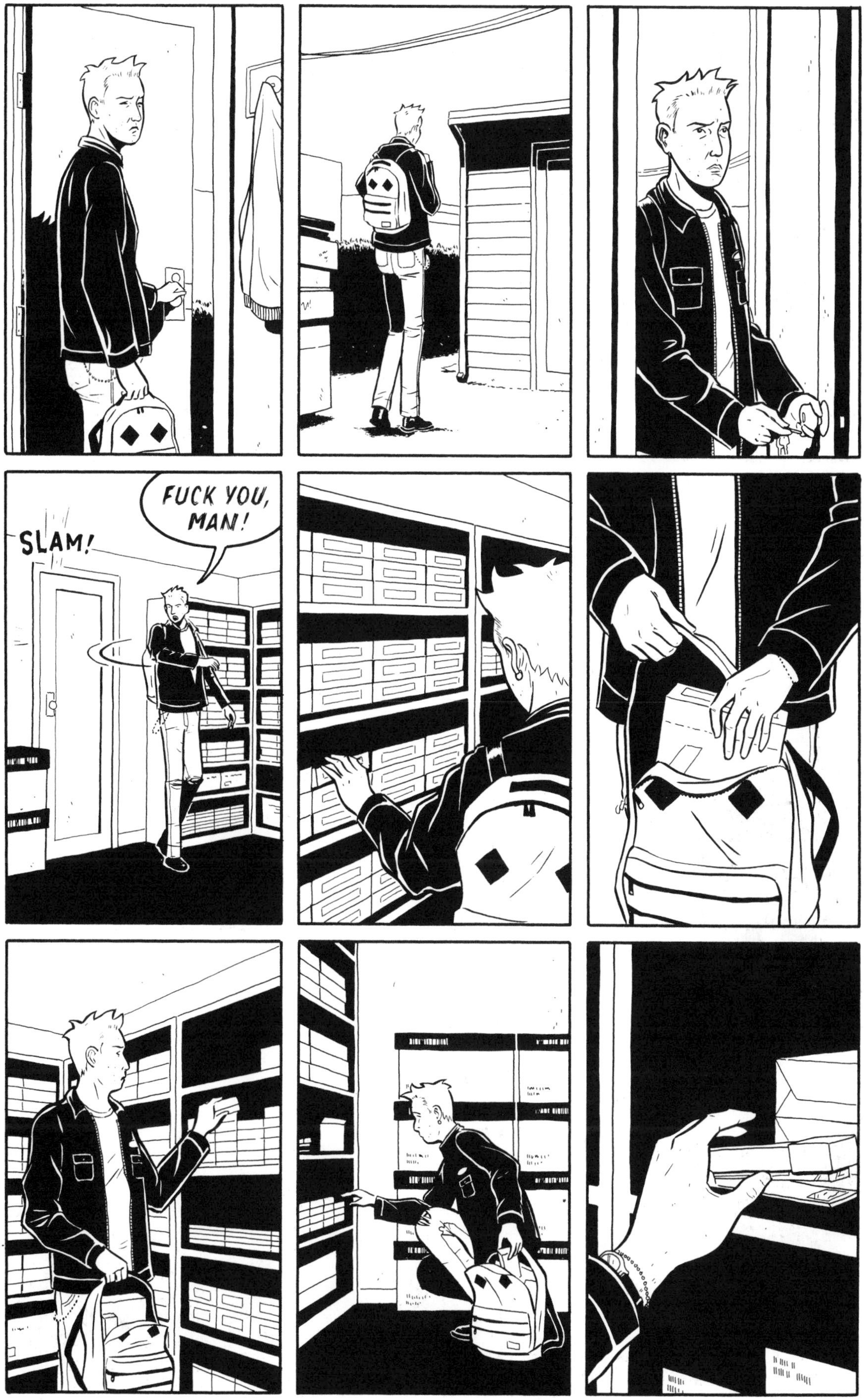
SLAM!
FUCK YOU, MAN!

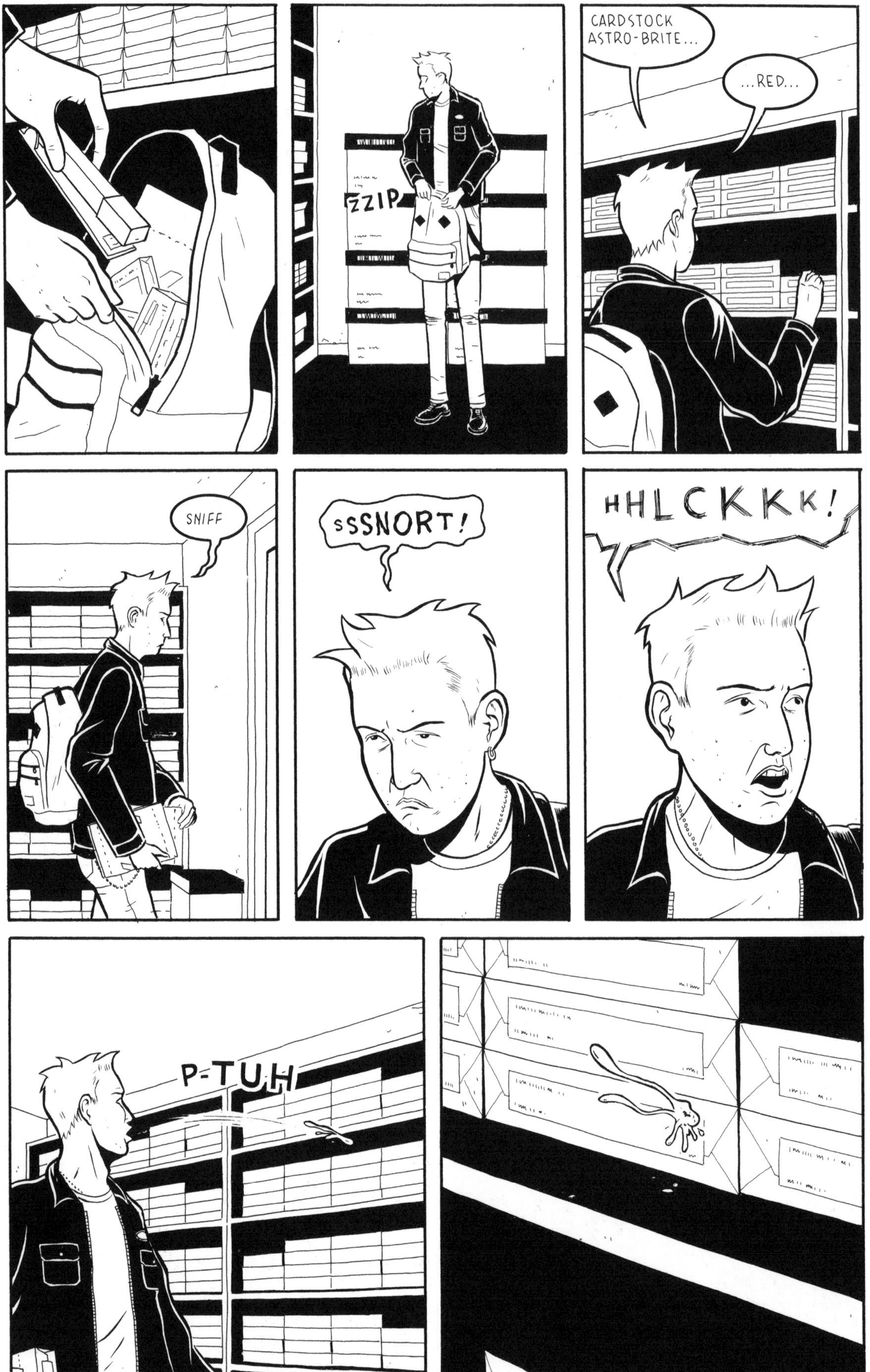
ZZIP
CARDSTOCK ASTRO-BRITE...
...RED...
SNIFF
sSSNORT!
HHLCKKK!
P-TUH

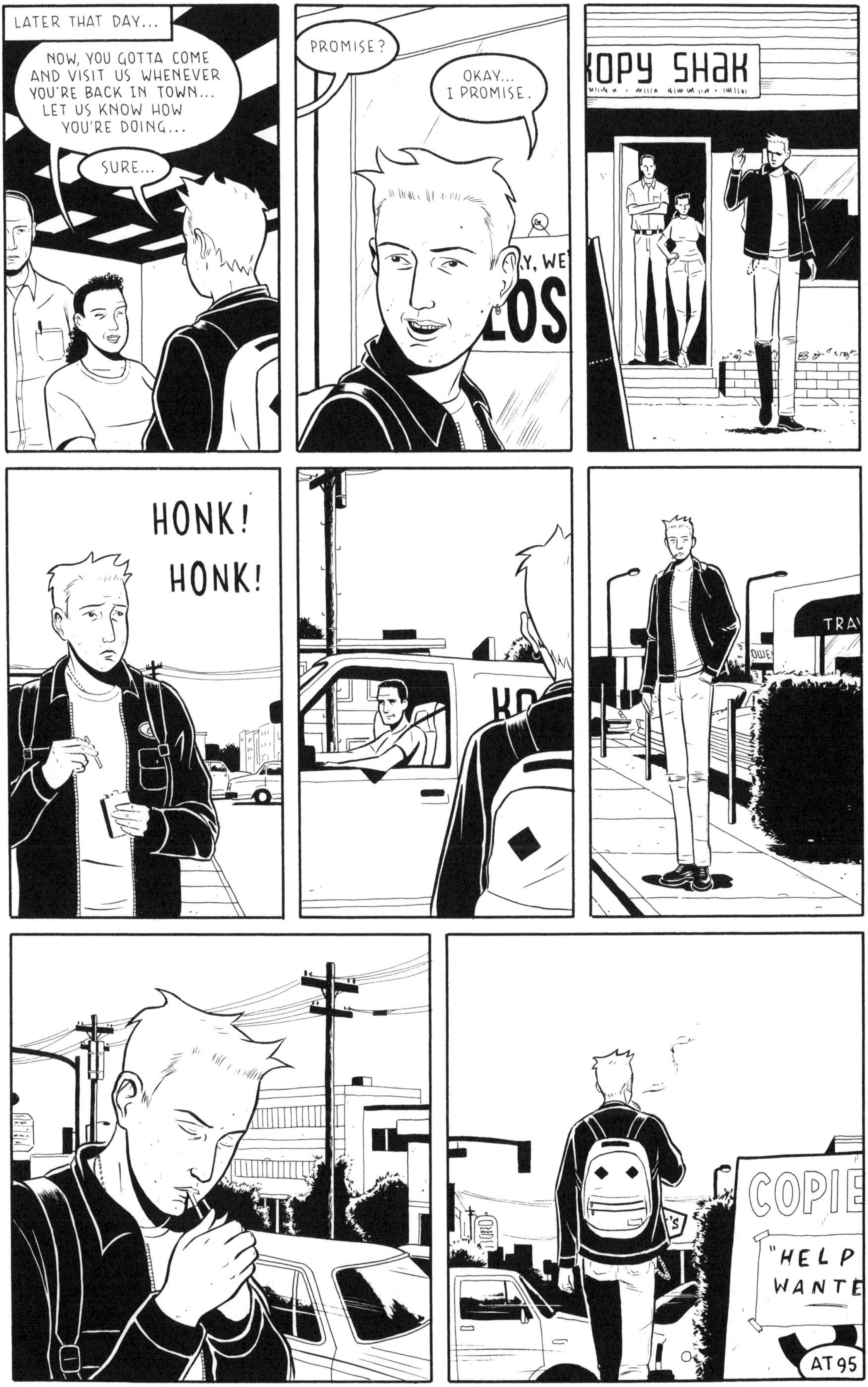
LATER THAT DAY...
NOW, YOU GOTTA COME AND VISIT US WHENEVER YOU'RE BACK IN TOWN... LET US KNOW HOW YOU'RE DOING...
SURE...
PROMISE?
OKAY... I PROMISE.
KOPY SHAK
HONK!
HONK!
"HELP
AT95

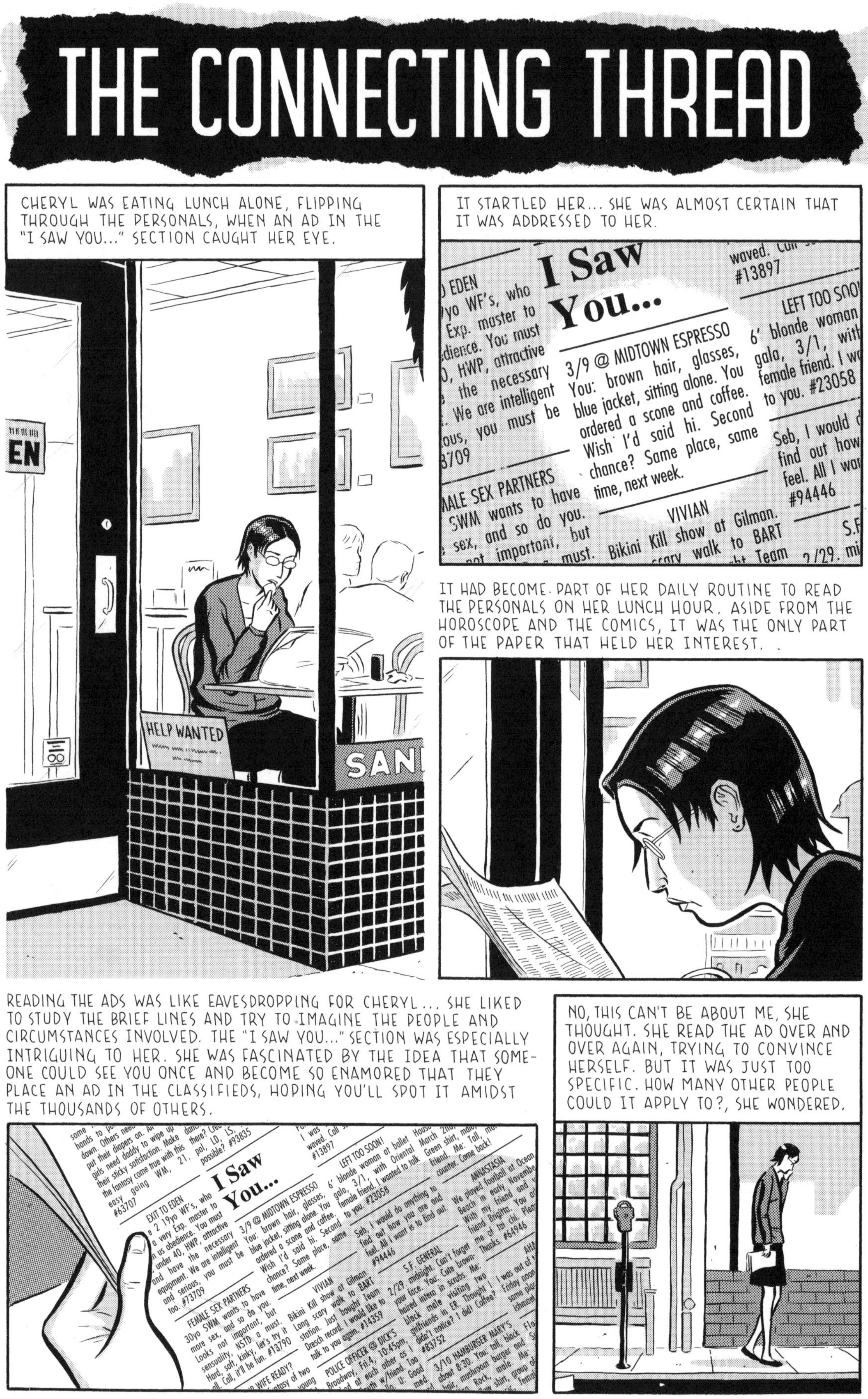

THE CONNECTING THREAD
CHERYL WAS EATING LUNCH ALONE, FLIPPING THROUGH THE PERSONALS, WHEN AN AD IN THE "I SAW YOU..." SECTION CAUGHT HER EYE.
EN
HELP WANTED
SAN
IT STARTLED HER... SHE WAS ALMOST CERTAIN THAT IT WAS ADDRESSED TO HER.
I Saw You...
3/9 @ MIDTOWN ESPRESSO
You: brown hair, glasses, blue jacket, sitting alone. You ordered a scone and coffee. Wish I'd said hi. Second chance? Same place, same time, next week.
LEFT TOO SOON!
6' blonde woman
#13897
#23058
#94446
VIVIAN
Bikini Kill show at Gilman.
IT HAD BECOME PART OF HER DAILY ROUTINE TO READ THE PERSONALS ON HER LUNCH HOUR. ASIDE FROM THE HOROSCOPE AND THE COMICS, IT WAS THE ONLY PART OF THE PAPER THAT HELD HER INTEREST.
READING THE ADS WAS LIKE EAVESDROPPING FOR CHERYL... SHE LIKED TO STUDY THE BRIEF LINES AND TRY TO IMAGINE THE PEOPLE AND CIRCUMSTANCES INVOLVED. THE "I SAW YOU..." SECTION WAS ESPECIALLY INTRIGUING TO HER. SHE WAS FASCINATED BY THE IDEA THAT SOMEONE COULD SEE YOU ONCE AND BECOME SO ENAMORED THAT THEY PLACE AN AD IN THE CLASSIFIEDS, HOPING YOU'LL SPOT IT AMIDST THE THOUSANDS OF OTHERS.
NO, THIS CAN'T BE ABOUT ME, SHE THOUGHT. SHE READ THE AD OVER AND OVER AGAIN, TRYING TO CONVINCE HERSELF. BUT IT WAS JUST TOO SPECIFIC. HOW MANY OTHER PEOPLE COULD IT APPLY TO?, SHE WONDERED.
I Saw You...
EXIT TO EDEN
3/9 @ MIDTOWN ESPRESSO
LEFT TOO SOON!
FEMALE SEX PARTNERS
VIVIAN
S.F. GENERAL
ANNASTASIA
POLICE OFFICER @ DICK'S
3/10 HAMBURGER MARY'S

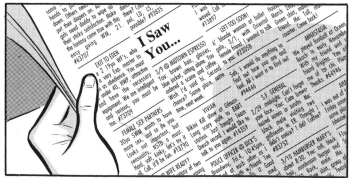

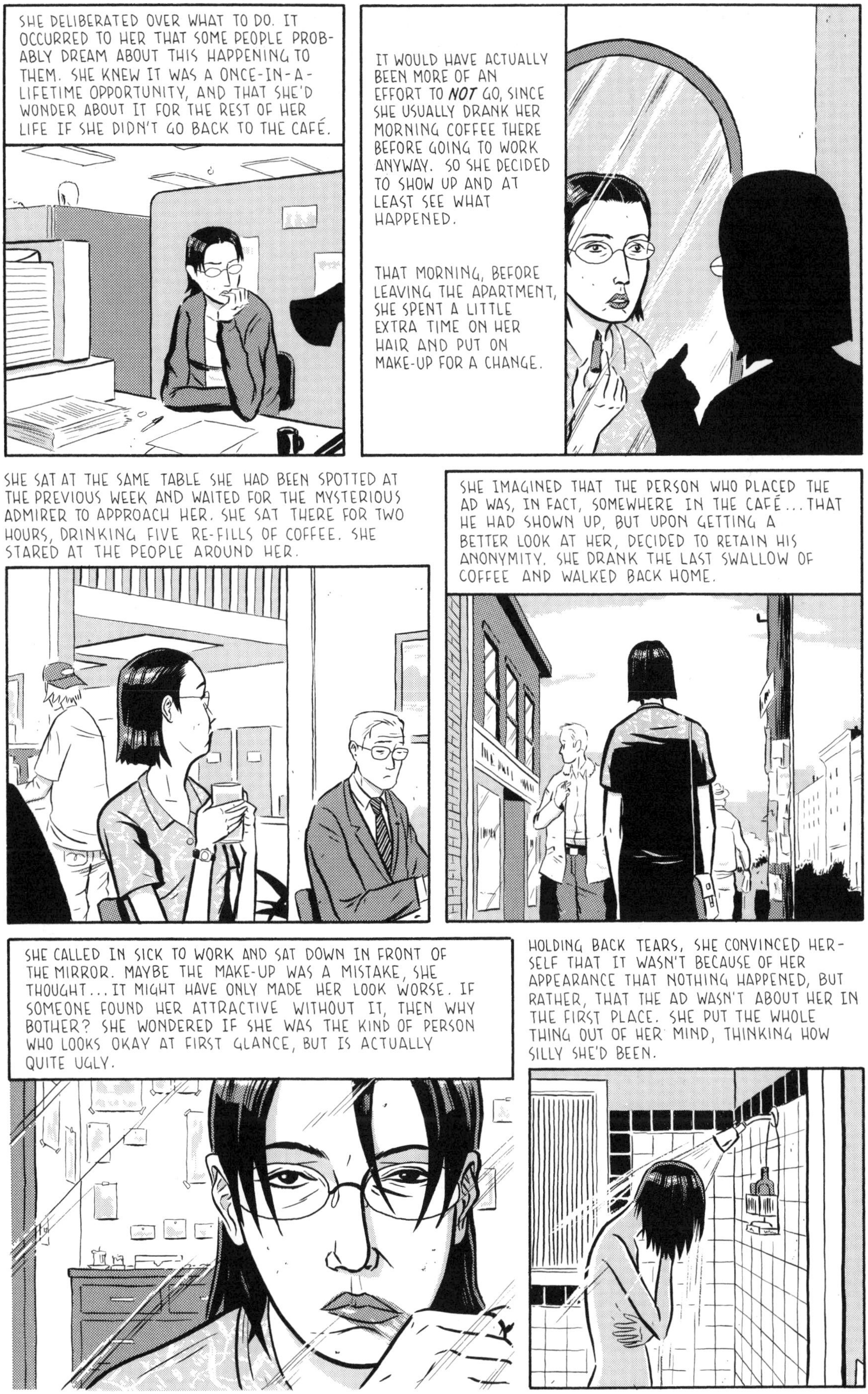
SHE DELIBERATED OVER WHAT TO DO. IT OCCURRED TO HER THAT SOME PEOPLE PROBABLY DREAM ABOUT THIS HAPPENING TO THEM. SHE KNEW IT WAS A ONCE-IN-A-LIFETIME OPPORTUNITY, AND THAT SHE'D WONDER ABOUT IT FOR THE REST OF HER LIFE IF SHE DIDN'T GO BACK TO THE CAFÉ.
IT WOULD HAVE ACTUALLY BEEN MORE OF AN EFFORT TO ***NOT*** GO, SINCE SHE USUALLY DRANK HER MORNING COFFEE THERE BEFORE GOING TO WORK ANYWAY. SO SHE DECIDED TO SHOW UP AND AT LEAST SEE WHAT HAPPENED.
THAT MORNING, BEFORE LEAVING THE APARTMENT, SHE SPENT A LITTLE EXTRA TIME ON HER HAIR AND PUT ON MAKE-UP FOR A CHANGE.
SHE SAT AT THE SAME TABLE SHE HAD BEEN SPOTTED AT THE PREVIOUS WEEK AND WAITED FOR THE MYSTERIOUS ADMIRER TO APPROACH HER. SHE SAT THERE FOR TWO HOURS, DRINKING FIVE RE-FILLS OF COFFEE. SHE STARED AT THE PEOPLE AROUND HER.
SHE IMAGINED THAT THE PERSON WHO PLACED THE AD WAS, IN FACT, SOMEWHERE IN THE CAFÉ... THAT HE HAD SHOWN UP, BUT UPON GETTING A BETTER LOOK AT HER, DECIDED TO RETAIN HIS ANONYMITY. SHE DRANK THE LAST SWALLOW OF COFFEE AND WALKED BACK HOME.
SHE CALLED IN SICK TO WORK AND SAT DOWN IN FRONT OF THE MIRROR. MAYBE THE MAKE-UP WAS A MISTAKE, SHE THOUGHT... IT MIGHT HAVE ONLY MADE HER LOOK WORSE. IF SOMEONE FOUND HER ATTRACTIVE WITHOUT IT, THEN WHY BOTHER? SHE WONDERED IF SHE WAS THE KIND OF PERSON WHO LOOKS OKAY AT FIRST GLANCE, BUT IS ACTUALLY QUITE UGLY.
HOLDING BACK TEARS, SHE CONVINCED HERSELF THAT IT WASN'T BECAUSE OF HER APPEARANCE THAT NOTHING HAPPENED, BUT RATHER, THAT THE AD WASN'T ABOUT HER IN THE FIRST PLACE. SHE PUT THE WHOLE THING OUT OF HER MIND, THINKING HOW SILLY SHE'D BEEN.

THE NEXT MORNING, FOR A CHANGE OF PACE, CHERYL WALKED THE EXTRA TWO BLOCKS TO A DIFFERENT CAFÉ BEFORE GOING TO WORK.

Ooh La LATTÉ

THREE DAYS LATER, ANOTHER AD IN THE "I SAW YOU..." SECTION CAUGHT HER ATTENTION.

s. SWM, 33,
orrid telephone
omen of color
. Only re-
imagination
ge, marital
mportant.

you never wait in stupid lines. You said
Don't make me wait either!
Let me lick you til you quiver.
#94198

MARCH 17 @ OOH LA LATTE
You: brown hair, glasses, grey sweater, bought a mocha to go. You left before I could say hi. Second chance? Same place, same time, next week.

Lady in white. We looked in each others eyes twice in front of elephant on Sunday. Who are you? #86221

AUTIFUL
m 45,
with my
ooking
for
and
that

#7, long lusc
olive color ey
eye contact &
you go to Dis
me? #74189

3/2 ITA

3/13. HOUSE ON

Caffe Cent

haired

SHE SUDDENLY FELT LIKE THE VICTIM OF A PRACTICAL JOKE...THAT SOMEWHERE, SOMEONE WAS LAUGHING HYSTERICALLY AT HER EXPENSE. BUT SHE COULDN'T THINK WHO IT COULD POSSIBLY BE.

IN THE WEEKS THAT FOLLOWED, SIMILAR ADS CONTINUED TO APPEAR, USUALLY EVERY OTHER DAY, SOMETIMES THREE DAYS APART. EACH TIME, THE TEXT ACCURATELY DE-SCRIBED CHERYL AND CITED A LOCA-TION WHERE SHE HAD RECENTLY BEEN.

AS A TEST, SHE CHANGED HER ROU-TINES, WALKED ALTERNATE ROUTES, AND DRESSED IN UNUSUAL OUTFITS.

THE ADS CONTINUED TO APPEAR, MAINTAINING THE SAME LEVEL OF ACCURACY.

I Saw You...

sub
You
drug

#06106

X-skater, "ski
MIA? Wha
happened;
haired "pu
through y
contact
Second
Sund
Com
ma

LIPS
minant, ex-
some SWM,
ubmissive fe-
safe S&M &
possible LTR.
caring, patient,
native. You are
attractive, and
, the unusual yes's,
l the devices okay.

MARCH 23 @ BUS STOP
Corner of College and Sierra.
You: brown hair, sunglasses, baseball cap, green jacket. You got on the 51 North. Wish I'd said hi. Second chance? Same place, same time, next week. #95768

BLUE-HAIRED BOY
3/15. I've seen
you twice, your purple doc's
match your hair. Think you're
utiful. Me: Bright

at Fantasy

M

CHERYL STARTED CARRYING A SMALL NOTEBOOK WITH HER, JOTTING DOWN BRIEF DESCRIPTIONS OF PEOPLE IN RESTAURANTS, ON THE BUS, ANYWHERE SHE WENT. SHE KEPT AN EYE OUT FOR ANY RECURRING FACES - THE CONNECTING THREAD THAT ELUDED HER.

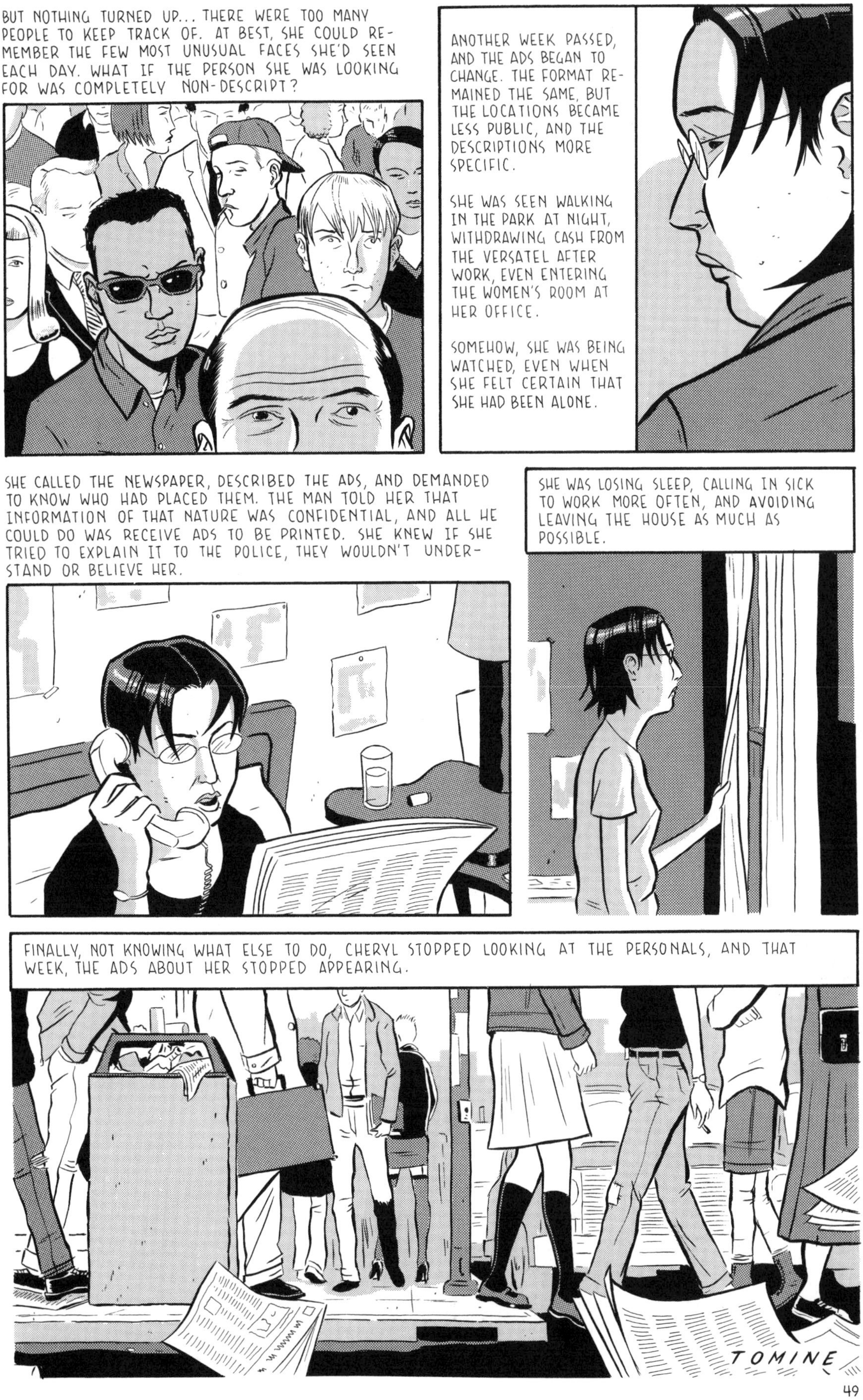
BUT NOTHING TURNED UP... THERE WERE TOO MANY PEOPLE TO KEEP TRACK OF. AT BEST, SHE COULD REMEMBER THE FEW MOST UNUSUAL FACES SHE'D SEEN EACH DAY. WHAT IF THE PERSON SHE WAS LOOKING FOR WAS COMPLETELY NON-DESCRIPT?
ANOTHER WEEK PASSED, AND THE ADS BEGAN TO CHANGE. THE FORMAT REMAINED THE SAME, BUT THE LOCATIONS BECAME LESS PUBLIC, AND THE DESCRIPTIONS MORE SPECIFIC.
SHE WAS SEEN WALKING IN THE PARK AT NIGHT, WITHDRAWING CASH FROM THE VERSATEL AFTER WORK, EVEN ENTERING THE WOMEN'S ROOM AT HER OFFICE.
SOMEHOW, SHE WAS BEING WATCHED, EVEN WHEN SHE FELT CERTAIN THAT SHE HAD BEEN ALONE.
SHE CALLED THE NEWSPAPER, DESCRIBED THE ADS, AND DEMANDED TO KNOW WHO HAD PLACED THEM. THE MAN TOLD HER THAT INFORMATION OF THAT NATURE WAS CONFIDENTIAL, AND ALL HE COULD DO WAS RECEIVE ADS TO BE PRINTED. SHE KNEW IF SHE TRIED TO EXPLAIN IT TO THE POLICE, THEY WOULDN'T UNDERSTAND OR BELIEVE HER.
SHE WAS LOSING SLEEP, CALLING IN SICK TO WORK MORE OFTEN, AND AVOIDING LEAVING THE HOUSE AS MUCH AS POSSIBLE.
FINALLY, NOT KNOWING WHAT ELSE TO DO, CHERYL STOPPED LOOKING AT THE PERSONALS, AND THAT WEEK, THE ADS ABOUT HER STOPPED APPEARING.
TOMINE

Pink Frosting

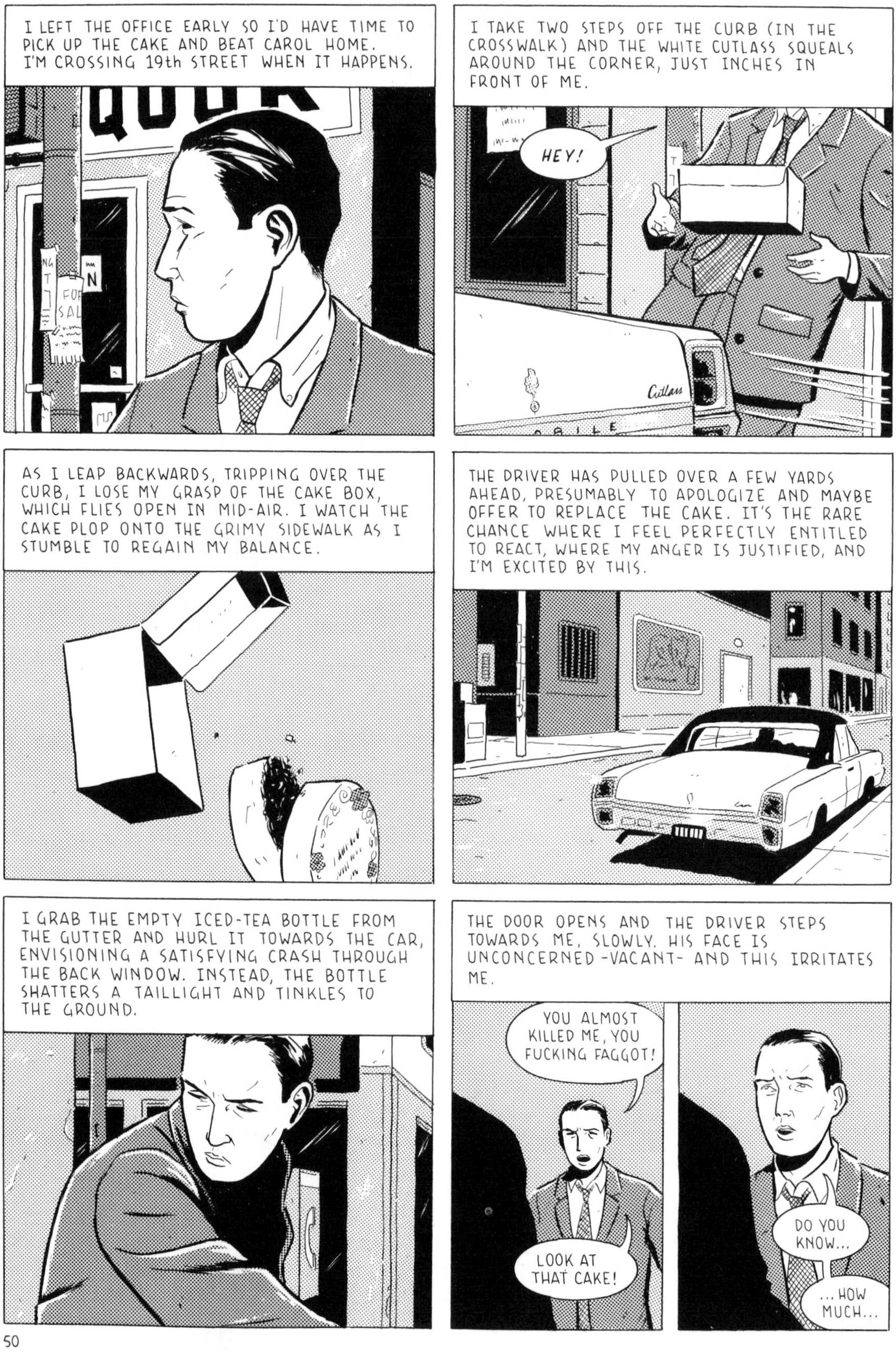
I LEFT THE OFFICE EARLY SO I'D HAVE TIME TO PICK UP THE CAKE AND BEAT CAROL HOME. I'M CROSSING 19th STREET WHEN IT HAPPENS.
I TAKE TWO STEPS OFF THE CURB (IN THE CROSSWALK) AND THE WHITE CUTLASS SQUEALS AROUND THE CORNER, JUST INCHES IN FRONT OF ME.
HEY!
Cutlass
AS I LEAP BACKWARDS, TRIPPING OVER THE CURB, I LOSE MY GRASP OF THE CAKE BOX, WHICH FLIES OPEN IN MID-AIR. I WATCH THE CAKE PLOP ONTO THE GRIMY SIDEWALK AS I STUMBLE TO REGAIN MY BALANCE.
THE DRIVER HAS PULLED OVER A FEW YARDS AHEAD, PRESUMABLY TO APOLOGIZE AND MAYBE OFFER TO REPLACE THE CAKE. IT'S THE RARE CHANCE WHERE I FEEL PERFECTLY ENTITLED TO REACT, WHERE MY ANGER IS JUSTIFIED, AND I'M EXCITED BY THIS.
I GRAB THE EMPTY ICED-TEA BOTTLE FROM THE GUTTER AND HURL IT TOWARDS THE CAR, ENVISIONING A SATISFYING CRASH THROUGH THE BACK WINDOW. INSTEAD, THE BOTTLE SHATTERS A TAILLIGHT AND TINKLES TO THE GROUND.
THE DOOR OPENS AND THE DRIVER STEPS TOWARDS ME, SLOWLY. HIS FACE IS UNCONCERNED -VACANT- AND THIS IRRITATES ME.
YOU ALMOST KILLED ME, YOU FUCKING FAGGOT!
LOOK AT THAT CAKE!
DO YOU KNOW...
...HOW MUCH...

IT ISN'T UNTIL A SPLIT-SECOND AFTERWARDS THAT I REALIZE I'VE BEEN HIT. MY NOSE EXPLODES AND I DROP TO THE PAVEMENT. IT OCCURS TO ME THAT IT'S THE FIRST TIME I'VE EVER REALLY BEEN PUNCHED.

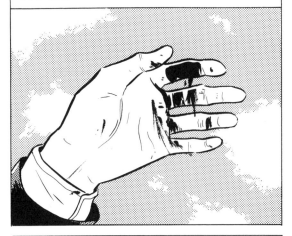

I KNOW I SHOULD GET UP AND PUNCH BACK OR RUN OR SAY SOMETHING, BUT PAIN AND DISBELIEF GRIP ME AND I JUST LIE THERE, SILENT. I CAN'T EVEN RESIST WHEN THE DRIVER DRAGS ME OFF THE SIDEWALK, INTO THE GUTTER.

HE SAYS SOMETHING THAT I DON'T QUITE UNDERSTAND, AND THEN SAYS IT AGAIN WHEN I DON'T RESPOND.

BITE THE CURB.

I LOOK UP AT HIS FACE AS HE REPEATS HIMSELF, THIS TIME MUCH LOUDER. I MAKE A SUDDEN MOVE TO GET UP AND HE KICKS ME HARD IN THE SIDE AND I WONDER WHY NO ONE IS DOING ANYTHING TO STOP THIS.

DO IT!

I GET UP ON MY HANDS AND KNEES AND CRAWL FORWARD, UNCERTAIN OF HIS INTENT. THE CURB IS SMEARED WITH PINK FROSTING FROM THE CAKE, AND I TASTE THE COMFORTING SWEETNESS AS MY TEETH SETTLE AGAINST THE CEMENT.

HE LIFTS ONE FOOT, RAISING IT BEHIND MY HEAD. RIGHT NOW, CAROL IS WALKING THROUGH THE FRONT DOOR. SHE LOOKS AROUND AT THE CREPE PAPER AND BALLOONS, AND FOR A MOMENT, WAITS FOR ME TO LEAP OUT AND YELL "SURPRISE!"

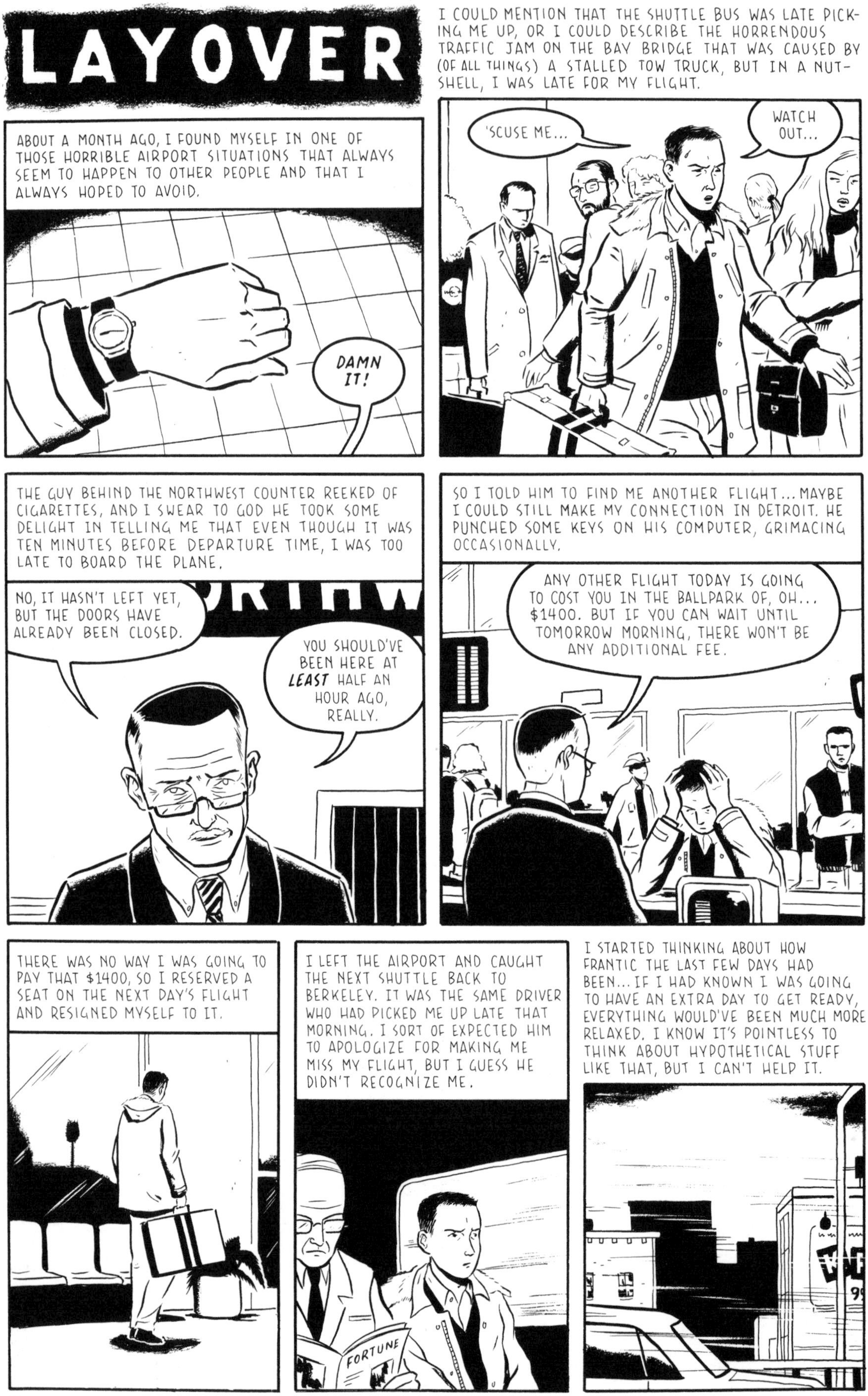
LAYOVER
I COULD MENTION THAT THE SHUTTLE BUS WAS LATE PICKING ME UP, OR I COULD DESCRIBE THE HORRENDOUS TRAFFIC JAM ON THE BAY BRIDGE THAT WAS CAUSED BY (OF ALL THINGS) A STALLED TOW TRUCK, BUT IN A NUTSHELL, I WAS LATE FOR MY FLIGHT.
ABOUT A MONTH AGO, I FOUND MYSELF IN ONE OF THOSE HORRIBLE AIRPORT SITUATIONS THAT ALWAYS SEEM TO HAPPEN TO OTHER PEOPLE AND THAT I ALWAYS HOPED TO AVOID.
DAMN IT!
'SCUSE ME...
WATCH OUT...
THE GUY BEHIND THE NORTHWEST COUNTER REEKED OF CIGARETTES, AND I SWEAR TO GOD HE TOOK SOME DELIGHT IN TELLING ME THAT EVEN THOUGH IT WAS TEN MINUTES BEFORE DEPARTURE TIME, I WAS TOO LATE TO BOARD THE PLANE.
NO, IT HASN'T LEFT YET, BUT THE DOORS HAVE ALREADY BEEN CLOSED.
YOU SHOULD'VE BEEN HERE AT **LEAST** HALF AN HOUR AGO, REALLY.
SO I TOLD HIM TO FIND ME ANOTHER FLIGHT... MAYBE I COULD STILL MAKE MY CONNECTION IN DETROIT. HE PUNCHED SOME KEYS ON HIS COMPUTER, GRIMACING OCCASIONALLY.
ANY OTHER FLIGHT TODAY IS GOING TO COST YOU IN THE BALLPARK OF, OH... $1400. BUT IF YOU CAN WAIT UNTIL TOMORROW MORNING, THERE WON'T BE ANY ADDITIONAL FEE.
THERE WAS NO WAY I WAS GOING TO PAY THAT $1400, SO I RESERVED A SEAT ON THE NEXT DAY'S FLIGHT AND RESIGNED MYSELF TO IT.
I LEFT THE AIRPORT AND CAUGHT THE NEXT SHUTTLE BACK TO BERKELEY. IT WAS THE SAME DRIVER WHO HAD PICKED ME UP LATE THAT MORNING. I SORT OF EXPECTED HIM TO APOLOGIZE FOR MAKING ME MISS MY FLIGHT, BUT I GUESS HE DIDN'T RECOGNIZE ME.
FORTUNE
I STARTED THINKING ABOUT HOW FRANTIC THE LAST FEW DAYS HAD BEEN... IF I HAD KNOWN I WAS GOING TO HAVE AN EXTRA DAY TO GET READY, EVERYTHING WOULD'VE BEEN MUCH MORE RELAXED. I KNOW IT'S POINTLESS TO THINK ABOUT HYPOTHETICAL STUFF LIKE THAT, BUT I CAN'T HELP IT.

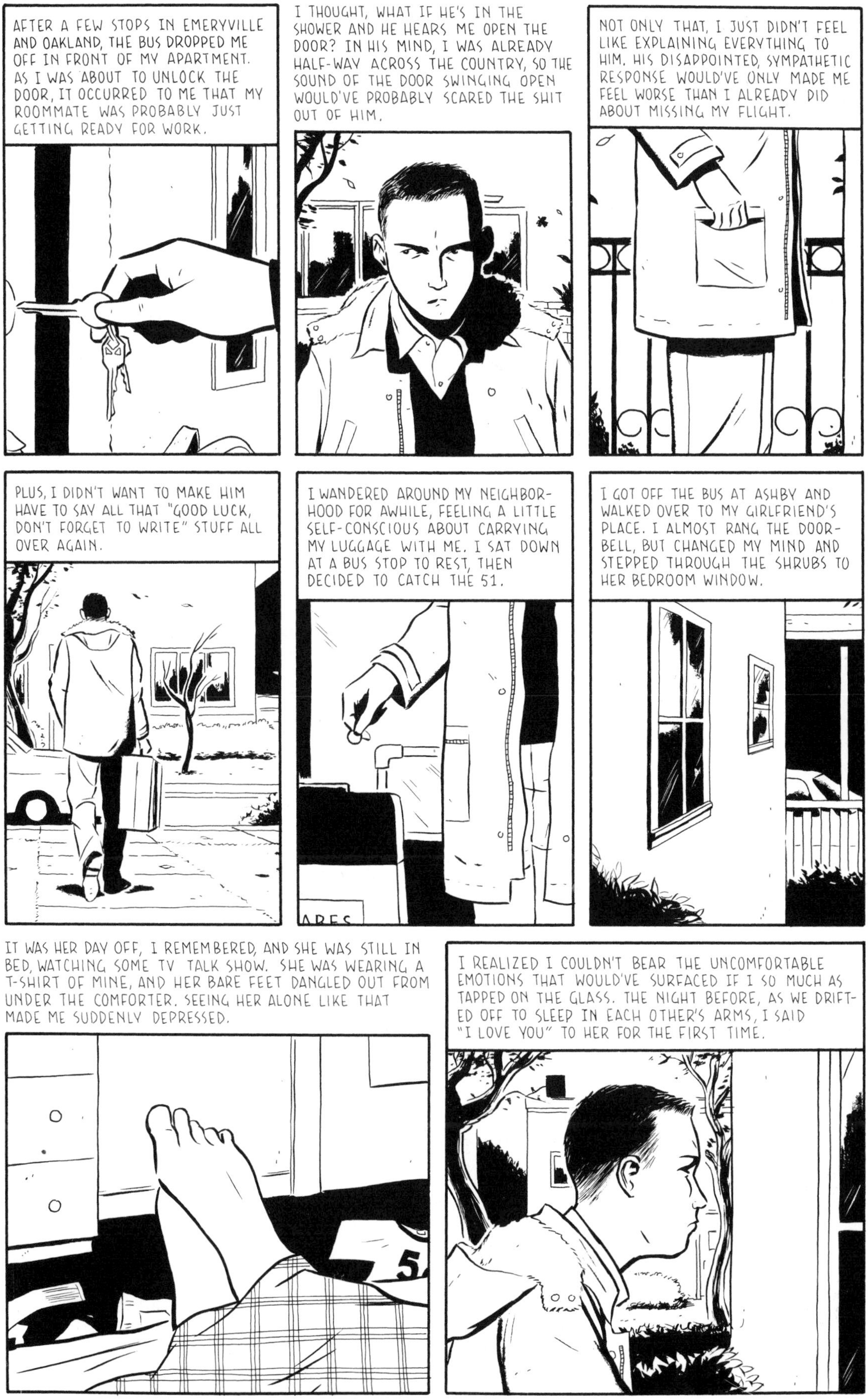

AFTER A FEW STOPS IN EMERYVILLE AND OAKLAND, THE BUS DROPPED ME OFF IN FRONT OF MY APARTMENT. AS I WAS ABOUT TO UNLOCK THE DOOR, IT OCCURRED TO ME THAT MY ROOMMATE WAS PROBABLY JUST GETTING READY FOR WORK.
I THOUGHT, WHAT IF HE'S IN THE SHOWER AND HE HEARS ME OPEN THE DOOR? IN HIS MIND, I WAS ALREADY HALF-WAY ACROSS THE COUNTRY, SO THE SOUND OF THE DOOR SWINGING OPEN WOULD'VE PROBABLY SCARED THE SHIT OUT OF HIM.
NOT ONLY THAT, I JUST DIDN'T FEEL LIKE EXPLAINING EVERYTHING TO HIM. HIS DISAPPOINTED, SYMPATHETIC RESPONSE WOULD'VE ONLY MADE ME FEEL WORSE THAN I ALREADY DID ABOUT MISSING MY FLIGHT.
PLUS, I DIDN'T WANT TO MAKE HIM HAVE TO SAY ALL THAT "GOOD LUCK, DON'T FORGET TO WRITE" STUFF ALL OVER AGAIN.
I WANDERED AROUND MY NEIGHBORHOOD FOR AWHILE, FEELING A LITTLE SELF-CONSCIOUS ABOUT CARRYING MY LUGGAGE WITH ME. I SAT DOWN AT A BUS STOP TO REST, THEN DECIDED TO CATCH THE 51.
I GOT OFF THE BUS AT ASHBY AND WALKED OVER TO MY GIRLFRIEND'S PLACE. I ALMOST RANG THE DOORBELL, BUT CHANGED MY MIND AND STEPPED THROUGH THE SHRUBS TO HER BEDROOM WINDOW.
IT WAS HER DAY OFF, I REMEMBERED, AND SHE WAS STILL IN BED, WATCHING SOME TV TALK SHOW. SHE WAS WEARING A T-SHIRT OF MINE, AND HER BARE FEET DANGLED OUT FROM UNDER THE COMFORTER. SEEING HER ALONE LIKE THAT MADE ME SUDDENLY DEPRESSED.
I REALIZED I COULDN'T BEAR THE UNCOMFORTABLE EMOTIONS THAT WOULD'VE SURFACED IF I SO MUCH AS TAPPED ON THE GLASS. THE NIGHT BEFORE, AS WE DRIFTED OFF TO SLEEP IN EACH OTHER'S ARMS, I SAID "I LOVE YOU" TO HER FOR THE FIRST TIME.

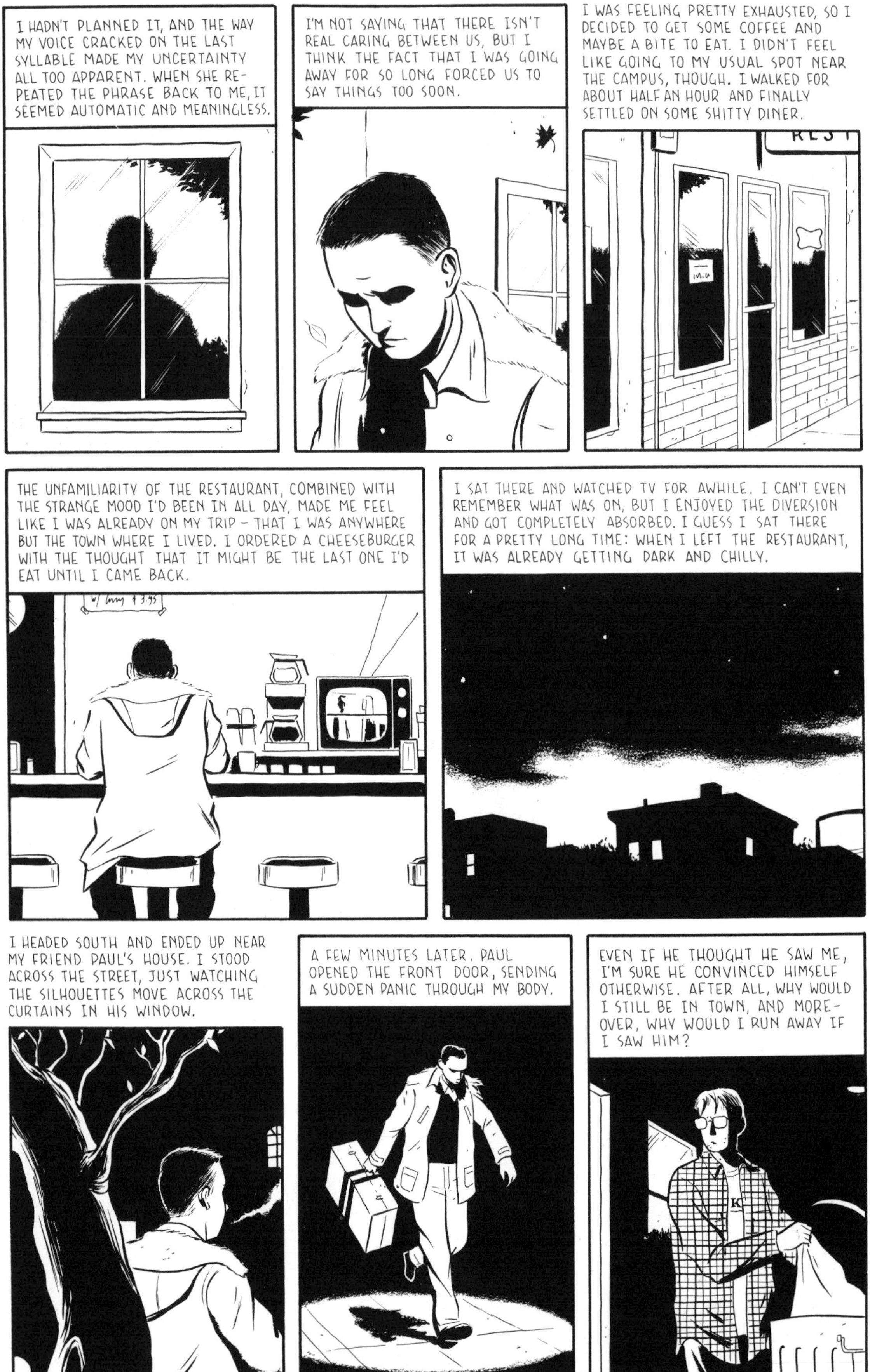
I HADN'T PLANNED IT, AND THE WAY MY VOICE CRACKED ON THE LAST SYLLABLE MADE MY UNCERTAINTY ALL TOO APPARENT. WHEN SHE RE-PEATED THE PHRASE BACK TO ME, IT SEEMED AUTOMATIC AND MEANINGLESS.
I'M NOT SAYING THAT THERE ISN'T REAL CARING BETWEEN US, BUT I THINK THE FACT THAT I WAS GOING AWAY FOR SO LONG FORCED US TO SAY THINGS TOO SOON.
I WAS FEELING PRETTY EXHAUSTED, SO I DECIDED TO GET SOME COFFEE AND MAYBE A BITE TO EAT. I DIDN'T FEEL LIKE GOING TO MY USUAL SPOT NEAR THE CAMPUS, THOUGH. I WALKED FOR ABOUT HALF AN HOUR AND FINALLY SETTLED ON SOME SHITTY DINER.
THE UNFAMILIARITY OF THE RESTAURANT, COMBINED WITH THE STRANGE MOOD I'D BEEN IN ALL DAY, MADE ME FEEL LIKE I WAS ALREADY ON MY TRIP – THAT I WAS ANYWHERE BUT THE TOWN WHERE I LIVED. I ORDERED A CHEESEBURGER WITH THE THOUGHT THAT IT MIGHT BE THE LAST ONE I'D EAT UNTIL I CAME BACK.
I SAT THERE AND WATCHED TV FOR AWHILE. I CAN'T EVEN REMEMBER WHAT WAS ON, BUT I ENJOYED THE DIVERSION AND GOT COMPLETELY ABSORBED. I GUESS I SAT THERE FOR A PRETTY LONG TIME: WHEN I LEFT THE RESTAURANT, IT WAS ALREADY GETTING DARK AND CHILLY.
I HEADED SOUTH AND ENDED UP NEAR MY FRIEND PAUL'S HOUSE. I STOOD ACROSS THE STREET, JUST WATCHING THE SILHOUETTES MOVE ACROSS THE CURTAINS IN HIS WINDOW.
A FEW MINUTES LATER, PAUL OPENED THE FRONT DOOR, SENDING A SUDDEN PANIC THROUGH MY BODY.
EVEN IF HE THOUGHT HE SAW ME, I'M SURE HE CONVINCED HIMSELF OTHERWISE. AFTER ALL, WHY WOULD I STILL BE IN TOWN, AND MORE-OVER, WHY WOULD I RUN AWAY IF I SAW HIM?

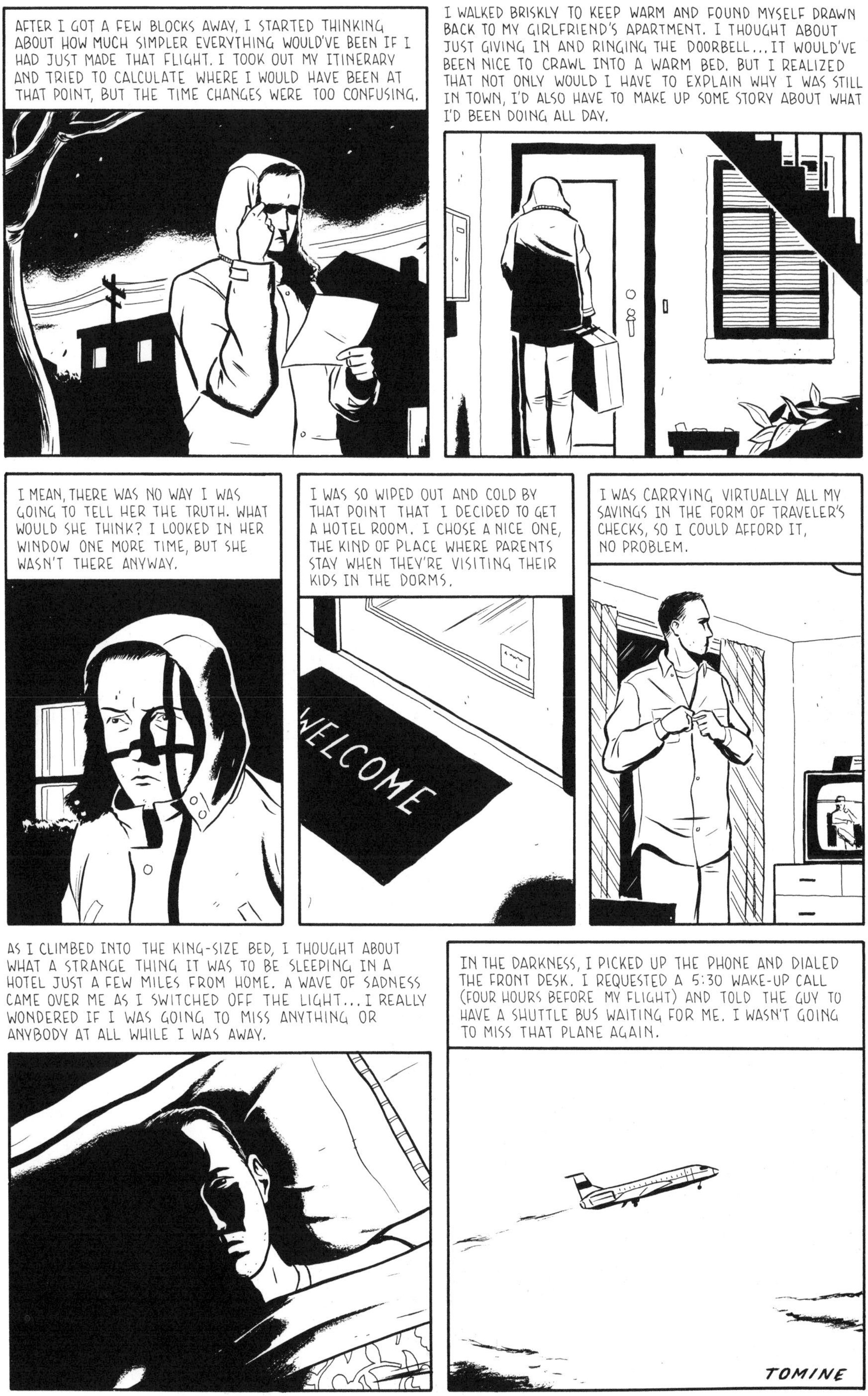
AFTER I GOT A FEW BLOCKS AWAY, I STARTED THINKING ABOUT HOW MUCH SIMPLER EVERYTHING WOULD'VE BEEN IF I HAD JUST MADE THAT FLIGHT. I TOOK OUT MY ITINERARY AND TRIED TO CALCULATE WHERE I WOULD HAVE BEEN AT THAT POINT, BUT THE TIME CHANGES WERE TOO CONFUSING.
I WALKED BRISKLY TO KEEP WARM AND FOUND MYSELF DRAWN BACK TO MY GIRLFRIEND'S APARTMENT. I THOUGHT ABOUT JUST GIVING IN AND RINGING THE DOORBELL... IT WOULD'VE BEEN NICE TO CRAWL INTO A WARM BED. BUT I REALIZED THAT NOT ONLY WOULD I HAVE TO EXPLAIN WHY I WAS STILL IN TOWN, I'D ALSO HAVE TO MAKE UP SOME STORY ABOUT WHAT I'D BEEN DOING ALL DAY.
I MEAN, THERE WAS NO WAY I WAS GOING TO TELL HER THE TRUTH. WHAT WOULD SHE THINK? I LOOKED IN HER WINDOW ONE MORE TIME, BUT SHE WASN'T THERE ANYWAY.
I WAS SO WIPED OUT AND COLD BY THAT POINT THAT I DECIDED TO GET A HOTEL ROOM. I CHOSE A NICE ONE, THE KIND OF PLACE WHERE PARENTS STAY WHEN THEY'RE VISITING THEIR KIDS IN THE DORMS.
WELCOME
I WAS CARRYING VIRTUALLY ALL MY SAVINGS IN THE FORM OF TRAVELER'S CHECKS, SO I COULD AFFORD IT, NO PROBLEM.
AS I CLIMBED INTO THE KING-SIZE BED, I THOUGHT ABOUT WHAT A STRANGE THING IT WAS TO BE SLEEPING IN A HOTEL JUST A FEW MILES FROM HOME. A WAVE OF SADNESS CAME OVER ME AS I SWITCHED OFF THE LIGHT... I REALLY WONDERED IF I WAS GOING TO MISS ANYTHING OR ANYBODY AT ALL WHILE I WAS AWAY.
IN THE DARKNESS, I PICKED UP THE PHONE AND DIALED THE FRONT DESK. I REQUESTED A 5:30 WAKE-UP CALL (FOUR HOURS BEFORE MY FLIGHT) AND TOLD THE GUY TO HAVE A SHUTTLE BUS WAITING FOR ME. I WASN'T GOING TO MISS THAT PLANE AGAIN.
TOMINE

SUPERMARKET

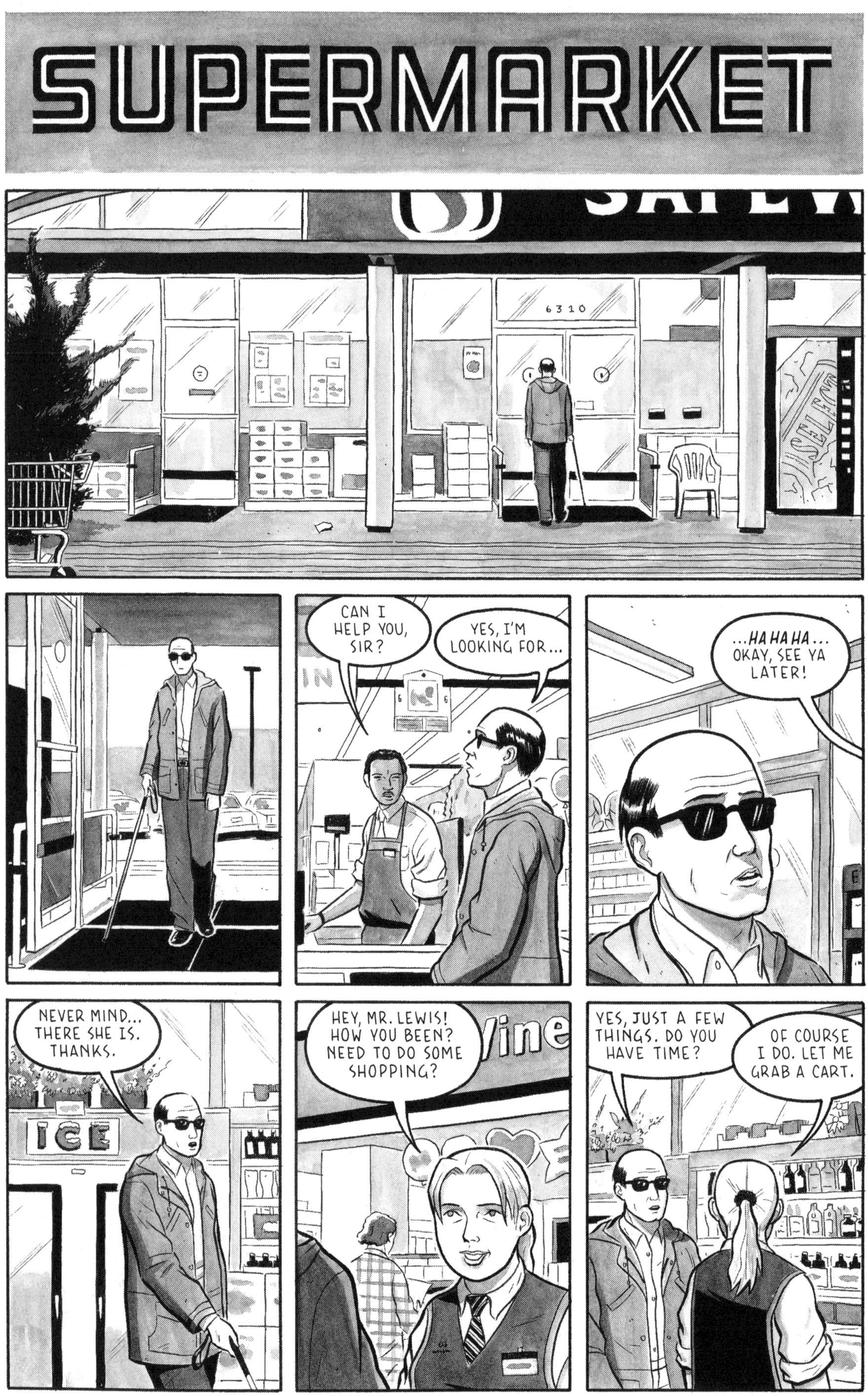
6310
CAN I HELP YOU, SIR?
YES, I'M LOOKING FOR...
...HA HA HA... OKAY, SEE YA LATER!
NEVER MIND... THERE SHE IS. THANKS.
ICE
HEY, MR. LEWIS! HOW YOU BEEN? NEED TO DO SOME SHOPPING?
YES, JUST A FEW THINGS. DO YOU HAVE TIME?
OF COURSE I DO. LET ME GRAB A CART.

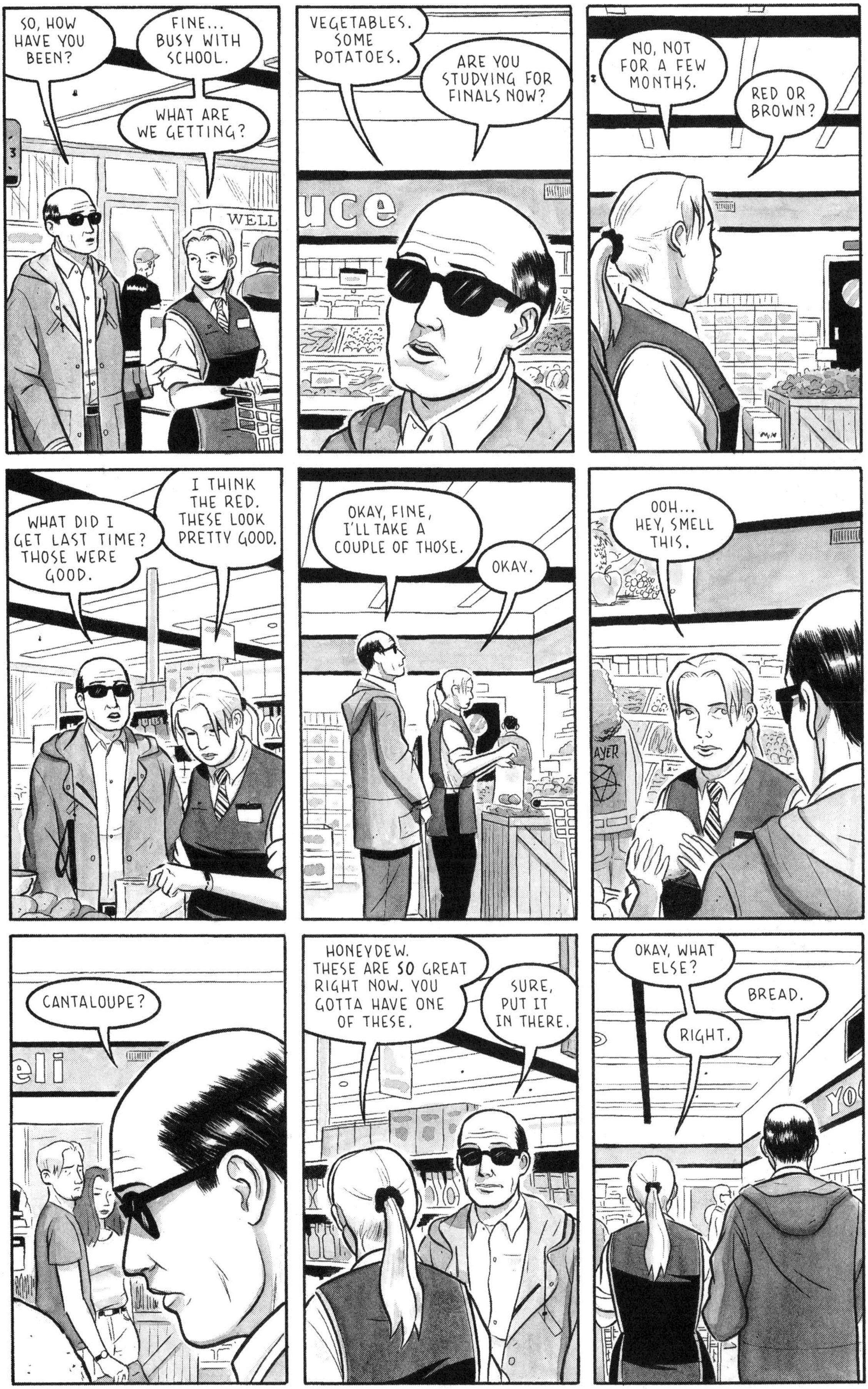
SO, HOW HAVE YOU BEEN?
FINE... BUSY WITH SCHOOL.
WHAT ARE WE GETTING?
VEGETABLES. SOME POTATOES.
ARE YOU STUDYING FOR FINALS NOW?
NO, NOT FOR A FEW MONTHS.
RED OR BROWN?
WHAT DID I GET LAST TIME? THOSE WERE GOOD.
I THINK THE RED. THESE LOOK PRETTY GOOD.
OKAY, FINE, I'LL TAKE A COUPLE OF THOSE.
OKAY.
OOH... HEY, SMELL THIS.
CANTALOUPE?
HONEYDEW. THESE ARE **SO** GREAT RIGHT NOW. YOU GOTTA HAVE ONE OF THESE.
SURE, PUT IT IN THERE.
OKAY, WHAT ELSE?
BREAD.
RIGHT.

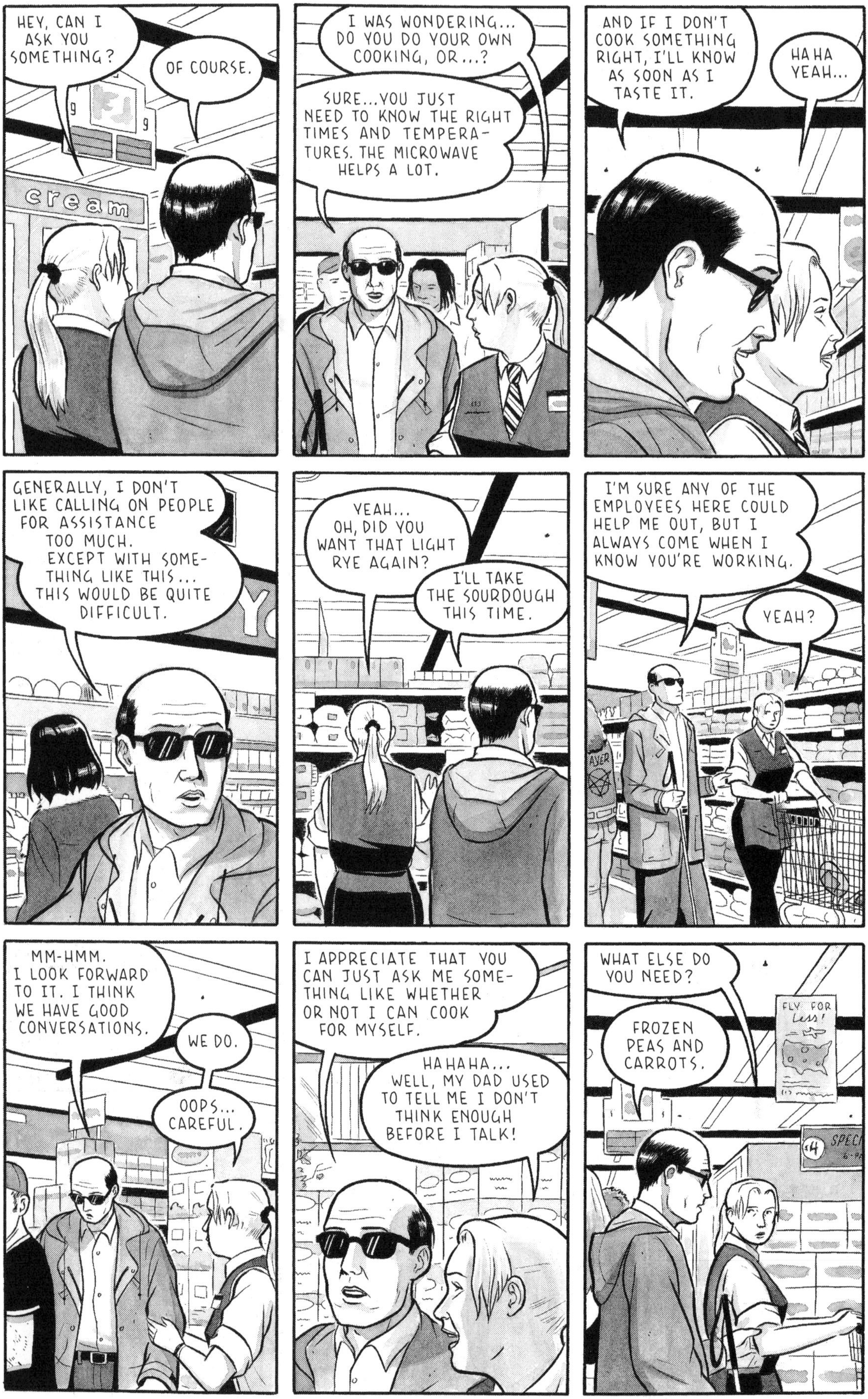
HEY, CAN I ASK YOU SOMETHING?
OF COURSE.
cream
I WAS WONDERING... DO YOU DO YOUR OWN COOKING, OR...?
SURE...YOU JUST NEED TO KNOW THE RIGHT TIMES AND TEMPERA-TURES. THE MICROWAVE HELPS A LOT.
AND IF I DON'T COOK SOMETHING RIGHT, I'LL KNOW AS SOON AS I TASTE IT.
HA HA YEAH...
GENERALLY, I DON'T LIKE CALLING ON PEOPLE FOR ASSISTANCE TOO MUCH. EXCEPT WITH SOME-THING LIKE THIS... THIS WOULD BE QUITE DIFFICULT.
YEAH... OH, DID YOU WANT THAT LIGHT RYE AGAIN?
I'LL TAKE THE SOURDOUGH THIS TIME.
I'M SURE ANY OF THE EMPLOYEES HERE COULD HELP ME OUT, BUT I ALWAYS COME WHEN I KNOW YOU'RE WORKING.
YEAH?
MM-HMM. I LOOK FORWARD TO IT. I THINK WE HAVE GOOD CONVERSATIONS.
WE DO.
OOPS... CAREFUL.
I APPRECIATE THAT YOU CAN JUST ASK ME SOME-THING LIKE WHETHER OR NOT I CAN COOK FOR MYSELF.
HAHAHA... WELL, MY DAD USED TO TELL ME I DON'T THINK ENOUGH BEFORE I TALK!
WHAT ELSE DO YOU NEED?
FROZEN PEAS AND CARROTS.
FLY FOR Less!

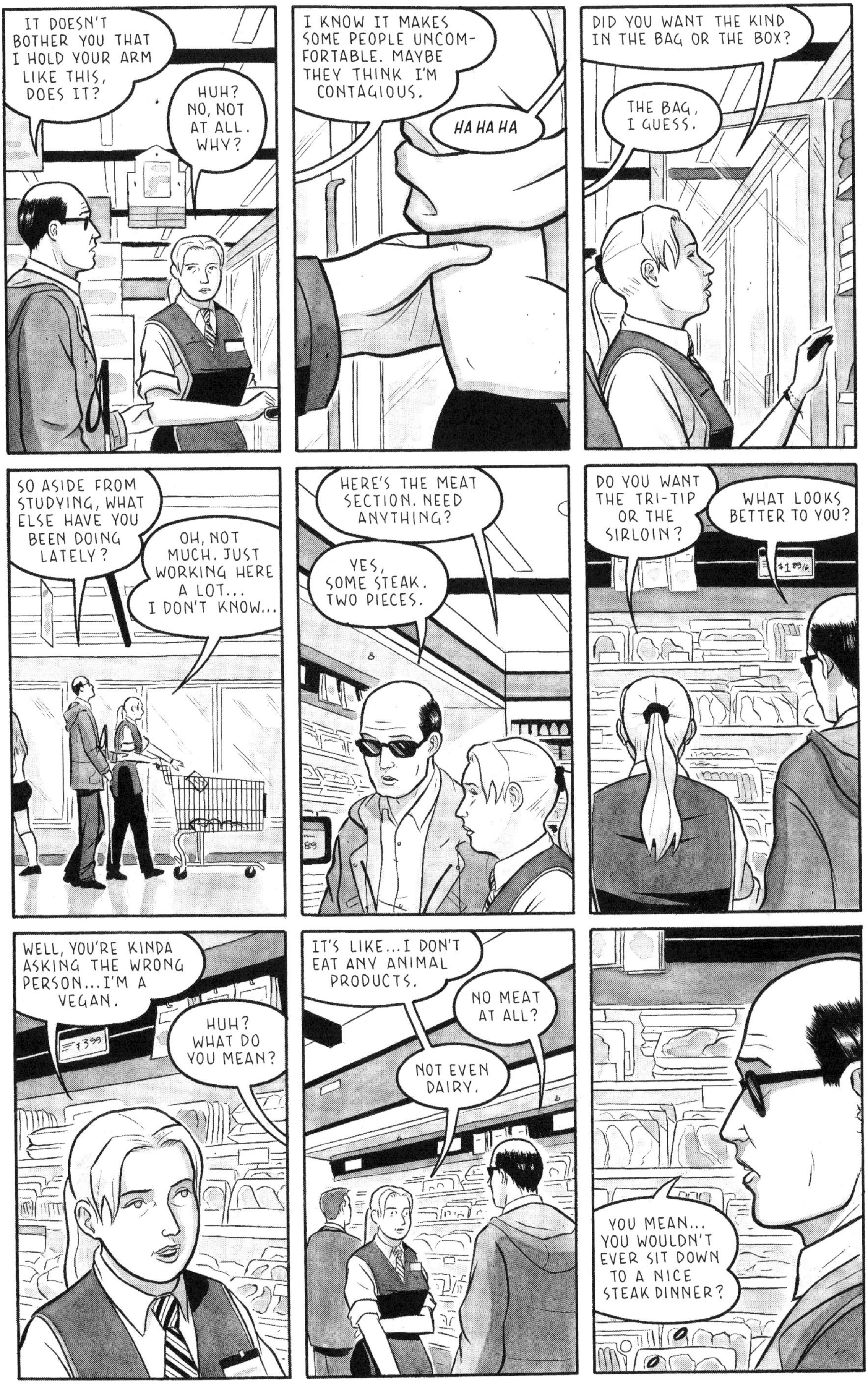
IT DOESN'T BOTHER YOU THAT I HOLD YOUR ARM LIKE THIS, DOES IT?
HUH? NO, NOT AT ALL. WHY?
I KNOW IT MAKES SOME PEOPLE UNCOMFORTABLE. MAYBE THEY THINK I'M CONTAGIOUS.
HA HA HA
DID YOU WANT THE KIND IN THE BAG OR THE BOX?
THE BAG, I GUESS.
SO ASIDE FROM STUDYING, WHAT ELSE HAVE YOU BEEN DOING LATELY?
OH, NOT MUCH. JUST WORKING HERE A LOT... I DON'T KNOW...
HERE'S THE MEAT SECTION. NEED ANYTHING?
YES, SOME STEAK. TWO PIECES.
DO YOU WANT THE TRI-TIP OR THE SIRLOIN?
WHAT LOOKS BETTER TO YOU?
WELL, YOU'RE KINDA ASKING THE WRONG PERSON...I'M A VEGAN.
HUH? WHAT DO YOU MEAN?
IT'S LIKE...I DON'T EAT ANY ANIMAL PRODUCTS.
NO MEAT AT ALL?
NOT EVEN DAIRY.
YOU MEAN... YOU WOULDN'T EVER SIT DOWN TO A NICE STEAK DINNER?

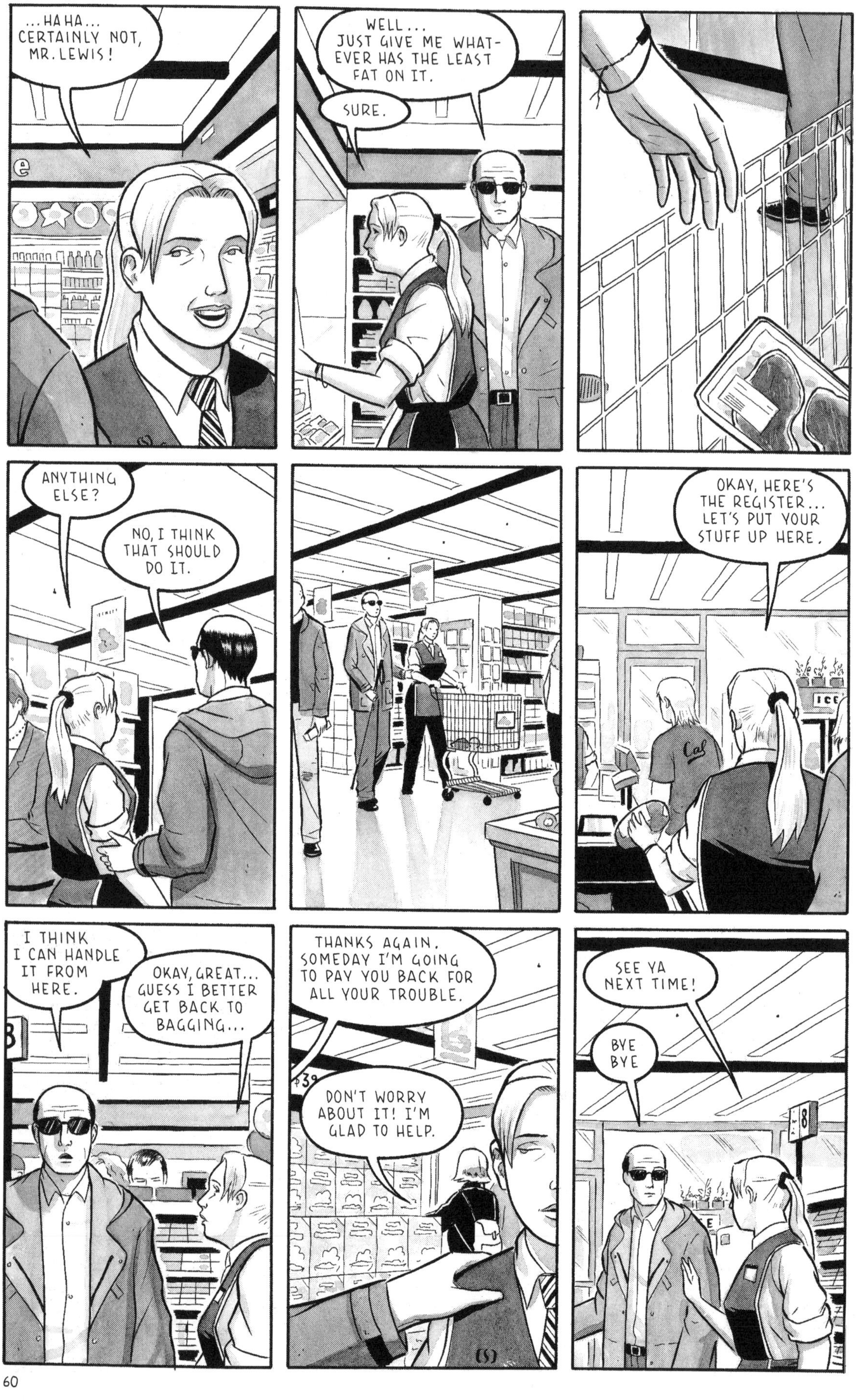
...HA HA... CERTAINLY NOT, MR. LEWIS!
WELL... JUST GIVE ME WHATEVER HAS THE LEAST FAT ON IT.
SURE.
ANYTHING ELSE?
NO, I THINK THAT SHOULD DO IT.
OKAY, HERE'S THE REGISTER... LET'S PUT YOUR STUFF UP HERE.
I THINK I CAN HANDLE IT FROM HERE.
OKAY, GREAT... GUESS I BETTER GET BACK TO BAGGING...
THANKS AGAIN. SOMEDAY I'M GOING TO PAY YOU BACK FOR ALL YOUR TROUBLE.
DON'T WORRY ABOUT IT! I'M GLAD TO HELP.
SEE YA NEXT TIME!
BYE BYE

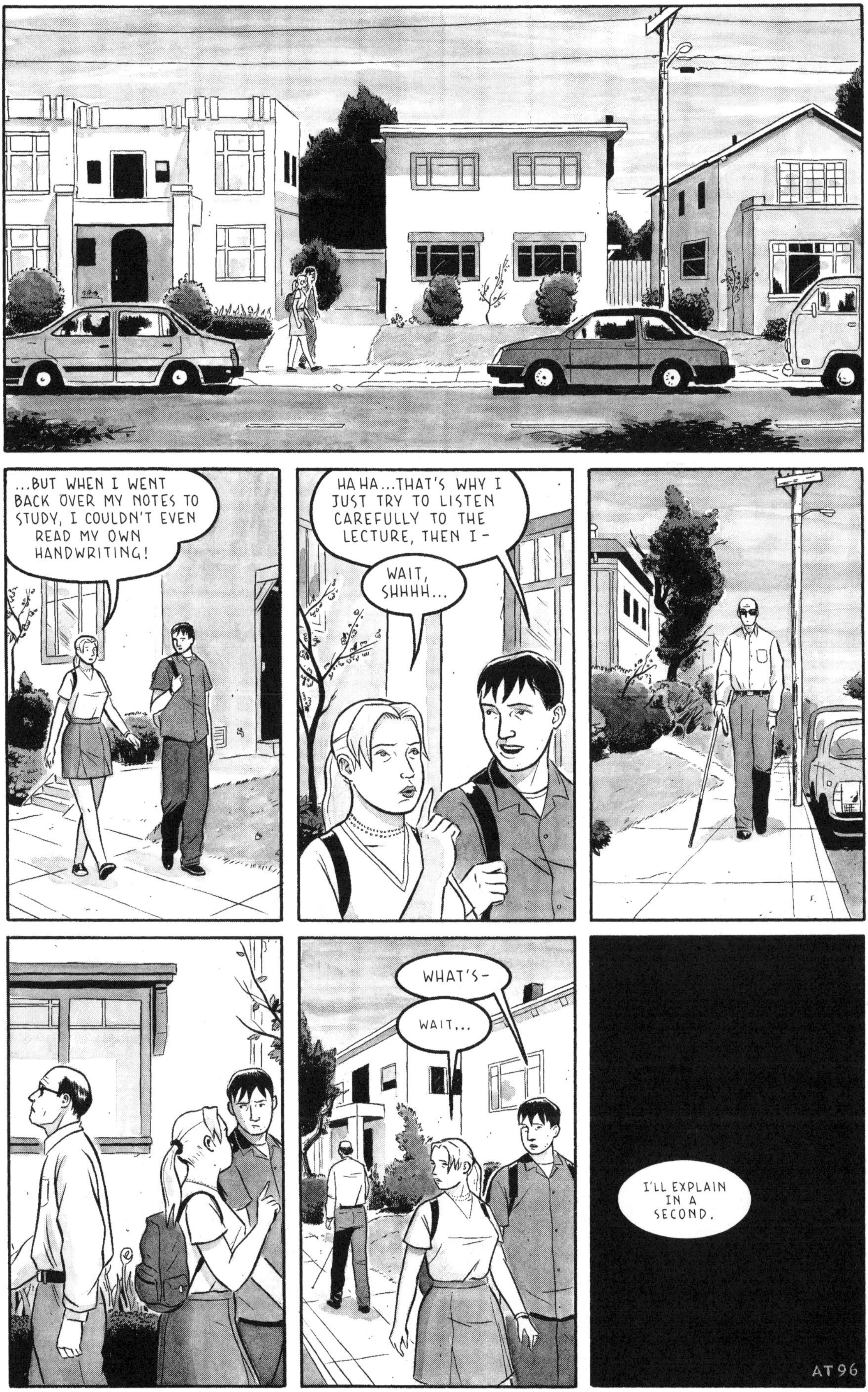

...BUT WHEN I WENT BACK OVER MY NOTES TO STUDY, I COULDN'T EVEN READ MY OWN HANDWRITING!
HA HA...THAT'S WHY I JUST TRY TO LISTEN CAREFULLY TO THE LECTURE, THEN I-
WAIT, SHHHH...
WHAT'S-
WAIT...
I'LL EXPLAIN IN A SECOND.
AT 96

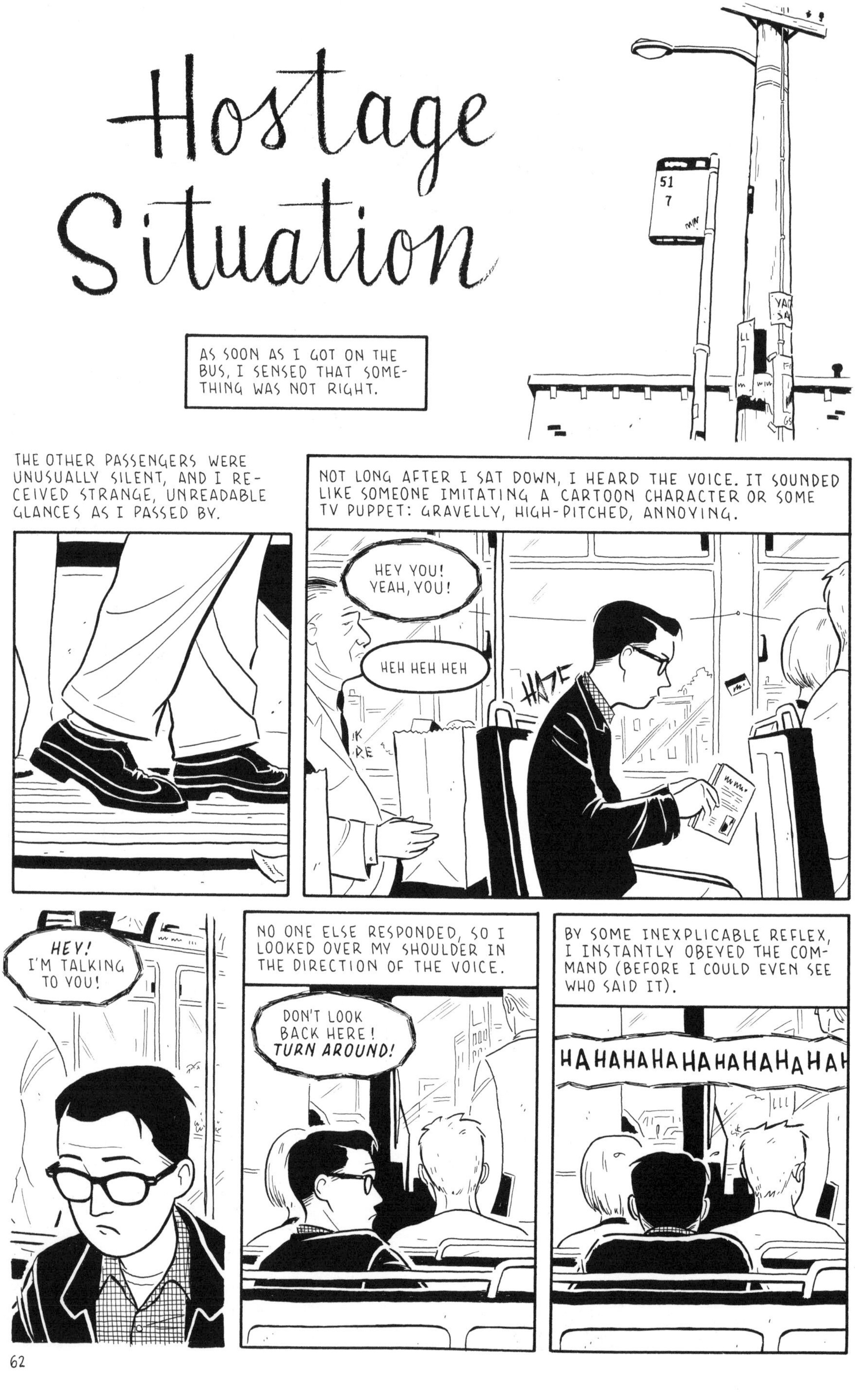
Hostage Situation
AS SOON AS I GOT ON THE BUS, I SENSED THAT SOMETHING WAS NOT RIGHT.
THE OTHER PASSENGERS WERE UNUSUALLY SILENT, AND I RECEIVED STRANGE, UNREADABLE GLANCES AS I PASSED BY.
NOT LONG AFTER I SAT DOWN, I HEARD THE VOICE. IT SOUNDED LIKE SOMEONE IMITATING A CARTOON CHARACTER OR SOME TV PUPPET: GRAVELLY, HIGH-PITCHED, ANNOYING.
HEY YOU! YEAH, YOU!
HEH HEH HEH
HEY! I'M TALKING TO YOU!
NO ONE ELSE RESPONDED, SO I LOOKED OVER MY SHOULDER IN THE DIRECTION OF THE VOICE.
DON'T LOOK BACK HERE! TURN AROUND!
BY SOME INEXPLICABLE REFLEX, I INSTANTLY OBEYED THE COMMAND (BEFORE I COULD EVEN SEE WHO SAID IT).
HAHAHAHAHAHAHAHAHAHAH

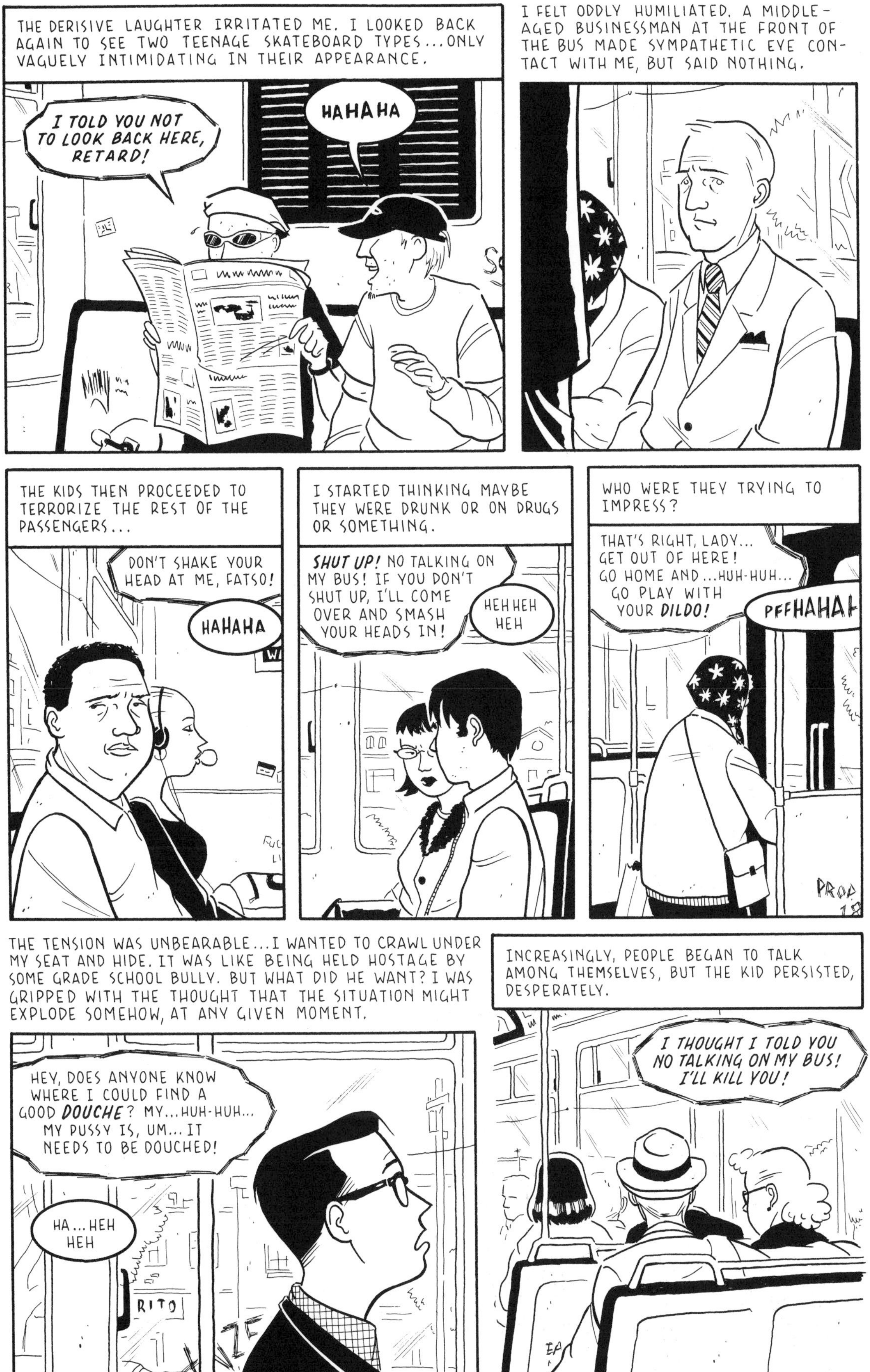
THE DERISIVE LAUGHTER IRRITATED ME. I LOOKED BACK AGAIN TO SEE TWO TEENAGE SKATEBOARD TYPES...ONLY VAGUELY INTIMIDATING IN THEIR APPEARANCE.
I TOLD YOU NOT TO LOOK BACK HERE, RETARD!
HAHAHA
I FELT ODDLY HUMILIATED. A MIDDLE-AGED BUSINESSMAN AT THE FRONT OF THE BUS MADE SYMPATHETIC EYE CONTACT WITH ME, BUT SAID NOTHING.
THE KIDS THEN PROCEEDED TO TERRORIZE THE REST OF THE PASSENGERS...
DON'T SHAKE YOUR HEAD AT ME, FATSO!
HAHAHA
I STARTED THINKING MAYBE THEY WERE DRUNK OR ON DRUGS OR SOMETHING.
SHUT UP! NO TALKING ON MY BUS! IF YOU DON'T SHUT UP, I'LL COME OVER AND SMASH YOUR HEADS IN!
HEH HEH HEH
WHO WERE THEY TRYING TO IMPRESS?
THAT'S RIGHT, LADY... GET OUT OF HERE! GO HOME AND...HUH-HUH... GO PLAY WITH YOUR DILDO!
PFFHAHAH
THE TENSION WAS UNBEARABLE...I WANTED TO CRAWL UNDER MY SEAT AND HIDE. IT WAS LIKE BEING HELD HOSTAGE BY SOME GRADE SCHOOL BULLY. BUT WHAT DID HE WANT? I WAS GRIPPED WITH THE THOUGHT THAT THE SITUATION MIGHT EXPLODE SOMEHOW, AT ANY GIVEN MOMENT.
HEY, DOES ANYONE KNOW WHERE I COULD FIND A GOOD DOUCHE? MY...HUH-HUH... MY PUSSY IS, UM...IT NEEDS TO BE DOUCHED!
HA...HEH HEH
INCREASINGLY, PEOPLE BEGAN TO TALK AMONG THEMSELVES, BUT THE KID PERSISTED, DESPERATELY.
I THOUGHT I TOLD YOU NO TALKING ON MY BUS! I'LL KILL YOU!

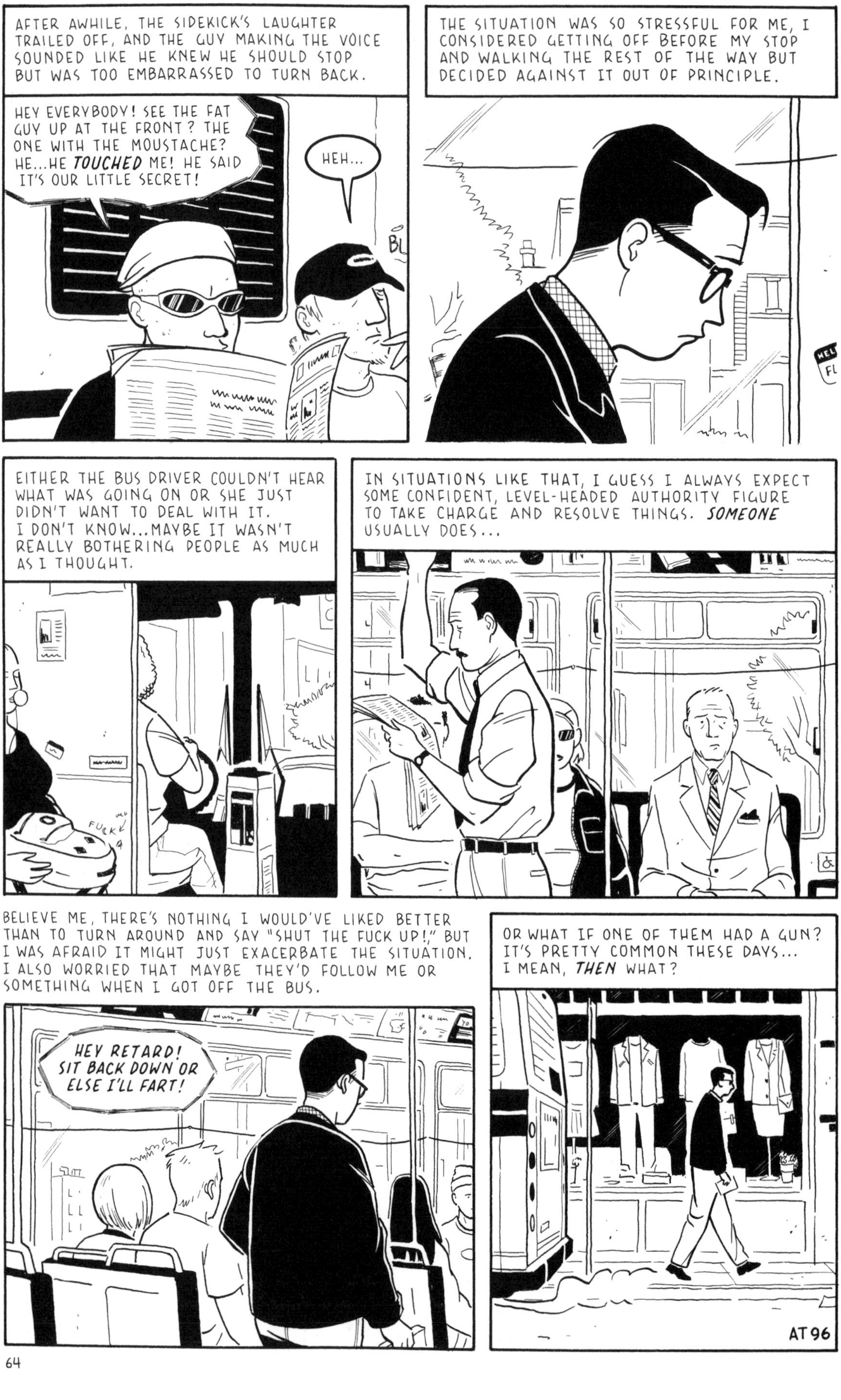
AFTER AWHILE, THE SIDEKICK'S LAUGHTER TRAILED OFF, AND THE GUY MAKING THE VOICE SOUNDED LIKE HE KNEW HE SHOULD STOP BUT WAS TOO EMBARRASSED TO TURN BACK.
HEY EVERYBODY! SEE THE FAT GUY UP AT THE FRONT? THE ONE WITH THE MOUSTACHE? HE...HE *TOUCHED* ME! HE SAID IT'S OUR LITTLE SECRET!
HEH...
THE SITUATION WAS SO STRESSFUL FOR ME, I CONSIDERED GETTING OFF BEFORE MY STOP AND WALKING THE REST OF THE WAY BUT DECIDED AGAINST IT OUT OF PRINCIPLE.
EITHER THE BUS DRIVER COULDN'T HEAR WHAT WAS GOING ON OR SHE JUST DIDN'T WANT TO DEAL WITH IT. I DON'T KNOW...MAYBE IT WASN'T REALLY BOTHERING PEOPLE AS MUCH AS I THOUGHT.
IN SITUATIONS LIKE THAT, I GUESS I ALWAYS EXPECT SOME CONFIDENT, LEVEL-HEADED AUTHORITY FIGURE TO TAKE CHARGE AND RESOLVE THINGS. *SOMEONE* USUALLY DOES...
BELIEVE ME, THERE'S NOTHING I WOULD'VE LIKED BETTER THAN TO TURN AROUND AND SAY "SHUT THE FUCK UP!," BUT I WAS AFRAID IT MIGHT JUST EXACERBATE THE SITUATION. I ALSO WORRIED THAT MAYBE THEY'D FOLLOW ME OR SOMETHING WHEN I GOT OFF THE BUS.
HEY RETARD! SIT BACK DOWN OR ELSE I'LL FART!
OR WHAT IF ONE OF THEM HAD A GUN? IT'S PRETTY COMMON THESE DAYS... I MEAN, *THEN* WHAT?
AT 96

DYLAN & DONOVAN

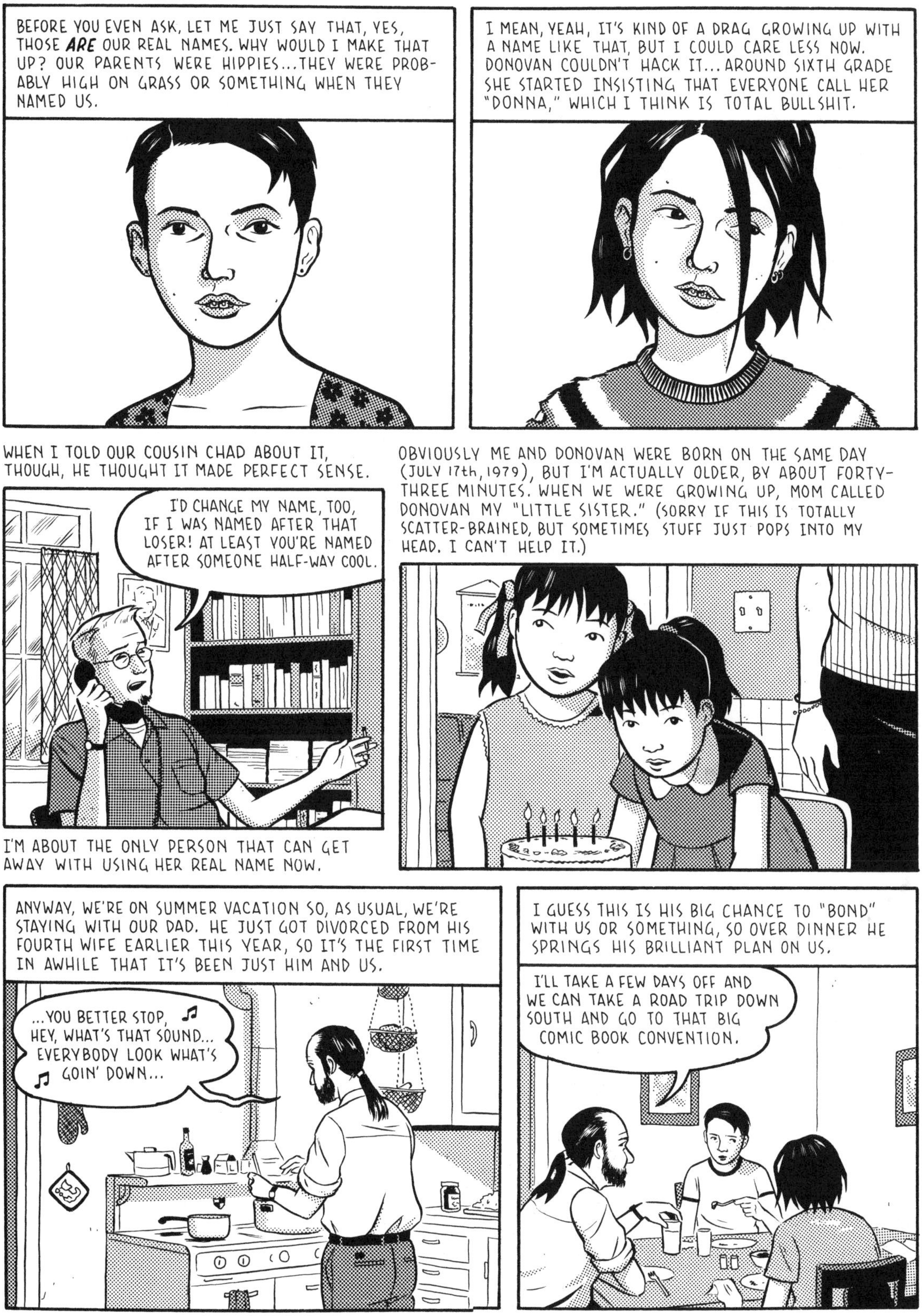

BEFORE YOU EVEN ASK, LET ME JUST SAY THAT, YES, THOSE ARE OUR REAL NAMES. WHY WOULD I MAKE THAT UP? OUR PARENTS WERE HIPPIES...THEY WERE PROBABLY HIGH ON GRASS OR SOMETHING WHEN THEY NAMED US.
I MEAN, YEAH, IT'S KIND OF A DRAG GROWING UP WITH A NAME LIKE THAT, BUT I COULD CARE LESS NOW. DONOVAN COULDN'T HACK IT... AROUND SIXTH GRADE SHE STARTED INSISTING THAT EVERYONE CALL HER "DONNA," WHICH I THINK IS TOTAL BULLSHIT.
WHEN I TOLD OUR COUSIN CHAD ABOUT IT, THOUGH, HE THOUGHT IT MADE PERFECT SENSE.
I'D CHANGE MY NAME, TOO, IF I WAS NAMED AFTER THAT LOSER! AT LEAST YOU'RE NAMED AFTER SOMEONE HALF-WAY COOL.
I'M ABOUT THE ONLY PERSON THAT CAN GET AWAY WITH USING HER REAL NAME NOW.
OBVIOUSLY ME AND DONOVAN WERE BORN ON THE SAME DAY (JULY 17th, 1979), BUT I'M ACTUALLY OLDER, BY ABOUT FORTY-THREE MINUTES. WHEN WE WERE GROWING UP, MOM CALLED DONOVAN MY "LITTLE SISTER." (SORRY IF THIS IS TOTALLY SCATTER-BRAINED, BUT SOMETIMES STUFF JUST POPS INTO MY HEAD. I CAN'T HELP IT.)
ANYWAY, WE'RE ON SUMMER VACATION SO, AS USUAL, WE'RE STAYING WITH OUR DAD. HE JUST GOT DIVORCED FROM HIS FOURTH WIFE EARLIER THIS YEAR, SO IT'S THE FIRST TIME IN AWHILE THAT IT'S BEEN JUST HIM AND US.
...YOU BETTER STOP, ♫ HEY, WHAT'S THAT SOUND... EVERYBODY LOOK WHAT'S ♫ GOIN' DOWN...
I GUESS THIS IS HIS BIG CHANCE TO "BOND" WITH US OR SOMETHING, SO OVER DINNER HE SPRINGS HIS BRILLIANT PLAN ON US.
I'LL TAKE A FEW DAYS OFF AND WE CAN TAKE A ROAD TRIP DOWN SOUTH AND GO TO THAT BIG COMIC BOOK CONVENTION.

CAN YOU BELIEVE THAT? THAT'S HIS IDEA OF A "FAMILY EXPERIENCE."
I MEAN, I GUESS IT'S COOLER THAN GOING ON SOME OUTDOORS-Y
CAMPING TRIP OR TAKING US TO A BASEBALL GAME OR SOME CRAP
LIKE THAT, BUT IT JUST SEEMS SO WEIRD.

WHAT DO YOU
THINK? HOW'S
THAT SOUND?

ALL RIGHT,
I GUESS.

I HATE LONG CAR
RIDES AND I HATE
THE KIND OF PEOPLE
WHO'D BE THERE.

NOW THAT'S TOTALLY THE KIND OF
THING THAT CRACKS ME UP ABOUT
DONOVAN. SHE USED TO *BEG* DAD TO
TAKE HER TO THAT CONVENTION
WHEN SHE WAS YOUNGER.

I MEAN, I THINK COMICS ARE ALL RIGHT AND EVERY-
THING, BUT DONOVAN IS OBSESSED WITH THEM. SHE
ADORES THEM. TO BE HONEST, I THINK DAD CAME UP
WITH THIS PLAN JUST TO MAKE HER HAPPY.

HA HA HA

I'M SERIOUS.

BUT SEE, THERE'S NOTHING SHE HATES MORE THAN
WHEN SOMEONE STARTS LIKING THE SAME THINGS
SHE LIKES, ESPECIALLY ADULTS. I MEAN, MY DAD
SHOULD'VE KNOWN THAT SHE WOULD INSTANTLY GET
PISSED OFF AT HIM FOR EVEN SUGGESTING THAT.

I THINK IT'LL BE A
BLAST! I CAN LOOK FOR
SOME OF THOSE OLD
"UNDERGROUNDS"...

GOD...

HE REALLY TRIES TO BE ONE OF THOSE "COOL" PARENTS WHO'S
ALL "IN TOUCH" WITH HIS KIDS AND EVERYTHING, WHICH CAN
BE TOTALLY ANNOYING AT TIMES. IT'S A SURE BET THAT
DONOVAN WON'T TALK ABOUT ANYTHING SHE'S INTERESTED
IN IF DAD ASKS HER ABOUT IT.

HEY, WHAT'S
THIS CD YOU'RE
LISTENING TO?

I DON'T
KNOW.

OKAY,
WELL...

GOOD NIGHT,
DONNA.

'NIGHT.

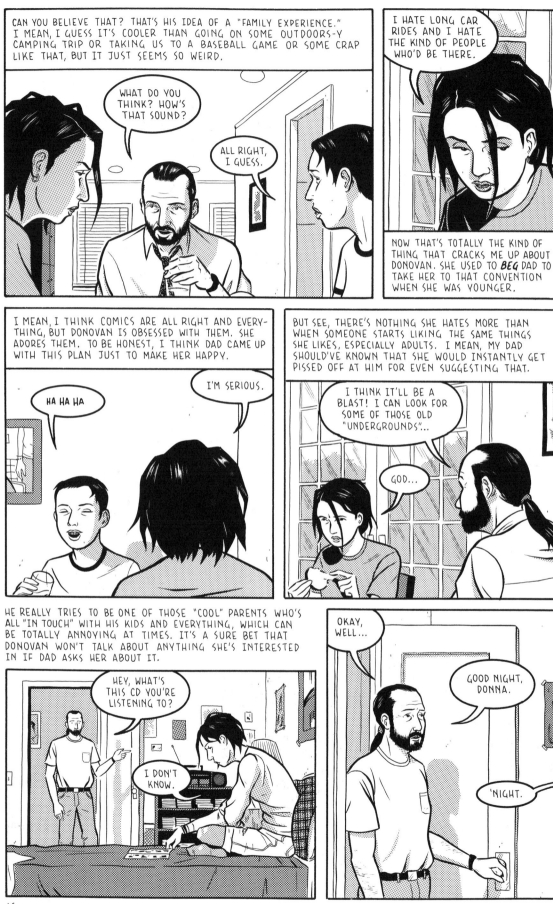

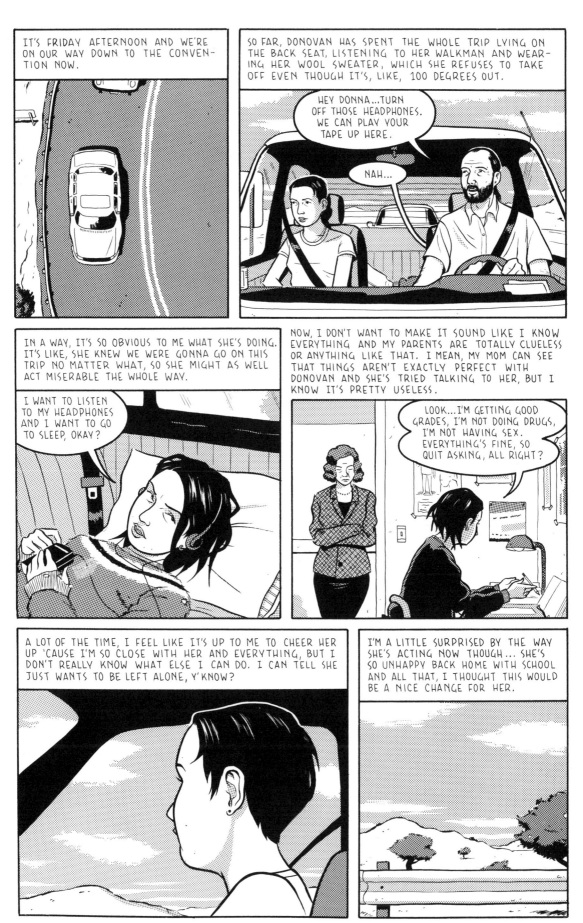

IT'S FRIDAY AFTERNOON AND WE'RE ON OUR WAY DOWN TO THE CONVENTION NOW.

SO FAR, DONOVAN HAS SPENT THE WHOLE TRIP LYING ON THE BACK SEAT, LISTENING TO HER WALKMAN AND WEARING HER WOOL SWEATER, WHICH SHE REFUSES TO TAKE OFF EVEN THOUGH IT'S, LIKE, 100 DEGREES OUT.

HEY DONNA...TURN OFF THOSE HEADPHONES. WE CAN PLAY YOUR TAPE UP HERE.

NAH...

IN A WAY, IT'S SO OBVIOUS TO ME WHAT SHE'S DOING. IT'S LIKE, SHE KNEW WE WERE GONNA GO ON THIS TRIP NO MATTER WHAT, SO SHE MIGHT AS WELL ACT MISERABLE THE WHOLE WAY.

I WANT TO LISTEN TO MY HEADPHONES AND I WANT TO GO TO SLEEP, OKAY?

NOW, I DON'T WANT TO MAKE IT SOUND LIKE I KNOW EVERYTHING AND MY PARENTS ARE TOTALLY CLUELESS OR ANYTHING LIKE THAT. I MEAN, MY MOM CAN SEE THAT THINGS AREN'T EXACTLY PERFECT WITH DONOVAN AND SHE'S TRIED TALKING TO HER, BUT I KNOW IT'S PRETTY USELESS.

LOOK...I'M GETTING GOOD GRADES, I'M NOT DOING DRUGS, I'M NOT HAVING SEX. EVERYTHING'S FINE, SO QUIT ASKING, ALL RIGHT?

A LOT OF THE TIME, I FEEL LIKE IT'S UP TO ME TO CHEER HER UP 'CAUSE I'M SO CLOSE WITH HER AND EVERYTHING, BUT I DON'T REALLY KNOW WHAT ELSE I CAN DO. I CAN TELL SHE JUST WANTS TO BE LEFT ALONE, Y'KNOW?

I'M A LITTLE SURPRISED BY THE WAY SHE'S ACTING NOW THOUGH... SHE'S SO UNHAPPY BACK HOME WITH SCHOOL AND ALL THAT, I THOUGHT THIS WOULD BE A NICE CHANGE FOR HER.

ACTUALLY, WE BOTH PRETTY MUCH DETEST SCHOOL. NOT SO MUCH THE STUDYING AND STUFF, BUT ALL THE CRAP THAT GOES WITH IT. THE SOCIAL STUFF. I GUESS I GET BY ALL RIGHT, BUT THE OTHER KIDS REALLY GIVE DONOVAN A HARD TIME.

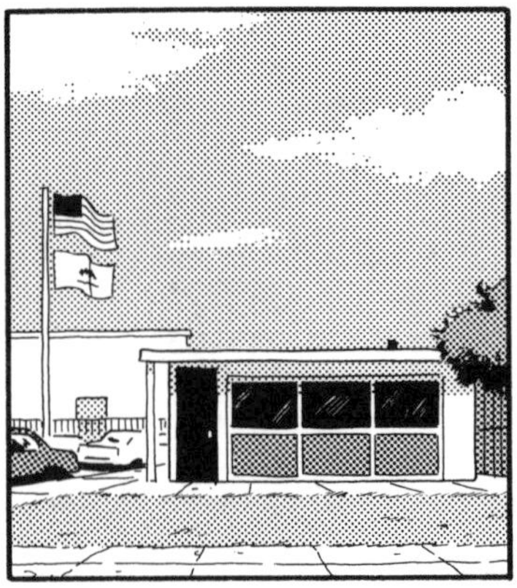

I MEAN, I THINK OF HER AS A PRETTY NORMAL PERSON, BUT I HAVE TO ADMIT SHE DOES SEEM KIND OF WEIRD IN CLASS. SHE USUALLY WON'T SAY ANYTHING, BUT WHEN SHE DOES START TALKING, IT'S PRETTY HARD TO SHUT HER UP. PLUS, SHE TALKS SUPER FAST AND SHE ACTS LIKE SHE'S SMARTER THAN EVERYONE ELSE. IT'S ALMOST LIKE SHE'S ***TRYING*** TO PISS PEOPLE OFF.

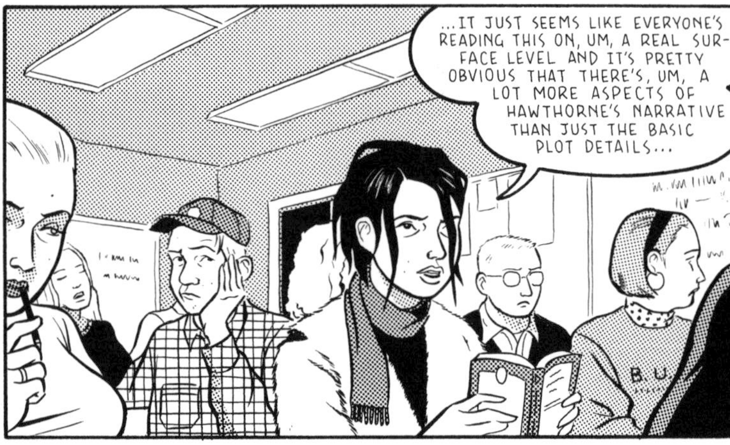
...IT JUST SEEMS LIKE EVERYONE'S READING THIS ON, UM, A REAL SURFACE LEVEL AND IT'S PRETTY OBVIOUS THAT THERE'S, UM, A LOT MORE ASPECTS OF HAWTHORNE'S NARRATIVE THAN JUST THE BASIC PLOT DETAILS...

YOU PROBABLY WON'T BELIEVE THIS, BUT FRESHMAN YEAR, DONOVAN WAS WALKING ACROSS THE CAMPUS AND SOME JOCK THREW A FIG NEWTON AT HER. HE WAS ON THE OPPOSITE SIDE OF THE QUAD AND STILL MANAGED TO HIT HER RIGHT IN THE FACE.

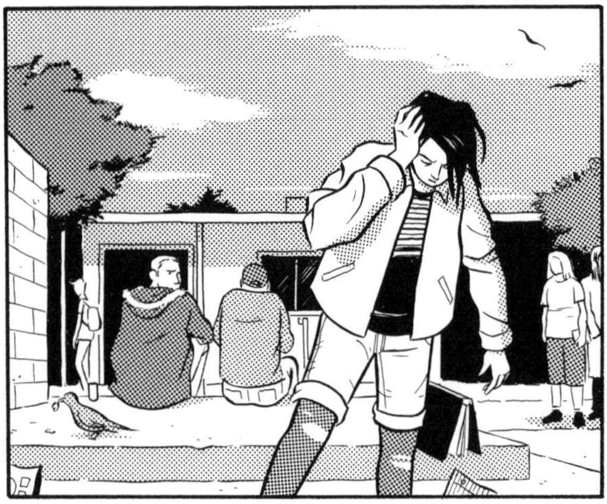

PEOPLE THOUGHT IT WAS SO FUNNY AND THEY COULDN'T BELIEVE, LIKE, WHAT AMAZING AIM THE GUY HAD. DONOVAN TOLD ME IT ACTUALLY HURT PRETTY BAD, AND THAT NIGHT, I IMAGINED MYSELF BEATING THE SHIT OUT OF THAT GUY OVER AND OVER AGAIN.

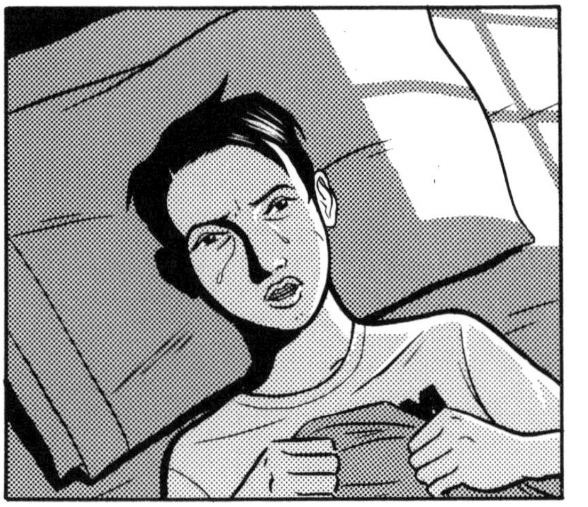

I'M SURE IF I DIDN'T SIT WITH HER EVERY DAY, DONOVAN WOULD JUST EAT LUNCH ALONE. I GUESS IT MIGHT FORCE HER TO MEET OTHER PEOPLE, BUT SHE'D OBVIOUSLY HATE ME FOR LIFE. EVEN WHEN WE DON'T REALLY TALK, I CAN TELL SHE'S GLAD I'M THERE.

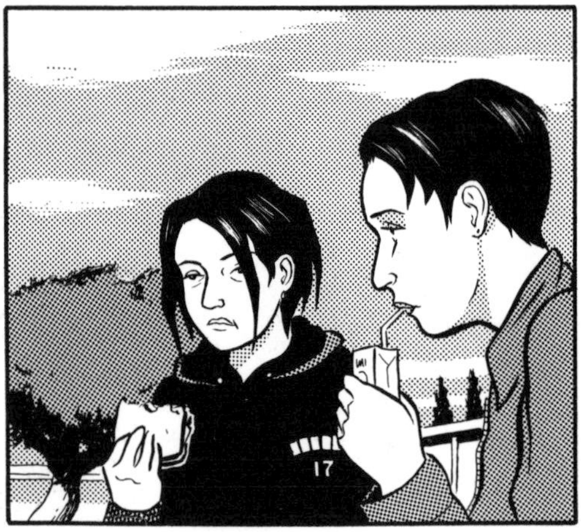

WHEN I WAS YOUNGER, I TRIED TO EXPLAIN TO MY MOM WHY ME AND DONOVAN ALWAYS EAT LUNCH BY OURSELVES. I TOLD HER WE SIT ALONE BECAUSE ALL THE OTHER KIDS HATE US, AND SHE TRIED TO CONVINCE ME THAT I HAD IT ALL WRONG.

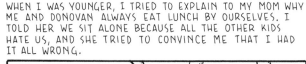

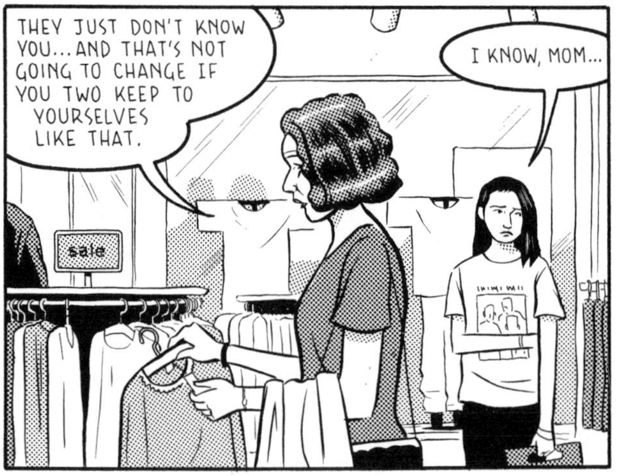
THEY JUST DON'T KNOW YOU...AND THAT'S NOT GOING TO CHANGE IF YOU TWO KEEP TO YOURSELVES LIKE THAT.
I KNOW, MOM...
sale

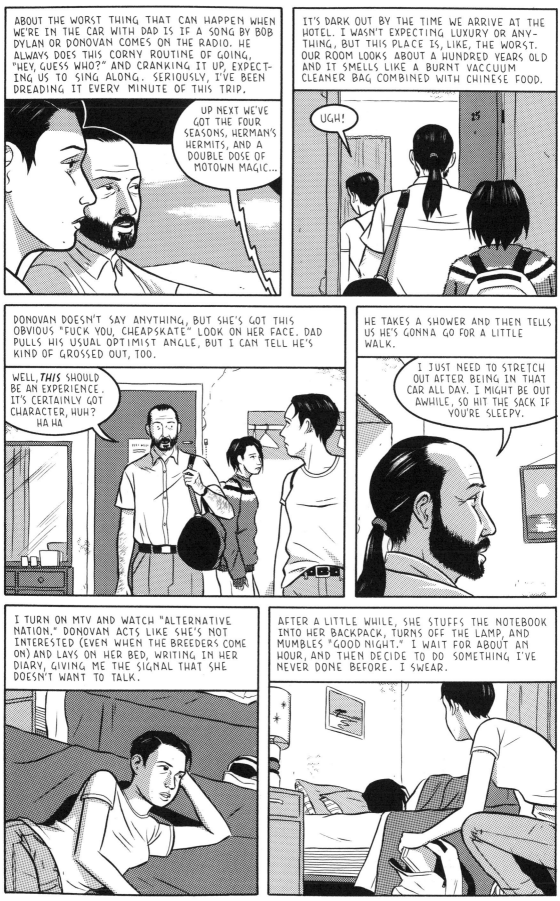

ABOUT THE WORST THING THAT CAN HAPPEN WHEN WE'RE IN THE CAR WITH DAD IS IF A SONG BY BOB DYLAN OR DONOVAN COMES ON THE RADIO. HE ALWAYS DOES THIS CORNY ROUTINE OF GOING, "HEY, GUESS WHO?" AND CRANKING IT UP, EXPECTING US TO SING ALONG. SERIOUSLY, I'VE BEEN DREADING IT EVERY MINUTE OF THIS TRIP.

UP NEXT WE'VE GOT THE FOUR SEASONS, HERMAN'S HERMITS, AND A DOUBLE DOSE OF MOTOWN MAGIC...

IT'S DARK OUT BY THE TIME WE ARRIVE AT THE HOTEL. I WASN'T EXPECTING LUXURY OR ANYTHING, BUT THIS PLACE IS, LIKE, THE WORST. OUR ROOM LOOKS ABOUT A HUNDRED YEARS OLD AND IT SMELLS LIKE A BURNT VACCUUM CLEANER BAG COMBINED WITH CHINESE FOOD.

UGH!

DONOVAN DOESN'T SAY ANYTHING, BUT SHE'S GOT THIS OBVIOUS "FUCK YOU, CHEAPSKATE" LOOK ON HER FACE. DAD PULLS HIS USUAL OPTIMIST ANGLE, BUT I CAN TELL HE'S KIND OF GROSSED OUT, TOO.

WELL, *THIS* SHOULD BE AN EXPERIENCE. IT'S CERTAINLY GOT CHARACTER, HUH? HA HA

HE TAKES A SHOWER AND THEN TELLS US HE'S GONNA GO FOR A LITTLE WALK.

I JUST NEED TO STRETCH OUT AFTER BEING IN THAT CAR ALL DAY. I MIGHT BE OUT AWHILE, SO HIT THE SACK IF YOU'RE SLEEPY.

I TURN ON MTV AND WATCH "ALTERNATIVE NATION." DONOVAN ACTS LIKE SHE'S NOT INTERESTED (EVEN WHEN THE BREEDERS COME ON) AND LAYS ON HER BED, WRITING IN HER DIARY, GIVING ME THE SIGNAL THAT SHE DOESN'T WANT TO TALK.

AFTER A LITTLE WHILE, SHE STUFFS THE NOTEBOOK INTO HER BACKPACK, TURNS OFF THE LAMP, AND MUMBLES "GOOD NIGHT." I WAIT FOR ABOUT AN HOUR, AND THEN DECIDE TO DO SOMETHING I'VE NEVER DONE BEFORE. I SWEAR.

YEAH, I GUESS IT'S PRETTY LAME AND SNOOP-Y OF ME, BUT I DO IT ONLY BECAUSE I'M CONCERNED. I FLIP THROUGH THE PAGES RANDOMLY, STARTING WITH THE MOST RECENT ENTRY AND SKIMMING BACKWARDS:

8/4 - LYING ON A BED IN A SCUMMY OLD HOTEL. DAD'S OUT WALKING AROUND, DYLAN'S WATCHING SOME CRAP ON TV. CONVENTION TOMORROW - SHOULD BE INTERESTING. THERE'S A COUPLE ARTISTS I *HAVE* TO MEET. IT'LL BE WEIRD TALKING TO THESE PEOPLE AFTER READING THEIR STUFF SO MUCH. DON'T FEEL LIKE WATCHING TV... GUESS I'LL CRASH OUT.

5/2 - WOKE UP AT 6:30, HIT SNOOZE TWICE. DYLAN WAS IN THE SHOWER, SO I HAD BREAKFAST: HONEY BUNCHES OF OATS, LOWFAT MILK, CONSTANT COMMENT TEA. AS I WAS EATING, REMEMBERED READING ABOUT SOME REGULATIONS THAT ALLOWED A CERTAIN AMOUNT OF RAT FECES IN EACH BOX OF CEREAL. ATE TWO MORE BOWLS.

4/29 (CONT'D) - I GUESS I USED TO WANT PEOPLE AT SCHOOL TO "ACCEPT" ME OR WHATEVER, BUT NOW, *FUCK IT.* MY NEW PLAN IS TO JUST IGNORE ALL OF THEM... I HATE THEIR OBNOXIOUSNESS AND STUPIDITY JUST AS MUCH AS THEY HATE MY SHYNESS AND INTELLIGENCE.

I KEEP TELLING MYSELF, NOT MUCH LONGER TO GO, ANYWAY. COLLEGE *WILL* BE DIFFERENT. CAN'T WAIT TO BE ON MY OWN, AROUND PEOPLE THAT KNOW MORE THAN ME FOR A CHANGE. COUNTING THE DAYS...

4/17 - DYLAN TRIED TO GET ME TO EAT LUNCH WITH SOME OTHER KIDS TODAY. I REFUSED, SO WE SAT IN OUR USUAL SPOT AND SHE WAS SILENT THE WHOLE TIME. *FUCK THAT* - I TOLD HER SHE CAN DO WHATEVER SHE WANTS, BUT SHE WON'T.

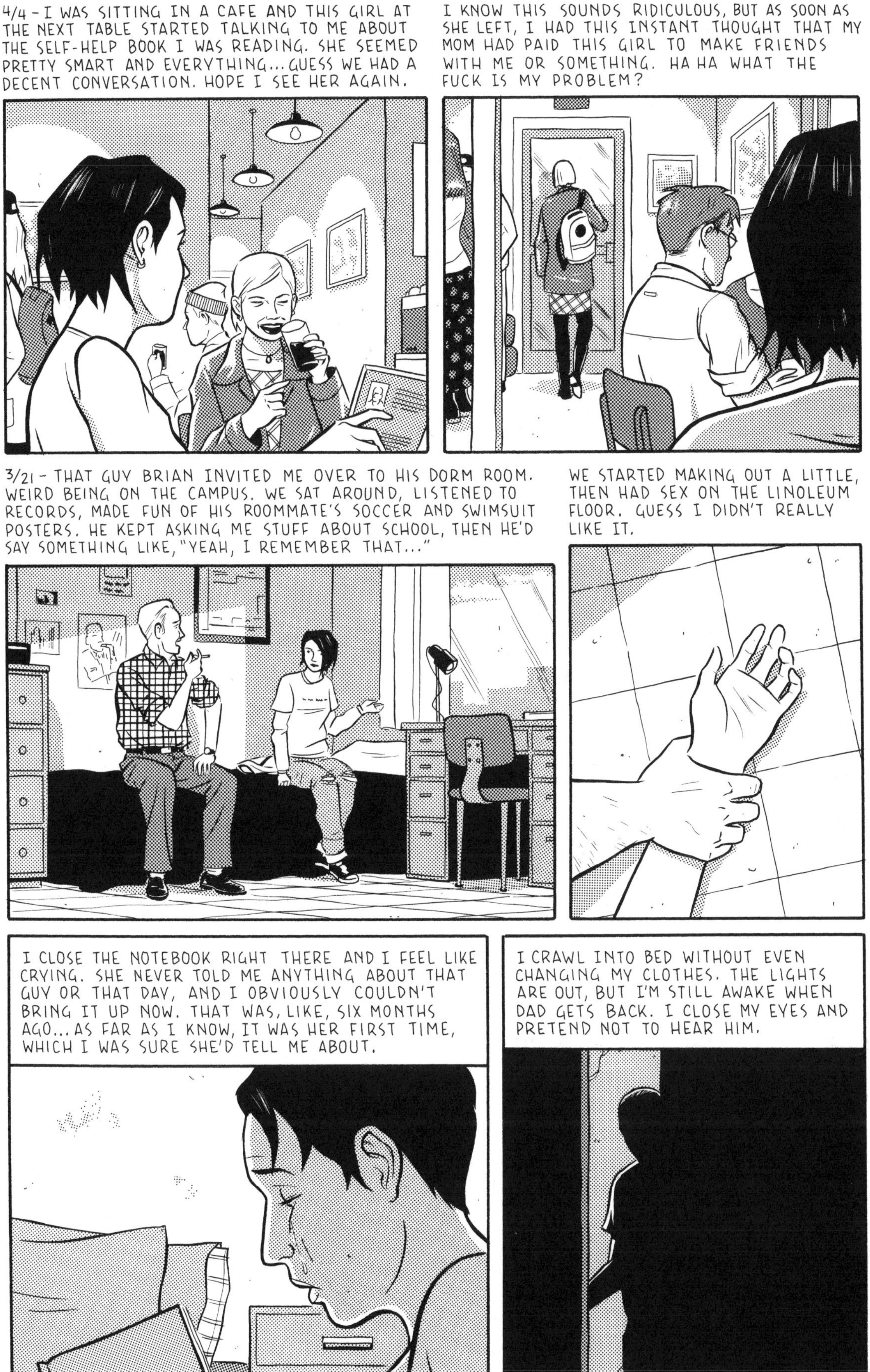
4/4 - I WAS SITTING IN A CAFE AND THIS GIRL AT THE NEXT TABLE STARTED TALKING TO ME ABOUT THE SELF-HELP BOOK I WAS READING. SHE SEEMED PRETTY SMART AND EVERYTHING... GUESS WE HAD A DECENT CONVERSATION. HOPE I SEE HER AGAIN.
I KNOW THIS SOUNDS RIDICULOUS, BUT AS SOON AS SHE LEFT, I HAD THIS INSTANT THOUGHT THAT MY MOM HAD PAID THIS GIRL TO MAKE FRIENDS WITH ME OR SOMETHING. HA HA WHAT THE FUCK IS MY PROBLEM?
3/21 - THAT GUY BRIAN INVITED ME OVER TO HIS DORM ROOM. WEIRD BEING ON THE CAMPUS. WE SAT AROUND, LISTENED TO RECORDS, MADE FUN OF HIS ROOMMATE'S SOCCER AND SWIMSUIT POSTERS. HE KEPT ASKING ME STUFF ABOUT SCHOOL, THEN HE'D SAY SOMETHING LIKE, "YEAH, I REMEMBER THAT..."
WE STARTED MAKING OUT A LITTLE, THEN HAD SEX ON THE LINOLEUM FLOOR. GUESS I DIDN'T REALLY LIKE IT.
I CLOSE THE NOTEBOOK RIGHT THERE AND I FEEL LIKE CRYING. SHE NEVER TOLD ME ANYTHING ABOUT THAT GUY OR THAT DAY, AND I OBVIOUSLY COULDN'T BRING IT UP NOW. THAT WAS, LIKE, SIX MONTHS AGO... AS FAR AS I KNOW, IT WAS HER FIRST TIME, WHICH I WAS SURE SHE'D TELL ME ABOUT.
I CRAWL INTO BED WITHOUT EVEN CHANGING MY CLOTHES. THE LIGHTS ARE OUT, BUT I'M STILL AWAKE WHEN DAD GETS BACK. I CLOSE MY EYES AND PRETEND NOT TO HEAR HIM.

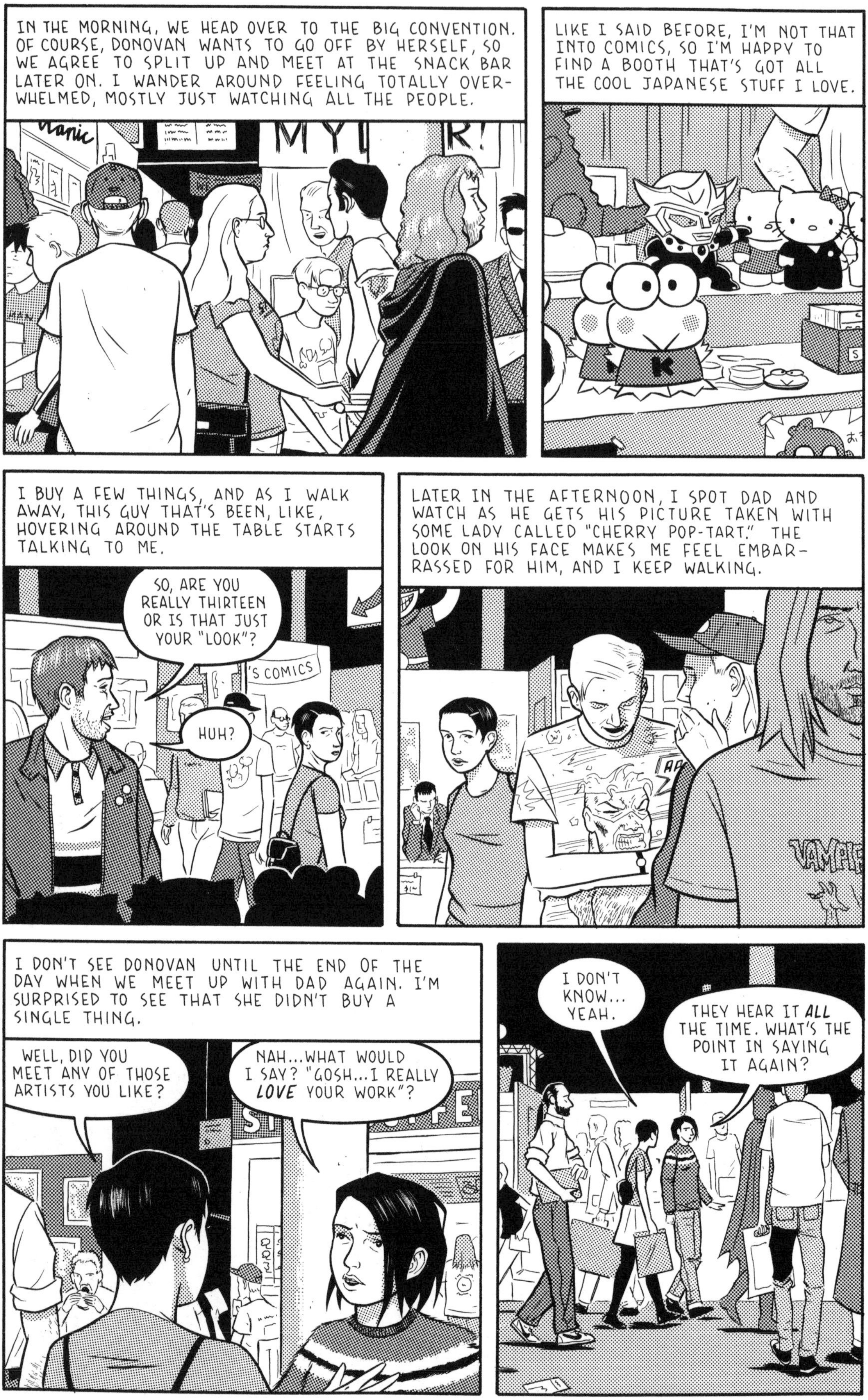
IN THE MORNING, WE HEAD OVER TO THE BIG CONVENTION. OF COURSE, DONOVAN WANTS TO GO OFF BY HERSELF, SO WE AGREE TO SPLIT UP AND MEET AT THE SNACK BAR LATER ON. I WANDER AROUND FEELING TOTALLY OVERWHELMED, MOSTLY JUST WATCHING ALL THE PEOPLE.
LIKE I SAID BEFORE, I'M NOT THAT INTO COMICS, SO I'M HAPPY TO FIND A BOOTH THAT'S GOT ALL THE COOL JAPANESE STUFF I LOVE.
I BUY A FEW THINGS, AND AS I WALK AWAY, THIS GUY THAT'S BEEN, LIKE, HOVERING AROUND THE TABLE STARTS TALKING TO ME.
SO, ARE YOU REALLY THIRTEEN OR IS THAT JUST YOUR "LOOK"?
'S COMICS
HUH?
LATER IN THE AFTERNOON, I SPOT DAD AND WATCH AS HE GETS HIS PICTURE TAKEN WITH SOME LADY CALLED "CHERRY POP-TART." THE LOOK ON HIS FACE MAKES ME FEEL EMBARRASSED FOR HIM, AND I KEEP WALKING.
I DON'T SEE DONOVAN UNTIL THE END OF THE DAY WHEN WE MEET UP WITH DAD AGAIN. I'M SURPRISED TO SEE THAT SHE DIDN'T BUY A SINGLE THING.
WELL, DID YOU MEET ANY OF THOSE ARTISTS YOU LIKE?
NAH...WHAT WOULD I SAY? "GOSH...I REALLY *LOVE* YOUR WORK"?
I DON'T KNOW... YEAH.
THEY HEAR IT *ALL* THE TIME. WHAT'S THE POINT IN SAYING IT AGAIN?

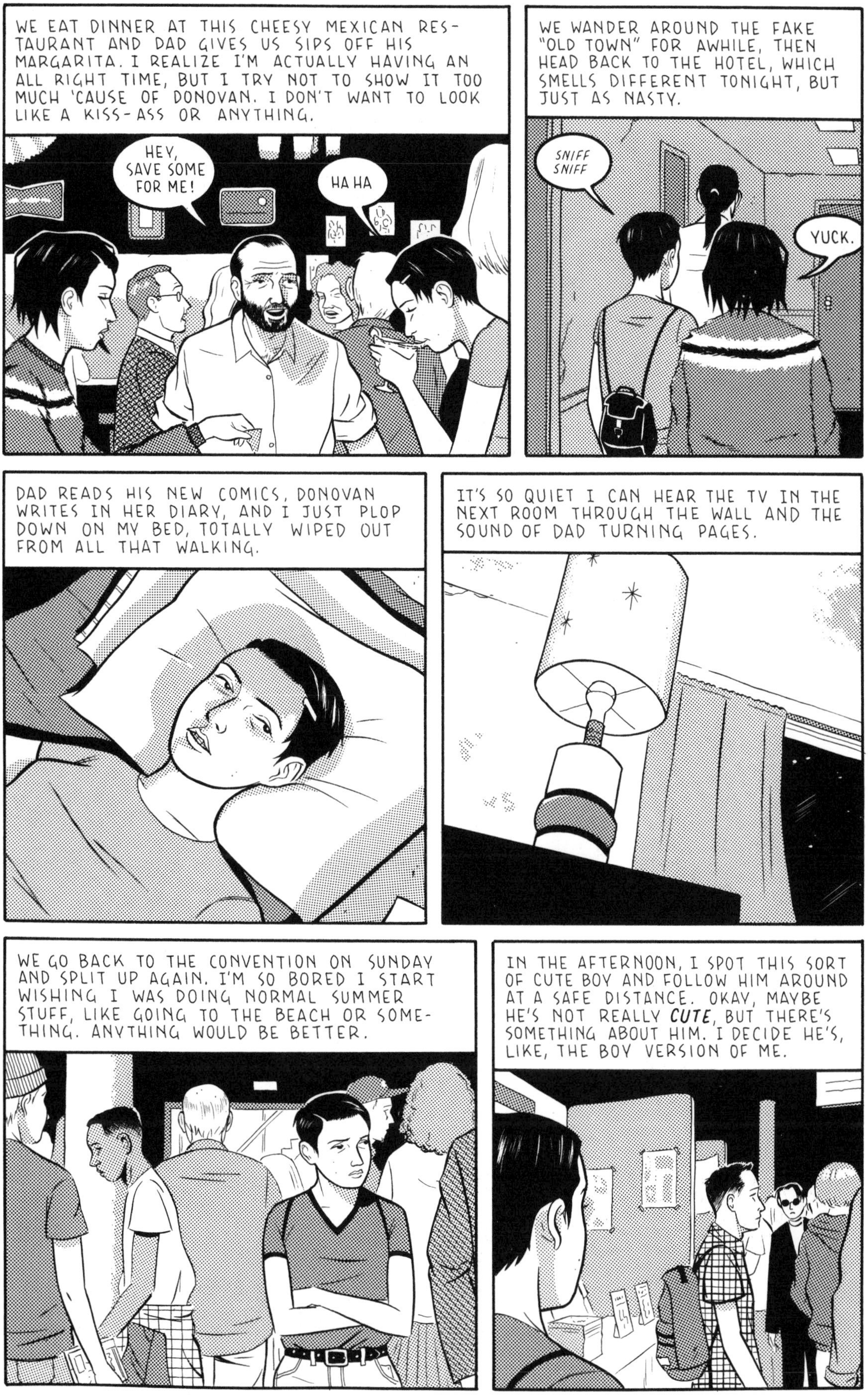
WE EAT DINNER AT THIS CHEESY MEXICAN RESTAURANT AND DAD GIVES US SIPS OFF HIS MARGARITA. I REALIZE I'M ACTUALLY HAVING AN ALL RIGHT TIME, BUT I TRY NOT TO SHOW IT TOO MUCH 'CAUSE OF DONOVAN. I DON'T WANT TO LOOK LIKE A KISS-ASS OR ANYTHING.
HEY, SAVE SOME FOR ME!
HA HA
WE WANDER AROUND THE FAKE "OLD TOWN" FOR AWHILE, THEN HEAD BACK TO THE HOTEL, WHICH SMELLS DIFFERENT TONIGHT, BUT JUST AS NASTY.
SNIFF SNIFF
YUCK.
DAD READS HIS NEW COMICS, DONOVAN WRITES IN HER DIARY, AND I JUST PLOP DOWN ON MY BED, TOTALLY WIPED OUT FROM ALL THAT WALKING.
IT'S SO QUIET I CAN HEAR THE TV IN THE NEXT ROOM THROUGH THE WALL AND THE SOUND OF DAD TURNING PAGES.
WE GO BACK TO THE CONVENTION ON SUNDAY AND SPLIT UP AGAIN. I'M SO BORED I START WISHING I WAS DOING NORMAL SUMMER STUFF, LIKE GOING TO THE BEACH OR SOMETHING. ANYTHING WOULD BE BETTER.
IN THE AFTERNOON, I SPOT THIS SORT OF CUTE BOY AND FOLLOW HIM AROUND AT A SAFE DISTANCE. OKAY, MAYBE HE'S NOT REALLY CUTE, BUT THERE'S SOMETHING ABOUT HIM. I DECIDE HE'S, LIKE, THE BOY VERSION OF ME.

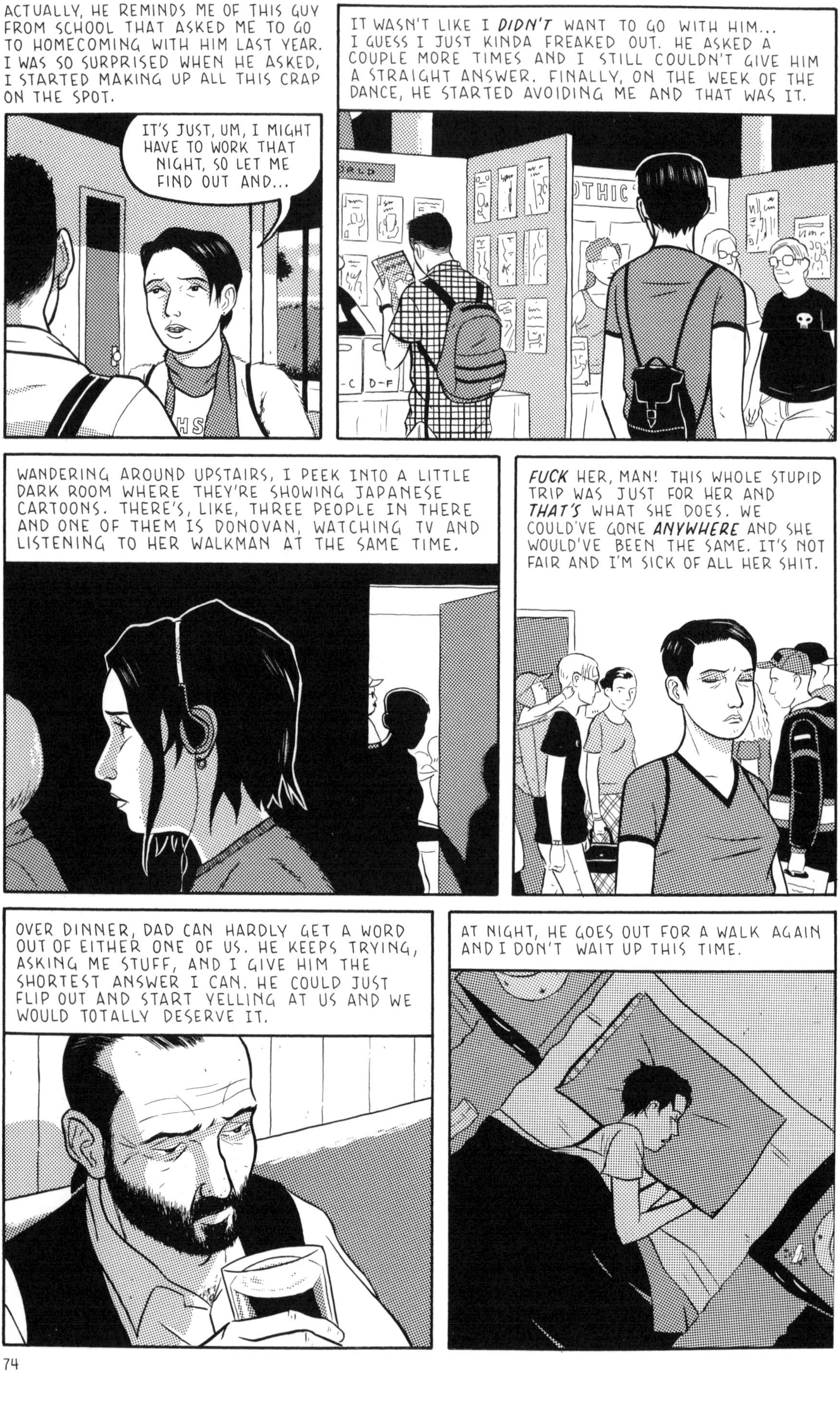
ACTUALLY, HE REMINDS ME OF THIS GUY FROM SCHOOL THAT ASKED ME TO GO TO HOMECOMING WITH HIM LAST YEAR. I WAS SO SURPRISED WHEN HE ASKED, I STARTED MAKING UP ALL THIS CRAP ON THE SPOT.
IT'S JUST, UM, I MIGHT HAVE TO WORK THAT NIGHT, SO LET ME FIND OUT AND...
IT WASN'T LIKE I *DIDN'T* WANT TO GO WITH HIM... I GUESS I JUST KINDA FREAKED OUT. HE ASKED A COUPLE MORE TIMES AND I STILL COULDN'T GIVE HIM A STRAIGHT ANSWER. FINALLY, ON THE WEEK OF THE DANCE, HE STARTED AVOIDING ME AND THAT WAS IT.
WANDERING AROUND UPSTAIRS, I PEEK INTO A LITTLE DARK ROOM WHERE THEY'RE SHOWING JAPANESE CARTOONS. THERE'S, LIKE, THREE PEOPLE IN THERE AND ONE OF THEM IS DONOVAN, WATCHING TV AND LISTENING TO HER WALKMAN AT THE SAME TIME.
FUCK HER, MAN! THIS WHOLE STUPID TRIP WAS JUST FOR HER AND ***THAT'S*** WHAT SHE DOES. WE COULD'VE GONE ***ANYWHERE*** AND SHE WOULD'VE BEEN THE SAME. IT'S NOT FAIR AND I'M SICK OF ALL HER SHIT.
OVER DINNER, DAD CAN HARDLY GET A WORD OUT OF EITHER ONE OF US. HE KEEPS TRYING, ASKING ME STUFF, AND I GIVE HIM THE SHORTEST ANSWER I CAN. HE COULD JUST FLIP OUT AND START YELLING AT US AND WE WOULD TOTALLY DESERVE IT.
AT NIGHT, HE GOES OUT FOR A WALK AGAIN AND I DON'T WAIT UP THIS TIME.

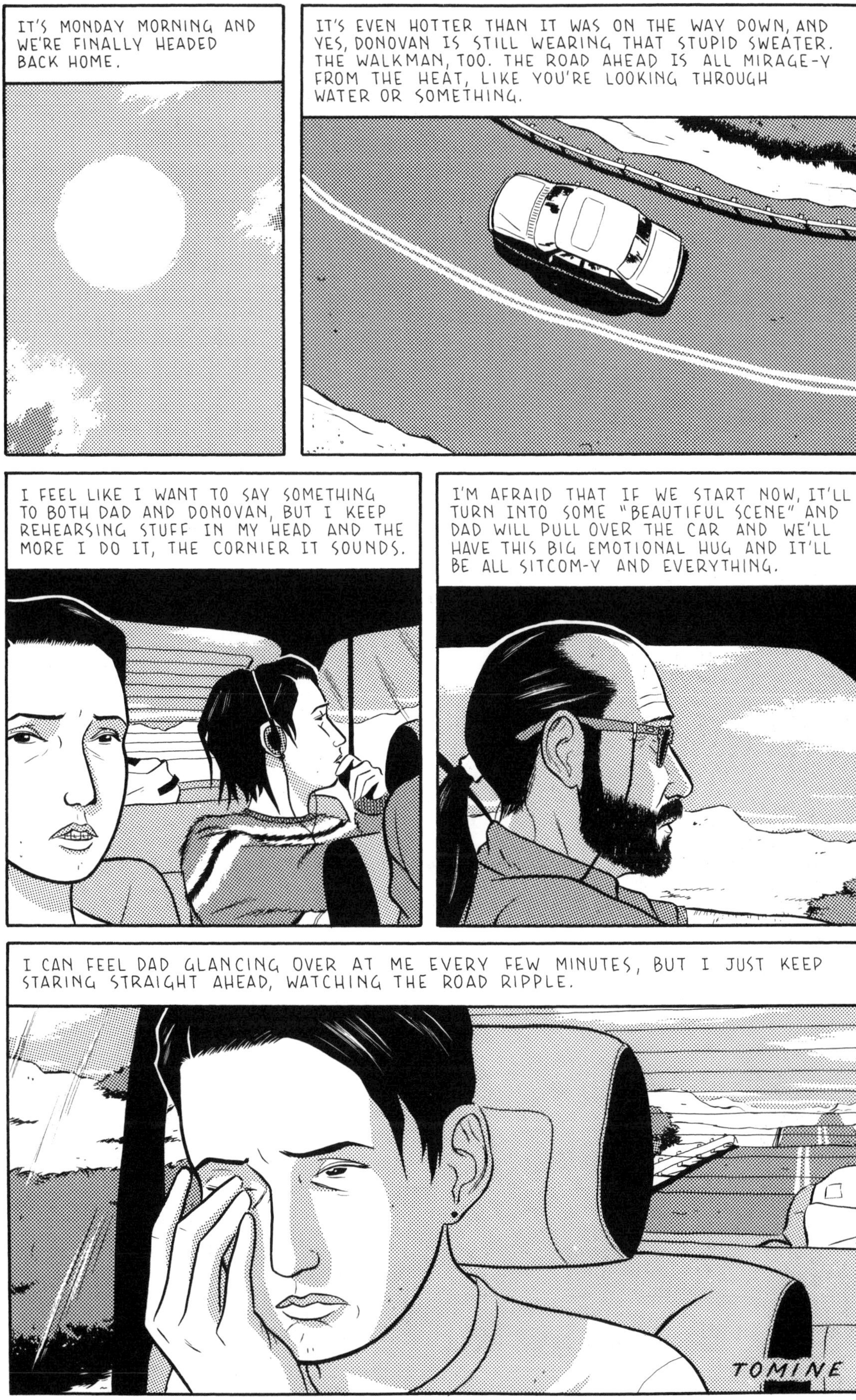
IT'S MONDAY MORNING AND WE'RE FINALLY HEADED BACK HOME.
IT'S EVEN HOTTER THAN IT WAS ON THE WAY DOWN, AND YES, DONOVAN IS STILL WEARING THAT STUPID SWEATER. THE WALKMAN, TOO. THE ROAD AHEAD IS ALL MIRAGE-Y FROM THE HEAT, LIKE YOU'RE LOOKING THROUGH WATER OR SOMETHING.
I FEEL LIKE I WANT TO SAY SOMETHING TO BOTH DAD AND DONOVAN, BUT I KEEP REHEARSING STUFF IN MY HEAD AND THE MORE I DO IT, THE CORNIER IT SOUNDS.
I'M AFRAID THAT IF WE START NOW, IT'LL TURN INTO SOME "BEAUTIFUL SCENE" AND DAD WILL PULL OVER THE CAR AND WE'LL HAVE THIS BIG EMOTIONAL HUG AND IT'LL BE ALL SITCOM-Y AND EVERYTHING.
I CAN FEEL DAD GLANCING OVER AT ME EVERY FEW MINUTES, BUT I JUST KEEP STARING STRAIGHT AHEAD, WATCHING THE ROAD RIPPLE.
TOMINE

Unfaded

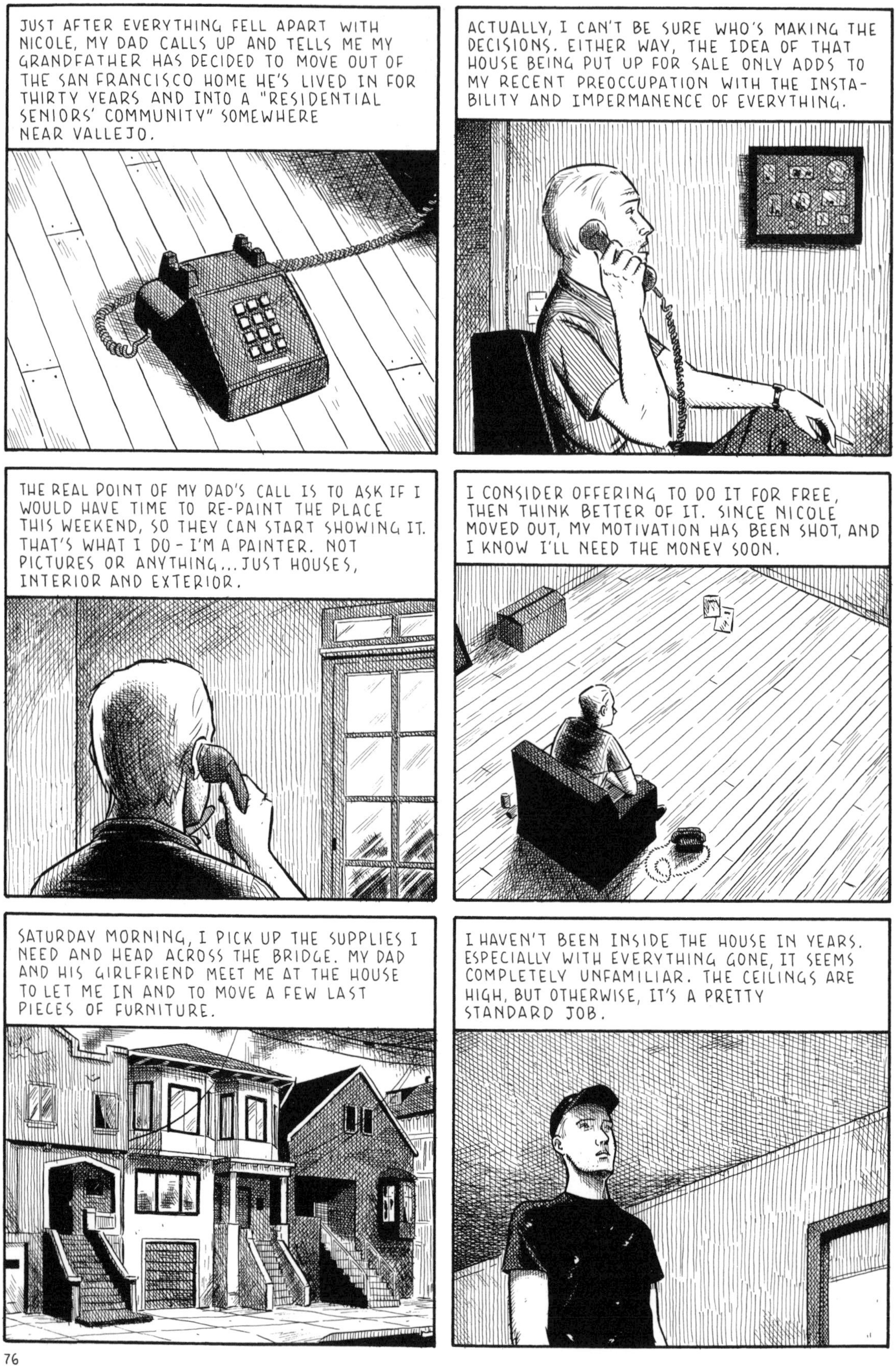
JUST AFTER EVERYTHING FELL APART WITH NICOLE, MY DAD CALLS UP AND TELLS ME MY GRANDFATHER HAS DECIDED TO MOVE OUT OF THE SAN FRANCISCO HOME HE'S LIVED IN FOR THIRTY YEARS AND INTO A "RESIDENTIAL SENIORS' COMMUNITY" SOMEWHERE NEAR VALLEJO.
ACTUALLY, I CAN'T BE SURE WHO'S MAKING THE DECISIONS. EITHER WAY, THE IDEA OF THAT HOUSE BEING PUT UP FOR SALE ONLY ADDS TO MY RECENT PREOCCUPATION WITH THE INSTA-BILITY AND IMPERMANENCE OF EVERYTHING.
THE REAL POINT OF MY DAD'S CALL IS TO ASK IF I WOULD HAVE TIME TO RE-PAINT THE PLACE THIS WEEKEND, SO THEY CAN START SHOWING IT. THAT'S WHAT I DO - I'M A PAINTER. NOT PICTURES OR ANYTHING... JUST HOUSES, INTERIOR AND EXTERIOR.
I CONSIDER OFFERING TO DO IT FOR FREE, THEN THINK BETTER OF IT. SINCE NICOLE MOVED OUT, MY MOTIVATION HAS BEEN SHOT, AND I KNOW I'LL NEED THE MONEY SOON.
SATURDAY MORNING, I PICK UP THE SUPPLIES I NEED AND HEAD ACROSS THE BRIDGE. MY DAD AND HIS GIRLFRIEND MEET ME AT THE HOUSE TO LET ME IN AND TO MOVE A FEW LAST PIECES OF FURNITURE.
I HAVEN'T BEEN INSIDE THE HOUSE IN YEARS. ESPECIALLY WITH EVERYTHING GONE, IT SEEMS COMPLETELY UNFAMILIAR. THE CEILINGS ARE HIGH, BUT OTHERWISE, IT'S A PRETTY STANDARD JOB.

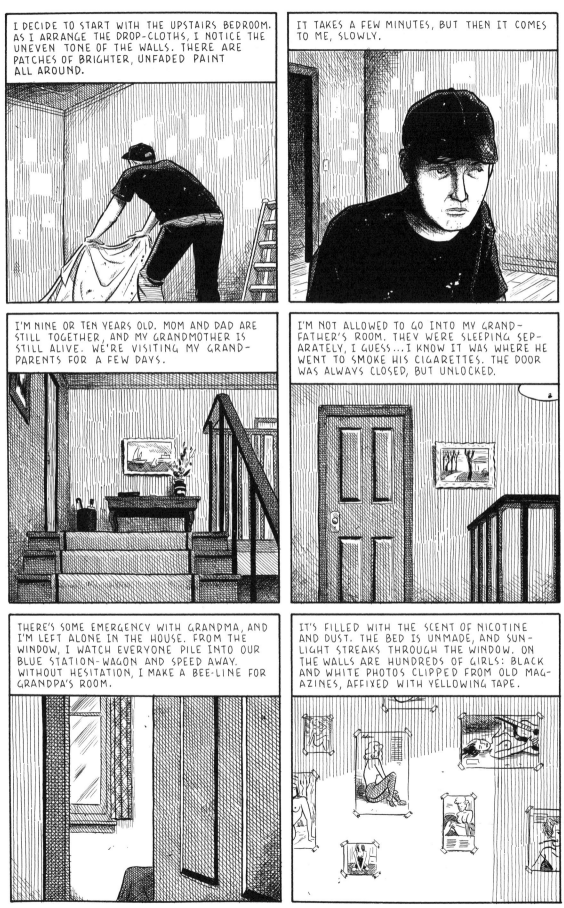

I DECIDE TO START WITH THE UPSTAIRS BEDROOM. AS I ARRANGE THE DROP-CLOTHS, I NOTICE THE UNEVEN TONE OF THE WALLS. THERE ARE PATCHES OF BRIGHTER, UNFADED PAINT ALL AROUND.

IT TAKES A FEW MINUTES, BUT THEN IT COMES TO ME, SLOWLY.

I'M NINE OR TEN YEARS OLD. MOM AND DAD ARE STILL TOGETHER, AND MY GRANDMOTHER IS STILL ALIVE. WE'RE VISITING MY GRAND-PARENTS FOR A FEW DAYS.

I'M NOT ALLOWED TO GO INTO MY GRAND-FATHER'S ROOM. THEY WERE SLEEPING SEP-ARATELY, I GUESS... I KNOW IT WAS WHERE HE WENT TO SMOKE HIS CIGARETTES. THE DOOR WAS ALWAYS CLOSED, BUT UNLOCKED.

THERE'S SOME EMERGENCY WITH GRANDMA, AND I'M LEFT ALONE IN THE HOUSE. FROM THE WINDOW, I WATCH EVERYONE PILE INTO OUR BLUE STATION-WAGON AND SPEED AWAY. WITHOUT HESITATION, I MAKE A BEE-LINE FOR GRANDPA'S ROOM.

IT'S FILLED WITH THE SCENT OF NICOTINE AND DUST. THE BED IS UNMADE, AND SUN-LIGHT STREAKS THROUGH THE WINDOW. ON THE WALLS ARE HUNDREDS OF GIRLS: BLACK AND WHITE PHOTOS CLIPPED FROM OLD MAG-AZINES, AFFIXED WITH YELLOWING TAPE.

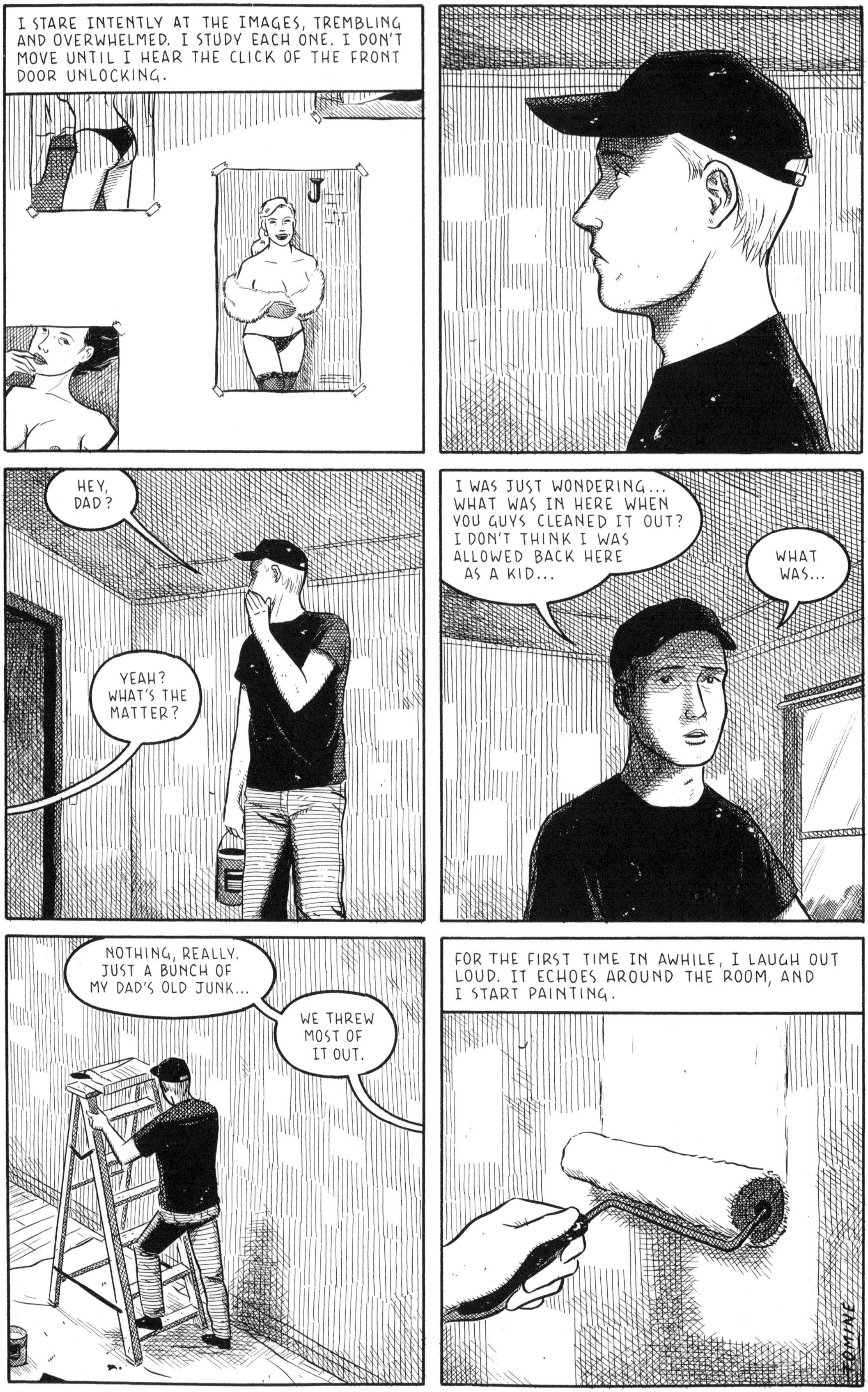
I STARE INTENTLY AT THE IMAGES, TREMBLING AND OVERWHELMED. I STUDY EACH ONE. I DON'T MOVE UNTIL I HEAR THE CLICK OF THE FRONT DOOR UNLOCKING.
HEY, DAD?
YEAH? WHAT'S THE MATTER?
I WAS JUST WONDERING... WHAT WAS IN HERE WHEN YOU GUYS CLEANED IT OUT? I DON'T THINK I WAS ALLOWED BACK HERE AS A KID...
WHAT WAS...
NOTHING, REALLY. JUST A BUNCH OF MY DAD'S OLD JUNK...
WE THREW MOST OF IT OUT.
FOR THE FIRST TIME IN AWHILE, I LAUGH OUT LOUD. IT ECHOES AROUND THE ROOM, AND I START PAINTING.
TOMINE

SIX DAY COLD

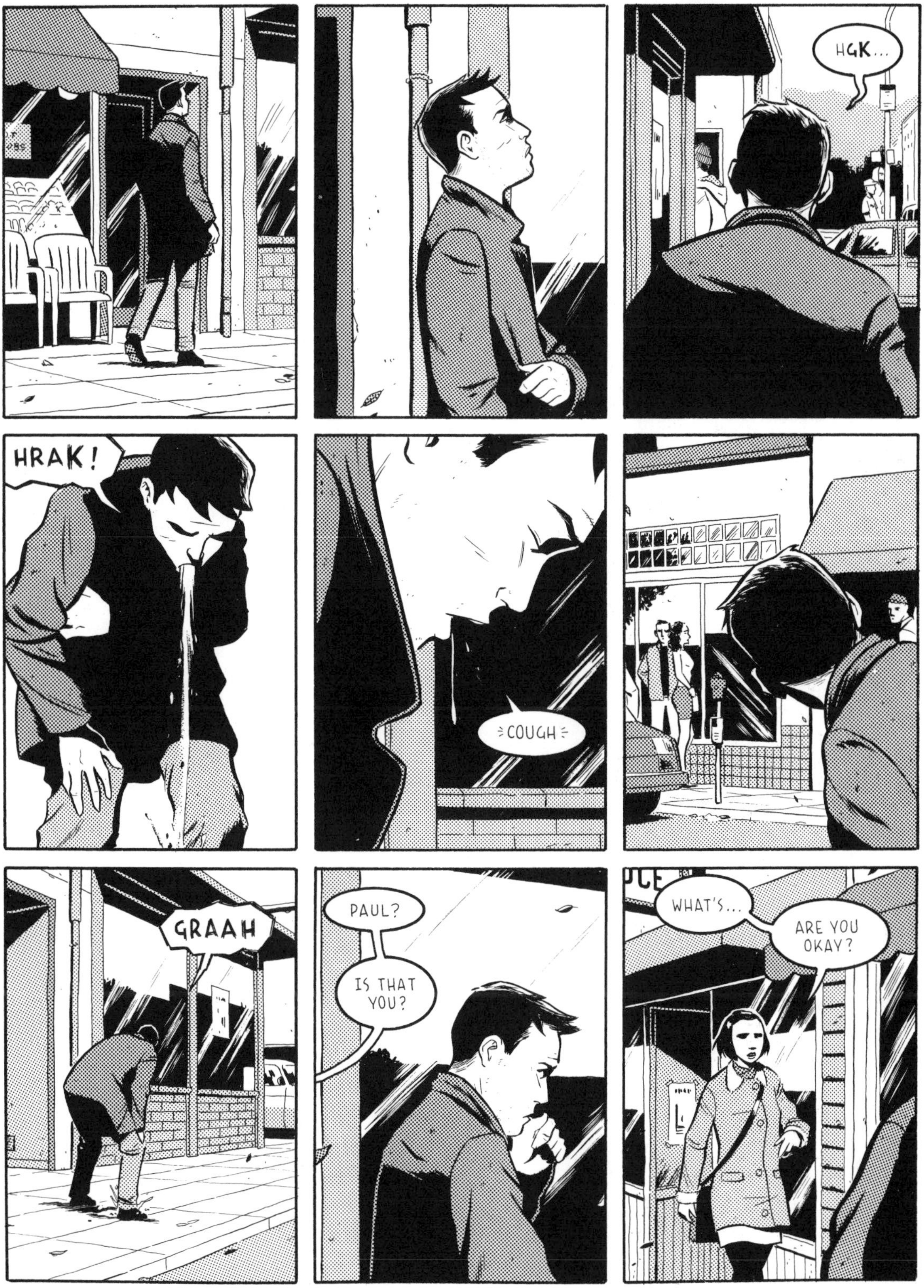
HGK...
HRAK!
COUGH
GRAAH
PAUL?
IS THAT YOU?
WHAT'S...
ARE YOU OKAY?

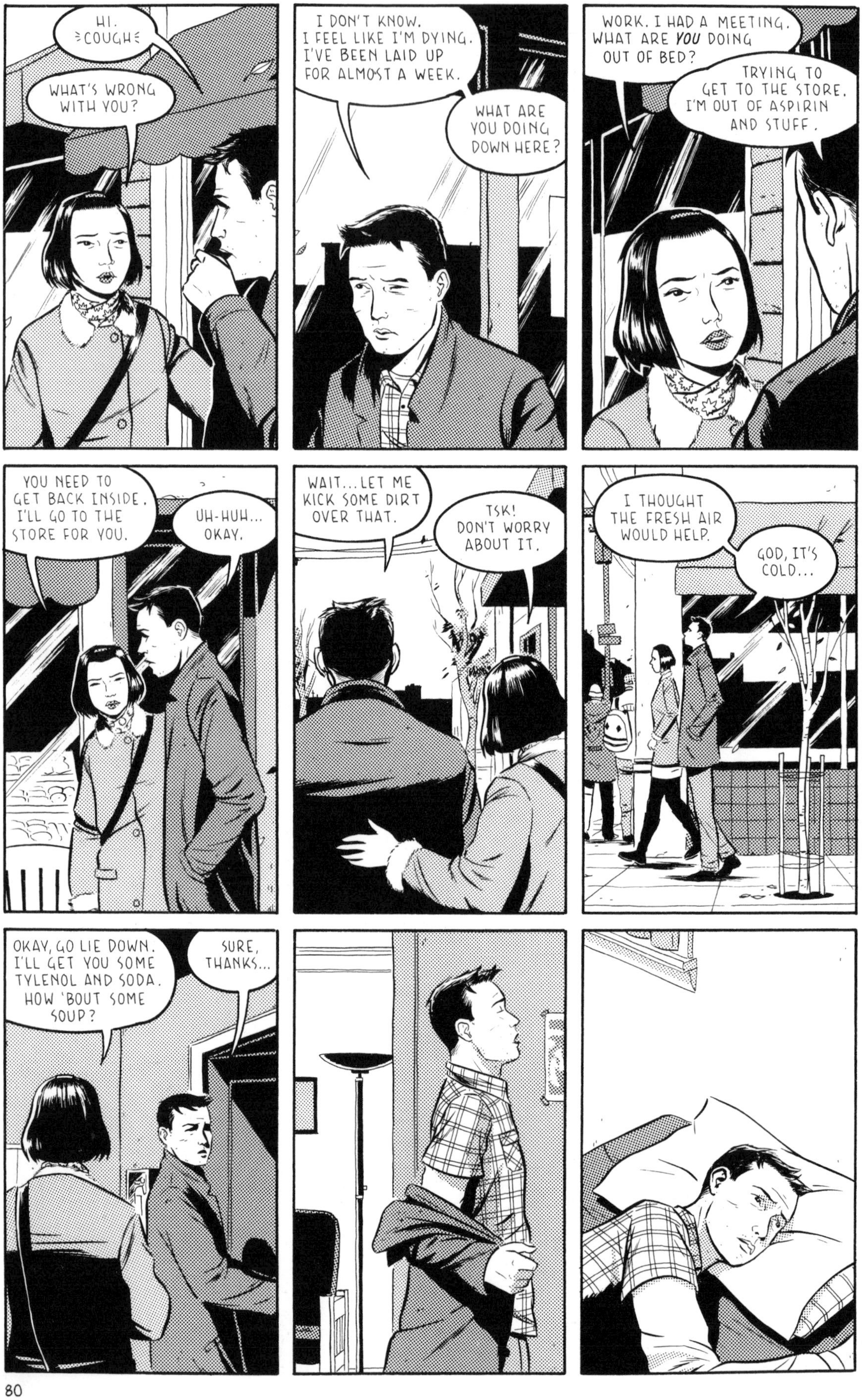
HI. ≷COUGH≶
WHAT'S WRONG WITH YOU?
I DON'T KNOW. I FEEL LIKE I'M DYING. I'VE BEEN LAID UP FOR ALMOST A WEEK.
WHAT ARE YOU DOING DOWN HERE?
WORK. I HAD A MEETING. WHAT ARE YOU DOING OUT OF BED?
TRYING TO GET TO THE STORE. I'M OUT OF ASPIRIN AND STUFF.
YOU NEED TO GET BACK INSIDE. I'LL GO TO THE STORE FOR YOU.
UH-HUH... OKAY.
WAIT... LET ME KICK SOME DIRT OVER THAT.
TSK! DON'T WORRY ABOUT IT.
I THOUGHT THE FRESH AIR WOULD HELP.
GOD, IT'S COLD...
OKAY, GO LIE DOWN. I'LL GET YOU SOME TYLENOL AND SODA. HOW 'BOUT SOME SOUP?
SURE, THANKS...

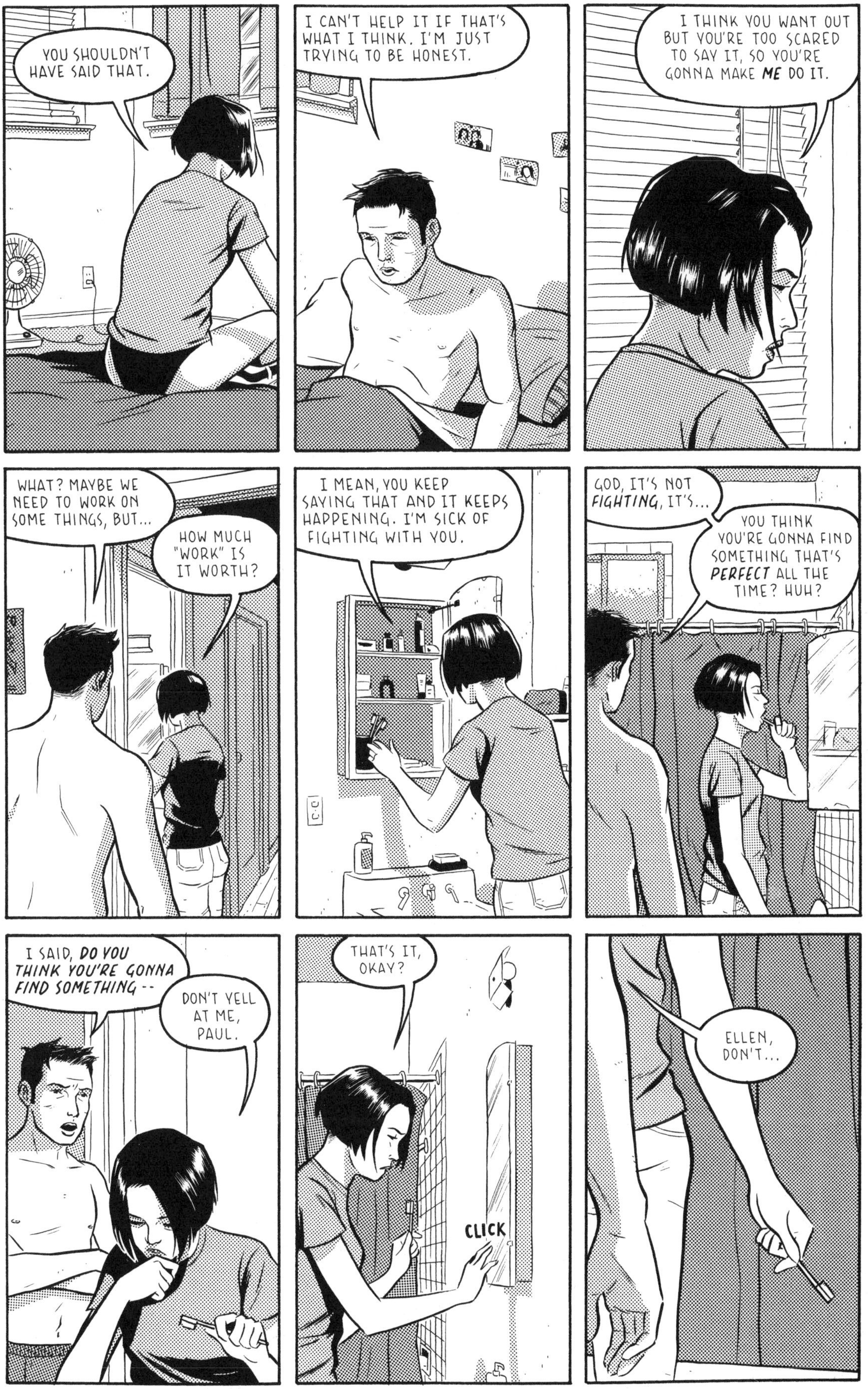
YOU SHOULDN'T HAVE SAID THAT.
I CAN'T HELP IT IF THAT'S WHAT I THINK. I'M JUST TRYING TO BE HONEST.
I THINK YOU WANT OUT BUT YOU'RE TOO SCARED TO SAY IT, SO YOU'RE GONNA MAKE **ME** DO IT.
WHAT? MAYBE WE NEED TO WORK ON SOME THINGS, BUT...
HOW MUCH "WORK" IS IT WORTH?
I MEAN, YOU KEEP SAYING THAT AND IT KEEPS HAPPENING. I'M SICK OF FIGHTING WITH YOU.
GOD, IT'S NOT *FIGHTING*, IT'S...
YOU THINK YOU'RE GONNA FIND SOMETHING THAT'S *PERFECT* ALL THE TIME? HUH?
I SAID, ***DO YOU THINK YOU'RE GONNA FIND SOMETHING*** --
DON'T YELL AT ME, PAUL.
THAT'S IT, OKAY?
CLICK
ELLEN, DON'T...

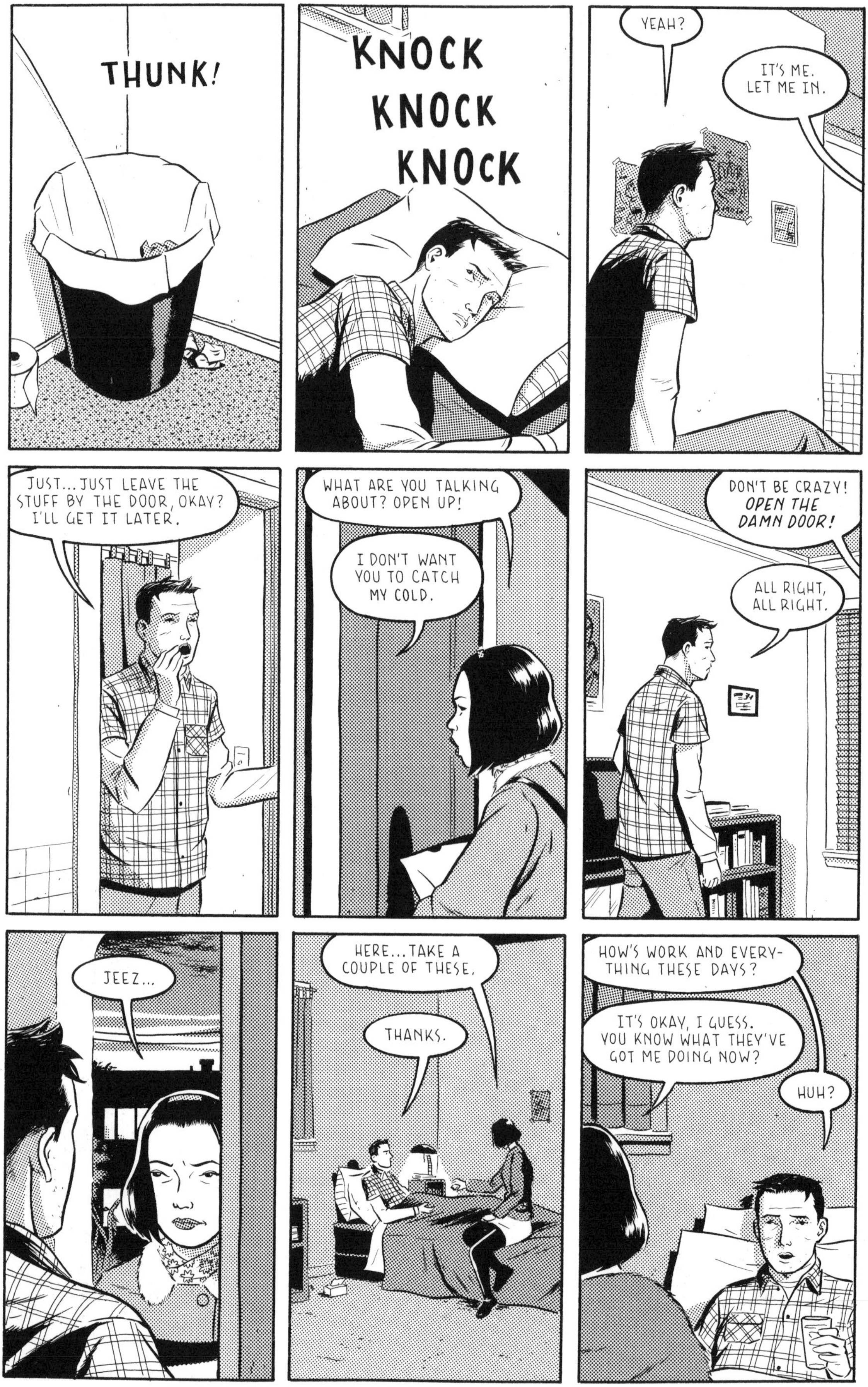
THUNK!
KNOCK KNOCK KNOCK
YEAH?
IT'S ME. LET ME IN.
JUST... JUST LEAVE THE STUFF BY THE DOOR, OKAY? I'LL GET IT LATER.
WHAT ARE YOU TALKING ABOUT? OPEN UP!
I DON'T WANT YOU TO CATCH MY COLD.
DON'T BE CRAZY! *OPEN THE DAMN DOOR!*
ALL RIGHT, ALL RIGHT.
JEEZ...
HERE... TAKE A COUPLE OF THESE.
THANKS.
HOW'S WORK AND EVERY-THING THESE DAYS?
IT'S OKAY, I GUESS. YOU KNOW WHAT THEY'VE GOT ME DOING NOW?
HUH?

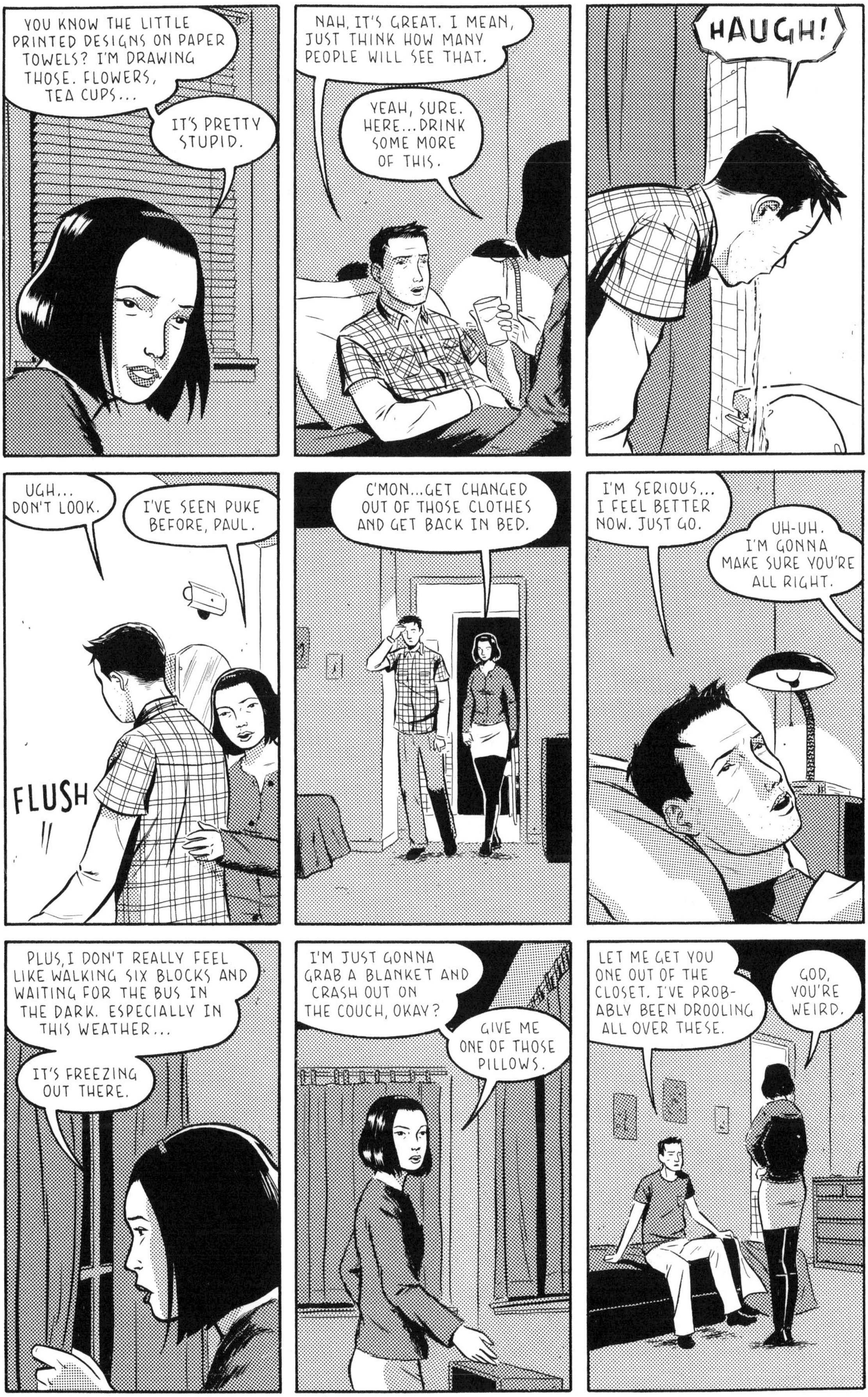
YOU KNOW THE LITTLE PRINTED DESIGNS ON PAPER TOWELS? I'M DRAWING THOSE. FLOWERS, TEA CUPS...
IT'S PRETTY STUPID.
NAH, IT'S GREAT. I MEAN, JUST THINK HOW MANY PEOPLE WILL SEE THAT.
YEAH, SURE. HERE...DRINK SOME MORE OF THIS.
HAUGH!
UGH... DON'T LOOK.
I'VE SEEN PUKE BEFORE, PAUL.
FLUSH
C'MON...GET CHANGED OUT OF THOSE CLOTHES AND GET BACK IN BED.
I'M SERIOUS... I FEEL BETTER NOW. JUST GO.
UH-UH. I'M GONNA MAKE SURE YOU'RE ALL RIGHT.
PLUS, I DON'T REALLY FEEL LIKE WALKING SIX BLOCKS AND WAITING FOR THE BUS IN THE DARK. ESPECIALLY IN THIS WEATHER...
IT'S FREEZING OUT THERE.
I'M JUST GONNA GRAB A BLANKET AND CRASH OUT ON THE COUCH, OKAY?
GIVE ME ONE OF THOSE PILLOWS.
LET ME GET YOU ONE OUT OF THE CLOSET. I'VE PROBABLY BEEN DROOLING ALL OVER THESE.
GOD, YOU'RE WEIRD.

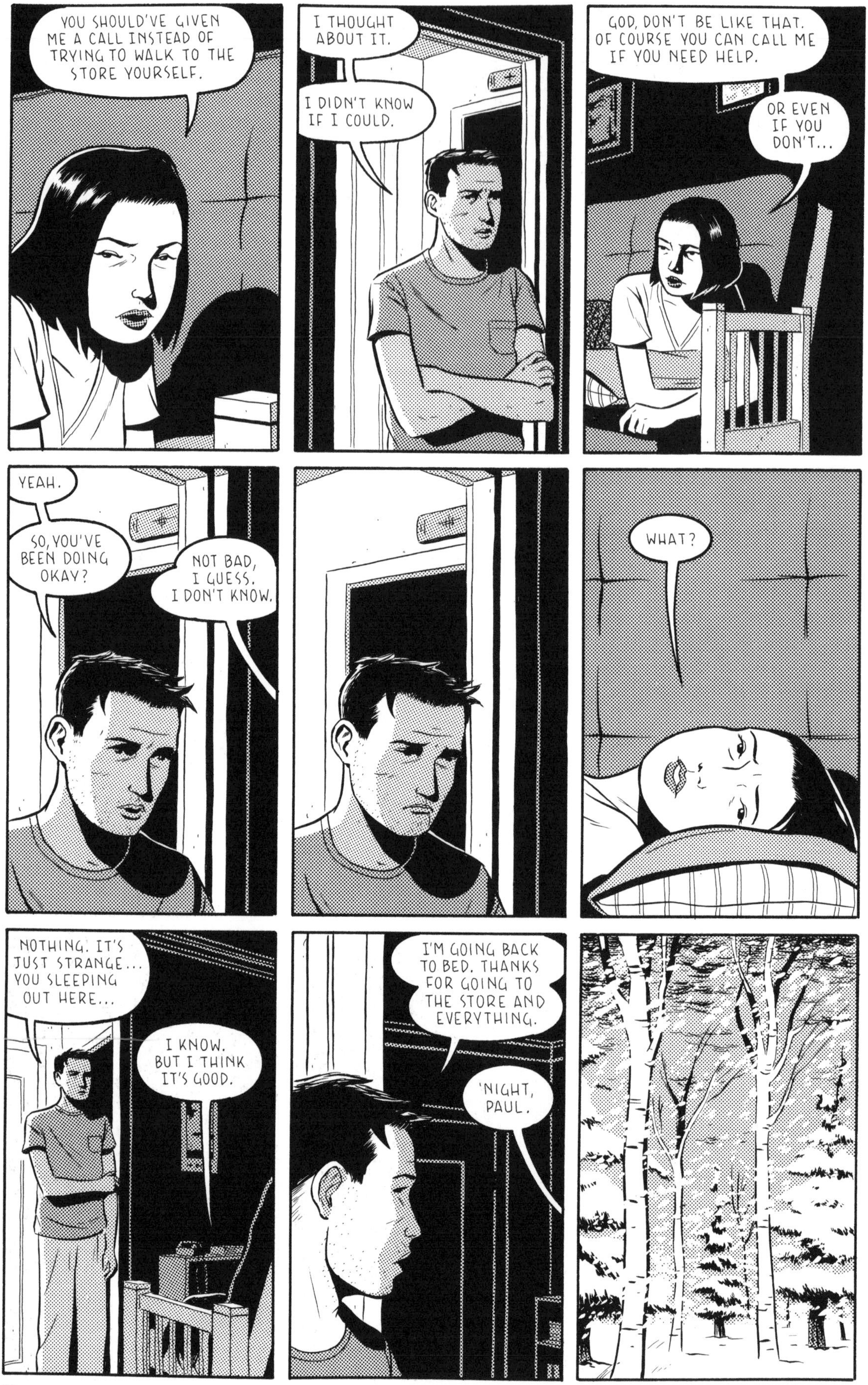
YOU SHOULD'VE GIVEN ME A CALL INSTEAD OF TRYING TO WALK TO THE STORE YOURSELF.
I THOUGHT ABOUT IT.
I DIDN'T KNOW IF I COULD.
GOD, DON'T BE LIKE THAT. OF COURSE YOU CAN CALL ME IF YOU NEED HELP.
OR EVEN IF YOU DON'T...
YEAH.
SO, YOU'VE BEEN DOING OKAY?
NOT BAD, I GUESS. I DON'T KNOW.
WHAT?
NOTHING. IT'S JUST STRANGE... YOU SLEEPING OUT HERE...
I KNOW. BUT I THINK IT'S GOOD.
I'M GOING BACK TO BED. THANKS FOR GOING TO THE STORE AND EVERYTHING.
'NIGHT, PAUL.

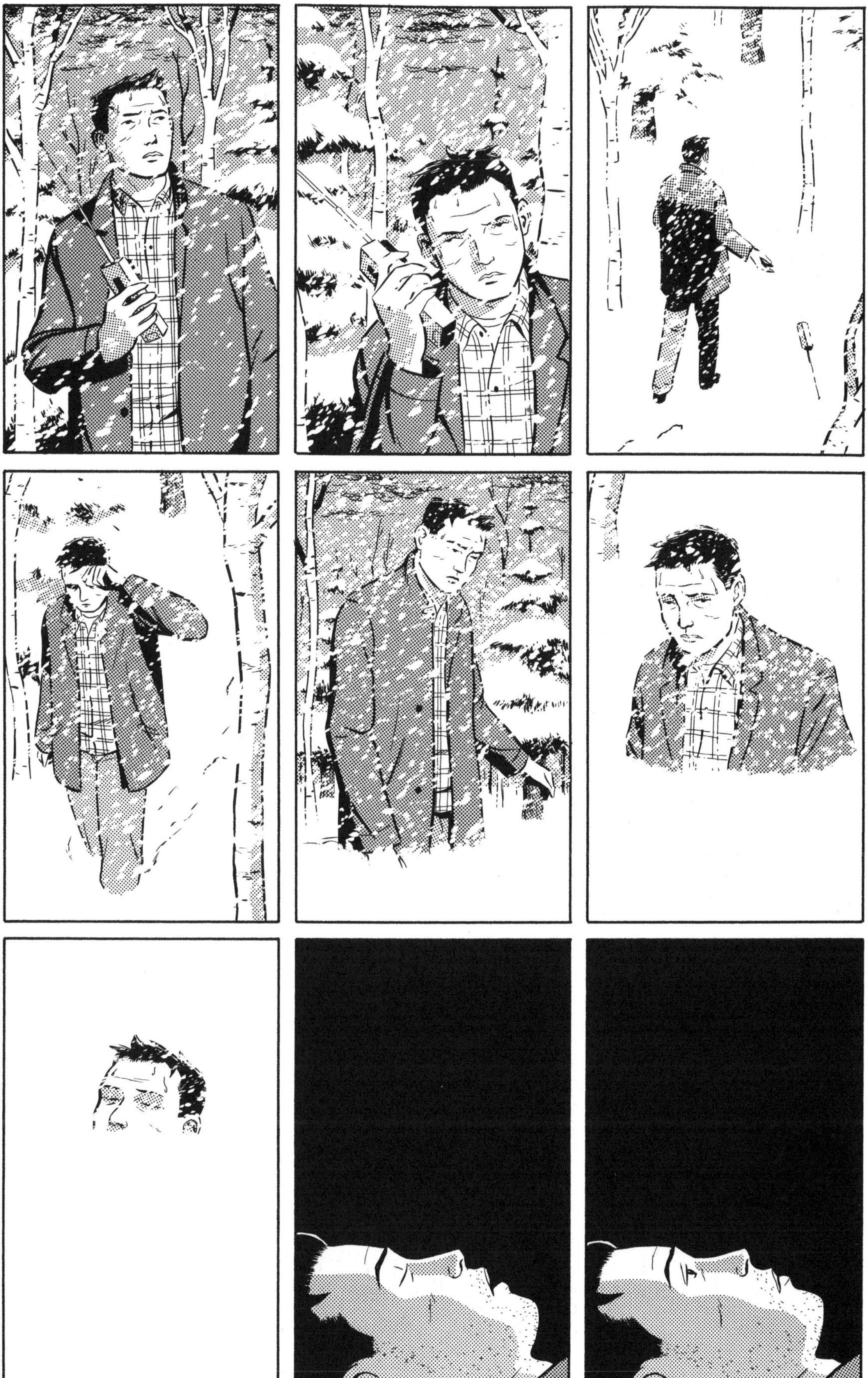

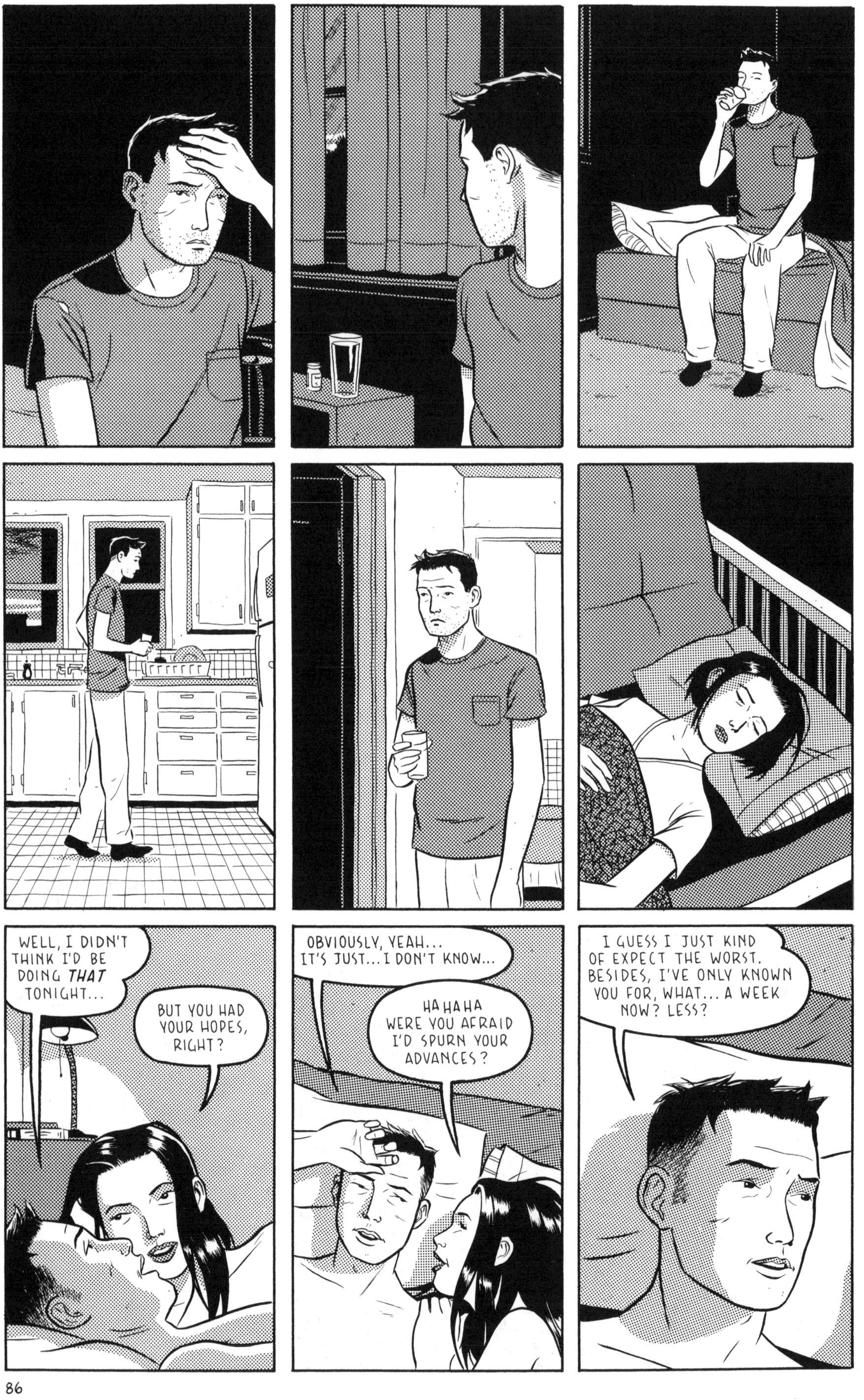
WELL, I DIDN'T THINK I'D BE DOING *THAT* TONIGHT...
BUT YOU HAD YOUR HOPES, RIGHT?
OBVIOUSLY, YEAH... IT'S JUST... I DON'T KNOW...
HA HA HA WERE YOU AFRAID I'D SPURN YOUR ADVANCES?
I GUESS I JUST KIND OF EXPECT THE WORST. BESIDES, I'VE ONLY KNOWN YOU FOR, WHAT... A WEEK NOW? LESS?

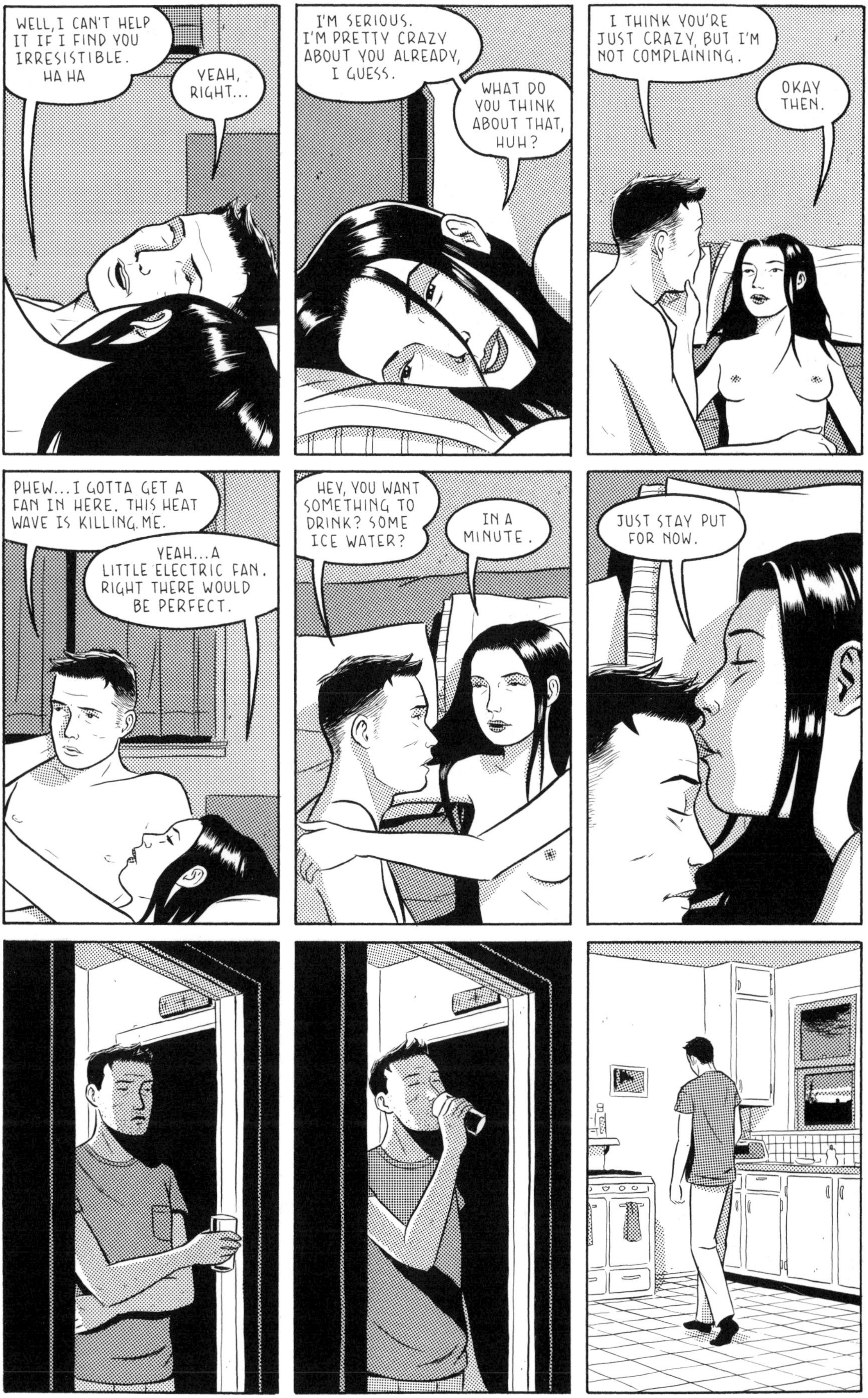
WELL, I CAN'T HELP IT IF I FIND YOU IRRESISTIBLE. HA HA
YEAH, RIGHT...
I'M SERIOUS. I'M PRETTY CRAZY ABOUT YOU ALREADY, I GUESS.
WHAT DO YOU THINK ABOUT THAT, HUH?
I THINK YOU'RE JUST CRAZY, BUT I'M NOT COMPLAINING.
OKAY THEN.
PHEW... I GOTTA GET A FAN IN HERE. THIS HEAT WAVE IS KILLING ME.
YEAH... A LITTLE ELECTRIC FAN. RIGHT THERE WOULD BE PERFECT.
HEY, YOU WANT SOMETHING TO DRINK? SOME ICE WATER?
IN A MINUTE.
JUST STAY PUT FOR NOW.

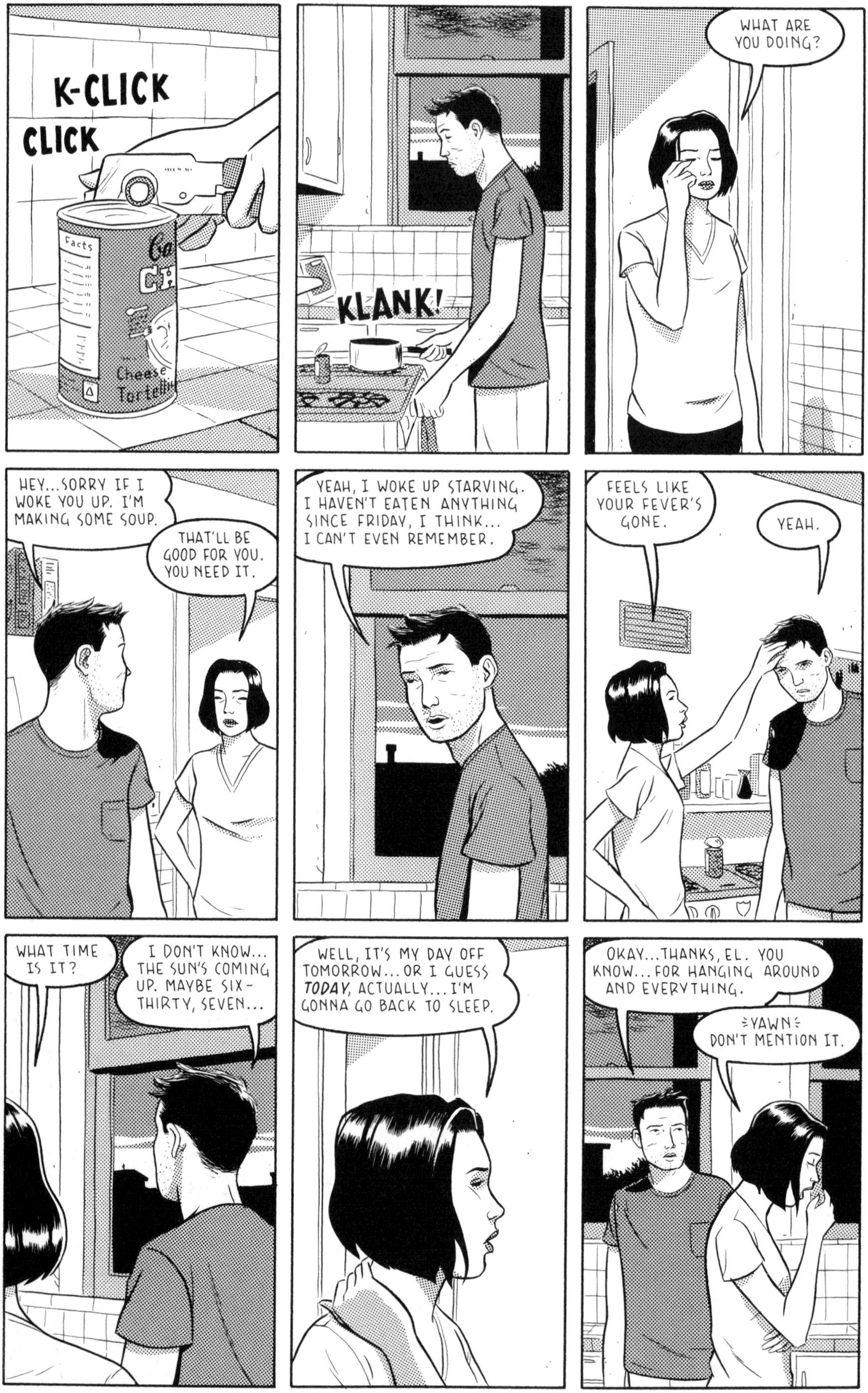
K-CLICK
CLICK
Facts
Cheese Tortell
KLANK!
WHAT ARE YOU DOING?
HEY...SORRY IF I WOKE YOU UP. I'M MAKING SOME SOUP.
THAT'LL BE GOOD FOR YOU. YOU NEED IT.
YEAH, I WOKE UP STARVING. I HAVEN'T EATEN ANYTHING SINCE FRIDAY, I THINK... I CAN'T EVEN REMEMBER.
FEELS LIKE YOUR FEVER'S GONE.
YEAH.
WHAT TIME IS IT?
I DON'T KNOW... THE SUN'S COMING UP. MAYBE SIX-THIRTY, SEVEN...
WELL, IT'S MY DAY OFF TOMORROW... OR I GUESS *TODAY*, ACTUALLY... I'M GONNA GO BACK TO SLEEP.
OKAY...THANKS, EL. YOU KNOW... FOR HANGING AROUND AND EVERYTHING.
≷YAWN≶ DON'T MENTION IT.

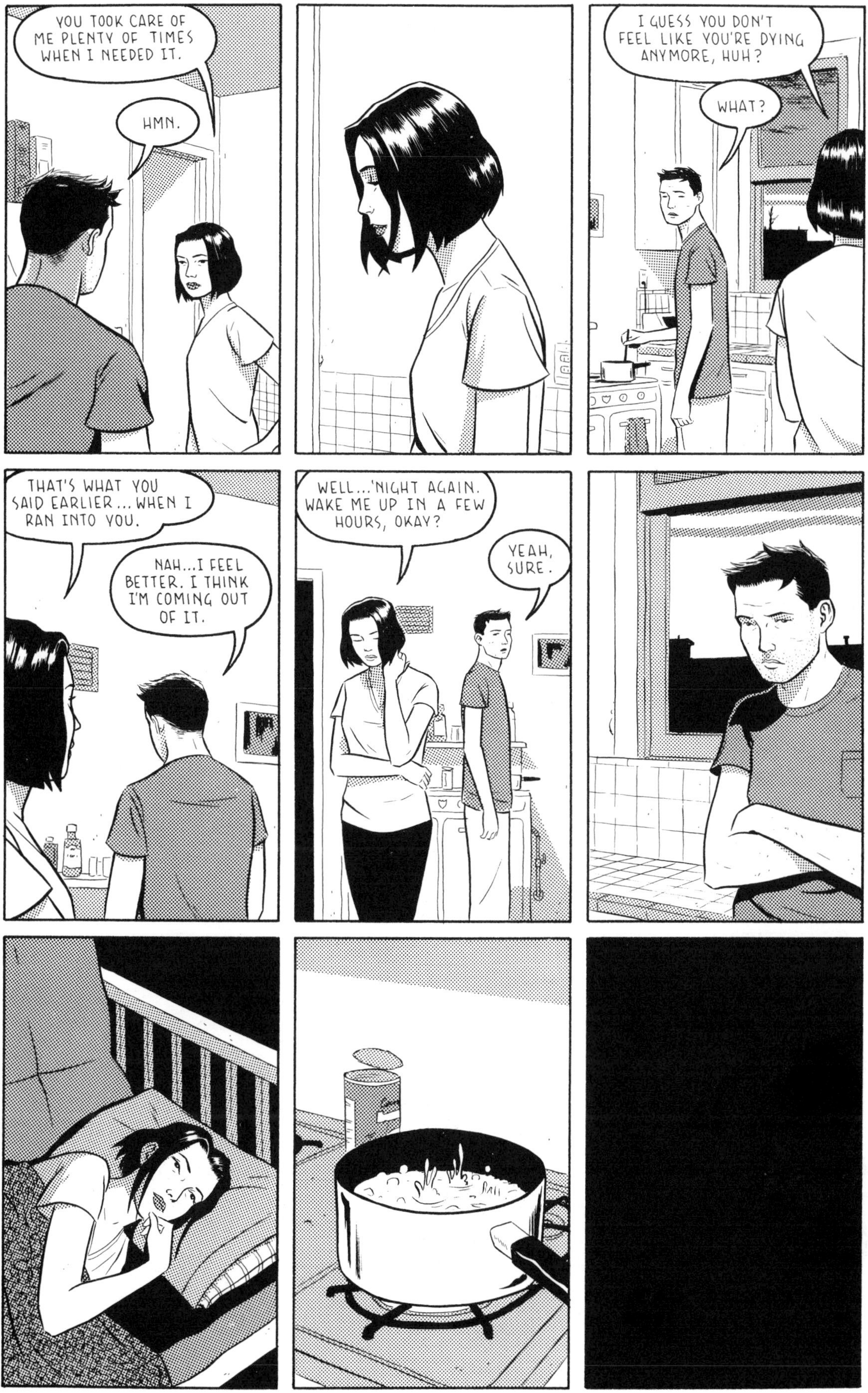
YOU TOOK CARE OF ME PLENTY OF TIMES WHEN I NEEDED IT.
HMN.
I GUESS YOU DON'T FEEL LIKE YOU'RE DYING ANYMORE, HUH?
WHAT?
THAT'S WHAT YOU SAID EARLIER... WHEN I RAN INTO YOU.
NAH... I FEEL BETTER. I THINK I'M COMING OUT OF IT.
WELL... 'NIGHT AGAIN. WAKE ME UP IN A FEW HOURS, OKAY?
YEAH, SURE.

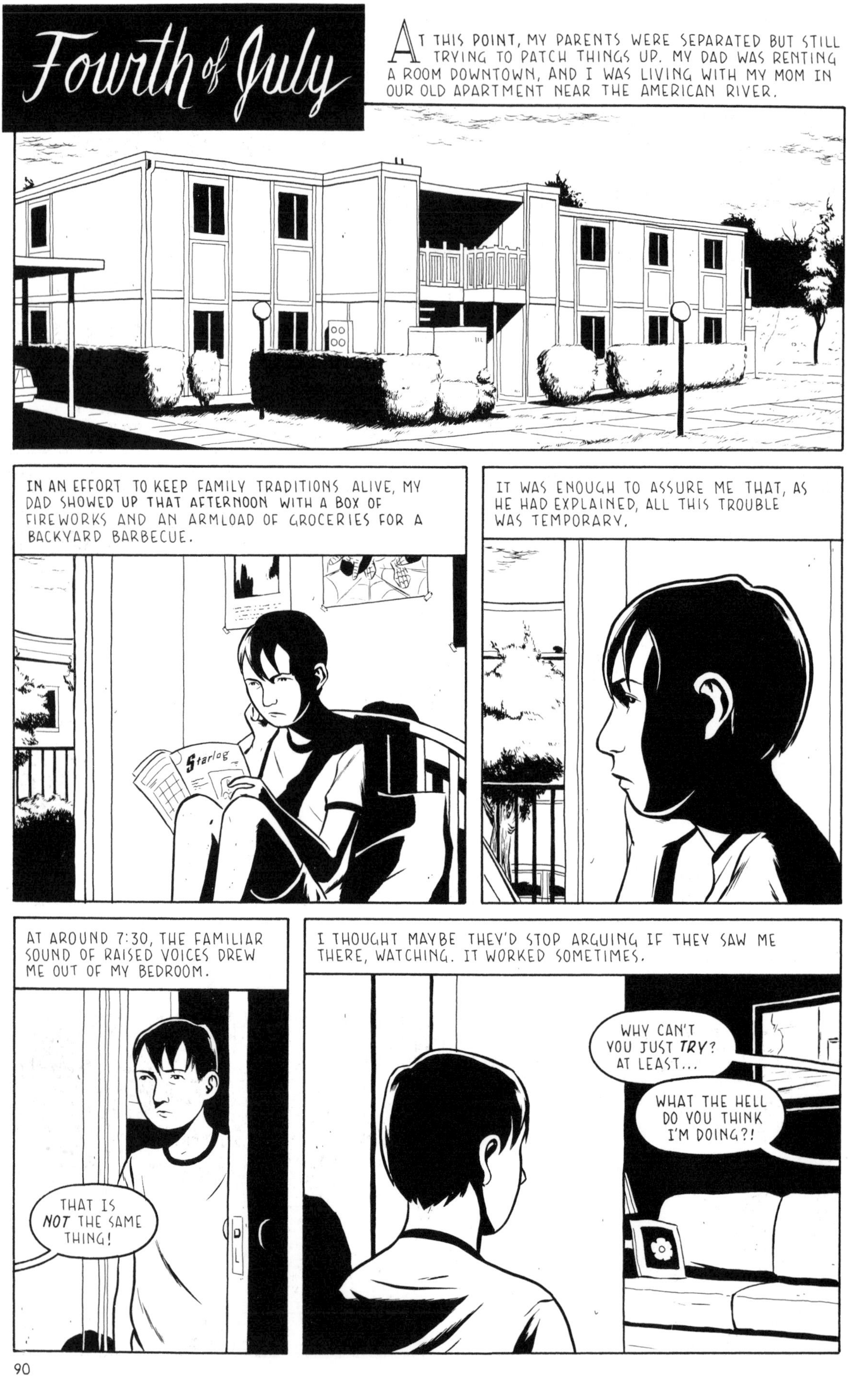
Fourth of July
AT THIS POINT, MY PARENTS WERE SEPARATED BUT STILL TRYING TO PATCH THINGS UP. MY DAD WAS RENTING A ROOM DOWNTOWN, AND I WAS LIVING WITH MY MOM IN OUR OLD APARTMENT NEAR THE AMERICAN RIVER.
IN AN EFFORT TO KEEP FAMILY TRADITIONS ALIVE, MY DAD SHOWED UP THAT AFTERNOON WITH A BOX OF FIREWORKS AND AN ARMLOAD OF GROCERIES FOR A BACKYARD BARBECUE.
Starlog
IT WAS ENOUGH TO ASSURE ME THAT, AS HE HAD EXPLAINED, ALL THIS TROUBLE WAS TEMPORARY.
AT AROUND 7:30, THE FAMILIAR SOUND OF RAISED VOICES DREW ME OUT OF MY BEDROOM.
THAT IS **NOT** THE SAME THING!
I THOUGHT MAYBE THEY'D STOP ARGUING IF THEY SAW ME THERE, WATCHING. IT WORKED SOMETIMES.
WHY CAN'T YOU JUST **TRY**? AT LEAST...
WHAT THE HELL DO YOU THINK I'M DOING?!

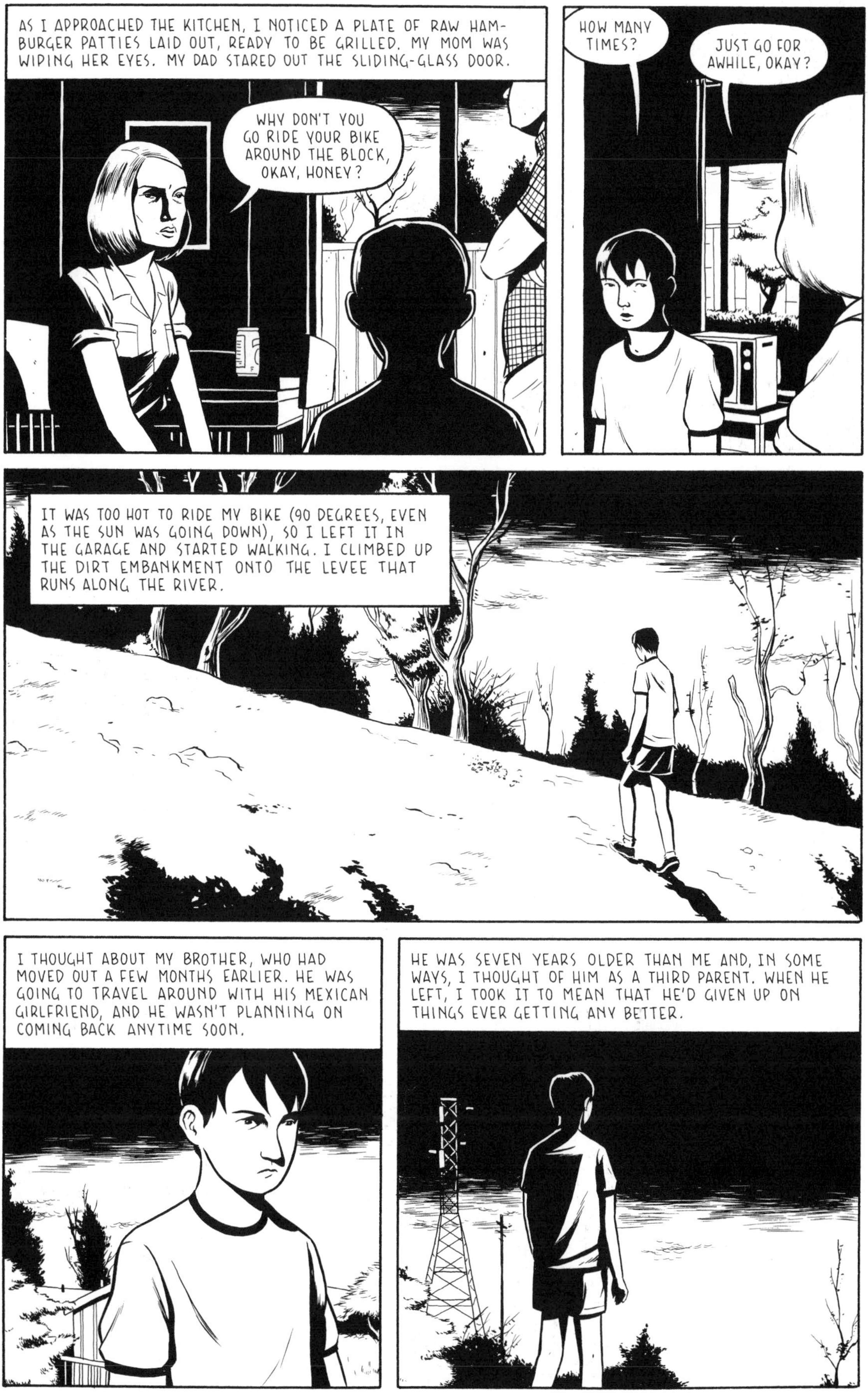

AS I APPROACHED THE KITCHEN, I NOTICED A PLATE OF RAW HAMBURGER PATTIES LAID OUT, READY TO BE GRILLED. MY MOM WAS WIPING HER EYES. MY DAD STARED OUT THE SLIDING-GLASS DOOR.
WHY DON'T YOU GO RIDE YOUR BIKE AROUND THE BLOCK, OKAY, HONEY?
HOW MANY TIMES?
JUST GO FOR AWHILE, OKAY?
IT WAS TOO HOT TO RIDE MY BIKE (90 DEGREES, EVEN AS THE SUN WAS GOING DOWN), SO I LEFT IT IN THE GARAGE AND STARTED WALKING. I CLIMBED UP THE DIRT EMBANKMENT ONTO THE LEVEE THAT RUNS ALONG THE RIVER.
I THOUGHT ABOUT MY BROTHER, WHO HAD MOVED OUT A FEW MONTHS EARLIER. HE WAS GOING TO TRAVEL AROUND WITH HIS MEXICAN GIRLFRIEND, AND HE WASN'T PLANNING ON COMING BACK ANYTIME SOON.
HE WAS SEVEN YEARS OLDER THAN ME AND, IN SOME WAYS, I THOUGHT OF HIM AS A THIRD PARENT. WHEN HE LEFT, I TOOK IT TO MEAN THAT HE'D GIVEN UP ON THINGS EVER GETTING ANY BETTER.

AS I WALKED ALONG THE LEVEE, I SAW PEOPLE DOWN BY THE WATER SETTING UP BLANKETS AND CHAIRS TO WATCH THE FIREWORKS THAT WOULD BE LAUNCHED FROM THE NEARBY FAIRGROUNDS. I COULD SMELL THE DRY FOXTAIL WEEDS AND THE CHARCOAL SMOKE ALL AROUND.

I DECIDED NOT TO GO BACK HOME RIGHT AWAY, BUT TO SIT DOWN AND TAKE IN THE FIREWORKS BY MYSELF. GENERALLY, I WAS HAPPIEST WHEN I WAS ALONE ANYWAY.

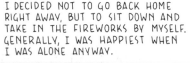

WHILE I SAT THERE WAITING FOR THE LAST OF THE SUNLIGHT TO FADE, I NOTICED SOMEONE WALKING UP FROM THE RIVERBANK TOWARDS ME. I RECOGNIZED THE KID FROM SCHOOL AND I KNEW HIS NAME WAS SUGGS, BUT THAT WAS IT.

THE LAST THING I WANTED TO DO AT THAT POINT WAS TALK TO SUGGS. I DIDN'T EVEN WANT TO SEE HIM, AND I DIDN'T WANT HIM TO SEE ME.

HEY. WHAT'CHA DOIN' HERE?

I LIVE AROUND HERE. I'M JUST WAITING FOR THE FIREWORKS, I GUESS.

BY YOURSELF?

UH-HUH.

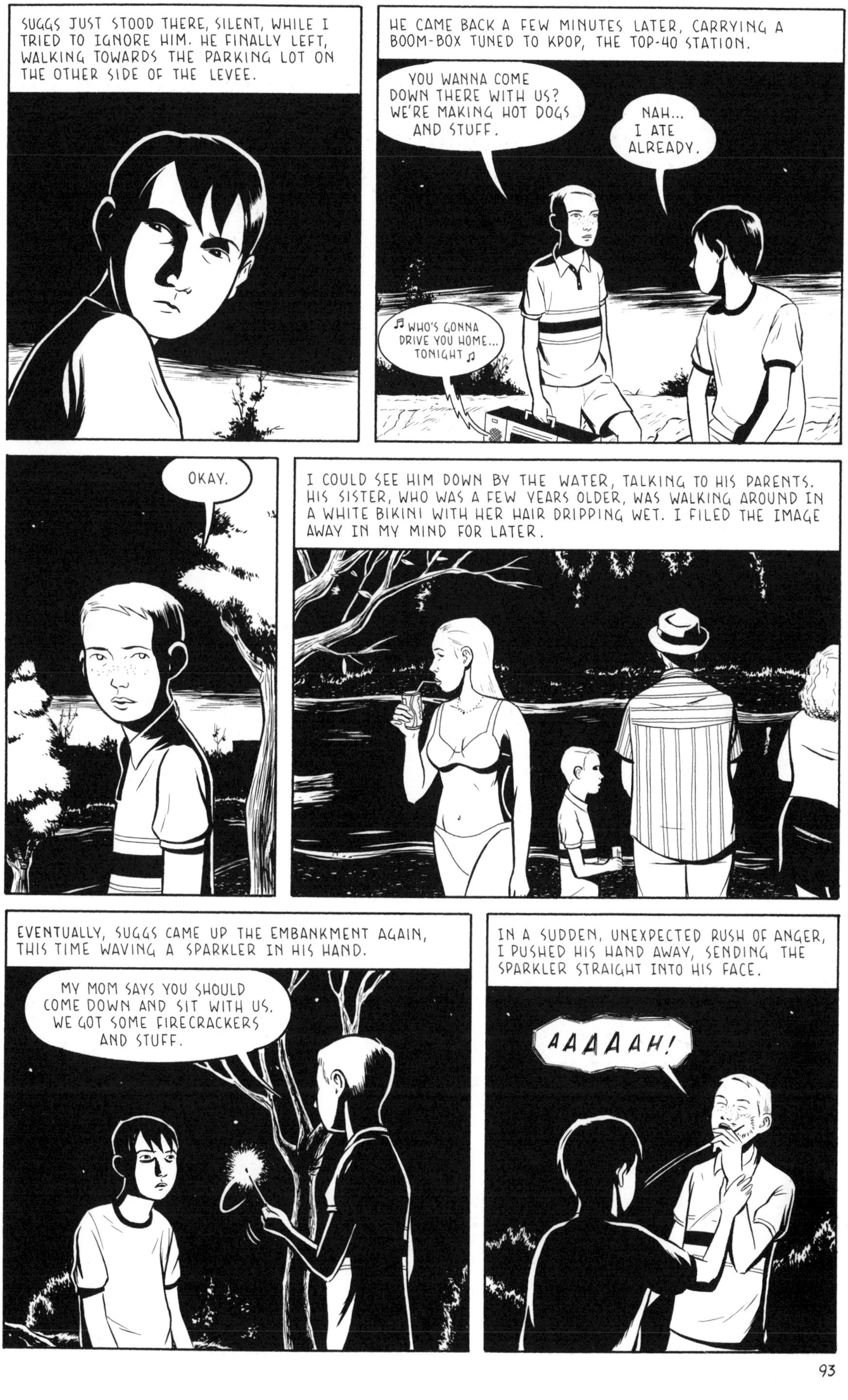
SUGGS JUST STOOD THERE, SILENT, WHILE I TRIED TO IGNORE HIM. HE FINALLY LEFT, WALKING TOWARDS THE PARKING LOT ON THE OTHER SIDE OF THE LEVEE.
HE CAME BACK A FEW MINUTES LATER, CARRYING A BOOM-BOX TUNED TO KPOP, THE TOP-40 STATION.
YOU WANNA COME DOWN THERE WITH US? WE'RE MAKING HOT DOGS AND STUFF.
NAH... I ATE ALREADY.
♫ WHO'S GONNA DRIVE YOU HOME... TONIGHT ♫
OKAY.
I COULD SEE HIM DOWN BY THE WATER, TALKING TO HIS PARENTS. HIS SISTER, WHO WAS A FEW YEARS OLDER, WAS WALKING AROUND IN A WHITE BIKINI WITH HER HAIR DRIPPING WET. I FILED THE IMAGE AWAY IN MY MIND FOR LATER.
EVENTUALLY, SUGGS CAME UP THE EMBANKMENT AGAIN, THIS TIME WAVING A SPARKLER IN HIS HAND.
MY MOM SAYS YOU SHOULD COME DOWN AND SIT WITH US. WE GOT SOME FIRECRACKERS AND STUFF.
IN A SUDDEN, UNEXPECTED RUSH OF ANGER, I PUSHED HIS HAND AWAY, SENDING THE SPARKLER STRAIGHT INTO HIS FACE.
AAAAAH!

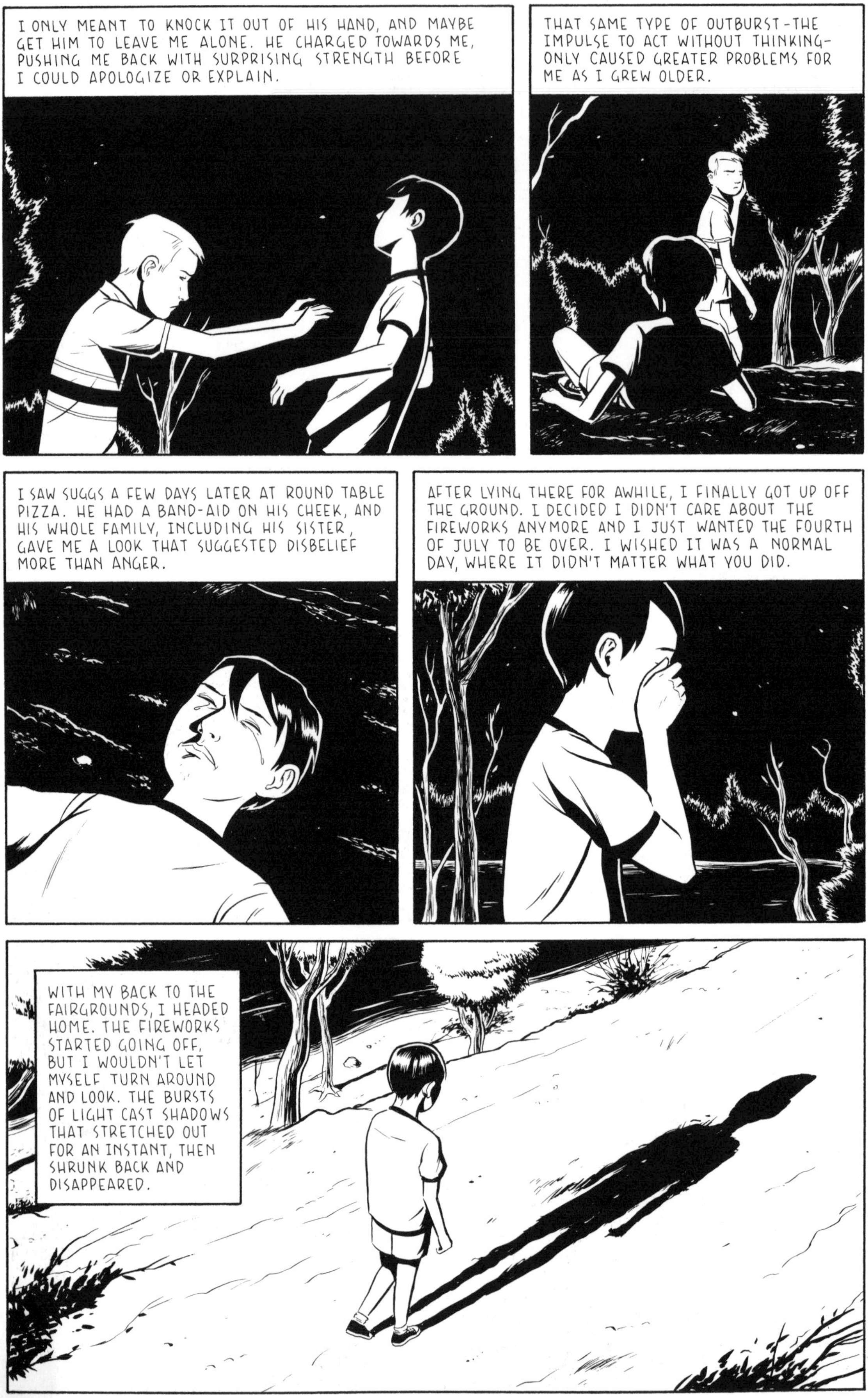
I ONLY MEANT TO KNOCK IT OUT OF HIS HAND, AND MAYBE GET HIM TO LEAVE ME ALONE. HE CHARGED TOWARDS ME, PUSHING ME BACK WITH SURPRISING STRENGTH BEFORE I COULD APOLOGIZE OR EXPLAIN.
THAT SAME TYPE OF OUTBURST-THE IMPULSE TO ACT WITHOUT THINKING-ONLY CAUSED GREATER PROBLEMS FOR ME AS I GREW OLDER.
I SAW SUGGS A FEW DAYS LATER AT ROUND TABLE PIZZA. HE HAD A BAND-AID ON HIS CHEEK, AND HIS WHOLE FAMILY, INCLUDING HIS SISTER, GAVE ME A LOOK THAT SUGGESTED DISBELIEF MORE THAN ANGER.
AFTER LYING THERE FOR AWHILE, I FINALLY GOT UP OFF THE GROUND. I DECIDED I DIDN'T CARE ABOUT THE FIREWORKS ANYMORE AND I JUST WANTED THE FOURTH OF JULY TO BE OVER. I WISHED IT WAS A NORMAL DAY, WHERE IT DIDN'T MATTER WHAT YOU DID.
WITH MY BACK TO THE FAIRGROUNDS, I HEADED HOME. THE FIREWORKS STARTED GOING OFF, BUT I WOULDN'T LET MYSELF TURN AROUND AND LOOK. THE BURSTS OF LIGHT CAST SHADOWS THAT STRETCHED OUT FOR AN INSTANT, THEN SHRUNK BACK AND DISAPPEARED.

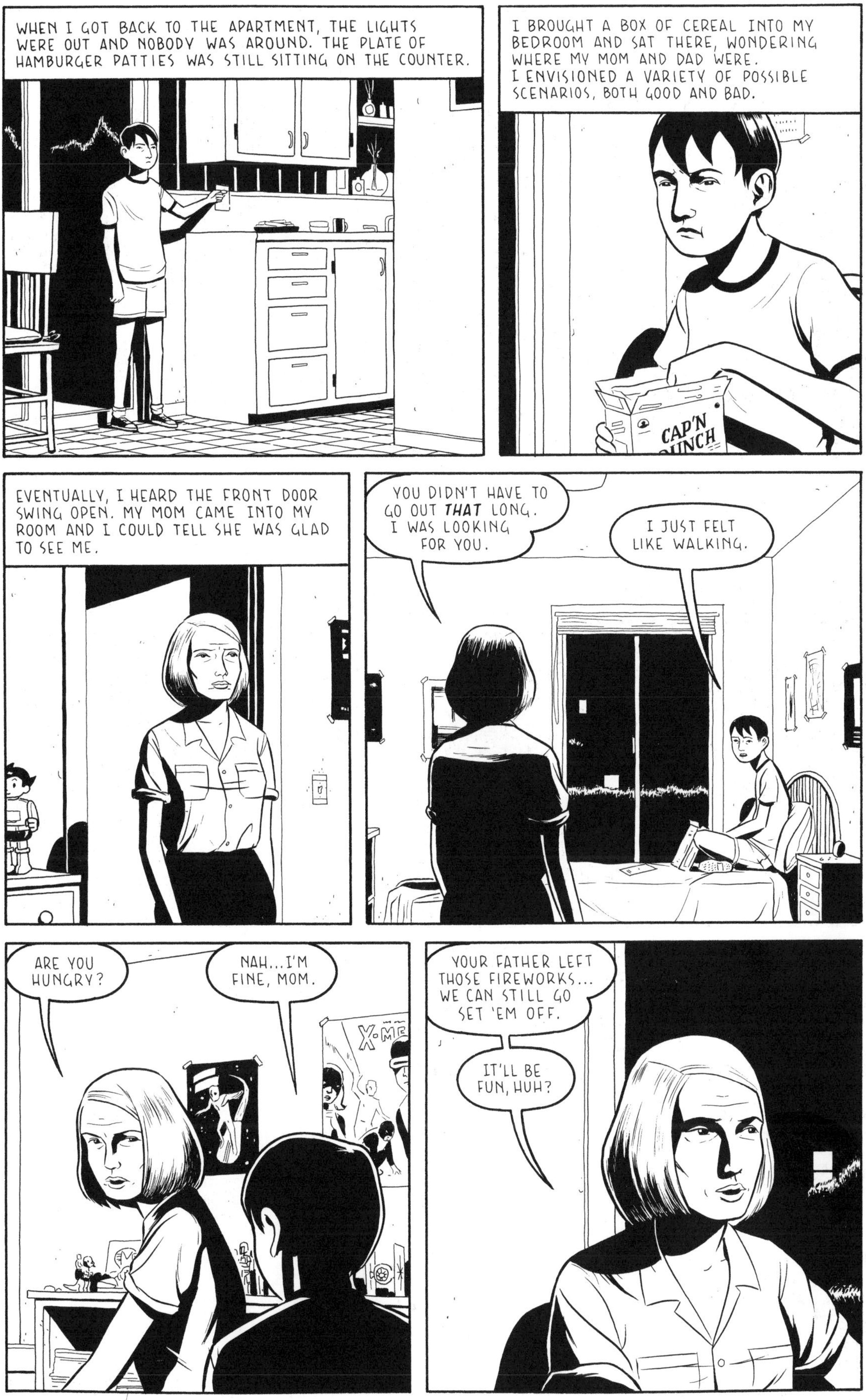
WHEN I GOT BACK TO THE APARTMENT, THE LIGHTS WERE OUT AND NOBODY WAS AROUND. THE PLATE OF HAMBURGER PATTIES WAS STILL SITTING ON THE COUNTER.
I BROUGHT A BOX OF CEREAL INTO MY BEDROOM AND SAT THERE, WONDERING WHERE MY MOM AND DAD WERE. I ENVISIONED A VARIETY OF POSSIBLE SCENARIOS, BOTH GOOD AND BAD.
CAP'N
EVENTUALLY, I HEARD THE FRONT DOOR SWING OPEN. MY MOM CAME INTO MY ROOM AND I COULD TELL SHE WAS GLAD TO SEE ME.
YOU DIDN'T HAVE TO GO OUT **THAT** LONG. I WAS LOOKING FOR YOU.
I JUST FELT LIKE WALKING.
ARE YOU HUNGRY?
NAH...I'M FINE, MOM.
YOUR FATHER LEFT THOSE FIREWORKS... WE CAN STILL GO SET 'EM OFF.
IT'LL BE FUN, HUH?

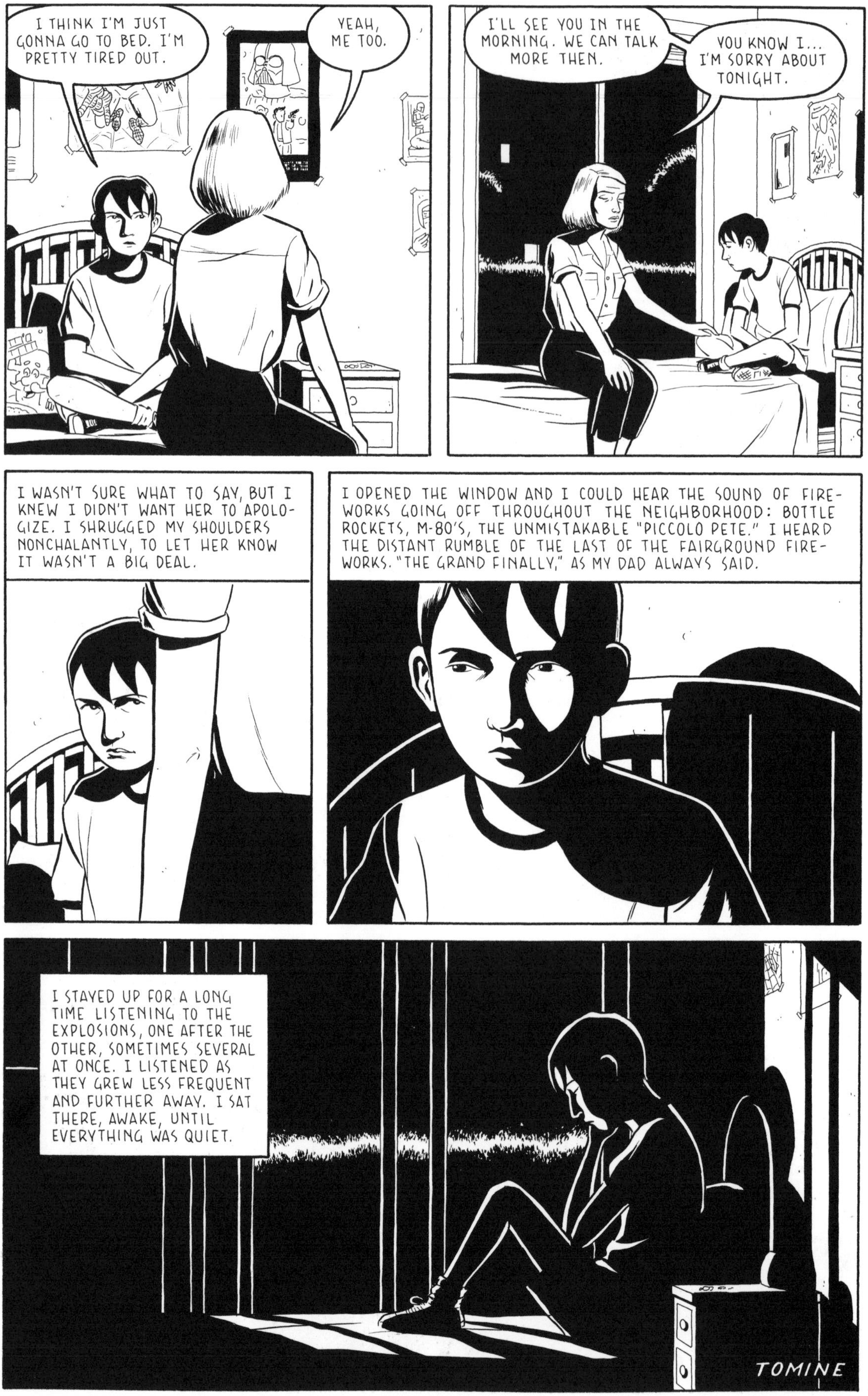
I THINK I'M JUST GONNA GO TO BED. I'M PRETTY TIRED OUT.
YEAH, ME TOO.
I'LL SEE YOU IN THE MORNING. WE CAN TALK MORE THEN.
YOU KNOW I... I'M SORRY ABOUT TONIGHT.
I WASN'T SURE WHAT TO SAY, BUT I KNEW I DIDN'T WANT HER TO APOLOGIZE. I SHRUGGED MY SHOULDERS NONCHALANTLY, TO LET HER KNOW IT WASN'T A BIG DEAL.
I OPENED THE WINDOW AND I COULD HEAR THE SOUND OF FIREWORKS GOING OFF THROUGHOUT THE NEIGHBORHOOD: BOTTLE ROCKETS, M-80'S, THE UNMISTAKABLE "PICCOLO PETE." I HEARD THE DISTANT RUMBLE OF THE LAST OF THE FAIRGROUND FIREWORKS. "THE GRAND FINALLY," AS MY DAD ALWAYS SAID.
I STAYED UP FOR A LONG TIME LISTENING TO THE EXPLOSIONS, ONE AFTER THE OTHER, SOMETIMES SEVERAL AT ONCE. I LISTENED AS THEY GREW LESS FREQUENT AND FURTHER AWAY. I SAT THERE, AWAKE, UNTIL EVERYTHING WAS QUIET.
TOMINE

HAZEL EYES

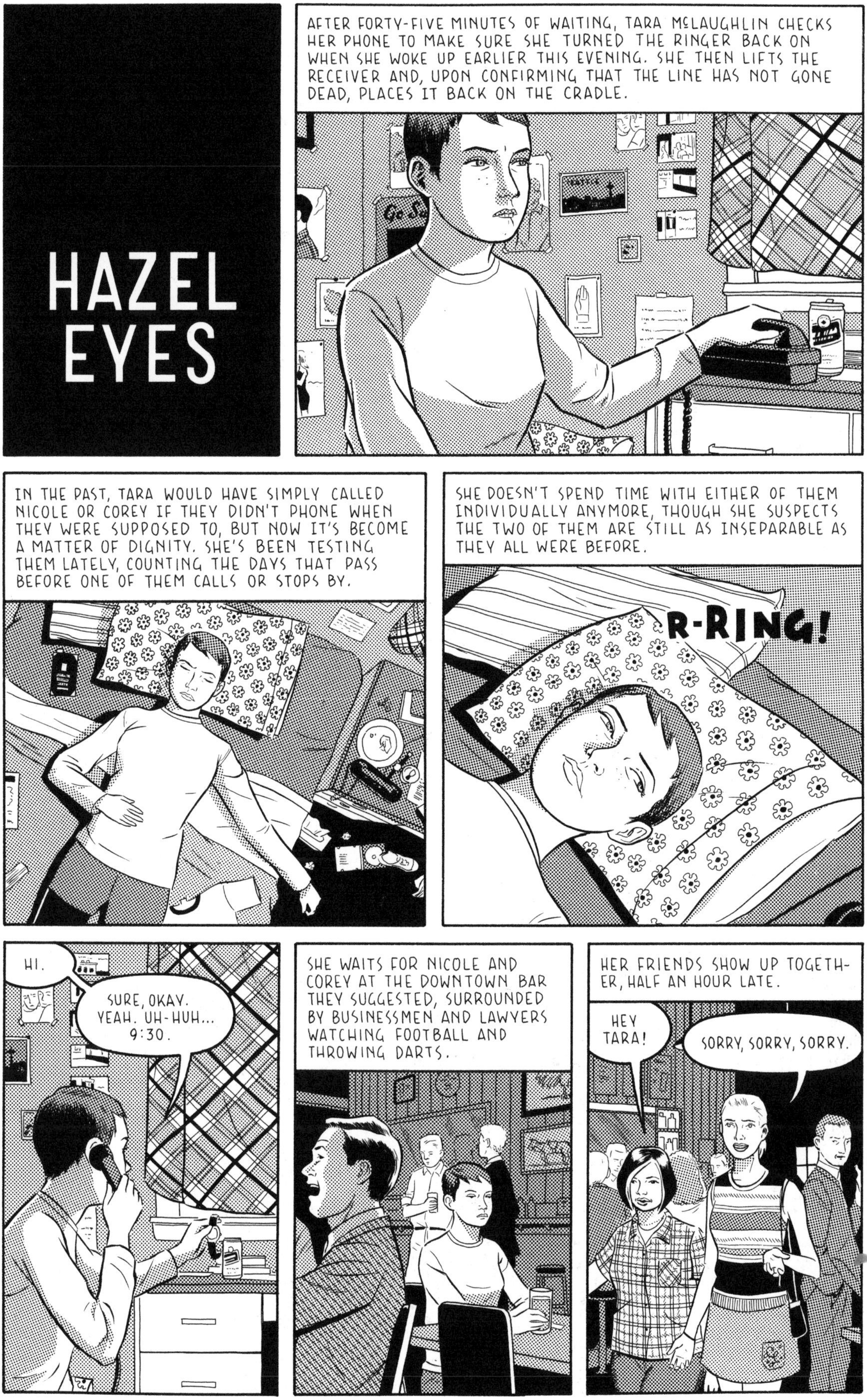
AFTER FORTY-FIVE MINUTES OF WAITING, TARA McLAUGHLIN CHECKS HER PHONE TO MAKE SURE SHE TURNED THE RINGER BACK ON WHEN SHE WOKE UP EARLIER THIS EVENING. SHE THEN LIFTS THE RECEIVER AND, UPON CONFIRMING THAT THE LINE HAS NOT GONE DEAD, PLACES IT BACK ON THE CRADLE.
IN THE PAST, TARA WOULD HAVE SIMPLY CALLED NICOLE OR COREY IF THEY DIDN'T PHONE WHEN THEY WERE SUPPOSED TO, BUT NOW IT'S BECOME A MATTER OF DIGNITY. SHE'S BEEN TESTING THEM LATELY, COUNTING THE DAYS THAT PASS BEFORE ONE OF THEM CALLS OR STOPS BY.
SHE DOESN'T SPEND TIME WITH EITHER OF THEM INDIVIDUALLY ANYMORE, THOUGH SHE SUSPECTS THE TWO OF THEM ARE STILL AS INSEPARABLE AS THEY ALL WERE BEFORE.
R-RING!
HI.
SURE, OKAY. YEAH. UH-HUH... 9:30.
SHE WAITS FOR NICOLE AND COREY AT THE DOWNTOWN BAR THEY SUGGESTED, SURROUNDED BY BUSINESSMEN AND LAWYERS WATCHING FOOTBALL AND THROWING DARTS.
HER FRIENDS SHOW UP TOGETHER, HALF AN HOUR LATE.
HEY TARA!
SORRY, SORRY, SORRY.

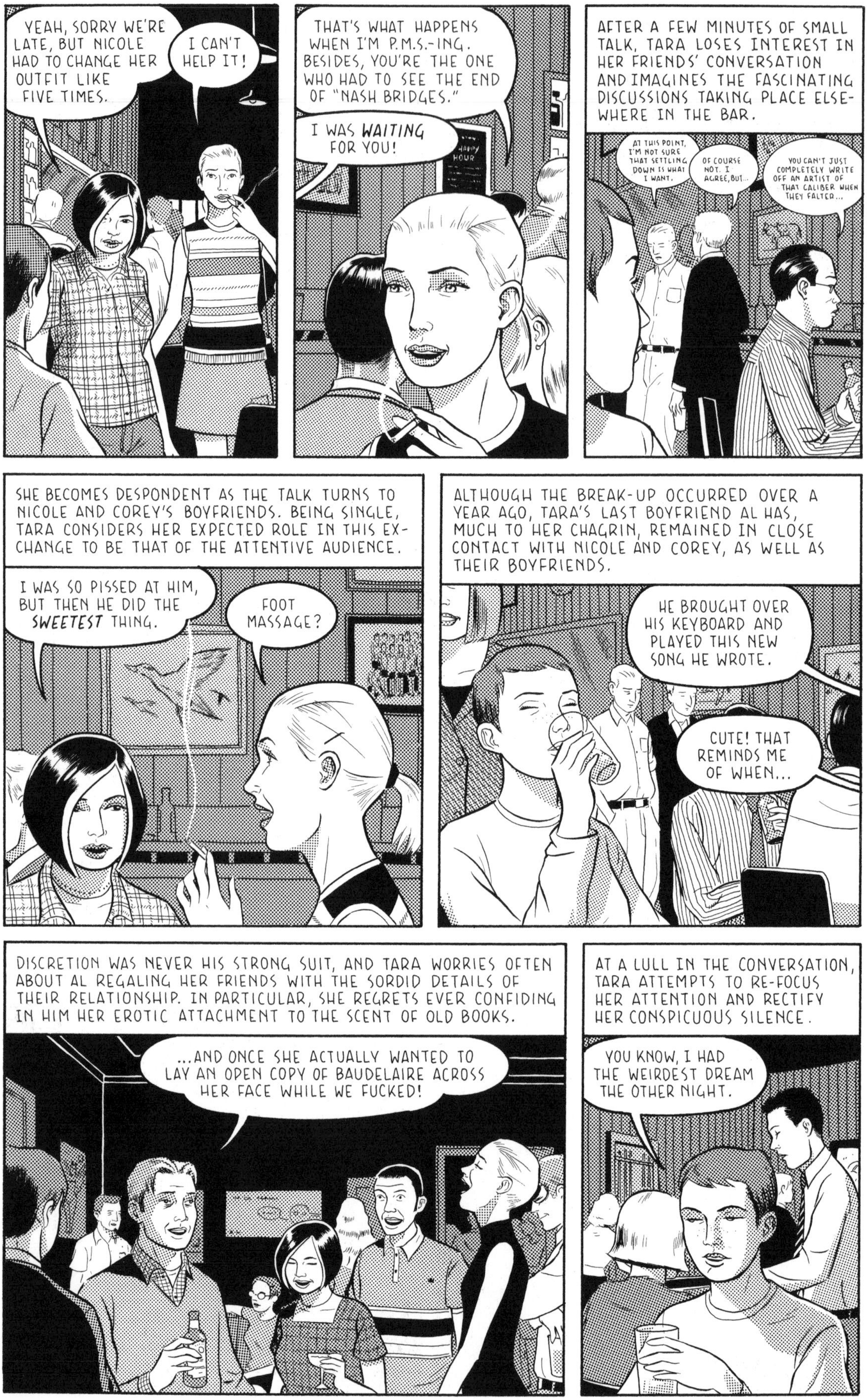
YEAH, SORRY WE'RE LATE, BUT NICOLE HAD TO CHANGE HER OUTFIT LIKE FIVE TIMES.
I CAN'T HELP IT!
THAT'S WHAT HAPPENS WHEN I'M P.M.S.-ING. BESIDES, YOU'RE THE ONE WHO HAD TO SEE THE END OF "NASH BRIDGES."
I WAS WAITING FOR YOU!
HAPPY HOUR
AFTER A FEW MINUTES OF SMALL TALK, TARA LOSES INTEREST IN HER FRIENDS' CONVERSATION AND IMAGINES THE FASCINATING DISCUSSIONS TAKING PLACE ELSE-WHERE IN THE BAR.
AT THIS POINT, I'M NOT SURE THAT SETTLING DOWN IS WHAT I WANT.
OF COURSE NOT. I AGREE, BUT...
YOU CAN'T JUST COMPLETELY WRITE OFF AN ARTIST OF THAT CALIBER WHEN THEY FALTER...
SHE BECOMES DESPONDENT AS THE TALK TURNS TO NICOLE AND COREY'S BOYFRIENDS. BEING SINGLE, TARA CONSIDERS HER EXPECTED ROLE IN THIS EX-CHANGE TO BE THAT OF THE ATTENTIVE AUDIENCE.
I WAS SO PISSED AT HIM, BUT THEN HE DID THE SWEETEST THING.
FOOT MASSAGE?
ALTHOUGH THE BREAK-UP OCCURRED OVER A YEAR AGO, TARA'S LAST BOYFRIEND AL HAS, MUCH TO HER CHAGRIN, REMAINED IN CLOSE CONTACT WITH NICOLE AND COREY, AS WELL AS THEIR BOYFRIENDS.
HE BROUGHT OVER HIS KEYBOARD AND PLAYED THIS NEW SONG HE WROTE.
CUTE! THAT REMINDS ME OF WHEN...
DISCRETION WAS NEVER HIS STRONG SUIT, AND TARA WORRIES OFTEN ABOUT AL REGALING HER FRIENDS WITH THE SORDID DETAILS OF THEIR RELATIONSHIP. IN PARTICULAR, SHE REGRETS EVER CONFIDING IN HIM HER EROTIC ATTACHMENT TO THE SCENT OF OLD BOOKS.
...AND ONCE SHE ACTUALLY WANTED TO LAY AN OPEN COPY OF BAUDELAIRE ACROSS HER FACE WHILE WE FUCKED!
AT A LULL IN THE CONVERSATION, TARA ATTEMPTS TO RE-FOCUS HER ATTENTION AND RECTIFY HER CONSPICUOUS SILENCE.
YOU KNOW, I HAD THE WEIRDEST DREAM THE OTHER NIGHT.

"IT WAS ABOUT AL. HE'D COMMITTED SOME CRIME AND WAS BEING SENT AWAY TO LIVE ON A DESERTED ISLAND SOMEWHERE. WE HAD JUST A FEW MINUTES TO TALK BEFORE THE COPS WERE GONNA HAUL HIM AWAY."

"HE TOLD ME THE THING HE WAS GONNA MISS THE MOST WAS LOOKING AT MY HAZEL EYES. I TOLD HIM THE THING I WAS GONNA MISS THE MOST WAS FEELING HIS SMOOTH SKIN."

"SO WE AGREED TO TRADE. HE STUCK HIS FINGERS INTO MY LEFT SOCKET AND PULLED OUT THE EYEBALL."

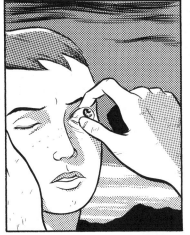

"THEN I DUG MY NAILS INTO HIS ARM AND PEELED OFF A CHUNK OF SKIN. THERE WASN'T ANY BLOOD OR ANYTHING..."

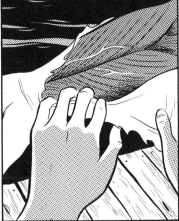

TARA'S VOICE TRAILS OFF AS SHE NOTICES NICOLE AND COREY EXCHANGE BRIEF, KNOWING GLANCES.

WHAT?

WHAT WAS THAT LOOK FOR?

NOTHING! IT'S JUST... YOU'RE ALWAYS HAVING THESE *FREAKY* DREAMS. THEY'RE SO...*VIVID.*

YEAH, I HARDLY *EVER* HAVE DREAMS LIKE THAT. IT'S ALMOST LIKE A MOVIE OR SOMETHING.

TARA FEELS A SWELL OF DEFENSIVENESS, BUT MAKES A CONCERTED EFFORT TO REMAIN AGREEABLE.

WELL, I TOLD YOU IT WAS PRETTY WEIRD.

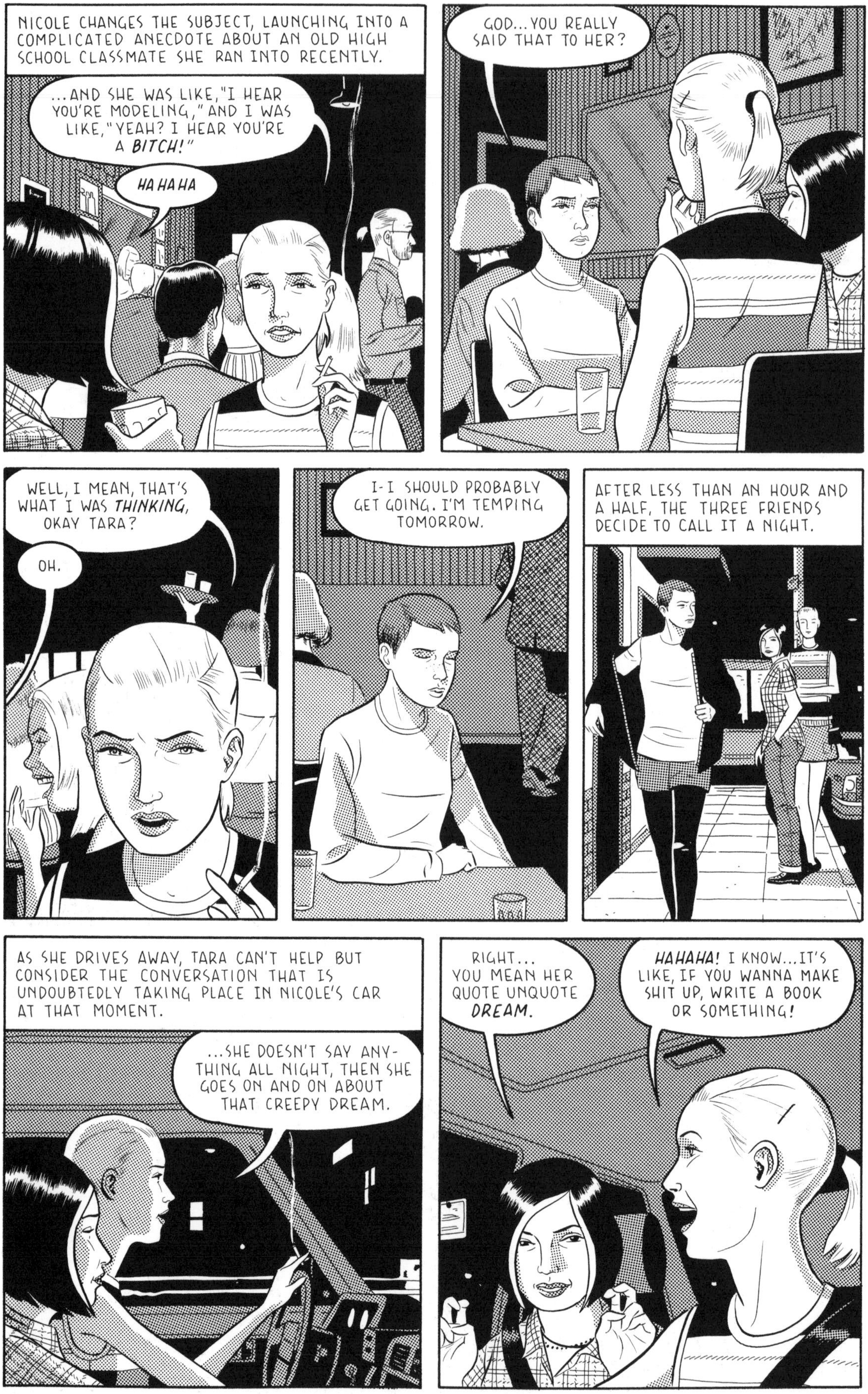
NICOLE CHANGES THE SUBJECT, LAUNCHING INTO A COMPLICATED ANECDOTE ABOUT AN OLD HIGH SCHOOL CLASSMATE SHE RAN INTO RECENTLY.
...AND SHE WAS LIKE, "I HEAR YOU'RE MODELING," AND I WAS LIKE, "YEAH? I HEAR YOU'RE A *BITCH!*"
HA HA HA
GOD... YOU REALLY SAID THAT TO HER?
WELL, I MEAN, THAT'S WHAT I WAS *THINKING*, OKAY TARA?
OH.
I-I SHOULD PROBABLY GET GOING. I'M TEMPING TOMORROW.
AFTER LESS THAN AN HOUR AND A HALF, THE THREE FRIENDS DECIDE TO CALL IT A NIGHT.
AS SHE DRIVES AWAY, TARA CAN'T HELP BUT CONSIDER THE CONVERSATION THAT IS UNDOUBTEDLY TAKING PLACE IN NICOLE'S CAR AT THAT MOMENT.
...SHE DOESN'T SAY ANYTHING ALL NIGHT, THEN SHE GOES ON AND ON ABOUT THAT CREEPY DREAM.
RIGHT... YOU MEAN HER QUOTE UNQUOTE **DREAM.**
HAHAHA! I KNOW...IT'S LIKE, IF YOU WANNA MAKE SHIT UP, WRITE A BOOK OR SOMETHING!

"AND PLUS, QUIT PATHETICALLY TALKING ABOUT A GUY WHO *DUMPED* YOU!"
"YEAH...LIKE TWO YEARS AGO!"

...FUCKING *HATE* YOU...

TARA DRIVES TO AN OLDER, EMPTIER BAR ON THE OUTSKIRTS OF TOWN AND EMBARKS ON A SERIES OF DRINKS, ALTERNATING VODKA GIMLETS AND BEER.

...BUT I MEAN, BACK IN SCHOOL, ME AND THIS GIRL AMBER WERE *CLOSE*. THAT'S WHY IT PISSED ME OFF SO MUCH.

MM-HMN?

SO ANYWAY, LAST WEEK I'M OVER AT LUCKY'S, AND GUESS WHO I BUMP INTO? IT'S AMBER, AND SHE JUST MOVED BACK FROM BOSTON.

SO SHE STARTS TALK- ING TO ME AND SHE'S LIKE, "I HEAR YOU'RE MODELING," AND I'M LIKE, "YEAH? I HEAR YOU'RE A *BITCH!*"

HMM.

HEY, LOOK AT MY EYES. SOMEBODY TOLD ME ONCE, "I CAN OVERLOOK ALL YOUR SHIT BECAUSE OF THEM."

HA HA

EXIT

YOU EVER HAVE THAT? WHERE JUST ONE GOOD THING ABOUT SOMEONE IS ENOUGH?

I DON'T KNOW... I GUESS...

LISTEN... YOU WANNA BUY ME A DRINK?

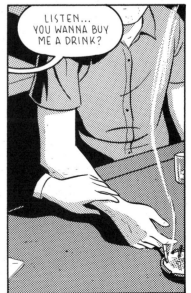

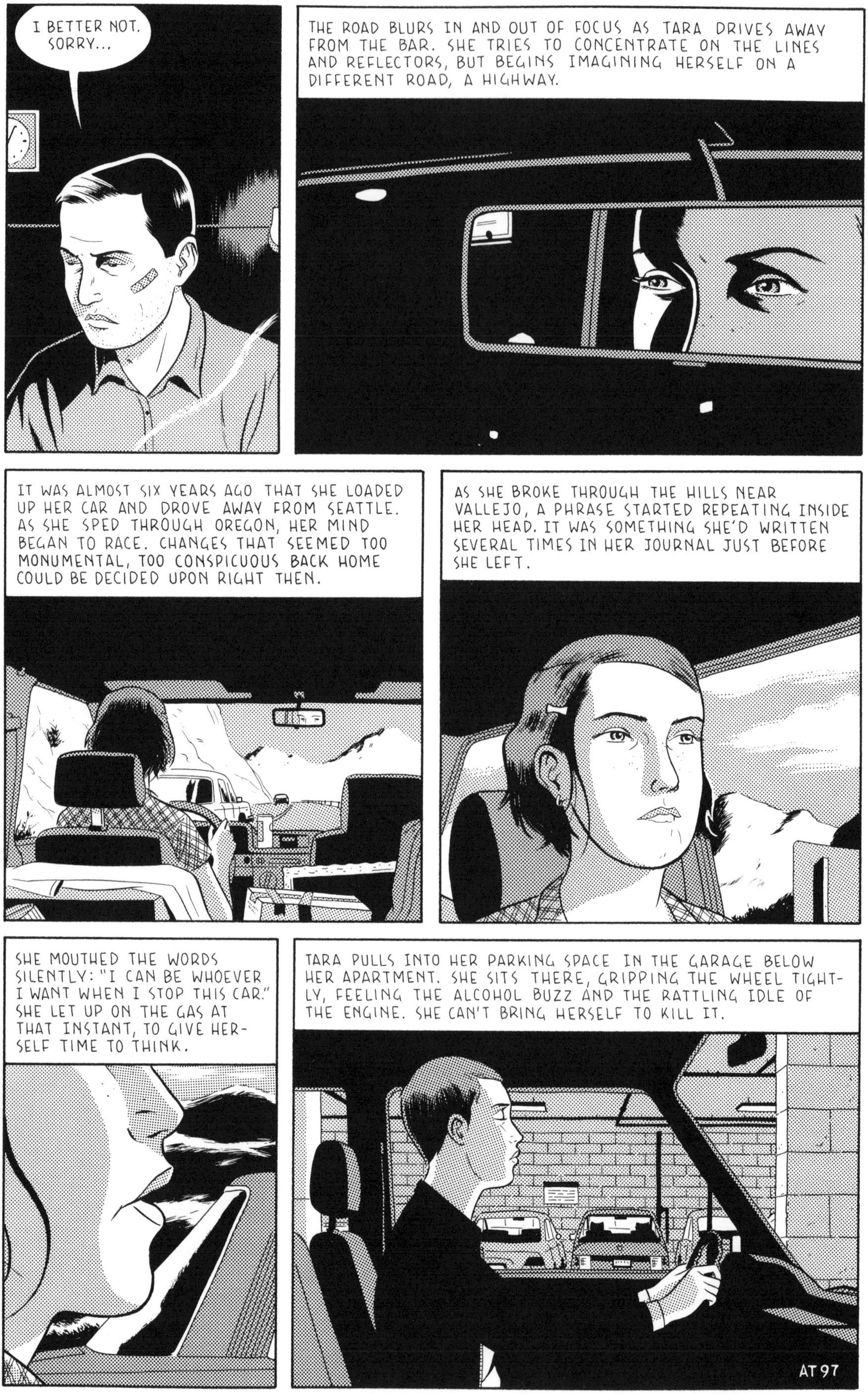
I BETTER NOT. SORRY...
THE ROAD BLURS IN AND OUT OF FOCUS AS TARA DRIVES AWAY FROM THE BAR. SHE TRIES TO CONCENTRATE ON THE LINES AND REFLECTORS, BUT BEGINS IMAGINING HERSELF ON A DIFFERENT ROAD, A HIGHWAY.
IT WAS ALMOST SIX YEARS AGO THAT SHE LOADED UP HER CAR AND DROVE AWAY FROM SEATTLE. AS SHE SPED THROUGH OREGON, HER MIND BEGAN TO RACE. CHANGES THAT SEEMED TOO MONUMENTAL, TOO CONSPICUOUS BACK HOME COULD BE DECIDED UPON RIGHT THEN.
AS SHE BROKE THROUGH THE HILLS NEAR VALLEJO, A PHRASE STARTED REPEATING INSIDE HER HEAD. IT WAS SOMETHING SHE'D WRITTEN SEVERAL TIMES IN HER JOURNAL JUST BEFORE SHE LEFT.
SHE MOUTHED THE WORDS SILENTLY: "I CAN BE WHOEVER I WANT WHEN I STOP THIS CAR." SHE LET UP ON THE GAS AT THAT INSTANT, TO GIVE HER-SELF TIME TO THINK.
TARA PULLS INTO HER PARKING SPACE IN THE GARAGE BELOW HER APARTMENT. SHE SITS THERE, GRIPPING THE WHEEL TIGHT-LY, FEELING THE ALCOHOL BUZZ AND THE RATTLING IDLE OF THE ENGINE. SHE CAN'T BRING HERSELF TO KILL IT.
AT97